Barr's Meadow

Kravitz and Sons LLC
1301 Farmville Blvd, Suite 104
Greenville, NC 27834

Published by Kravitz and Sons LLC.

ISBN: 979-8-89639-196-8   (sc)
ISBN: 979-8-89639-195-1   (e)

Library of Congress Control Number: 2025914867

Julian's Private Scrapbook
Book 1
Barr's Meadow

Special Edition

a summer frolic
by
Eldot

Kravitz & Sons
INNOVATORS IN PUBLISHING, MARKETING AND ADVERTISING

To MES with gratitude for his example and support
—Eldot

Barr's Meadow: (Julian's Private Scrapbook: Part One)
Eldot
Xlibris, 248 pages, (paperback) $15.99, 978-1-4691-4512-9
(Reviewed: December 2013)

Pleasant, nostalgic and ingenuous, *Barr's Meadow* is set at a Boy Scout camp in the early '60s, the fictional story of a gay young man named Julian.

Julian, nearly 13, is handsome, enthusiastic and affable, as well as a skilled artist. Julian has a crush on Scoutmaster Mark. Mark who, while married, has been open to same-gender sex in the past has resolved to confront this with sensitivity and fraternal affection, realizing that Julian's trusting nature could make him the victim of more predatory scouts.

Author Eldot (who writes under one name) explores the daily activities of scout camp and the politics of sex between teenage boys. The author focuses mostly on the gay characters and Julian's sexual thoughts, but this is not really gay erotica (although the back cover warns: "Not for sale to persons under 18"). With the exception of two somewhat explicit (though not heightened) passages, it reflects on same-gender, male sexuality while generally avoiding the salacious.

Eldot gets inside the heads of the characters, including Julian and Mark, as in: "Mark stepped around to the other side of the bed and watched Julian hustle. He bounced on his toes unconsciously. He had faced the unknown here and it had gone very well. I was right about this."

Barr's Meadow is comparable to other teenage boy coming-of-age narratives, such as *The Last Picture Show*, minus the cynicism, sophistication or relative depth. This doesn't mean that it's poorly crafted; only that Eldot's prose is simple, direct and seeks to examine the lives and thoughts of guys who are only beginning to view the world with introspection. Eldot walks the precarious line between making the boys evolved and depicting them as saints. He allows them moments of tenderness and nurturing without suggesting their virility has been tainted.

Barr's Meadow, the first in a series, never breaks through to the transcendent realms of literary brilliance, but it is intelligent, moving, well-grounded and memorable.

TITLE INFORMATION

BARR'S MEADOW
Eldot

BOOK REVIEW

A debut novel tells the story of a young gay Scout's sexual awakening at camp.

Twelve-year-old Julian Forrest has been raised by his single mother, never knowing his father. He loves drawing and being a Cub Scout. He has even made a Scouting journal full of drawings of his activities. He has recently become aware of his sexual desire, which is wound up in his habit of watching a neighbor, the adult Mark Schaefer, come home from work every day. When Mark comes over to the house to invite Julian to join his Scouting troop, the youngster can barely contain his excitement—or hide his erection.

Two years later, Julian gets to attend the annual two-week Scouting summer camp at Walker Lake. By this point, Mark is aware of Julian's crush, though he is unsure how to proceed: "What bothered Mark—a little, not a lot—was that Julian had become a presence in his thoughts…*at this point it's only a presence…but it's something new… it felt pleasant, it made him feel light.*" The first two days at Walker Lake will prove transformative for many people, including Nick Harrison and Tom Dawson, members of the troop's leadership patrol. In the allmale environment of a Scouting camp, Julian quickly discovers some of the rules of his new masculinity—and a few things about his burgeoning sexuality as well.

Set in the 1960s, this series opener deftly depicts feelings of childhood nostalgia, as evidenced in Eldot's wistful prose: "At last the sausage patties and pancakes were ready and waiting in the oven. Julian helped Danny put out the OJ and milk. *oh! a bubbling sound— the coffee!* He rushed over to the stove to watch." But the author dwells heavily on the sexual thoughts of several characters, including the teenage Julian. While these aren't necessarily erotic, there is an undeniable romanticism to them. This will likely make many readers decidedly uncomfortable, particularly those scenes that deal with the attraction between minors and adults. Eldot may argue that he's depicting an experience common to young gay men, but if this book isn't crossing a line, it's walking right up to it.

An uneven coming-of-age tale.

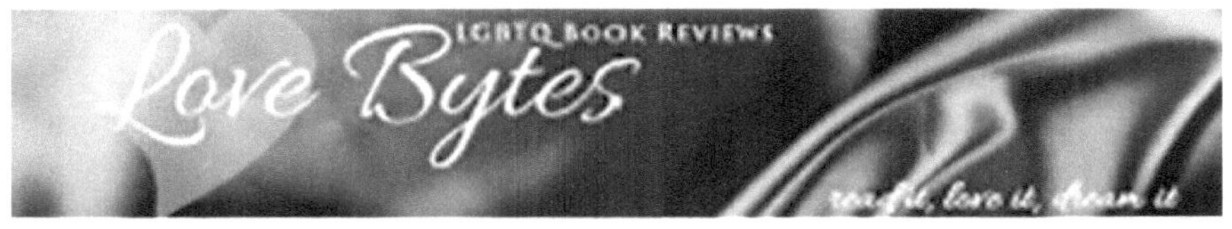

We received this book as part of a request from the author to review the five book series. Nothing odd about that, it happens all the time. I pride myself on being honest, so here goes. This is the first book I've read in a long time that I finished still having absolutely no idea how I would rate it, nor even what I would say in the review.

Barr's Meadow: Julian's Private Scrapbook Part One is the first book in a five book series set at a Boy Scout camp in North Carolina in the early 1960's which follows the adventures of a boy named Julian on his first trip to summer camp.

Let me tell you, I went to summer camp, both Boy Scouts and 4H every year from about 8 until about 15, and I never saw any of the extracurricular activities going on in this book! I wish!

Barr's Meadow begins with us learning that Julian has a crush on an adult male neighbor, Mark, who is also the Boy Scout Leader of Troop 9. Julian used to have a crush on a boy named Danny who lives directly behind them, but he has moved on to gazing at Mark every day when he gets off the city bus and walks down the street to his house.

Mark has noticed the boy, on occasion, looking out the window as he walks by, but hasn't met him until Mark stops by to recruit Julian for his Scout Troop. Julian's mother sees Mark as a surrogate adult male figure, Mark sees himself as more a big brother, Julian see him as hotness personified.

Things get interesting when they get to camp for a two week period. Mark is afraid of something happening to Julian, so he promotes him and moves him to stay in his own cabin, away from the other boys. That doesn't stop some of the other boys, the neighbor Danny included, from plotting how they are going to get into Julian's pants.

My one issue with this book, and what might keep me from reading the others, is the intense amount of detail. The entire book is dedicated to the leadup with Julian becoming a Boy Scout, and then the first two days at camp. The book contains some sex between teenagers, and an, as yet, unrequited lust for the adult scout leader, but nothing that should shock anyone reading books in this genre.

I liked the book, it contained far above average writing, although in my opinion too detailed. I would say that this book would be perfect reading for someone who enjoys a lot of minutiae and background details.

After reflecting on it, and writing this review I've decided that I'm giving it a "Liked It/Above Average" rating. If you decide to pick it up for a read, let me know what your thoughts were.

This book was provided free in exchange for a fair and honest review for LoveBytes. The story for much of the time follows the innocent activities at camp, but also frequently follows the intimate pursuits of the boys, and the developing relationship between Julian and Mark. It is well written and often quite funny, especially when the writer takes us into the minds of the various characters and we glimpse what is happening there. (Benjamin)

Author's note:

Barr's Meadow is a revision of *Julian's Private Scrapbook, Book 1,* the first book in a five part series. It includes the first two days of a two week summer camp. Books 2, 3 and 4 cover the story and activities of the following 12 days, Book 5, *The Champions*, concludes the set with the final three days of the camp. A preface explains the reasoning behind this new presentation.

Because there are so many characters, a descriptive index is provided. To assist readers with references to life in the 1960s, a glossary is provided as well— lifting an explanatory burden from an already long narrative. These are entirely auxiliary items, not required to understand or enjoy the fun and frolics. The placement of this story in a scout camp has not been made with permission. The story is not about any organization or its activities, goals, or personnel. It is about specific fictional characters and what is happening in their lives outside of the scouting domain. Presumably much of what the characters do would not be approved or condoned by any scout organization, and nowhere is such a thing suggested or inferred. But in the time and place where this story takes place, as in much of the developed world, the scouting enterprise was so universal and ubiquitous that scout camp was nearly generic. It is a logical setting in which to focus on these characters' lives. The scout organization in this story, entirely fictional as well, is depicted with respect and admiration whenever and wherever it is mentioned.

Though a work of fiction, its source is true-life experience. Similarities to actual persons and places are coincidental. Some of the locations exist, but are used fictitiously.

Publisher's Note:

This book is intended for a mature audience. The subject is sensitive and somewhat controversial. It is not written to serve or encourage prurient interests; it contains no pornography or graphic language, but there are several intimate male/male passages. Readers who are offended by that should be prepared to skip over a few passages or not read this book. All the characters were 60 years of age or older at the time the story first appeared.

prefatory note for the revised edition

Society has come a long way since the first appearance of this story ten years ago—from unmentionable taboo to socially relevant, the subject and purpose has always been to shed light on an awkward reality: it is nearly commonplace for a young person to develop a crush on a coach, teacher, scoutmaster, priest—or a relative, cousin, or neighbor. The object of affection does not need to be in a position of authority, but he or she often is. What has remained largely in the dark and unaddressed is the adolescent's perspective in a coming of age story that involves this awkward social taboo. Times have changed rapidly: at last, film and television series now deal openly with many of the issues explored in the Julian books—this Special Edition is offered in support of that trend.

Too often the story is distorted into one of tragic loss, cruelty, melodrama or perversion. Often it is a morality tale, told by sage minds to instruct or scold; rather than help society grow and become whole, they would prefer to manipulate and control. Or, it is profiteers seeking sensational material to maximize sales. Sometimes one encounters a memoir that is tender, special and sympathetic. Those come closest to dealing directly with the subject. Perhaps that is because they are fact based.

Meanwhile, what is behind the latest story of teen suicide we see in the media? That question is never addressed—it too is largely a taboo area. Recent campaigns to deal with bullying are welcome, but they are after the fact for many, and they sidestep one of the core issues: why has this young person fallen in love with the "wrong" person? That question is not allowed. How then, can it be answered? It never is. Instead, it is met with the pointed finger of blind prejudice. The object of affection is condemned outright without trial or chance to offer a defense, and the youth's views are never considered.

Often the victims have done nothing at all other than be born. They are presumed guilty because they surely will be eventually. The doctrine of original sin has been perverted and loosed on society. It is applied sanctimoniously without regulation or supervision.

Society has not allowed itself to look through the eyes of the adolescent at the needs and drives they feel. That has been outsourced to the clinical psychologists; society generally prefers to avoid it—simply wait it out and hope for the best. It is dealt with by meaningless phrases like "You'll grow out of this..." or "Take my word for it; one day you'll understand..." or "This is for your own good..."

Nothing is more annoying than being patronized. The good intent is compromised by the personal offense it gives. It is a form of cowardice. The recipient, regardless of age, is ill served—and they realize that at some point. They may forgive it eventually, making excuses or allowances—or they may resent it bitterly. The point is, the unexplained problem does not always go away; it could fester into something even more difficult to manage.

The Julian's Private Scrapbook series takes an unusual approach to addressing this social quandary: it is a romantic comedy. Throw out the villains and bullies and the prejudices—take a look at life afresh. Maybe if we look at life without the standard societal dressings and assumptions, we can learn something that will help us get beyond this unpleasant and hostile defect in our culture. We can rediscover what in life is beautiful and natural and fun.

It is not possible of course to guard against everything. There are wildly diverging tastes and interests. To accommodate them all is impossible. There are those who regard bare ankles as obscene—others find them arousing; they are neither to most people. But this book has no special agenda; it seeks to help and to inform by looking at that taboo head on, through the eyes of the smitten. It does so by using comedy and everyday foibles, and it tries always to be honest as well as entertaining. That means it walks a fine line somewhere between the bare ankle and the style of sock fashioned to cover it.

The reader will have to decide for himself whether to read some of the passages. Everyone has his own line, ultimately. If it isn't to your liking, skip to the next scene or put it away. It is meant to amuse and entertain while serving a social purpose, without making any apologies.

Before you begin reading, a word from Eldot about the style…

Here's a heads up about a few unusual devices employed in the revised version of Julian's story. The goal has been to maximize the reader's ability to get inside the characters while retaining the advantage of being an observer outside.

Standard narrative practice is to place the reader either inside or out, not both: inside means using the **first person**, seeing only what the character sees—usually a single character. Outside means using the **third person** point of view, seeing the character and the world of the story from outside, akin to watching a film.

The original version of *Barr's Meadow* employed an experimental style that intermingled first and third person usage; the goal was to enable the reader to get an inside-the-character perspective while retaining the advantages of seeing the character from the outside. The device was not a complete success—it achieved the goal, but at a cost—it was awkward in places and to some readers, somewhat annoying.

The revision has dealt with that problem directly by employing visual clues. All first person point of view elements are in *italics*. No other use of italics is permitted. If italics would usually be employed to express emphasis or stress, **boldface** is used instead.

Fonts:

Times New Roman: all narrative and character content, all third person point of view in standard Times, sentences are capitalized; all first person is in *italics*, sentences are not capitalized.

Optima: sound effects, noise, anything heard that isn't or can't be identified by quotation marks; these are placed between arrow brackets: > > squipp-squipp… < < and > > **whack!** < <

Lucida Handwriting: is used to indicate a dream stream-ofconsciousness; this is always first person point of view.

American Typewriter indicates quoting a handwritten word, phrase or sentence.

Here's a sample using two of these, quoted from chapter 1:

He went over by the bathtub and stood on his mom's scales. Breaking the hundred pound barrier a few months back was a milestone. Last week he was up to one hundred and one pounds. He always took off his clothes for this… didn't want to fudge anything. He stood on the scale until the cylinder thingy came to a full stop. If he leaned a little one way or the other it changed quite a bit. He wiggled and wagged until it stayed in one place.

> > *thunk… thunk… thunk… thunk-thunk…* < <

The bounce sounded soft and springy. *yep. still 101— unless I lean to the right a little. then it's 102. that's about right.* He didn't have a particular goal in mind, except to be more than 98 pounds. He wasn't skinny or fat… just average.

The third person-first person mix is easy to see; the goal is to enhance the reader's engagement with characters.

This technique has been utilized in varying degrees. In many places it is not used at all, in others it is extensive. Generally, the goal has been to get the reader into the character's perception while keeping the ability to see things from the outside.

So when you run across this phenomenon, you'll know what's going on—I hope it makes the experience of Julian's Private Scrapbook even more fun.

Table of Contents

Extras

Key to Symbols

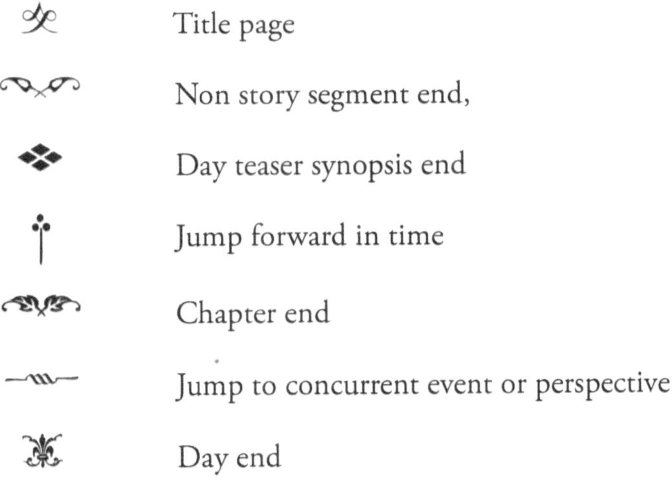

✄	Title page
∿	Non story segment end,
❖	Day teaser synopsis end
†	Jump forward in time
∿	Chapter end
⸺	Jump to concurrent event or perspective
⚜	Day end

Part 1: Germination

1 *Julian*   2 *Mark*

Julian Forrest can hardly wait: he is about to become a teenager at last. He and his mother live in a modest bungalow on Holly Street. Seven years ago they moved here from Joliet, Illinois. After an unpleasant divorce, **Francine** and her infant found sanctuary at her childhood home.

In the spring of 1952 her elderly parents passed away. It wasn't a surprise when her mother went, but a few weeks later her father, as if duty bound, joined his cherished wife. Fortunately, they left Francine with enough to get a fresh start. She moved with her child that summer, just after his fifth birthday. She needed to break with the past, and she wanted her son to grow up in a safer place, free from urban perils and influences.

A close friend she met in college offered an opportunity to join her real estate firm. Geraldine lived in a small town in central North Carolina—just the kind of environment Francine was looking for. The local parish of the same church her family had been in for generations welcomed her, and soon she established herself in the community.

The popular scoutmaster of the boy scout troop sponsored by their church resides several houses down the street. **Mark** Schaefer is a manager in Oglivy & Tucker's Emporium, a locally owned department store. His wife of three years is a registered nurse, studying to become a physician.

It is spring, 1960. The events described in this segment take place almost two years before the main story.

1 *Julian*

Julian Forrest stood on the small stool and examined his face in the bathroom mirror. The bright bulb on each side made it possible to see details very clearly. He was checking to see if there was any sign at all of a whisker. He wanted to be the very first to notice such a thing. Slowly he slid his fingers along the left cheek.

hmm… still perfectly smooth…

He figured he'd feel **something**, maybe little bumps when the whiskers were on the way. He tilted his head upward to examine under his chin. *where will they show up first?* That was not a question he wanted to ask anyone. Being so undeveloped was bad enough without drawing attention to it… but it had to happen pretty soon, didn't it? He was almost thirteen years old.

"I'm as good as thirteen…" The sound of his voice sounded strangely loud in the small room. Julian enjoyed talking to himself sometimes. It helped him sort things out… and he could say whatever he wanted when nobody else was around.

Only five weeks to go, then he'd be thirteen for **real**. *and, I'll be in the eighth grade next year. **finally**.* He smoothed the gentle wave above his eyes. He liked how it looked, actually—his hair was light blond. His deep brown eyes and blackish brown eyebrows were special, according to some people. *what's the big deal about that?* They said it was unusual with blond hair like his. That's what the moms said, anyway. All the moms said he was **beautiful**.

"Blaah!" He made an ugly face at himself and poked out his tongue.

All through grade school he had to put up with them always making a fuss over him. He got fed up with it; they'd come over and visit, sometimes one at a time, sometimes two or three at a time. There was never any place to hide. They always made him stand there and listen, and pretend to be pleased and say nice things back, and report on this and that, and tell what he was good at in school or who his favorite girlfriend was. It was worse when he had to go someplace with his mom... then he was stuck; he had to stay there as long as she did. Finally, all that tapered off this year... now he could pay attention to things that interested him, like making model planes, and cub scouts. The more the ladies let him alone, the better he liked it.

Mrs. Harris did talk one time about his beard; she thought when it came in it would be blond, like his head.

hmm...

He tightened his upper lip by pulling it down.

nope. nothing there yet, either... I wonder if Mrs. Harris is right. personally, I'd like it to be dark brown like my eyebrows. hmm...

He just noticed the area of very fine hair in front of his left ear.

almost white. He turned his head back and forth slowly... *interesting. disappears from view if the light isn't just right.* He stroked the one just like it on the right side— *so fine it's hard to feel it at all... Geraldine calls it peach fuzz. maybe those teeny hairs are like baby teeth or something... maybe that's where the whiskers will appear first.* He frowned at that idea... did that mean his whiskers would be white?

He was pleased right now, because he had just checked his height. Another eighth of an inch was all he needed to make five feet. He kept track of this by using his mom's hand mirror. He had marked the feet and inches on the doorframe of his closet, and when he held the mirror just right, he could see how he was doing. He hoped to make five feet by his birthday. He intended to reach six feet eventually. Then he could stop using this silly stool, for one thing. He was growing fast. His mom clucked her tongue about his pants getting too short already. She thought he should wear them out first, at least. She **really** moaned about the shoes. *the last two pairs are still good, except for being too small.* But she was pleased all the same. He loved it when she complained about things like that, because it showed that she was pleased without doing all that gooey gushing she did with the other moms.

He went over by the bathtub and stood on his mom's scales. Breaking the hundred pound barrier a few months back was a milestone.

Last week he was up to one hundred and one pounds. He always took off his clothes for this… didn't want to fudge anything. He stood on the scale until the cylinder thingy came to a full stop. If he leaned a little one way or the other it changed quite a bit. He wiggled and wagged until it stayed in one place.

>> *thunk… thunk… thunk… thunk-thunk…* <<

The bounce sounded soft and springy. *yep. still 101—unless I lean to the right a little. then it's 102. that's about right.* He didn't have a particular goal in mind, except to be more than 98 pounds. He wasn't skinny or fat… just average

He stepped off the scale and looked down again. That wagging felt good. He did it some more. *I'll get a stiffy if I keep this up. might as well… Mom won't be home for another couple of hours.* He watched it grow as he wagged back and forth slowly. He swung it in time with the song that was playing on the radio in the kitchen; his mom always had that playing whether she was home or not. She said it scared away the burglars. Julian smiled… his mom had some funny ideas sometimes.

"I bet nobody else in town is all that worried about burglars."

He raised his arms and watched the magical transformation take place. He liked the way it felt when his dick grew hard. He wouldn't mind if it felt like that all the time, actually… *ooo… it's poking straight out already. amazing how much larger it gets.*

Julian had just begun puberty. At first he didn't understand what was going on with that. But then he listened carefully to some of the things the other boys, the big boys, joked about.

boy, it's lucky I started Junior High when I did.

Now it made sense; since he learned how to jack off, he understood a lot more. Doing that had become a favorite pastime, in fact. He paid close attention now; listening to the older guys talk in P.E. class and during lunch was a good way to pick up something new like that. Most times they didn't know he was even listening. He tried to be cool and not be noticed. That's one secret he had learned: stay alert and pay attention, and keep his mouth shut. Some things they talked about still didn't make any sense. He figured that some day he'd find out all about it. So far he didn't know anybody among his friends who paid attention to such things.

they aren't ready yet, probably.

His dick was completely hard now—just as **Sixteen Tons** finished on the radio. Trying to keep time was fun—*actually, that song is kind of comical for this.* He went back to his bedroom to get his ruler. He placed the end against his tummy and leaned it against the tip. *just about... four and a half... no, it's four and three quarter inches long.* He pushed it down... *five and one half that way.* Next he put the end down at the bottom and rolled it up along the outside to the tip. That measurement was five and five eights from the sack to the tip... no big change there either. *so if I average the two, I'm five and a... quarter? close enough.* He measured this every month, at least. *it's very thick now when it gets hard. how do you measure that, anyway?* He wrapped his fingers around; his fingertips still went all the way around at the very bottom. *how large is it going to get?* He had seen a few of the big kids a couple of times at PE; some of them made his eyes pop out. And they weren't even stiff. Where did it go when they put on their shorts? They were hairy down there, too. He never got to look up close, of course. *man, when mine isn't stiff, it practically disappears, even without shorts on.*

He sat on the edge of his bed and picked the hand mirror back up... one side magnified things. He lifted his left foot up onto the bed and held the mirror just right, under his bent knee. He had a few hairs there, but nothing that counted... real fine soft ones, super short... almost invisible—they've been there a long time. *kind of like the ones on the side of my face, only a little longer and more spaced apart. ooo! a few new ones... real tiny, but dark like my eyebrows. that's a good sign.*

"You sure take your time!"

do they make anything that makes them grow faster, like lawn food or something? He ran his forefinger across his sack. *ooo!* That made his stiffy bounce... *that's fun.* It tickled if he touched the hairs too softly. He chuckled; now Perry Como was singing away in the kitchen, putting stars into his pocket, completely unaware of what was going on in Julian's room. He enjoyed this weekly inventory ritual. *why is the skin down there so different, anyway? sometimes it's so thick and wrinkly.* He flipped the mirror and looked. *huh. without a magnifying glass, I have practically no hair on my body except on top of my head.* The only place that fact bothered him was at PE Class. *at least I'm not the only one who's still mostly bald down below.*

should I jack off or not, now that I'm all ready? I'm shooting bigger blobs now... one of these days I'll measure that, too. I wonder if I could ever shoot a cup full. I'll make that one of my goals. well, maybe not a whole cup... he giggled. *that would take more than my two balls could ever hold.* He was able to shoot twice a day sometimes. He stroked himself a few times. He was curious about how much others shot, especially those big guys. He was too chicken to ask anyone about that kind of thing. He figured he'd hear about it eventually if he paid attention. He looked down as he pulled the skin up past the sensitive edge at the top... *why does it curve up, anyway?*

He decided to wait and do this later. He wasn't in the mood right this minute. *besides, Mark will be coming home soon... I have to be in position.* Julian always watched Mark get off the bus and walk to his house at the end of the block. Somehow, the day wouldn't finish right if he missed seeing his hero arrive back home safe and sound. He pulled on his red and brown striped t-shirt; it was one of his favorites. *mmm.* It felt good when he pulled on his skivvies with a stiffy going. *oh—* He grabbed the hand mirror. *what does that look like from a distance? hmm... nothing to brag about.* Sometimes his stiffy didn't show at all, which was lucky if he was in the wrong place. *better finish dressing—hafta return the hand mirror to mom's dresser and grab the small stool from the bathroom.*

The thing he didn't like about his mom's room was the smell of that powder stuff she used. She had a bunch of other uggy things too, but she kept them covered up, at least. He put the mirror down on the dressing table where she always kept it—right next to that powder puff thing. *p.u.* This is one room where he never lingered.

He stopped off at the bathroom for the stool and hustled out to the front room. His viewing position was next to the drape on the left side of the picture window. *I love this drape.* When he was little he could hide behind it completely and fool his mom. He did that a lot, until one day she saw his toes poking out from under. *haven't played that game in a long time.* He had the pattern memorized—magnolias, ingeniously woven into the thick fabric. The light blue color was like being out under the sky... he placed the stool close to the window and began his daily vigil.

Julian first saw Mark in church one Sunday when the whole scout troop went together; they always did that on the first Sunday of the month.

The scouts got to carry the flags in the procession. He never forgot that. Soon after, he joined Cubs. Mark looked so tall and imposing. Julian knew his name because he heard all the scouts call him Mark; Julian didn't know his last name. For a long while Julian fantasized about him, wishing he were his father. The reason was, he saw him getting off the bus every day when he came home from work. He saw a movie one time that made him feel so good—it had a scene like that. The father tipped the hat up on the back of his head, picked the boy up and swung him around... *like Grandpa used to, sort of.* That was one thing he had never been able to do, of course, greet his father—except in his imagination.

He learned Mark's schedule by heart: he went to work before Julian was up, even. He rode the bus both ways, and got home at 4:30 p.m. Julian always waited at the window to watch him come home. He didn't know where Mark worked, but he was always dressed up in a suit and tie. For a long time, he had the urge to run up to the bus stop and give Mark a big hug and bring him home, like that boy in the movie. He didn't dare, because Mark didn't even know who he was. One time he found out that Mark already had a wife, so he gave up that idea. But he still liked to think about it sometimes. He liked it best on the hot days, because Mark always had his suit coat flopped over one shoulder and his shirtsleeves were partly rolled up. That looked cool.

Julian looked over at Grandpa's wall clock: fifteen minutes until the bus is supposed to arrive... *better stay put.* One time he missed it because the bus was early, and that was on a Monday like today. The whole day went bad after that. He decided to sit and daydream while he waited... *the radio is too loud; makes it hard to think. I'll leave it alone for now.*

> > *Que sera, sera; whatever will be will be...* < <

they must play that one every hour. He liked it well enough, except they kept repeating the same words so much it kind of got boring. *I'll turn it down after Mark gets off the bus—just a little; the burglars will still be able to hear it.*

Sitting on the stool felt neat; about half as high as a chair, the green paint had some chips and scrapes, but was still strong as could be. *which is surprising, since I made it myself almost three years ago.* That was his first year in Cubs. *this year is okay, but now that Larry is gone it's boring a lot of the time.* Julian could see his knees reflected faintly in the window. *hmm... my knees seem to be sort of flat and wide when I sit like this—they aren't pointy like some knees I've seen. Larry's were sort of pointy, come to think about it. I sort of like the pointy ones. oh well. they don't look so bad when I have pants on.* They made a good rest for elbows. *Luckily, this window goes almost to the floor—* It made watching for Mark easy. When he was little he used to lie on his tummy and peek over the windowsill.

Julian lived with his mother. His father had gone away when he was only a baby. Julian had never met him and had no idea where he lived… he'd never seen a picture of him, even. The only thing he knew for sure was that his father had given him his unique name. He had never met anyone else who had his name, and he liked that. He didn't know for sure, but he didn't think he was named after his father; he wasn't ever called a "junior," at least. Sometimes, he wondered if he looked like his father. No one ever said. He figured he might, since he didn't look much like his mother, except for the color of his eyes. One time he asked her about it and she put him off. She didn't want to talk about his father at all. It didn't bother him much, really, except that he'd met some of his friends' fathers, and they were pretty cool. But his mom was super cool herself, so he figured he was pretty lucky, overall. Still, it would be nice if she had— well, a husband. It couldn't be Mark, of course; but maybe she could find someone. She was lonely at times, even if she tried to pretend she wasn't. She didn't want another husband, though; that was one of those things he didn't understand yet.

His mom was an Assistant in Geraldine's real estate office. *one day she's going to be an agent herself.* Geraldine was a friend of his mom's from college; he was supposed to call her "Aunt Geraldine," which he did just to please her. Might as well, since he didn't have any actual aunts. She was real nice, but sometimes she could be annoying— *she likes to pet me on the head all the time. she likes my hair. well, hers is sort of... stringy.* A lot of strays were always waving loose under the bun in the back. *she probably can't see them.* Sometimes she dyed it different colors—it was probably sort of brown, naturally. Last time he saw her it was a deep red brown, like his mom's big cedar chest. Luckily, she didn't ask his opinion about it.

it's nicer to be home after school. I can do stuff I want, like making model airplanes. His mom always left her office to pick him up after school. She dropped him off at school each morning too, so he never walked there. But she usually had to go back to work, though, like she did today. At first she used to take him to her office, but there wasn't anything for him to do. Four hours was a long time, too. He was sort of a pest, probably. He filled up all the coloring books they had, which maybe was a bad thing. There wasn't anything left for the kids who came in with their parents. So, she gave up on that idea, and brought him home after school and went back to the office. She came back home around six o'clock in the evening on those days. The rule was that Julian had to be in the neighborhood after school. *she's a fanatic about that, for some reason.*

He had to be at home, or with one of the neighborhood kids who had a mom there. *trouble is, all the kids around here my age are girls.* He got tired of playing with them a long time ago. *all they ever want to do is play Dress Up, House, or Doctor. talk about **boring**!* Once in a while he could talk them into a cartoon show on TV. Somebody said those would be in color real soon now. *I'd just as soon stay at home and work on hobbies and cub scouts and stuff. it's been over a year since I had to go over to Lucy's.* What a relief. Her mom had a real tizzy the time Lucy got into her makeup and perfume. *ug and p. u! why do girls like that stuff, anyway? her cat's okay, for a cat. I like dogs better. maybe someday mom will get us a puppy. I bet she'd like it, once it was here a while. the boy across the back fence has a dog. I like to watch them play in their back yard sometimes.*

On Sundays he and his mom went to church, like they used to with Grandma where they came from. *gosh... it's sort of hard to remember her and Grandpa Oscar now—* They died a long time ago. They were so nice. But they were really old. *they sure made a fuss over us at that big service at St. Edward's.* This church is a lot smaller. *they're nice here too, and going here is okay—unless the moms huddle too long afterwards. I hate standing there in a cloud of stinky perfume. they always talk about stupid things like stopping runs in their socks.* Julian laughed out loud. *if they'd wear real socks, they wouldn't have that problem!*

He was always glad to get out of there and come home to work on building his clubhouse or to draw. *I'm getting pretty good at that. the scrapbook is kind of full again.* His teachers said he had talent. *maybe so... I like building things better, actually. trouble is, I'm all out of boards. so far, I'm the only member of my clubhouse.* He sort of patterned it after a comic book he used to have—or was it a cartoon on TV? He wasn't sure. *anyway, mine isn't in a tree.* What cartoon was that? *hmm. lately, TV's been sort of boring.* But there were a lot of scrap boards in the back, and some old tools in the garage. He didn't know where they came from—probably from an old fence. They were here when he and his mom moved from Joliet. She said he could do whatever he wanted with them.

So when the Cubs met here, they helped build the clubhouse with those old boards—it was one of the Den projects. He joined the Cub Scouts when he was nine years old, and now he had completed his Webelos level. His mom was a Den Mother part of one year, and that was the best. That's when he was a Bear Cub. They had most of the meetings at his house or in the back yard. Jeremy and Sid were Bear Cubs too, and they helped out most of all, except for Larry, of course... *I really miss Larry...* They moved up north somewhere last summer. Larry was good at making model planes. *Larry and I earned three silver arrow points that year, too.*

The sound of air brakes snapped Julian back to the present. The bus had just stopped. He watched intently. *there he is!* Mark held a shopping bag in his left hand. *he's helping Miss Carter down the steps. she's the nice old lady that lives across the street. oh! he's going to help her get home. wonderful.* This meant he would see him longer... usually all he got to see was Mark walking to his front door, down at the other end of the block.

Mark wore his light blue sports coat today! wow. makes him look like the President. I like that outfit... looks light and airy. someday I'll get one just like it. He watched Mark help Miss Carter cross the street. They had to walk real slow. It was funny in a way because Mark is so much taller... he must be over six feet tall. *oh-oh...* The cars are backed up going both ways now.

"You should help Miss Carter too, if you get the chance." *there's a picture of that in one of my manuals... do I need to have my uniform on to do that?* Sometimes kids weren't paid attention to unless they had a uniform or a flag.

Now that the year was almost over, Julian was at the end of being a Cub Scout. He and Sid had talked some about what to do next... Sid said he was going to join the troop that Mark ran at the church... *maybe I could too. It would be the perfect thing to do. Danny belongs to it.* Danny lived in the house across the back fence. Julian didn't know him too well because he was a couple of years older. But he had seen him in his scout uniform a couple of times. It looked impressive. *oh! Mark's coming back... he looks so cool!* His maroon tie waved back and forth as he trotted across the street.

Julian blushed suddenly: Mark just waved as he walked by! Julian didn't think about being seen in the window. He waved back, sort of. Mark continued down the sidewalk to his house. He didn't look back. Julian felt pleasantly warm. Mark had never done that before. Probably had never noticed him before even... it must have looked pretty funny, just a head peeking over two knees.

> > *When the moon hits you eye like a big pizza pie...* < <

Julian had to go turn down that blamed radio! He wanted to concentrate on what had just taken place.

2   *Mark*

Mark moved the slide up on the scout kerchief as he made his final spot check in front of the bathroom mirror. This was usually the last step in his routine before leaving the house for an official function. Tonight was probably his final recruiting visit for the year. He checked everything again, just to be sure. He believed strongly that his personal appearance must be immaculate when he went to the home of the prospective scout to meet him and his parents. It set the standard for the scout, and established a clear image in the minds of the parents. *mmm... missed a bit on the left sideburn... that's easy to fix.*

Tonight's visit was unusual because it was so close by: *it's with that blond boy near the bus stop on the Tenth Street corner. Danny has been urging this for weeks.* Mark had a vague idea of what he looked like. He had seen him looking out the window a few days ago. The Den Mother backed up Danny's opinion, so presumably the boy would be good for the troop. *if not, I have a waiting list.* He was able to be selective, a luxury some troops didn't have. He preferred to get the new ones lined up before school was out and the families were off on vacation. Breaking in Tenderfoot scouts was always better in the fall, along with the start of school.

there... sideburn trimmed properly. He picked up his scoutmaster's briefcase on the way to the door. *don't need coat and hat...*

—✺—

Julian enjoyed helping his mom do the supper dishes... they were just about finished. He still had to use the stool to put some away, which was getting to be a pain. He'd built this stool in his Wolf Den, and it was about time to let it have some time off. *I have to admit everything can't go on the bottom shelf. this casserole pan is worth the trouble—scalloped potatoes!* Supper tonight was one of his favorites—ham and peas.

there's Perry Como again, singing about catching falling stars and putting them in his pocket... that's a pretty silly idea. the melody is good, though, easy to remember. they play that song three or four times every day, just about.

> > **binggg-bongg!** < < The doorbell rang.

"Will you go and answer it, please, Julian? I'll be there in a minute." She untied her apron and reached over to turn the radio off.

Julian put the dishtowel on its rack and went to the front door, humming along the unfinished part of Perry Como's song. He opened it, and about fainted: who else but Mark was there, in person! Julian was shocked and pleased all at the same time. He was tongue-tied. Mark was smiling at him! Luckily, his mother had just stepped behind.

"Why, hello." Francine recognized her neighbor, of course. He had called a week ago about this visit. On purpose, she had not told Julian he was coming; she wanted it to be a surprise. "Well, Julian, are you going to invite Mr. Schaefer in?"

"Um… oh, yeah." Julian stepped back. "Please come in." He just noticed something important: *he has his **Scoutmaster** uniform on!* His heart began to race.

"Thank you, very much," he offered Julian his handshake. "I'm Mark."

Julian took his hand. "Um… I'm Julian." *Mom called him Mr. ... umm... what did she say? boy... his hand is warm... his handshake is **strong**.* A tingle ran up his spine… he felt his face turn red… couldn't help it… those bright blue eyes… electrifying. Julian had never imagined standing this close… he was frozen in place.

"I'm pleased to meet you, Julian." *what exotic eyes this boy has... a little shy, but that's usual at first meetings.*

"Would you like a cup of coffee?" Francine often found that was a good way to break the ice.

"Please." Mark was pleasantly surprised. She seemed younger than she sounded on the phone. *doesn't look like a typical housewife at all, more like a professional woman.* Her brunette hair was arranged handsomely. Very different from the boy's wavy golden blond.

She gestured for Mark to follow her into the kitchen.

Mark smiled at Julian again as he passed by. He noted the well-kept living room—tidy, it had the look of a single child house; nothing was out of place, no toys were scattered about, the house was quiet. The furnishings were very old fashioned and conservative, well cared for.

Julian watched the scoutmaster follow his mom into the kitchen. *he's so **tall**! boy am I glad mom came up behind when she did. I didn't know what to say, exactly.* He followed along. He wasn't sure what to do with his hands.

"Thank you." Mark was grateful she had chosen a mug—saucers were never comfortable to use. "I'm glad I didn't interrupt your supper." The room was warm and just as tidy as the living room. A faint aroma lingered from the meal just completed, but he couldn't quite identify it; obviously, the dishes had just been finished. He shook his head, declining her offer of cream or sugar. He took a polite sniff: freshly brewed. *excellent.* He gave a thumb up.

"Let's go back to the living room." It interested her to see his preferences and manners. He took his coffee black. That seemed to fit his rather military bearing. She led him into the living room and sat in the side chair on the far side of the ottoman. It was clear that he was to be seated in the other.

Julian felt awkward... *where should I sit? oh... on the floor by Grandma's giant footstool...*

"Julian, bring your scrapbook here and show it to the scoutmaster." *that will make a favorable impression.* She sensed that it would take a few minutes for Julian to adjust. Her boy wasn't shy, but he wasn't inclined to be forward in presenting himself. *his scrapbook is the perfect conversation piece.*

ohmygosh! Julian did not expect this—he was afraid at first. Hardly anyone else had ever looked at it—his mom, and Mrs. Harris. Quietly, he walked toward his bedroom. He didn't have any time to think about this; he didn't know what else to do. *maybe if I'd known, I could have made it look nicer, somehow.*

"Julian is devoted to his scouting. He has a complete chronicle of everything…"

Julian walked as carefully as he could. He wanted to hear every word. He just realized how important this was: Mark—the **Scoutmaster**—had come to talk about joining the scout troop! *boy, I don't want to foul this up…* He picked his Cub Scout Scrapbook up off his dresser… *the cover is chipped—I should have made a new one.* The leather strings were new this year—the old ones were too short.

He returned to the living room—he paused for a moment. It was hard to believe his eyes—he never expected to see such a thing: Mark, the Scoutmaster, sitting right there! Julian felt so unprepared… he made himself move forward. He placed his scrapbook down carefully, facing the guest. *boy… he's looking straight at me.* Julian was used to seeing him through his fantasy front window; *seeing him up close is like a dream or something.*

"The first part is pretty bad… I was just a new Cub then, and I didn't know what to do, exactly." *should I sit down?* He looked at his mom. She smiled and nodded for him to sit at her feet.

Julian got down on his knees and watched Mark study his sketch of the Wolf Badge. There were some magazine pictures cut out, and a snapshot of his Den in Mrs. Benson's back yard, with a copy of the Pack Awards Program. *I wish I did more…* There were work sheets and a few project sketches… only seven pages for that year. *I forgot to keep some stuff… no Bobcat at all. I mostly forgot about that, it went so fast.*

His mom helped him a little when he did the Bear part; *it's a lot longer—twenty pages, almost.*

Mark was very impressed. "I see a lot more drawings in this section. Your drawings of the bear are really special, Julian." He examined one closely. *remarkable… the paper's too thick for these to have been traced.*

Julian blushed a little at the compliment. He'd found a National Geographic article on bears. He couldn't cut the pictures out, so he drew copies as well as he could. The pages made an odd sound when Mark turned them. *they're heavy… some are overloaded*—Julian was afraid something would get unstuck and fall out. *it's so quiet… oh, yeah: the radio is off for a change.* Grandpa's wall clock sounded extra loud all of a sudden. He could hear the pendulum—it seemed to be keeping track of Mark's slow examination of his drawings.

"Tell me about this one, Julian." The large drawing of gnarled driftwood on a sandy beach was striking—not what one would expect to find in a Cub Scout scrapbook.

"Oh… that's when the Bears went to the beach. I saw that washed up on the shore. It looked kinda different from all the others. It was sort of cool the way it twisted all around like that. So I drew it up." Julian was slightly embarrassed. *I could do a better job now… I never thought about redoing it before…*

Mark was fascinated by this remarkable book. He was compelled to look all the way through. The boy's Lion and Webelos pages were outstanding—even more drawings and cartoons. Clearly, Julian took pride in his work—and his work was impressive. He had not expected to see such a thorough production. This was beyond being a scrapbook. The descriptive paragraphs, even though they were hand printed, were thought out rather well; the events carefully remembered. Amazingly, the only photograph was a copy of the group picture Sherri Harris had given to all the den members. The sketches told the story of the year very well. The handmade wooden binding suited the contents perfectly.

"This is quite an achievement… maybe you could make a book like this for Troop 9 if you decide to join." Mark closed the scrapbook and moved it to the center of the ottoman. Julian's expression was priceless… *the picture of eager, unspoiled youth*—Mark had an odd sensation just now: the three of them gathered around this ottoman reminded him of a Norman Rockwell painting—proud mother, eager boy, corny scoutmaster, photo of grandparents under the lamp on the side table, braided oval rug in the center… *well, it feels good to be in this picture.*

Julian felt his cheeks go all pink again. *as if there was any question about that! all the parents want their son to be a member of Troop 9; they all think Mark is the best Scoutmaster anywhere.* The sound of his voice—not what he was saying, but the tones, the sound itself… *so interesting, so smooth…* the words faded into the background. The sound made Julian feel wonderful.

As Mark talked to his mom, Julian studied his face. He had never been this close. He was in the perfect spot: he settled down just at the side of the ottoman, propped his elbows on his knees and put his arms up into a triangle; his hands made a perfect chin cradle. While the Scoutmaster told his mom all about the High Adventure Program, Julian examined every inch of his face. *cool, the way his hair parts on one side.* Light brown, soft looking, with some gentle waves that reached down to the red and gold scout kerchief. *whoa...* a fine line revealed where he shaved his chin... *and around his mouth*—what a wondrous discovery. It was fascinating to watch his lips move as he talked. The whisker pores! *interesting: faint, invisible unless I sit close up... no actual whiskers are poking out.* He had not noticed before that Mark had to shave; he couldn't tell from a distance. The mustache line over the upper lip was fascinating... it moved and undulated when Mark talked. *what would he look like if he didn't shave? his Adam's apple is really cool... no whisker traces there.* The straight line at the bottom of the sideburn was perfect. Julian looked back over to his eyes... they're such a bright blue; they sparkle. *oh*— the Scoutmaster caught him staring— *he smiled!* Julian blushed; he felt warm all over. He had to look away for a second—but looked back when he thought it was safe. *wow, this is so... I don't know the word... this is one of the best nights ever.*

"Julian, will you go into the kitchen and fetch the coffee, please? We need a refill." Francine was impressed with the thoroughness of this man... and his attention to detail. *his outstanding reputation is understandable.*

Julian couldn't see what they liked about that stuff. As he stood up he noticed an awkward thing: he had a stiffy. *lucky nobody's looking.* When he went into the kitchen he reached down and pointed it up. He was glad for the chance to straighten it up, actually, because it would go down quicker that way... *it's harder to tell when it's pointed straight up.* He didn't want to take a chance. It depended on which pair of pants he had on. *these are only fair... I'll keep my hand in front just to be safe.* He'd been having that problem lately. It happened at school, pretty often now. It would just pop up by itself. He never knew why.

Sometimes he thought there was a secret crew down there cranking the handle on a large round winch wheel, just to have fun. He could hear the crew chief ordering them to 'Pull!' on one side, and 'Push!' on the other. As the cable grew more taut, one revolution of the winch at a time, up it went until it stood tall, nice and hard. When they were done cranking the wheel, the crew stood with their hands on their hips, proud as could be. They all had stiffies too. One time he was in a study period when he thought that, and he giggled at the idea, by mistake. Everybody looked at him wondering why he had laughed. He just blushed and buried his face in the book. Thankfully, nobody ever asked what was so funny. He liked getting stiffies, really, because they felt so good.

He heard his mom talking about him to the Scoutmaster; she always did that, and it was sort of annoying. To hear her tell, he was the most beautiful most talented best kid in the world, blah blah blah. Why did moms always do that? He thought she had stopped it years back. *but here she is, doing it all over again. I hope she doesn't overdo it and make the Scoutmaster sorry he came over.* He unplugged the coffee pot and hurried back to the living room.

He filled their cups; at least they had changed the subject... *phew, this stuff smells strong... oh!* The scoutmaster had just looked at him and smiled. It was only a glance, but... Julian turned back to the kitchen quick. *that look, that smile!* It made his stiffy come right back. *ooo... be careful! wow...* He almost dropped the coffee.

The Scoutmaster explained how to fill out all the forms. "It's easier if you're a Cub...*"*

Julian strained to hear every word as he put the pot back on the counter and re-inserted the power cord. He tried to imagine what it would be like at a meeting of Troop 9. *it's a lot bigger than the Webelos Den, maybe four or five times bigger.* They met every Tuesday night at the parish hall meeting room. He heard they had a great time—and they had lots of hikes and campouts. He hurried to get back in there and study Mark some more... he held his hand in front.

He settled back down, and looked at the Scoutmaster's large hands. Fine hairs appeared just above the knuckles. They lay flat against the skin. *how cool could anybody's fingers be, anyway?* He glanced at his own fingers: hairless, of course, just like everything else. They're about half the size! His eye moved up to the wrist... a wristwatch peeked out from under the edge of the cuff. The olive green shirt was pressed and really spiffy looking. A red and white patch on his shoulder said "9." *hmm... they should have used gold instead of white, like on the other patches.* White looked all wrong... the scout kerchief was bright red and gold. He glanced down to the shoes—real shiny, dark brown. The socks were the same olive green as the shirt... Julian wanted to reach over and touch the crease to see what it felt like. They weren't like any pants he had seen before.

"Why don't you show Mr. Schaefer your room, Julian? I think you'll be interested," she told the scoutmaster. "His room is a regular museum of scouting."

oh, no! my room is too messy! He wasn't expecting this; models and kits were spread out everywhere. *worktable is a complete jumble…* His bed was made, and that was about it.

"What a great idea!" Mark looked at Julian with an eager smile and lifted his eyebrows. "I'd really like that, Julian. Would you mind?"

The Scoutmaster's look into his eyes was electrifying. Julian had another of those sudden get warm all over feelings; he almost dizzied. "Uhh… sure! But it's a little messed up right now—I was working on a plane—" he got up to lead them, and—*oh, no! I still have a stiffy!* Clumsily, he tried to cover it with his left hand. *they're looking the other way—maybe they didn't notice.*

His mother took over the tour, thankfully. First she went to the closet. She pulled out his shirt and showed all the patches and points she had sewn on. The Webelos Arrow was the last one. Julian was proud enough of it, but it looked a little silly, now that he saw the dark olive green Scoutmaster's uniform. *man, that's **really** cool.* She showed the Scoutmaster the big bulletin board; it had all the things stuck on it that were too bulky to fit into the scrapbook. *it's packed full of stuff—I should thin it out… a lot of school stuff too.* A couple of big drawings had an A on one corner, along with Mrs. Connor's comments. He always wished that was on the back, because he didn't want to brag. But he was proud of the large drawing of a boat with a sail. He had seen that on a field trip when he was in the fifth grade.

His mother explained about these things. She was doing her usual flattery, but at least it gave him a chance to stand back and fix his "problem" again. Then he glanced over at his bed and blanched. It was made, all right, but the box of Kleenex was lying right beside his pillow… *no way to get it out of sight now.* The wastebasket was on the other side of the bed; that helped. *maybe the Scoutmaster won't see it. maybe he won't know why it's on my bed.* Julian snuck a glance— *he's looking at the models suspended in the air above the bed. maybe he hasn't seen the Kleenex.*

The imaginative arrangement of the hanging models reminded Mark of his own when he was an Air Scout. He had a squadron of F-86 Sabre jets in pursuit of a MiG-17. It had taken a week to get them hung just right. *these are more like an air show parade.*

Julian was amazed that the Scoutmaster was so interested in his models. Sometimes he liked to lie on his bed and look up and pretend they were flying. *maybe they should be farther apart.* He looked back to see what Mark thought—*he's looking right at me!* Julian froze—that blue sparkle! It's more than that—it's a **dazzle**. Julian just now thought about that stupid song—it kept repeating catch a falling star... never let it fade away. The melody echoed in his head... *what's that song about?*

Mark reached over and put his hand on Julian's shoulder. "I'm really impressed, Julian," He pinched his thumb and forefinger together slightly, and smiled. "Tell me about your models."

Electric, that's what it was. That pinch was like nothing he had ever felt. It was sort of a tickle... only not the kind that makes you want to laugh and squirm all around. It was soothing in a way. It curled up from behind his right ear around the back of his neck up to his head. His stiffy really loved it, too. He looked the Scoutmaster in the eye... he was immobilized briefly, focused on the intense blue... *he's raising his eyebrows, questioning or something... oh! he asked about the models! boy, I'm really messing up.*

"I... uh... I got started last summer just before I was a Lion in Cubs," Julian stammered. He recovered fast. "I like the old time one best," he pointed at the Red Baron's Fokker Dr1. He kneeled down by the edge of his shelf unit so that he could hand it to the Scoutmaster to look at up close.

"I used to make models myself, you know." Mark knelt down next to Julian to examine them closely. Some of these models were new to him. "I see you've painted these insignias yourself." *this really brings back some memories.*

"Yeah... I wish they were better. The ones in the box wouldn't stay on. I need a smaller brush, I guess."

"Next time try wiping the surface clean with some alcohol while you're soaking the decal; you can't always see the fingerprints you leave while assembling the parts. Fingerprint oil can stop the decal from contacting the surface." Mark picked up that tip at Johnny's Toy Shop. *a great place to get models.*

It was fantastic that the Scoutmaster liked this kind of thing. Since Larry moved, no one else he knew was interested in them. *he examines them so carefully, close up.* While Mark was examining the wheels on the P-51, Julian noticed an **amazing** thing: an aroma unlike anything he had ever smelled before. It was like that touch, somehow. Julian wanted to smell him for an hour, at least. He did not want the Scoutmaster to stand up. But he did. He had looked at all the models.

"Well, I have certainly enjoyed meeting you both." Mark looked Julian in the eye once again. The boy's intense stare was startling. He hadn't seen anything quite like it before. "And thanks for the excellent coffee, Mrs. Forrest." *what a pleasure, what a surprise, this visit. this boy will be a real asset to the troop.*

Julian tagged along behind as his mother conducted the Scoutmaster to the door. He was still a little overwhelmed by everything.

"Thanks again." Mark gave her a short bow; he stepped onto the porch and turned to Julian. He stood at attention. He gave the scout salute briefly, then a big grin. "See ya later," he winked his left eye. He turned and went down the steps.

They watched him walk the short distance back to his own house.

"What do you think, Julian? You certainly want to join his troop, don't you?" Francine was delighted; Julian was quite awed by the scoutmaster. She'd never seen him so taken.

Julian was still blushing, still savoring things… his mind was full of impressions and feelings, all going at once… *that wink! the way he looked at me!* Julian replayed every minute. He spoke slowly. "He is **so** cool, Mom, isn't he?" He extended this moment for as long as he could… until Mark disappeared into his house. Julian looked up at his mother and jumped up and down. "I can, can't I? Yes, yes, yess! This is the **coolest!**"

He ran into his bedroom and jumped onto the bed. He buried his face in his pillow and hollered for joy. He sat up at once and took a deep breath. He said loudly, "Yes!" His model airplanes swung back and forth wildly as if they shared his excitement—his dive onto the bed had caused a sudden breeze.

Francine was amused and delighted. It gave her such a boost to see Julian this happy. And she was very impressed with Mark Schaefer. He was quite a bit younger than she had expected; ten or twelve years younger than herself, at least. Probably not thirty yet, but certainly an able and centered person. The wedding band was not a surprise; she couldn't tell if the insignia on the other ring was an official scout item, or from a college fraternity. She closed the door.

Yes, this was the right thing for her son; he was going to need a man to lead him through the trials of adolescence. She didn't regret her decision to remain completely out of touch with Adrian after the divorce, but she could see now that not knowing his father had been a handicap of sorts. *well, Julian seems to have done well enough without Adrian so far. he looks more like his father all the time, which is a good thing, in itself. but now he needs a male role model—a stable, reliable one.* Mark Schaefer's arrival was exactly what she needed. *he's nearly the opposite of Julian's father.* She felt relieved and fortunate. Moving to this town had always been the right decision, but now more than ever, she felt secure. *I must thank Geraldine again*; she made it possible to start a life here for Julian and herself. *it is a wonderful town.*

Julian calmed down and sat on the side of his bed. *everything is so wonderful…* he closed his eyes and tried to recreate the sensations… The Scoutmaster's flashing blue sparkle, his touch, his **magic** touch… and the **smell!** *boy. oh.* He looked down: his stiffy was really throbbing. *boyohboy…* he wanted to do it this minute, while these thoughts were strong and fresh. *but mom might come in… yikes!* Could he wait? *how can I do this? if I close the door, she'll wonder why… ooo…*

Part 2: Sunday

Julian has been in the scout troop for nearly two years. Scouting was his primary focus from the first day; his first year was the best year in his life, with one exception: he was unable to attend summer camp. He worked hard and saved all the next year and is on the verge of fulfilling his great dream at last: two weeks with his idol. His attraction to the scoutmaster has become an obsession. Getting Mark's personal attention is his primary goal.

After a year of hard work, he conquered the arduous swimming requirements for First Class rank: he is now prepared for the annual summer camp at Walker Lake. He has been unable to think about much else for weeks.

Mark is in a quandary about how to handle Julian's crush. A major decision is made.

Several other scouts in the troop are introduced. Many of them will be important in the events of the next two weeks. Central in this chapter:

Sid Thomas and **Jeremy** Baker are Julian's closest friends, and they are in his patrol. They moved up from the same Cub Scout pack.

Tom Dawson, **Danny** Laskey and **Nick** Harrison are members of the Flaming Arrow, the exclusive troop leadership patrol.

3   *departing for camp*

Something was missing—he could feel it in his gut. Mark stood in the center of his bedroom, hands on his hips. He'd been going over the recent troop activities in his mind while he lined everything up. He reviewed his progress again... he'd assembled everything needed for summer camp, as usual—*what's so different this time?* His papers, supplies and manuals were packed, and his other gear was collected. He was in a strange frame of mind about camp this time—*why am I...* he couldn't seem to define **what** he was feeling. He couldn't focus on things as usual; it was almost as if he wasn't ready, or something... but that was ridiculous. Well, it had been an odd year, after all.

He scratched his head and surveyed the nearly completed packing again. His dress uniform was pressed and ready to be placed on top. The clothes dryer had to complete its cycle before he could finish... his running sweats and headband were there along with his workout socks. *everything else is done; I haven't forgotten a thing.* He shook his head. He went to the basement to check.

The healthy rumble and tumble sound told him everything was going well down here... *mm... five minutes left on the dial... might as well wait for it.* He sat cross legged on the floor with his back against the washing machine... the air was a little less steamy and cloying down low.

He stared across the room, not focusing on anything in particular. A few seconds went by. *hmm...* being ready had an unexpected side effect: nothing to do. He was a patient man generally, but unaccustomed to simply waiting—it made him feel useless... *should have brought along a magazine. no point in going for one... the machine would be done by the time I got back. relax, Mark; it'll do you some good.* He smiled... *Mom always said that when I was a kid. so did Erik. they were always right. what's five minutes?*

He took a deep breath and exhaled... a relaxation routine usually worked. He closed his eyes; the buzzer would sound soon enough.

Another deep breath. The drone of the dryer and the sound of soft cottons being jumbled and fluffed encouraged reverie...

His thoughts returned to the issue that had preoccupied him from time to time for weeks. The visit last week to see the Troop 9 Scrapbook was the most awkward yet. Julian was no longer able to disguise his erections. Sometimes it almost seemed intentional. Mark was sure Francine did not know how serious Julian's preoccupation had become. He tilted his head, uncertain... could it be a real live crush? He noticed it first when he visited to look at the new scrapbook. He discounted it at the time... *erections at that age are always unpredictable and random.* When it occurred to him that it might be a response to his own presence, he was mildly amused; *I assumed it would pass.* Instead, it had intensified.

Francine makes light of it; she thinks Julian's "hero worship" is amusing. she's of the opinion that Julian merely puts me in place of the father he's never known. I thought she was right at first... made sense. now I'm not so sure. it's a convenient enough explanation, so I've let it rest at that. I'm not anywhere close to being old enough; big brother, maybe.

Mark understood Julian better now—that was why he had been careful always to visit when his mother was at home. He'd been afraid that if he was to drop in when Julian was alone... well, he had a gut feeling—Julian might accidentally on purpose do something. Mark wasn't ready for that, at all.

His own response had gone through a curious evolution. He was flattered for a time, then bemused; for a brief time he was annoyed. Lately, however, he felt a responsibility. Julian had connected with his—he didn't have the term handy. He remembered something from Psych 101... instinct? No, wrong word. Anyway, something related to the drive adult birds feel—shelter the vulnerable chicks before they leave the nest. Something separate from parenting, but similar in a way. Nursing dogs adopt kittens sometimes and let them become one of the litter... that kind of thing. Julian needed guidance, direction. *Francine is partly correct... he's never had a father or a brother to guide him.* Mark frowned... *I didn't pay very good attention in that class...* he tilted his head upward—his train of thought shifted; *around that time, I met Erik.* He shook his head—he didn't need to dwell on that.

Mark now had an expectation, almost, like being given a new assignment, a new job. It wasn't defined in his mind yet. He had to admit that was one reason he made those home visits—curiosity, as much as anything. And, living so near made dropping in a given, almost. He enjoyed the visits, actually. *Francine is always fun. it's good to know your neighbors.* Still, he needed to be careful... there were inherent dangers; he couldn't very well give circumstances free reign. *that's why this two-week camp is somewhat worrisome. I won't have Francine there to duck behind if Julian... well, gets out of line.* He had no specific plan in mind. *aha!* He nodded affirmatively... *that's probably why I'm so unsettled about camp this year.* He was used to setting and meeting goals, not drifting about.

hum... his finger had drawn a spiral in the dust on the floor... *is there a hole in the lint trap or something?*

"When do you need to be there?" Pat called down the stairs.

"No later than eight, but seven thirty would be ideal, if you can." Mark wanted to be there early, actually, to make sure the bus and truck are positioned properly. They needed to be clear of the parking lot before the crowd arrived for the nine o'clock service.

"Fine; I'll be in the study. Just let me know when." Pat had a study group meeting, but it wasn't until two thirty. She'd be able to make that easily.

Mark was grateful that Pat was so wrapped up in her grad studies. It was a perfect counterpart to his involvement in scouting. *in a couple of years, she'll have to intern somewhere. that's going to be interesting to arrange... we might have to get a second car.*

Mark never had to worry about his marriage, such as it was. As far as Pat was concerned, whatever he wanted or needed he could have, as long as it didn't get in the way of her career. Romance had never been an issue. They had both needed to satisfy their families' need more than their own, so four years ago the "social contract" was arranged to everyone's satisfaction. *luckily, we get along fabulously.*

And, it gave Mark latitude to indulge in his fondness for scouting. Anyway, Francine had never shown any signs of... well, personal interest. Julian, on the other hand... that's another matter. What bothered Mark—a little, not a lot—was that Julian had become a presence in his thoughts... *at this point it's only a presence... but it's something new...* it felt pleasant,

it made him feel light. He had no experience handling this kind of thing.…
he felt drawn by the challenge. He looked forward to those home visits.
they're a great alternative to TV westerns, come to that.

He recognized that what he felt inside had a vague connection with
the memory of his college romance. Erik wasn't a romance: he was a **life**.
When Erik was killed, Mark had closed himself from any further
emotional opportunity. But that was nearly six years ago. Time had
allowed him to move on, he supposed, in many ways. It had been a while
since he had felt that emptiness and hurt—or dwelt on it, at least. He
didn't feel guilty about not thinking about Erik so often, which was
probably a good thing.

*maybe that's why I'm more conscious of Julian's… **energy**, shall I
say: it's consistent and constant.* And after, what… ten months? *maybe
longer…* It was impossible for Mark to ignore or dismiss it entirely. It
had to be faced and dealt with, somehow. *summer camp is an ideal place
for that—is it the right time, though? probably…* in another year, what
could it lead to? Some way had to be found to get Julian redirected before
he did something unfortunate.

>> **ZZZZ…** <<   The buzzer went off suddenly.

Mark jumped up at once, his reverie shattered. *I have to unload this
machine and finish packing!* Quiet at last— *what a relief…* that droning
sound had become oppressive. *after this I'll wait upstairs.*

He skipped every other step: "Hasten, Jason, time's a-wastin." Mark
often used his scout admonitions on himself. Back in his room, he emptied
the basket across his bed; the clothes would cool as he sorted and folded.
He sniffed at a T-shirt briefly. He checked the weave—a habit he brought
home from work. *this is not domestic…* He pulled at the fabric in both
directions. *hmm.* He examined the ticking around the neck: *asian?* His
expertise was legend at the store. He was now Director of Purchasing at
Oglivy's. He sniffed again; *that was stupid: fabric softener always makes
everything come out smelling the same. hmm. thin ticking… probably
from west India—it will be interesting to see how long this holds up.* No
information on the label. *I don't recall buying this—*probably out of one
of the sample lots. Imports were getting more common these days. *they
should require them to be identified on the label.*

Now then: back to the matter at hand. Julian getting hard every time
they crossed paths would not be so good at camp. *the campsite*

assignment will be key...   Barr's Meadow would be perfect, but I can't take that for granted.   In any case, he had found a way to keep Julian's mind on scouting, much of the time, at least. Having Nick be a mentor will help. He can supervise Julian's work on the newsletter during his spare time; *Nick will appreciate being able to hand that entire assignment off, eventually.*   Mark enjoyed keeping promotions a last minute surprise... *Julian's reaction will be fun to see.*

he's made First Class... there'll be plenty to keep him busy.   Mark counted out seven pair of socks—*I'll stuff these down the sidewalls of the pack...* two days per pair; experience and hygiene had taught him long ago: bring plenty of socks... *there's enough of the unknown about this to make it a true challenge.*   He paused for a second. Another consideration just came to mind: the built in "hazards" of a scout camp. Five or six hundred horny adolescent boys gathered in the same vicinity meant that a certain amount of "extra-curricular" activity was to be expected. Two weeks is long enough to do a lot of playing around… Mark knew this from his own experience. His instinct was to protect Julian somehow—at least from anything major. *hmm.*   He was more eager to get started now. How well could he shield Julian? More than a few heads will turn to look— *classic beauty replaced his boyish good looks more every day. before long he's going to draw a crowd of followers. in another year, he'll be irresistible.*   Mark's sense of danger was alerted. He had an image of a pack of wolves panting heavily as they stalked an unsuspecting fawn. He cinched the top strap tightly and gave it a firm pat.

There: his duffel, backpack and travel case were packed. "Time to hit the trail." He donned his Pershing campaign hat; *Pat enjoys seeing me in this. it does make me a bit of a cartoon. well, it's a good costume, so what the heck?*   He chuckled. At least he didn't take himself too seriously. 'Onward, men,' he commanded silently.

—⁓—

Julian stared at the number circled in red on his wall calendar: **9**. He always liked that number. *my birthday is July 9... must be my lucky number or something. Troop 9, June 9... both those are lucky, for sure...* The second Sunday in June was here **at last**. School was out for the summer—Julian's great dream was about to come true. The troop was about to leave for summer camp. *I get to spend two full weeks with Mark!*

this is going to be so much better than those weekend campouts. He had gone to every one of those… each had two or three pages in the Troop Nine Scrapbook that he had started. But they always treated him like a little kid on those trips. Just when he thought they were going to talk about something interesting, they'd see him and shush right up. He got to see Mark take his jeans off a couple of times, though. *that was really hot!* He was always over at a different tent, of course. The big kids surrounded him all the time. But Mark was always interested in the scrapbook, and that's when Julian got to sit next to him.

oh. I'm about to get a stiffy just thinking about it. He shook his head to clear his thoughts. *I don't need to mess up things today, of all days. 'specially by having to hide a stiffy from everybody.*

Julian inhaled deep… *mmm.* Neat's-foot oil. What a nifty smell. He looked down. *my feet are so huge.* He rocked back and forth to test his new hiking boots. They were rigid and heavy and **big**—out of place inside the house. They were laced up and ready to go. He stepped over to the bed—

>> *squip-p-p-p… squip-p-p-p squip-p-p-p… squip—* <<

The thick soles made an exotic, muscular sound on the hardwood floor… *these are so cool.* Before on a hike, all he had was tennies. *these have deep treads like truck tires!* He sat on the edge of the bed and checked his list again.

Everything was packed; his new duffel bag was filled and stuffed into his backpack; his sleeping bag, extra blanket, pillow, and scout equipment were ready. During the week his mother had helped him get all his things together. He was so anxious he could hardly stand the wait. He wore his official kerchief, all his patches were sewn on, and he had on his brand new pair of olive green scout shorts… *the red ribbing along the pocket tops is so cool.* That gave him a pair in reserve, which was probably a good idea. *two weeks is a long time for one pair to hold out.* His floppies were tucked in, just in case there's a beach to play on. He had his tennies and six pair of sox. He had his new Troop 9 T-shirts, the ones with a monogrammed pocket, and his scout cap. He had six new pair of Hanes skivvies—his saggy old Fruit of the Looms were being retired from duty. He had his toiletry kit, including a tube of sun cream—*Mom insisted on that.* He had extra batteries to go with his flashlight; he had his emergency kit and wallet—*Mom gave me twenty-five dollars!* That was really amazing. *that's more money all at one time than I've ever had in my life!* He had his special box of pencils and notebooks. He kept out his new drawing tablet so he could do a sketch for the scrapbook on the bus. He had packed and repacked at least four times. He'd never been so ready in his life

The radio volume in the kitchen increased abruptly. Julian looked up.

"Julian?" Francine called out from the living room. "Are you ready? We should go."

I knew it! she always turns it up whenever we leave the house. Julian grabbed his pack and headed for the door. "Here I come!" His boots clomped down the hallway—it sounded like the whole Wolf patrol was along. *they almost drown out Mom's radio, they're so loud.*

Julian loaded his pack onto the back seat, and climbed in front with his mom. He had his new tablet and his sack lunch up here with him— *I need these on the bus.* He pulled the checklist out of his shirt pocket and studied it again while they drove to the church parking lot. He'd read it a million times, but… anyway, he didn't want to think about anything else right now.

Francine looked over at Julian, amused… *such an intense boy. he looks so handsome in his new uniform. what will he look like after two weeks in the wild?* She couldn't imagine the challenge Mark faced, herding nearly fifty of these bundles of energy. She waved at a car waiting to turn into traffic… *it's Louise West bringing her two boys along. they're older than Julian. how Louise can keep straight which boy is which is a mystery. how fast they've grown up! Julian will be their size all too soon.* She had mixed feelings about that—she adored her little boy. He was growing into a man so much sooner than she had expected. What a week he had, getting ready.

It had been a busy week for her too. Geraldine had a special vacation planned during Julian's time at camp. She was nearly ready, but she didn't want Julian to know she would be going out of town while he was away, so her preparations were very discreet. Her main purpose in life was to keep him safe and free—including from having worries about her. She had reservations about this, but Geraldine had prevailed, arguing that it would be just as well to have something to do besides worry about Julian for two weeks. Geraldine knew her too well. Francine reasoned that she could focus on their secret little jaunt after Julian was safely on his way. *it's a comfort knowing that Mark is in charge.* She slowed—the parking lot was up ahead already—it wasn't a long drive, less than two miles. It was swarming with scouts and parents. She found a place to park. It felt strange to be arriving here early on Sunday; *I have to come back for church in a few minutes.*

"Ooo! We're here!" Julian was so hyped up about the trip that they'd arrived before he knew it; he hadn't seen a thing along the way. He looked around—scouts everywhere! A **lot** more than they had on campouts! *yikes!* He craned his neck to look—*where's Mark? ah! there he is, all dressed in his summer uniform, with his clipboard, checking off the names of everyone as they get aboard. he has one of those wide rim hats on! looks like Sergeant Preston! he always looks so cool. boy! half the troop must be here. yow! what if I'm too late! ooo! I have to hurry!*

His mom had barely shut off the ignition when he opened the door. "Well, here goes!" He got out and unloaded his pack from the back seat— he had to get it over to the truck, quick... the troop luggage and supplies were being carried to camp in Murray Farm's big red stake truck. A couple of patrol leaders were up there stacking everything by patrol.

"Not so fast..." Francine checked to see that the sleeping bag was tied on securely, and the nametag was in order... everything was being stacked together. *so many of these duffels and sleeping bags look identical.*

"Give me a hug, please." He wouldn't think of it until later... this was just about the biggest thing in his life right now, and she wanted it to be as fun as possible for him. Forgetting to give a hug would begin to nag at Julian. *he's always a very considerate and thoughtful boy, but sometimes he forgets until later, and feels guilty.*

Julian stopped fidgeting and put down his tablet and sack lunch. He looked at his mother and smiled happily, gratefully. She had her turquoise blue business suit on this morning—one of his favorites. He hugged her vigorously. He was almost as tall now—he didn't have to stand on his toes any more. "Thanks, Mom... it's okay if you have some fun, too." He didn't tell her to go and live it up, or anything like that, even though he wished she would. *she'll probably read another book or something. she's so wonderful.* He never had to worry about her. He kissed her lightly on the lips. That meant a lot to her. It meant a lot to him too, actually.

She escorted him to the line at the bus. The boy in front of them was much taller; that was comforting, in a way. She put her hands on Julian's shoulders; they were next. Mark had been over to the house so often she was unable to be formal with him. "Good morning, Mark." She found his official hat charming.

Mark looked up from his clipboard and smiled warmly; he had become a friend of the family. "Hello, Francine... are you all ready for a boy-free two weeks?"

She laughed. She had not thought of it that way. "Here's hoping you have good weather the whole time." She pushed Julian forward gently, delivering him into Mark's care. She did a last minute tug on his kerchief—a wrinkle had appeared. *silly, of course, to fuss... mothers do things like that automatically. my boy looks perfect, as always.*

Julian looked into Mark's face and gave a "Here I am, the Cheshire Cat" grin. Julian's eyes, however, communicated something deeper. Looking directly into Mark's sparkling blue eyes nearly always gave him a stiffy, and today was no exception. *I'm standing so close...* Julian blushed and looked down. *oh! Mark has on shorts too. wow... they show more than the long pants.* The angle of the bright morning sun helped highlight the contours... Julian's glance had landed where it usually did, and he was especially intrigued by what he saw this morning.

Mark had been expecting a look like this from Julian, but it was still difficult to keep his eyes steady; instinct warned that he was facing more than a promising young scout. It was a mix that he had no experience with, and the challenge was invigorating. The sentiment emanated from what appeared to be the face of pure innocence. He put his hand on Julian's shoulder and gave his customary greeting. "Welcome aboard, Julian."

He felt a small pang of conscience. *I know better than to do that. the blush is subtle this morning.* Julian's second look at him was more gentle... *brown eyes can be so mellow.* Mark smiled and patted Julian's shoulder, nudging him toward the bus door. "You're the second Wolf here. Casey's on board already."

Francine resisted the urge to give Julian a final hug and watched him lunge eagerly for the bus door. She gave Mark a parting smile; *my boy is in safe hands. now I can focus on Geraldine's madcap adventure plans.*

Mark smiled at her, like a good neighbor and scoutmaster should. He was grateful that Francine was here... oddly enough, he felt safer when she was present. He also felt a secret thrill—*the challenge is at hand. now I have to figure out what to do—at camp I'm on my own. can't worry about that now...* A line of eager boys were waiting to be greeted. "Good morning, Jeremy. Hello, Mrs. Baker—good to see you again."

—⁓—

Julian leapt up the steps and raced down the aisle; he had been planning this trip very carefully. He knew just where he was going to sit: right in front of the emergency exit on the driver's side. That was where he could watch Mark the best. *yay! it's still empty.* He scooted in and sat by the window. He put his lunch and tablet on the seat and adjusted his stiffy quickly. Luckily, once he did that the fly design of his new shorts hid things pretty well when he was seated. *when I don't have anything else to do, I'll draw a couple of sketches for the scrapbook.* He looked out the window. *there she is...* he bounced up and down happily and waved at his mom, and she blew him a kiss. He watched her go to the car. *why is she leaving? church starts in a few minutes... oh! she forgot her hat!* He chuckled. Just as she drove by he realized... *I've never been away from home for more than one night. she'll be okay... she might have some peace and quiet for a change—although I'm not much of a noisemaker any more.* He hadn't worked on the clubhouse in over a year. And Geraldine said she'd have her crew take care of the lawn. *she's nice, actually.*

Jeremy settled in beside him. He was in the Wolf patrol too; they'd been friends ever since his second year of Cubs. Jeremy was usually very serious about things. Julian remembered their first meeting in the troop. He had called Mark 'Mister Schaefer.' Mark looked left, then right, and said "Who? Where is he? I don't see his name here!" Sometimes Mark really broke him up. He wanted the scouts to call him Mark. It felt funny to do that at first, but after a while, it seemed just right. He checked to see if Mark was on board yet... *nope. still checking scouts in.*

Sid took the seat in front of Julian with a flourish. He bounced on the bench seat a couple of times to test its hardness. *ugh... the church bus is just like a school bus: the usual hard-as-a-rock seat: two hours plus of torture. I'll have T.B. before we get out of town.* He leaned against the panel under the window and sat with his legs stretched out. *I'll take up the whole bench for as long as I can. at least there aren't any cracks in the leather—or whatever this dark green stuff is. fake leather, for sure.* He looked over the seatback at his two buddies.

"Hiya, Doodles." Sid glanced at Julian's sketch tablet. He scooted the glasses up on his nose. Sid was partial to Julian because he could always take a joke.

"Hi, Sid." Good old Sid, with his wide grin and buck teeth. Julian liked Sid a lot. *He's such a wise guy, always dreaming up a gag to pull or a wisecrack to make. Julian wondered sometimes if Sid spent time making them up so that he'd have them all ready when the time came.* "Did you get it, like you hoped?"

Sid swung up on his knees and leaned over the back of the seat. "Yess! Eat your hearts out," he grinned. His father had given him a classy new air mattress.

"How much did it cost?" Jeremy was a little envious.

"Not my department. I'd just as soon stay in the dark; don't want to feel guilty or anything." That was a huge fib. "I tested it, of course. I may be tempted to rent it out, actually. I could get rich by the end of camp." He glanced at the kid who had just sat down and taken the aisle side of the seat. *looks okay, but... three hours is a while to sit next to somebody.*

Julian and Jeremy gave each other a "fat chance!" look. Sid had looked away and missed it. Julian was glad for him. Sid was the skinniest boy he knew, and he needed an air mattress if anybody did. *those canvas cots are probably okay, but after a while, like two weeks, they might be a little tough to take. I've been wondering about that... but no way I'd ever be able to afford an air mattress; it's pointless to think about it.*

Julian kept an eye up front. The file of scouts had ended. Mark was still outside, but the bus looked full now. There was a lot of talking and joking. Julian looked around at the packed bus—everybody was excited and talking. He felt a wave of something go through him suddenly, making his face flush: he was so glad to be here. Scouts was just about the most fun thing he had ever done in his life. He would always be a boy scout. He could hardly wait for the trip to start. He had to make himself sit still and not yell out how happy he was.

—∽∞∽—

The last scout had just signed in.   Mark checked his watch. *excellent. we'll be able to leave on time.* He stepped over to the truck.

"That's the last one, Jer," He slapped the panel next to the door. "We'll make one stop along the way. Do you want to join us, or drive straight through?"

"Reckon I'll go right to the camp. I've been there often enough." He had his thermos and sack lunch along; that's all he needed. He'd been making this run eight or nine years now.

"Right. See you in a few hours." Mark waved him forward. *good... the truck might be a little slow.* He wanted it there when the bus arrived. *with the lunch stop, we'll be well over three hours.* He scanned the crowd to see if there was a board member or anyone that needed attention. He had a standing agreement with Father Wilson to refrain from giving a prayerful sendoff; they got enough of that during the year. The priest was probably relieved anyway, since he had to start another service in about twenty minutes. *nope; all clear.* He gave a general wave and smile.

Mark sprang up the bus steps. His patrol leaders were clustered up front, awaiting instructions... he was rarin' to go, himself. He did a quick glance to see if he could spot Julian. *ah... a few rows back. that's a relief. at least he won't be staring at me from directly across the aisle. he's surrounded by his Wolf patrol buddies.*

"Thanks, boys." Mark took off his hat. "After we get underway, come forward one at a time. I have a few things to go over with each of you. It won't take very long. Bring along your patrol rosters." He put his hat on the front end of the bench. *these things are such a nuisance.*

"Regular patrol order?" Dale would be second if that was the case.

"Yes, let's do it that way. Nathan, when we get out onto the open highway, you can start off." Mark watched them go to their seats; they were all eager to get going. He sat down and opened his briefcase; he wanted it handy for the patrol leader conferences. He'd saved some things until now purposely... perfect way to take the edge off the long drive and freshly energize his leaders.

—⚉—

Julian watched intently. He worried for a minute—Mark might not sit on the front bench across from the driver. That was the one seat that was turned outward facing the aisle. He was counting on Mark to sit there, with his satchel and papers. *oh—the patrol leaders are coming down the aisle to take their seats... would Mark sit where... yes! he did! perfect. I'll be able to look at him for most of the drive to camp.* He gave a big sigh of relief. *Mark's hat is on the bench—no one else is going to sit there.* Julian smiled with satisfaction. He got the tablet ready.

During the past year Julian had fallen into this habit of staring at Mark; he couldn't get enough. His crush had become a secret obsession. What was tricky was not being obvious about it. He'd heard a couple of embarrassing wisecracks about always being such a silly puppy whenever Mark was close by; but he'd gotten better at being cool about it... like finding this seat. Other than an occasional nodding head or someone walking up the aisle, he had only to look ahead, and no one would know what he was looking at. *'course, I'm about fifteen feet away, so it isn't perfect. but it's darn good.*

His fantasy life had evolved wonderfully during the year, and he imagined new scenarios often. Being able to watch Mark today was going to inspire some new ones. *besides, once everyone is settled in for the drive, I can flip over to my secret reserved sketches.* A few months back he had begun to make drawings of Mark from memory, imagining him without anything on. He had seen a book of drawings in the library that gave him the idea. He had to admit that sometimes these drawings turned him on. He hadn't tried to draw any front views, though... too chicken. But he did have a couple of rear views. If he looked at those for too long, he would often get a stiffy.

4   *the bus ride*

Mark moved the briefcase over to his left so that Danny could assist once they were underway; his new Senior Patrol Leader needed to be in on these tent and buddy assignments. "George, I hope you're prepared for this." This was his first experience driving the troop. "Might be a little noisy." Mark nodded forward, indicating it was time to get underway.

"Can't be any worse than a rally bus, can it?" He'd been driving for eleven years, so he'd seen it all; this bunch was well behaved so far; usually he had to stand up and shout out the rules and make threats before he could get started. Not today. He'd had one eye on the mirror all along. He didn't see any problem kids at all. He turned the key and put it into first gear. *this rig is only what—two, three years old? as good as new. we'll have no troubles.* He adjusted his Dodgers cap and engaged the clutch pedal.

—⁂—

wow! Julian sat up straight: the gearbox made such a racket—its grinding made the floor vibrate, like it was right under his feet. *Mark gave the driver the signal to go!* Julian braced himself as the bus lurched forward; *the bus is in a hurry to get going, too.* The scouts waved at their parents as the bus pulled out, and the driver beeped the horn. His mom had already gone, but he looked out and waved anyway. They were off on the long drive, at last. He scootched his buns back and forth, trying to get comfy. *boy. this seat is hard; I'm not used to school bus seats.*

He checked to see what his friends were doing: Jeremy had his scout manual open to the chapter about merit badges—engrossed already; Sid was talking to the kid that sat down next to him—*a Tenderfoot... Panther patch on his shoulder... can't hear what they're saying... bus is too noisy. too many conversations going on all at once—no way to sort anything out.*

He opened his tablet to a blank page. *I'll draw for a while.* He started to sketch a bus going down the highway. *I'll put some funny faces in the windows, and some arms waving. darn... this is tricky, with the bus bouncing so much. when we get onto the highway it will smooth out, probably.*

He checked to see what Mark was doing... *talking to the Tiger Patrol Leader; talking about stuff on a clipboard. ooo... Mark's new scout shorts! almost like mine... belt buckle is a lot fancier... pockets look the same, with that special scout top. look at his knees! pointy, like Larry! my favorite.* Julian had only seen Mark in short pants once before. *this will be a huge help... too bad he's wearing the long socks though. shins and calves are all covered up.* He looked up to Mark's lap. *hmm. this is way better than I expected. what exactly is causing that bulge? is it part air, like in my shorts, or is Mark that big? hard to tell...* the fabric looked new, stiff.

Julian watched Mark's crotch intently when the patrol leaders weren't blocking the view... luckily, they didn't hang around very long. He had never been able to do this for any length of time before. Every shift he detected under the olive green cloth was a clue to what was in there... they did fit rather tightly. Julian was convinced that there wasn't any air down there at all. But he couldn't quite translate the shifting bulge into a comprehensible shape. He pictured in his mind the view he got earlier outside the bus... *Mark is big all right.* He studied it carefully...

After a while Julian lost track of time; his eyes glazed over gradually... he started to nod off. With a sudden jerk he stopped his head from falling forward. *how long have I been—ohmygosh!* Mark had just fanned his legs back and forth—a small space opened up along the inside of his left thigh... Julian was glued: *will that open any wider?* Another stiffy just got started. *I love getting those.* The leg motion had proven it, too: *that's all Mark; no air. wow.* Julian was wide awake again.

—ɷ—

When he was talking to the patrol leaders one at a time, Mark happened to glance over at Julian; it looked like he was at work on something—sketching in his tablet. Mark figured he was doing something for the scrapbook—an excellent use of his time. Julian was often hard at work drawing, and the scrapbook was excellent. Many of the boys had commented about it. *it grows better, in fact. he clearly has the talent for a career in illustrating or commercial art.* Mark had entertained the idea of suggesting him to the advertising manager at Oglivy's. In a year he could, probably… Oglivy's has a rule about employees being at least 15. That's not so far off.

After a while Mark wondered if Julian was just sketching. The occasional glances his way had increased… they had become an extended study. He was disappointed, but not surprised. *so, Julian is as obsessed as ever.* Mark stared ahead blankly; he had no idea what to do about this— there was no way to hide, nowhere to go—he glanced around the bus— there were a few empty seats, but what would moving to one of those achieve? It would only raise questions. Besides, then Julian might be continually craning his neck and attracting attention. *no, I have to do what I always do at meetings—play stupid. maybe I can figure out what to do before we get to camp.*

He puzzled about the problem, but nothing emerged that made any sense. Instinct told him that he had to remain aloof and appear unaware. How to do that when it felt so dishonest and unconvincing… *I'm not exactly a clueless old fogey… if I'm too dumb, I'm afraid Julian might do something bolder just to get my attention. this is a tough one. I feel like I'm on a tightrope or something. well, keep at it, Mark…* He was confident something would come to mind, eventually; *lots of miles to go— we'll get there.*

He fanned his left leg unconsciously—he had developed one of those annoying underwear problems. Fanning usually released things… *no luck. oop—* he glanced back to check—*oh dear: Julian's eyes just opened wide.* Mark glanced away quickly—*I forgot I was on display. I did not expect this… what am I going to do? other than put up with a pinched scrotum, that is.*

The pinch seemed to get worse. Mark realized that he shouldn't encourage Julian by providing a show. He folded his hands in his lap for a while. It had to appear that he was just riding on the bus like everyone else. He wasn't sure what Julian could see at this distance… *I don't dare fix things while he's staring—exasperating… like having an itch on the tip of your nose when you're hands are full and you can't do a thing.*

He refrained from looking at Julian; his peripheral view was no help, either. But he had to assume that he was still the main exhibit. He had no experience dealing with this kind of thing. As far as he could tell, Julian was being **completely** consistent… there had been no counter indications about his focus. *this is just more of the same… Julian's been undressing me with his eyes for months.* Mark took stock of himself; he didn't feel tempted, at least. *if Julian were a few years older, I might be worried…* He wasn't about to be taken over by forbidden urges… he never had been. *unlike Julian, I'm not subject to uncontrollable sudden erections.*

His eyes wowed: that would be almost impossible to mask while sitting here. *Julian is funny at times, as a matter of fact.* He shook his head. *it's easy to forget what it was like to be that age. I used to have that problem myself… I'd always get one on a bus—no way to stop it. well, enough of this: time to pay attention to the job, Mark. it's not that big a deal, anyway; what can he possibly see from that far away?*

Mark picked up his clipboard and flipped to a blank sheet. *there's no need for anyone to be checking in… maybe I can jot down a few ideas… might as well get something accomplished. I wish there was a way to know where we'll be assigned this year; makes a huge difference in how to plan the day… hiking time from the various camps varies.* His memory wandered to previous years. *all told I've been in… let's see… Owl—that was the worst. Alligator, Bobcat… Shawnee camp is nice, except for the climb up there and the water problem. Barr's Meadow is the best, of course. I doubt that we'll get that two years in a row… we had nearly two hours extra every day because of saved travel time.*

Mark spent several minutes jotting down random ideas, but he wasn't achieving much. *maybe I should have brought a book.* He never did that for some reason. He exhaled deeply and sat back in a slouch—*this bench is so uncomfortable.* He put down the clipboard and stretched his arms on the back of the bench seat. *these are not designed for long distance travel.*

Without thinking, he had spread his legs wide apart. Suddenly he remembered… he glanced back toward the emergency exit: the wide-open eyes had been joined by a dropped jaw. *what!?* He looked down to his lap. *there's nothing wrong—everything looks fine.*

Mark looked across the bus and thought it over; *this is ridiculous. Julian would need binoculars to make anything out… besides, the angle can't be that good anyway. his imagination must be on overtime. in any case, Julian mustn't realize that he's been observed. I'll hold this pose for a minute, then sit up.* He tried to recall—*did I ever have a fixation like Julian has?* He couldn't think of one. That's one reason this was so hard to understand. *aha—yes. Erik accused me of having a one-track mind once. hmm… this isn't the first time Julian has triggered those memories. they make me feel good… very good.* He identified with Julian, to a degree; he had been the same way once—Erik was four years older, and Mark was putty in his hands from the very first.

Mark shook his head. He had to review the situation. *I must challenge myself here. I've never had to deal with anyone like Julian before… I need to be clear about what's going on in his head. goal: confirm what I think Julian really needs. I need to feel sure before I can decide what to do about it. I can't confront him—that would backfire; but if I'm right, somehow I have to redirect him.*

now I need to circulate and touch base personally with each scout. There were forty-five boys to worry about, not just one.

—⚊⚊—

Julian had seen, actually seen, Mark's skivvies as he looked up his leg. It was too dark to tell much detail, but he'd gotten a fair idea of how huge those balls were. The bulge was real, all right, no doubt about that. He was so grateful for that best ever look-see. If only Mark would sit back like that more often. He fantasized for a minute about crawling up the aisle on his hands and knees for a close look. He imagined Mark fanning his leg as he got closer…*oop. Mark just stood up. what's going on now? he's talking to the guys in the front… huh… he moved to the next seat… he's stopping by every row! looks like he's going to talk to everybody personally!*

Mark's every move was followed with rapt fascination. *he is so cool…* When he crouched down in the aisle to talk to a scout, when he bent over to talk to a scout sitting by the window, Julian preserved it in memory. *wow… the back of his thighs and knees… and his rear: what would that look like, bare?* Julian had trouble picturing that. The new shorts made him look all flat.

Mark enjoyed touching base like this. It provided a good snapshot of what was going on. *ah, yes… Doug and Paul are doing something with a stopwatch.*   Mark was rather pleased with them.   *they're the proof.* Encouraging scouts to make friends in different patrols was good for the overall troop morale. He believed that competition should be made constructive. Friendly rivalry helped remove the negative aspects of competition. The seats the scouts had chosen for this trip showed several other examples. This larger sense of identity assisted greatly in the competitions with the other troops at the camp. Mark had noted from time to time that other troops got so bogged down with their internal competition, it was easy for Troop Nine to walk away with a win.

Julian observed that when Mark stood upright the bulge didn't show that much… *except sometimes when he moves just right.   Mark has a pretty big one, all right. look at his arm, the way it reaches out and rests on the back of that seat. I'm so glad his shirt is short sleeved today. he's cool from every angle, no doubt about it.*

Mark moved to the next seat; a game of Blackjack was in progress. "What's the score?" *I enjoyed that game when I was a scout.*

"He's up by five." Casey was suspicious of Robin's good luck. He dealt him the face up card: the queen of clubs. He dealt himself an eight.

"Some of us are born lucky," Robin said smugly. "Blackjack!" He smiled at Casey gratefully as he flipped over the ace of diamonds. Now he was up by six. He looked forward to collecting his "winnings" after they arrived. *Casey's always very good at that… yes he is.*

Mark patted Casey on the shoulder. "Hang in there. He'll get his eventually." This was another inter-patrol success. He felt for Casey; he had often been on the losing side of Blackjack. He moved to the next row.

Julian's heart rate increased… his nostrils flared… Mark had reached the row in front of him! *his hand is right there, inches away, resting on the seat behind Sid's right shoulder. I love the way the veins stand out on the back of his hand. if only I could reach out and stroke that arm…* Julian started his study at the fingernails, as he did whenever he was this close… Every time he'd see a new detail and add it to the drawing… now they were aimed downward and pressing the back of the seat. *what a strong hand!* His eye moved past the wrist and followed its course over to the elbow. *mmm!*   The way his bicep emerged from the sleeve was tantalizing. The shoulder looked **so** strong… the neck, the ear, the lips… the blue eyes. Julian was hard again, of course. He fanned his legs unconsciously. This was the best treat yet, seeing Mark up close like this. *how long will he... oop. here he comes.*

Mark had been anticipating this stop; Julian was in the next row. He'd been able to resist looking at him, but it was difficult. He placed his hand on the metal ridge between the two boys as he had at each row; he held it fast, as if it were a safety rail. His hand squeezed the seatback tight—his thumb drawing a surprised groan from the stiff leatherette upholstery. "Jeremy... what are you going to work on first?" He noticed the leaflet in Jeremy's hand. "Let's see." Jeremy had the new Canoeing merit badge pamphlet. "Excellent. They have a couple dozen really fine canoes on the lake. Are you all signed up?"

"Yeah... I got Kurt to go in with me."

"Great! He's pretty husky. You'll do well, I know." Mark gave Jeremy a friendly tap on the shoulder with his right hand.

Julian was frozen... ever since Mark had squeezed the seatback he'd held his breath... he'd felt the cushion press inward by his shoulder—now it was being released... its subtle stretching sound served notice that...

Mark put his hand on Julian's shoulder briefly, as was his custom. He forced himself to hold it there—he felt it was wise to relate to Julian as he always did. "Can I see what you've been drawing, Julian?" *play dumb, Mark, play dumb.*

Julian flooded with what he knew not, but it was wonderful. Mark's hand! When he squeezed just a little, it caused that exquisite tickle. He looked up into Mark's face. *wow.* It was only a second, but it seemed like an hour. Julian was able to recover somehow, and tilted the tablet to show the drawing of the bus. He didn't try to hide his stiffy.

"Hey, you're up to the minute!" Mark took the tablet and held it close to his face with both hands. *it's a cartoon!* His grin was spontaneous. *remarkable detail as always...* "Let's see if I can recognize anyone; the faces are a little small. Is that Tom?" He extended the tablet and pointed to a face in the back window.

Julian nodded. He reached over and pointed to one in the center. "That one's supposed to be Sid." His fingertip touched Mark's thumb.

> > *snap!* < <

They looked at each other, startled. A spark of static electricity had discharged as their fingers touched.

Julian would remember that for the rest of his life!

"Whoa!" Mark laughed. *I haven't had one of those in a while.* The spark was a remarkable coincidence. Mark refused to think of it as anything else. It brought back a memory. A wonderful memory of a night six years ago. He returned the tablet, and he gave Julian a wink as usual. He looked him right in the eye longer than he intended. He pinched Julian's shoulder again before he stood back. He was reassured, actually. Julian's cartoon was terrific. *that wasn't so hard after all; went better than I expected.*

"Hey, Jason!" Mark turned to the scout on the other side of the aisle and punched him lightly on the shoulder. *time to get better acquainted with Jason... no time like the present.*

Julian took a while to calm down. Mark's departing touch left him all abuzz. With any luck no one was looking at him: *I must be red as a radish.* His ears were roaring. The tingle had become a jolt that ran full length from his right ear, around his neck, down his back to his butt, and back up the front to the tip of his raging dick. He was even short of breath. It increased the impact and strength of that **magical** spark. He'd had static sparks before... but this one was so different. And when he kept touching the side of Mark's thumb, it was as if he was being charged, or something. He examined his fingertip. It looked the same as always. *what would happen if I shook Mark's hand?* He imagined himself jittering wildly up and down, as if he were being electrocuted. He chuckled aloud at the image.

"What?" Jeremy thought for a second that Julian was chuckling at him.

That shattered the trance. "Oh. Nothin'. I just thought of something. No big deal." He folded his hands in his lap… he needed to cover his pulsing crotch. He squeezed the heels of his palms around it as he looked out the window at the landscape flowing by. The far away things seemed to be posing grandly for him, while the things up close were a blur of colors, light and dark. That's what his brain was like right now: a total blur! He checked to see if Jeremy was watching… *nope; he's back in his booklet.* Slowly Julian picked up his tablet and opened to the special drawings. He tilted it so that Jeremy wouldn't see them if he should look over. He glanced around; Mark's back was turned; he was talking to the scout one row back on the other side of the bus. Julian had to check something in his sketches. *the nose is not right at all... and the elbow is awful! the eyes, they look nice; yes... I have those right...*

—⚹—

Mark turned back to the other side of the bus to talk with Tony Johnson. He happened to glance to the right, at the back of Julian's head. The sketchpad caught his eye—the page that Julian was looking at... the bus cartoon had been replaced by something else. He looked just long enough to realize what it was. *wow. so that's what he's been working on—a portrait! I've been all wrong...* Mark was embarrassed—and a little ashamed. He hadn't given Julian enough credit. *that's why he's been studying me so intensely! I have to find a way to see that. that's not a cartoon...* He turned away. *I'd better not be caught seeing it.*

"Hey, Tony. Great to see you! Still going for the First Aid Badge?" Out of the corner of his eye he saw the tablet flip closed. He was confident Julian didn't know he'd seen the portrait.

"Yeah. I know a lot of it already, o'course. And I'm signed up for Rowing with Andy." Tony was even up on his demerits now... *maybe I can gain a few points during camp. Mark always gives me a chance.*

Mark continued his brief chat with each scout, all the way to the back. His top two leaders occupied the bench that stretched across the rear of the bus. Something was wrong; they weren't cheerful and up like the rest of the boys. *looks like they're in bad shape.* What could the problem be? Tom, his Junior Assistant Scoutmaster, leaned against the right wall, left foot up on the bench. Nick, the Troop Scribe, sat facing him on the opposite side. His right knee lay flat on the bench, his foot resting on his left knee. He rocked his left foot on the floor, preoccupied. Mark sat between them.

"So, what are you two laughing so hard about, anyway?"

That broke them up. The gloomy mood dissolved instantly. Tom had not been paying attention to Mark's approach.

Mark hit Tom's toe with his right fist. "Really... anything I can do? You're on in..." Mark checked his watch... "about 75 minutes."

"I'm sorry, Mark. I don't have a good excuse. The last couple of weeks of school were sort of bum, I guess. I'll get over it. Actually, I'm counting on camp to come to my rescue." Tom was embarrassed. He forgot that Mark would be doing his check-in tour. *I should have been paying attention.* But he was glad Mark was here. He needed to shape up. He couldn't tell Mark what was wrong, of course. The recent failures of his after school exploits in Hayden Woods weren't something Mark could fix, anyway. *I'll figure it out. now that we're at camp, I'll find a nice fresh pair first thing.* "Mark?"

"Yeah, shoot."

"What did you do, after you finished your Junior Assistant Scoutmaster duty?" *that's a good place to point Mark's attention...* Tom adjusted his sock top unconsciously.

Mark understood at once. Tom was almost ready to leave the nest and didn't know quite how to deal with it. His Junior Assistant Scoutmaster needed a little TLC right now. Mark was confident he'd be okay. "Well, I wasn't quite as good as you are; I shuffled over to an Air Explorer troop for a while instead of becoming a hotshot JA like you. Then I just went on to college. You've gotten to the very top with a year left to go, too. Not too bad, kiddo."

Tom blushed at the compliment. He didn't know what to say. The idea that he might be a better scout than Mark was ridiculous. Mark sure knew how to pump him up. He pursed his lips and shrugged. He didn't want to say anything stupid or corny.

"Once things get going this week, we can sit down for a talk. I'll give it some thought. Until then, your job is to inspire this bunch to have the best two weeks of their life." He gestured to the boys seated in front of them. "Right?" He gave Tom's toe a harder tap with his fist.

"You got it. Thanks, Mark." Tom sat up, very relieved. Mark was brilliant when it came to pointing his head right. *actually, I will do better now.* He felt motivated, encouraged. *not only that, I'll check out some of the prospects at the trailhead... might help one or two put on their pack...*

"What about you, Chuckles?" Mark bumped his left thigh against Nick's foot and gave him a grin.

Nick laughed again. "I've got no troubles. And I have too much to do; maybe I can figure a way to con Tom into giving me a hand." He wasn't serious; he was so grateful to Mark for erasing Tom's bad mood; he'd been trying unsuccessfully to do that the whole trip. When Tom was happy, Nick was happy... and **ready**.

"I, of course, did not hear that." Mark winked and slapped his calf gently. He stood up. "See you guys later—we have a lunch stop coming up real soon. Tom, be sure to give Danny an assignment—like helping round everyone up afterward." They had to be careful, or they'd be late for the opening ceremony at Camp Walker. He gave Tom a thumbs-up sign and stood to leave.

Tom nodded with a big smile. When Mark headed back to the front, he glanced over at Nick. *look at that grin... hafta do something about that!* "Hey, Chuckles!" Tom attacked with rough tickles under the arms. Mark had loosed him on the world again... Nick was too handy to leave be. He loved to tease Nick, anyway.

Mark had gone about six feet when Tom pounced. He smiled. *I, of course, did not hear that.* He moved to the front of the bus, slowly, glancing at each of the boys again... double-checking to see if he needed to touch base a second time with anyone. He saw the wavy golden hair on the port side... *maybe I'll get another look at that drawing...* he was buoyed unexpectedly by that glimpse... that was a total surprise. *how do I find a way to have a look... hmm...* the tablet was closed. *ah well. onward, men... an opportunity might come along. two weeks is two weeks.* Being the subject of a portrait was something that had never entered his mind. He was conflicted, somehow... this required some careful thought.

Nick tried, but not hard, to fend Tom off. He laughed, and protested just enough to keep him on the attack. *man, I'm so grateful to Mark. he erased Tom's frump. the rest of the trip will be good. maybe better than good.* Tom had given him a hard-on again.

5   *arrival at Camp Walker*

> > **whap!** < <

oh! the slapping sound... what the... notebook fell onto the floor... musta started to nod off or something... slipped from my lap. don't see where it went... hafta get on hands and knees to look. where'd it go? dark down here... huh... not under the seat... peek around behind Jeremy' legs... not there either. musta slid into the aisle... squeeze past Jeremy... careful, careful... gotta miss his feet. darn floor keeps pitching back and forth... hard to keep steady. boy... not here either. maybe it slid toward the front —woop... have to lean on a seat for a second... don't wanna tip over. hmm. just got a hot idea: why not keep on going... maybe... check both sides first... see if anybody's paying attention... not much farther. maybe just a small peek... you don't want Mark catching you crawling on hands and knees like this... dang! why is the floor pitching again...

> > **ker-whunk!** < <

"Ow!" Julian was jostled awake suddenly. His head had knocked sharply against the ledge under the window—the bus had driven over a large hole in the road. Wide awake now, he reestablished his bearings quickly—he was embarrassed at having dozed off. *I heard my tablet fall to the floor. ah!* The corner was just visible part way under Sid's seat. He reached down... *gosh, this is like the dream I had just now.* He sat back up and looked around. The bus was going down a gravel road. *trees everywhere...* He looked forward. Mark was still there, watching out the front window. *I was sound asleep!* Julian was amazed… he looked around the bus. He had company: others were just waking up too.

"We must be getting close." Jeremy didn't mention that Julian's hair was pressed flat on the left side. Julian had been asleep quite a while.

"Yeah." *what have I missed?* "Did you go to sleep too?"

"Nope. I always stay awake when I'm on trips." Jeremy took pride in that fact.

Julian usually did too. The last thing he remembered was watching Mark sitting with his left leg crossed over his right. It was annoying, because he couldn't see under there from this angle. *musta dozed off... it got so boring.* He watched the trees go by… *wow...* The ditch alongside the road was deep and wide; the road was narrow and full of potholes. *kinda scary...* he could visualize the bus slipping off the edge. *they need to do something about that.* Julian rubbed his head where it had hit the window frame. *not too bad...no bump. sure be glad when the bus is through swaying back and forth so much... the noise it makes on this road!* The seats all squeaked and groaned from the stress, compounding the impact of the sound. His butt was half numb, but the vibrations had given him a stiffy… *that part's nice.*

—⁓—

Mark looked at his watch. *we're late.* Stopping to get something to drink with forty-six sack lunches took longer than planned; it had turned into a potty break as well. *we've missed the general assembly and announcements.* He stood as they pulled up behind the truck and rested his left hand on the back of the driver's seat.

"It looks like we have the turnaround all to ourselves, George."

"Yep. You want me in front or behind the truck?" This was his first time here.

"Just behind will be fine. Leave a few feet between, six or eight." Mark turned to speak to the troop as the bus came to a stop.

"Welcome to Camp Walker, boys. Tom and the patrol leaders will go first and unload the truck. When you have all your gear, go to the center of the turnaround and be ready to fall in." Mark gestured to the leaders to come forward and go to the truck. "They have coffee and facilities, George, if you and Jer want. It's only a short hike in."

"Thanks, Mark." *stretching these old legs is a good idea. we'll walk in after the scouts are on their way. Jer knows his way around the place… at least we don't have to carry backpacks.* He kept his eye on the mirror—an occupational habit.

Mark glanced down the aisle... He was grateful that Julian had dozed off; being a prime exhibit had gotten a little tiring. He'd been able, finally, to free his pinched scrotum… no telling what the effect of witnessing that would have been. He looked forward to welcoming Julian to the camp. *somehow, I want to get a good look at that portrait.* He put his left foot on the first step down so that he could stand without stooping. Greeting the boys as they disembarked gave them an upbeat feeling after the long ride.

Julian was relieved somewhat… his stiffy had almost gone down. He was about to walk right by Mark, and these shorts didn't hide things too well when he was standing. He always tried to hide it, especially from Mark. The trouble was, he usually got one all over again whenever Mark was close, especially if he looked him in the eye. Julian was like a moth flying around a candle when it came to Mark's eyes. He always looked and he always got zapped.

Julian's hair betrayed that he'd just awakened from a nap... his appearance was slightly comical… quite harmless. Mark looked directly into Julian's deep brown eyes… he couldn't resist winking. The instant flush of color made him feel naughty... it was hard to keep a straight face.

wow. Julian inhaled deep as he went past... boy, did he want to reach out and touch... Mark was very close by the steps. As usual, he chickened out. The swelling below was automatic—*trouble is, it feels so good.* He followed behind Jeremy in a daze. *that was one of the best winks in my whole life!* He held his tablet in front. He couldn't adjust anything here without being noticed.

He walked over to fetch his backpack. It felt good to be moving around; he rubbed his butt vigorously—it was still half numb… *such a **hard** seat.* He looked around. *the air up here sure smells good...* The trees on the edge of the clearing revealed only a trace of a breeze. Small white clouds overhead were scattered like random tufts of cotton. A nice summery day; best of all, the noise of the bus was over with.

"You got T.B. too," Sid empathized, massaging his backside with both hands.

"Teebee?"

"Yeah: Tired Butt. I always get it on school buses."

"Oh. Yeah." Julian nodded. "Next time I'll carry a pillow, that's for sure." *they should put that on the travel sheet, come to think about it.* He had a pillow all squished up tight in his sleeping bag, where it did him no good at all.

Sid just noticed Julian's fancy boots; he was envious, a little. "Some clog-hoppers." The track Julian left was impressive. "Where'd ya get those?"

Julian looked down. The boots looked too big, actually. "Outdoor Store—early birthday present." *amazing how easy it is to walk in these... I expected them to be heavy or something. they don't squeak out here, either.*

Sid fished for a wisecrack but nothing came to him. He knew those boots cost more than his air mattress. But he wasn't about to trade.

Mark kept an eye on how well the patrol leaders worked as a team. *they're certainly in high spirits.* He'd have commendations and points to award at tonight's dismissal. He stepped toward the tailgate and reached out—the Badger Patrol Leader passed him his pack. "Thanks, Arnie." He carried it to the south end of the turnaround and set it to the side. The open truck had allowed a considerable layer of dust to build up. *nothing for it... unpaved roads do that.* He did a few stretches... after the long drive, that hard seat took a toll. *well, the hike will limber everyone up.* He secured his travel case to the pack—keeping arms free on a trail was one of the basics. He glanced up at the sky: *weather looks perfect.* The dust stirred up by the bus was dissipating slowly... it formed into a spiral as the wind higher up grabbed hold. The tops of the large beech trees seemed to be sweeping the air clean—the dust dissolved as it sped away. *the hike will be easy... it's still plenty cool—between 70 and 75. it's good to be back up here.*

Tom helped the truck driver fasten the tailgate. *it's great to be here finally—that bench seat was pretty bad; being able to stretch out my legs as far as I want was worth it. my fourth camp!* He intended to make it the best yet, because it would probably be his last. He'd scanned the field from the flatbed and spotted three that were just what he needed... *plenty for a start.* He grabbed his pack and stepped over next to Mark; everyone had his gear.

Mark donned his Pershing: "Assemble the troop." He glanced at his watch and grimaced. The assembly must be letting out right about now.

"Troop 9!" Tom called out. "Fall in, by patrol."

Julian thought this was so cool. This is how they always started—the patrols would all line up by rank. The rank was based on how they had done during the year, and so there was a first, second, third and so forth. The Wolf patrol was number four. Julian's place was in the center of the second row. There were six patrols now, one more than a year ago—seven counting the Flaming Arrow leaders. The last three in rank had to stand behind the first three. The patrol leaders took roll and reported back as they were called on. Of course, everybody was present.

"All present and accounted for," Tom reported. Mark returned Tom's salute and nodded. Tom faced the troop: "At Ease."

Julian loved to stand like this, legs apart and hands behind the back. It was comfortable, and he could look around, especially at Mark. He glanced down at his front... *oo-boy. lucky I'm in the back row.* His point was still clearly visible. *it would show if I was in front... should be gone soon... especially if I don't look at Mark that much.*

Mark addressed the troop: "We have less than a mile to hike. We'll march in single file by patrol ranking. You will not need to be in step until I give the order. I'll call a halt just before we arrive in front of the HQ building. From that point on, you are to be as sharp as possible. While I check in and get our campsite assignment and other information, you'll have a few minutes to use the washroom or stop by the Trading Post. We'll march to the campsite in line formation. Remember, please... from here on, our movements could be watched and evaluated. We are the returning champs again; I know you'll each do your part to keep us on top." He looked across the troop... three of the new scouts had on their caps. *bad idea on the trail.* "For this hike, secure your cap under your belt. You won't need that until tonight." He nodded to Tom.

"Attention! Right Face! Mount up!"

The troop reached to the right, hoisted their backpacks, put them on and waited for the signal.

Mark put on his pack; another bus was coming down the road. *at least my boys won't be the last to arrive.* He stepped briskly to the left front of the formation; he raised his right arm high and paused for several seconds. When it was completely silent, he dropped his arm sharply forward and began the hike. They went around the gate onto the trail that ran along the access road. Only service and emergency vehicles were allowed to drive into the camp.

While the others started off, Julian retied his hiking boots quickly—they had loosened on the drive. He finished just in time. His pack was lighter than usual. They didn't have to tote in any grub or cooking utensils or tents, or patrol gear. That made this an easy hike—and quiet—no swinging pots or banging pans. *this trail is practically a highway! too dusty, though... a lot of scouts today... hey! we're going downhill... that will make it easy.*

Tom's Junior Assistant duties were usually gratifying in some way, but being at the end of the line was a mixed blessing today. There wasn't enough breeze to keep the dust blown to the side, so he and a big portion of the troop had to walk through a dust cloud. *it's better than rain—this trail would be a mud pie in five seconds.* He could still indulge himself by admiring the view of the yummy butt just in front of him… the backpack didn't cover everything, thankfully. Watching what young buns do as they walk along a trail was as good a pastime as any he could imagine. The pair directly in front of him he discovered last summer. *now that Danny's in the same patrol, it would be better to look for someone new. the next ones up are an old favorite; I can go there most any time—Nick always pleases.* The brief tussle on the bus had warmed him up good… *got him a little horny too. giving Nick a hard-on is always fun.* Tom had been frustrated for several weeks now: the failure to find any prospects to join in his favorite satisfaction had gone on for too long. Maybe it was because school was almost out. *anyway, I need to get my rocks off the right way—it's critical. no need to be choosy; lots of new ones this year—new ones are always the best.*

After they had been on the trail for five minutes, Mark spoke to the patrol leader of the Panthers, who was right behind him. "Nathan, are you ready for the first call?"

"Yes, Sir!"

"Proceed." Mark raised his arms into a V sign. That alerted the troop that the patrol calls were about to begin. This was a chance to earn points for their patrol. Uniformity and homogeneity of sound along with the loudest volume earned a ten point bonus.

Nathan held his arms straight out to the sides, extending three fingers. This was a silent command to his patrol to give the patrol roar three times. He counted ten and dropped his arms back down. The Panthers did their big cat roar, in unison. Its screech was one of the hardest to do. It was one reason they were the top patrol. They did three.

In sequence, each patrol did its special roar or call—a tradition they enjoyed. It gave some variety, and built troop spirit. When the new Zebra patrol had finished its whinny, Mark cued the troop for the wrap-up by raising his arms back into the V. He held for ten seconds; when they dropped, the whole troop chanted "9!" three times. They would perform this routine again just as they entered camp.

Marker cairns along the trail enabled Mark to select the perfect place to pause the march. The 100 yard marker was ahead, about six feet out from a white pine; he raised his right arm. Each patrol leader raised his right arm as well, enabling everyone to know when to halt. He dropped his arm, and the patrol leaders followed suit. The troop came to a sharp uniform stop.

Mark stepped off the trail into the road so that he could see the entire line. "Troop 9, Attention!" He paused. "Dress Forward, Dress!" The scouts extended their arms forward to make the spacing uniform. When he was satisfied, he gave the final instruction. "We will enter camp in step and follow regulation drill procedure, as we practiced at the last meeting. Assemble your colors." He gestured for Danny to come forward, and he returned to the front of the line.

As the Senior Patrol Leader, Danny was assigned the duty of bearing the official Troop Flag. He stepped to the front and assembled the pole sections, then attached the flag. The assistant patrol leaders assembled their patrol flags in the same manner. When Danny was ready, he stepped three paces in front of the troop and stood at attention.

Mark waited for all the flags to be in place; he stepped behind Danny and raised his arm. He held for ten, then commanded, "Forward, March!"

Danny had a major case of goose bumps. He had never had this honor before. He had practiced it all week, and was ready. *awkward, with a pack on... I don't mind.* Walking right in front of Mark was a little scary… any mistake he made would be seen immediately.

At the 50 yard cairn Mark held his arms in the V form again, and the patrol yells began in sequence. They went perfectly—the rehearsal had been a good idea. Just as the Zebras were on the last whinny, Mark quietly gave the stop order to Danny—he had just passed the HQ entrance. Mark held his right arm up high. The first patrol came to a parade stop in the two rank formation. They continued to march in place as each patrol moved into position. Danny knew to do an about face without a command, and he faced the troop, marching in place.

—∭—

Camp Director Jorgensen lowered his field glasses when Troop 9 drew close. He had been alerted when he heard the patrol chants in the distance. Only two scoutmasters at camp practiced this maneuver. Mark Schaefer's troop always excelled. As he watched, he shook his head. "If only I had a way to record this entrance." As Camp Director, he had to maintain a neutral position, but it was clear to him that 9 would prevail again this year. *it's unfortunate they're an hour late, but that won't be held against them; two other troops are late—they all have a long drive.* He returned downstairs to his office. He wanted to greet Mark personally.

—∭—

Mark turned to face the troop and raised his arms into the V. They chanted '9!' in unison. "Troop 9, Halt!" He marched sharply to the center and faced the troop; he gestured to Danny and Tom to join him at the front.

Mark spoke loud and clear: "Assistant Scoutmaster, you may give the order."

"Troop 9, Left Face!" Tom checked to see that all were in good order. He asked Mark in a low voice, "how long?"

"Make it fifteen minutes." *it will take longer with all these tanks to be emptied, but they'll hurry better with a deadline.*

"We will reassemble in fifteen minutes," Tom announced. "Troop, Dismount and Dismiss!"

The troop took a step back, turned to the rear and fell out. They removed their packs and left them in place. Those who knew their way around led the first timers within their patrols into the HQ building. The only indoor plumbing available to campers was across from the Trading Post or in the staff facilities upstairs.

Mark helped Danny unfold the troop flag stand; the patrol leaders stepped forward to place their flags in the slots. Mark went inside to the Director's office. The scarcity of scouts here, as well as his watch, told him that they were too late to make the opening assembly, as he had feared. The stares they had drawn from a few Junior Counselors nearby confirmed as much.

Julian wasn't in a hurry to go anywhere. He kneaded his shoulders where the pack straps had been rubbing.... luckily, he didn't need padding, because it wasn't too heavy. Still, they did sort of make an impression. For the time being his pack made a suitable perch. While Mark and the others were inside, he took the opportunity to gaze at the magnificent lake. He had not expected it to be so **large**. *everything here is huge! those trees off to the right have to be over a hundred feet high.* He had to let all this settle in his head before he could think about what to draw. *the headquarters building is as big as our church. what all could be inside there? as soon as the crowd at the doorway thins out I'll peek inside and see what it's like. I expected some kind of frontier outpost, not a huge building like this!* He retied the rawhide lacing on his left boot; the hike in had loosened it up too much... his boots felt heavier now, too. *wow... look down there!* At the bottom of the slope, a gigantic dock was swarming with scouts. *they're swimming already!*

Camp Walker

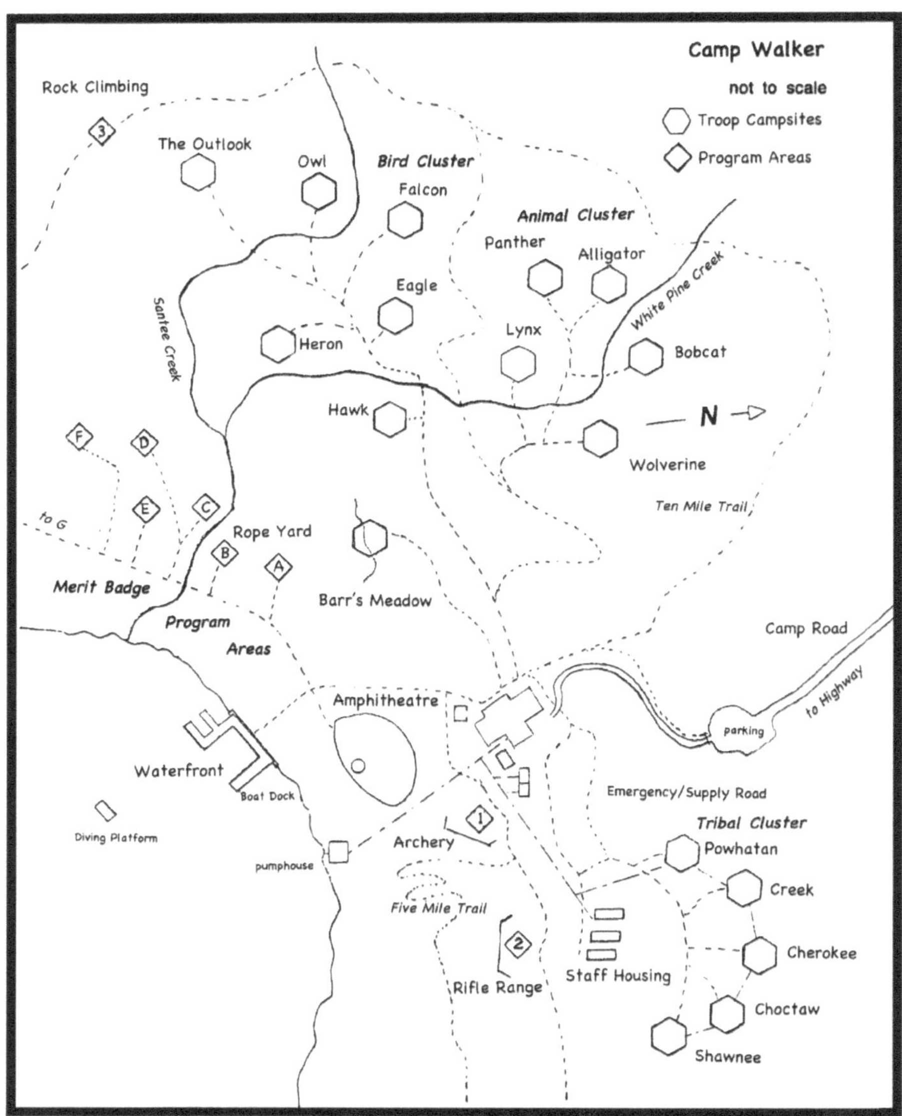

Camp Walker is in the Blue Ridge Mountains near the Nantahala
National Forest in western North Carolina and the

Chattahoochee National Forest in northern Georgia. The extensive acreage has areas for a variety of activity, large and small. Each troop in the Council has a reserved campsite for the two weeks. Trails to the sites radiate from the central headquarter buildings. A separate permanent village serves the counselors and staff. Each camp session averages between five and eight hundred scouts, or up to seventeen troops. Nearly a hundred miles of internal trails connect the camps and provide for training and hiking activity.

Areas for large multi-troop assemblies and recreational fields are located south of the HQ, adjacent to over a mile of lakeshore. When not in use by the scouts, parts of the facility are leased to outside groups. Prior to Affirmative Action in 1970, the camp observed the late nineteenth and early twentieth century hygienic custom of naked swimming at segregated sites. No women were on the staff; as a rule, female visitors were not allowed to enter the swim area.

After Mark had met with the Camp Director, he returned to the entrance landing and waved Tom over. "Find Danny and round everyone up. We need to shake a leg."

Mark had set a rapid pace, but he should have made it even faster. The hike to the campsite would be more rigorous. They were about an hour behind; unfortunately, their showy entrance went unseen by the other troops this year. The lunch break had cost them a good point opportunity. He opened his case and put the new documents on top where he could grab them quickly.

When the troop was assembled, Tom ordered it to attention. He reported to Mark with a smart salute. "The troop is ready."

Mark returned Tom's salute and addressed the troop. "I have great news! We're lucky enough to get Barr's Meadow again this year. It's one of the best campsites, and we got it because we came out on top last year. By the end of the camp, those of you who are new will see how fortunate we are. I believe you will come out on top again this year." He turned to Tom. "Junior Assistant, Lead the Troop Cheer."

Tom led the Troop Cheer, then ordered, "At Ease!" He assumed the at ease position, facing the troop.

Mark continued. "We're running late; the others are already getting settled in. You have just enough time to hike to the Meadow and get your tent and cot assignments. We'll hike in formation, but break step after the patrol calls. Patrol leaders, you'll get your slips from Tom when we arrive. After you stow your gear, you need to get to the lake as soon as you can— swimming certification is required for **everyone**. Be sure to take your registration form with you.

"We'll return here for the opening night activities. It will start with a big barbecue. After that, the first night Campfire Assembly will be held in the amphitheater. The Tiger patrol will be presenting our part of the program. You all know about that!"

Everyone laughed. The Tigers had developed a great comic skit that won top honors at the last Troop Theme Assembly.

Mark nodded to Tom.

"Troop 9, Mount up!" Tom and Danny handed the patrol flag bearers their standards after they'd hoisted their packs.

Julian made sure his tablet was still secure under the rope. He stooped to put on his pack. Sid's new bright blue-green air mattress was visible, tucked under the sleeping bag. "Is it very heavy?"

"What? Oh, the mattress. Probably ten pounds or so." He exaggerated on purpose. "If you want to carry it in, I'll let you use it one night." He didn't want to be taken up on the offer.

Julian chuckled. He couldn't think of anything witty, so he pushed in behind Sid's knees just enough to make him dip involuntarily.

Mark scanned the troop; when they were ready he ordered Tom to bring them to attention. He nodded to Danny to move to the front with the flag. "Right Face!" He stepped behind Danny and held his right arm up for ten seconds. "Forward, March!" He lowered his arm smartly, and the hike to Barr's Meadow began, each patrol peeling off into the line in order. They were being watched; this could get them an easy twenty-five points.

—ᴍ—

Jorgensen had reclaimed his viewpoint at the second floor conference room window; he brought a couple of staff members along. They watched as the Junior Assistant fell in place at the end of the line.

"I want you to hear the patrols, Fred." He'd asked Mark to repeat the calls as they left for their campsite. Barr's Meadow is the closest and most convenient campsite to HQ.

The small group watched Troop 9 march in step to the start of their trail. Mark was still in their sight when he raised his arm into the V. The performance was flawless.

Jorgensen smiled. *too bad I'm not a betting man.* Troop 9 was certain to win the overall point total again this year. Having the patrol flags hoisted high during their chant was a nice touch.

6   *Barr's Meadow*

The trail entered the idyllic meadow campsite from the east after passing through a mixed stand of white pine, hemlock, poplar and an occasional large red oak. A small mountain stream bubbled up from a spring about a hundred feet upslope of the westernmost campsite. Crystal clear and cold, it was so pure that campers could drink directly from the grassy banks without fear. It meandered lazily between the campsites and went back underground before entering the lake underwater half a mile to the southeast.

Near the camp's assembly area Mark raised his arm to the halt position. He turned and waited for the last scout to stop.

"At ease." He nodded to Tom at the end of the string. As Tom came forward, Mark took off his pack and retrieved the handouts from his case. Tom stepped forward, removed his pack, and took the handouts.

"Troop, dismissed!" Mark stood at ease and observed the process: Tom handed each patrol leader his instruction sheet and site assignment. It was a pleasure to see them function so smartly. It gave the boys a sense of order and purpose to see him paying close attention. As Tom headed back, Mark grabbed his pack and headed for the cabin, pleased; the Troop was a little late, but they'd make up for it soon enough.

Tom led the other two members of the Flaming Arrow patrol upslope to the leadership camp; each patrol leader led his boys across the meadow to their camp.

"Wolves, follow me." Stuart Walker, Julian's patrol leader, led them up to the first trail junction where they turned left.

Julian stole a glance to the right. Mark was walking toward a cabin, carrying his pack by one of the straps. *wow... Mark has a **cabin**!*

Barr's Meadow

To keep the meadow as natural as possible, campers were expected to use the trails and paths at all times. The system of paths and carefully fashioned water access points were designed centuries ago by an unknown tribe of Cherokees.

The latrine was downslope of the campsite string, near the entrance trail. It had a set of six stalls next to a urinal trough. It was maintained by Camp Walker, not the client campers. No individual camp facilities were permitted, but each camp had a waste disposal bin. Refuse had to be packed out weekly to a central collection area at HQ by each camp. Patrol leaders generally assigned this duty to scouts needing to erase Demerit Points. No burning or burial pits were permitted.

Near the latrine, a general use shower platform with two separate shower spaces was supplied with cold water from an overhead tank. Scouts worked the built in hand pump to fill the tank. No laundry facilities were available in the camps. Each troop had a two hour block reserved mid way during the two weeks in the HQ laundry room. The troop campfire assembly area was on the other side of the trail, farther uphill.

Each patrol campsite consisted of three tents grouped around a picnic table and cooking area. All scouts were assigned to a two or three man wall tent. Each person was supplied a folding canvas cot and a footlocker for clothes and personal belongings. A network of footpaths connected the individual campsites to each other, the latrine, and to the main trail. Thirty to forty feet of meadow separated the camps. No camps were closer than twenty feet from the spring fed creek. Except for a few yellow birch trees and some scrub pine, the meadow was open.

A small marshy zone above the latrine had dried up years ago. All the other campsites at Walker were in forest locations.

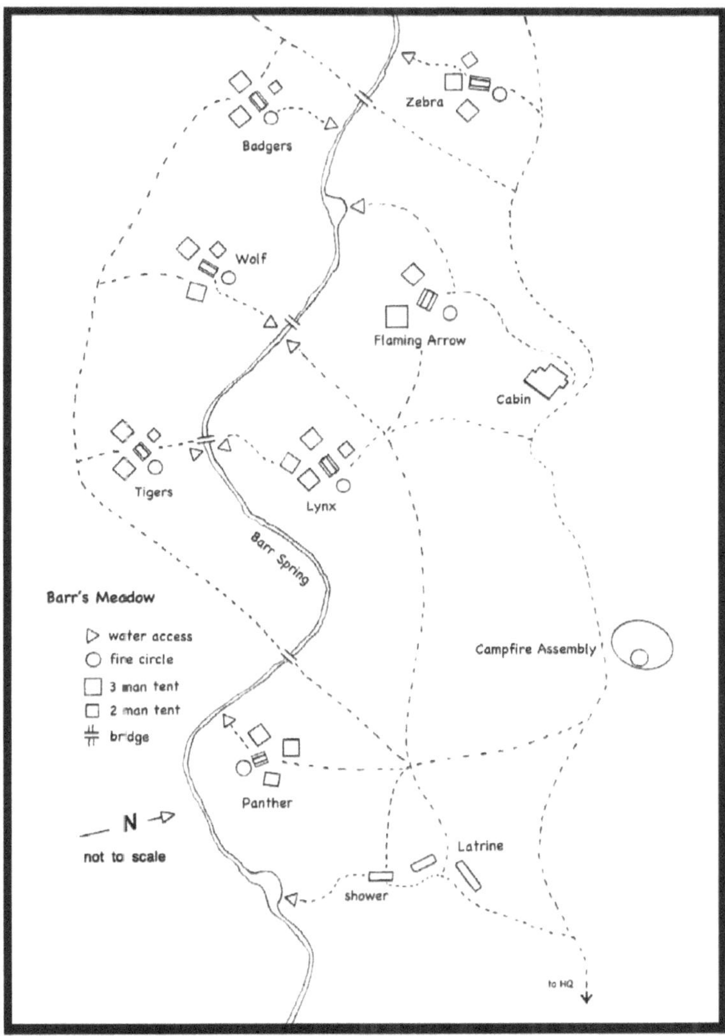

Campfires were not in routine use because of the high fire danger. Only a couple of the merit badge classes were allowed to build a fire. Strictly regulated troop campfires were allowed if it wasn't windy.

Barr's Meadow featured a small one-room cabin with an indoor bathroom. Four campsites with a cabin were available at Camp Walker, but this one was the best. It had its own well, electric pump, and water heater. The site was a favorite during the winter and outside groups paid a premium to use it. The small fireplace on the west wall was for wintertime use only.

The path to the Wolf camp curved southward below the cabin. The fourth tent cluster was across the creek in the southwest center of the meadow. One two man and two three man wall tents were arranged around the eating area; the standard picnic style table had attached benches. A portable propane camp stove stood in the stone campfire ring near the table. Norman, the Assistant Patrol Leader, installed the patrol flag; the mounting clamp was on the outer corner of the tent he shared with Stuart.

Julian was assigned the space in the back of one of the large tents; Sid and Jeremy were along the sides. *oh...* He put his pack down. *cots are all folded up!* He kneeled down. *I've never set up one of these. how does this work, anyway?* He spotted a hinge. *okay... that's where to—*

"Patrol, Fall In!" Stu barked.

it's time already? I haven't even got started. Julian frowned. *that means I have to set this up after the swimming certification.* He fished out his registration form—it was kind of wrinkled up. He tried to smooth it out while he stepped out into the line between Sid and Jeremy.

Stu held up his instruction sheet. "At Ease. We don't need to go in strict formation, but we'll go in a line, by patrol— he looked at Julian and his pals: "we're s'posed to stay on the established paths when we're in the meadow. 'Sides, we have to stand in a line when we get to the lake, anyway. Got your registration forms?"

Everyone waved his form in the air.

"Good." Stu followed the list on the handout. "Now, as to rules: no swim suits are allowed; if you need sun cream, take it along. There's no shade anywhere close by. First timers, you've been assigned a special Buddy to show you what to do; they'll get into line with you. When you get to the gate, turn in your form. The Counselor will give you a blank

Buddy Badge. You take your clothes off at that point. The cubbyholes could be taken already so you have to be careful where you put your stuff; be sure it doesn't get lost or mixed up with somebody else's. Oh: take your towel along, unless you want to get back into your clothes while you're still wet. When you've qualified, you're s'posed to wait on the slope for the rest of the troop to finish. Tom will assemble us there. They'll take roll at the end. If anyone wanders off, we'll lose **mucho** points. That happens, and you'll have Tom on your case. That you **don't** want."

Sid raised his hand. "What if ya hafta go?"

"Oh yeah, that's a good point… they have latrines there, but there's always too many guys, so you get to wait, usually. I recommend you take care of that here, first thing. You need to?"

"Could be; it was a long ride, y'know." Sid crossed his legs dramatically. Jeremy and Julian giggled. Sid could count on them to appreciate his performance.

Stu could stand to spend a minute at the pissing trough himself. "Right. So we'll stop by ours on the way there. Glad you thought of that. By the way: don't get caught taking a leak out in the brush. Everything is latrine only, all the time. **Beaucoup** demerits there. Everybody ready?" He looked over to the other camps—they were on the move. He planned to catch up on the main trail. "Quick: grab your towels and fall back in."

They scurried back to the tents to grab a towel. Julian's wasn't exactly on top, either—it was right in the middle of his duffel bag. He tugged everything out a layer at a time until he found his orange towel. *what a mess! hafta put it all straight later, I guess.* He grabbed his tablet too. *boy, there's a lot of stuff to remember… oh…* at his right, Sid had grabbed his tube of sun cream. *hmm... better not fish around for mine—* the toiletry kit was at the very bottom. *everybody's waiting!* He hurried back to the patrol line.

"Okay: we'll peel off at the latrine first, then go to the lake second. Forward!" Stu waved his arm, and they hurried over the bridge and fell in behind the Lynx.

—⚊—

Mark placed his gear on the bed. *here at last. what a relief to have the boys on task... now I can make some plans.* Jorgensen's welcome was a very nice surprise. It boosted Mark's self-confidence enormously. Being assigned the Meadow again was wonderful. And, it removed the main obstacle to what he had in mind. After all, privacy would be an absolute necessity if he were to talk to Julian directly, openly. He was growing bolder about this, but still... he sniffed the air. *phew! needs to be aired out... it's stale and musty in here.* He opened the curtains wide and swung the windows open full. He'd spent last summer camp here, so he knew how to deal with the air problem. The afternoon breeze would ream the place out while he got squared away... the bathroom door was already open. Last year he felt awkward about having a cabin all to himself, at least at first. But he learned that the relative privacy it afforded became valuable as time went on—to the boys as well as himself. And, since he was able to set a personal example for hardiness at the campouts during the rest of the year, doing that here wasn't an issue.

This year, being in the cabin could make all the difference in dealing with Julian. Having a private conversation in most camps was all but impossible. *I have a hunch I'll need several.* Diverting Julian wasn't likely to be an easy task. On the other hand, the boy was young, not yet fixed in his ways. Mark had no experience with this kind of problem, but he was confident of success, given the advantages he would have here, away from the everyday distractions back home.

He returned to the door and swung it open wide. Tom and the Flaming Arrows were passing by on the way to lead the troop down to the lake. This is one reason he was glad he had Tom as a Junior Assistant Scoutmaster: his ability to manage the entire troop for big blocks of time, like this afternoon. Thanks to Tom, Mark would have a couple of hours free for planning and plain old brainstorming. He had quite a bit to do today, too. *first, a quick look...* he stepped down the trail a few yards where he could see the boys better. They always performed best when they knew he was watching—it made sense to establish a high standard from the start.

Lines of scouts leaving their camps simultaneously looked impressive; Tom was down below, waiting to lead them to the lake. *there he is...* Julian was second from the end of the Wolf patrol line. His golden hair always stood out. As his patrol passed by the Lynx camp, Julian turned toward the cabin and looked—and waved eagerly. Mark waved back; he could see that his return wave was a boost. Julian's waving like that worried Mark... *he's too open with his feelings.* The urge to protect him grew more every time Julian displayed his sentiment—it broadcast vulnerability. A scout that openly showed affection and dependence could get into trouble. Julian had drawn some notice during the year. *well, let's hope we find a fix for that this week.*

The blond head bobbing happily down the trail reminded Mark of his own very first day at camp. *I wasn't as self-assured as Julian is... I was a Tenderfoot my first year... surrounded by giants.* He returned to the cabin; he had to unpack, get organized and set the place in order—supper duty was only a couple of hours away.

so, we're at camp at last. I have to decide for certain which way to go with this. Mark stepped over to the bed and opened the straps. Clothes first... he pulled at the top dresser drawer.

> > *scree—eep!* < <

I forgot this was so badly fit—this had annoyed him last year, no end. *I'll have to get some sandpaper... the workshop must have something that will do the job.* Last summer's system worked fine: socks and briefs in the top drawer; T-shirts in the second. The lower two were perfect for papers and manuals. He took his second shirt to the clothes rack. *where are all the hangers? some overachiever has cleaned house. maybe I can pick up a few in the HQ staff lounge. I should hang up my long pants...*

The drawing he had glimpsed on the bus flashed into his mind. Flattering... maybe it indicated a way to approach this. He had gotten to know Julian moderately well. Visiting him at home and talking with his mother was fun—he looked forward to it. Admittedly he had grown fond of Julian. He'd done his best to remain aloof, but it was difficult. Especially when he caught Julian staring at him. On occasion it was obvious the boy was aroused. Proximity exacerbated Julian's difficulty, so he remained as distant as he could particularly during Troop activities. Generally, Julian was oblivious to how he appeared. Mark didn't want other scouts to pick up on Julian's staring and make fun of him. Mark had not allowed himself to show any visible response or receptivity, of course. *I haven't ever encouraged Julian.*

Mark had never had any "improper" relations with a scout—never been tempted, even. *but Julian is different.. I feel closer in a way... almost like family.* He worked to avoid any opportunity for Julian to be close by for any length of time, especially in public. Increasingly, Julian made him remember Erik. He had thought that was a closed chapter; the pain of the loss he had suffered had taken a long time to fade. Lately, somehow, Julian triggered memories of the happiness he had known. He appreciated Julian for that. For some reason, thankfully, the pain did not return.

He took his case and papers over to the table. *ah... the camp schedule... fancy this year.* He looked up—*where to post it...* He unfolded it as he walked across the room. *perfect spot, right here. masking tape: there used to be some...* he went to the cupboard by the door. *yep... all kinds of tape here.* He grabbed a roll and mounted the poster sized schedule on the west wall next to the window.

He returned to the table and opened the briefcase. He paused for a minute—an idea came to him. He did an about face and stared at the wall where he had just posted the schedule. The entire west side of the room was empty. *I wonder...* he put his hands on his hips. *you know, that could be the answer. there's plenty of room... hmm.*

Mark continued to settle in; toiletry kit was next. *into the bathroom, men...* the shaving gear needed to be set out. He opened the medicine cabinet mirror—the last occupant had left some things behind. "tsk-tsk." *could just pitch them out... nah.* Tossing things like that out meant carrying them to the HQ. The camps didn't have a standard garbage setup. *no hurry. anyway, this stuff might come in handy for the next guy... looks like some of this has been here a while.* The pit stick looked familiar. He took off the cap... *thought so... this was here a year ago!* He shook his head. *come to think about it, who needs deodorant at a scout camp?* He consolidated everything onto the top two shelves, above the first aid supplies. *those look vintage too...* He put his toothpaste and toothbrush on the bottom shelf. *luckily, I don't need a whole bunch of space.* He closed the mirror and caught a glimpse of his face... *hmm... hair could use smoothing out.*

As he ran his pocket comb across the top of his head, he caught a glimpse of his eyes tracking the comb. He had a moment of flippant self-examination. "Well, smart guy, have you decided what to do, or not?" Mark looked at himself. The glimpse of his portrait on the bus came to mind. "What do you suppose Julian's pencil did to you"? He smiled at his reflection, then paused. Looking at himself was not something he did, other than to shave, or comb his hair, or straighten his tie. Looking into his own eyes was startling—disconcerting. He couldn't hold his gaze in place for long. He dropped his eyes down toward the basin, unfocused.

He inhaled deep, and exhaled. He did not want to examine what he was feeling right now. He backed away from it, instinctively. Too often in the past that path led to painful memories. *you have a job in the here and now, Mark.* He restored control to the everyday part of his mind. He asked the question again: *have you decided what to do, or not?*

maybe so, maybe so. the minute Jorgensen told me we had the Meadow I realized that I had the perfect opportunity to face the problem— the cabin is ideal. the table is perfect for his drawing and scrapbook work. why should I worry, really? as long as he's on task and focused, everything will be fine. and, he'll be out of harm's way during the night. one less thing to worry about... I owe that to Francine.

no need to feel queasy about it: it isn't that scary; I don't need anyone to help. Francine wouldn't be any help anyway if she were here. what I need to do is plan it. there's plenty of time for that. He looked up again as if to answer that guy in the mirror and nodded. *this will work. it's sensible and obvious if you look at it objectively.* His eye was distracted by what he saw behind. The towel rack on the wall... *it's fitted out for two... like a classy beach resort.* Mark smirked; clearly, the cabin had no objections.

I'll decide for certain this afternoon, at the barbecue.

7   *first day*

In Julian's opinion, swim certification was badly organized. You had to stand around most of the time and wait. First you stood in line to sign in and get a badge. That part took an hour, at least. *well, there is an ocean of scouts here... nobody said the camp would be this **big**... that's why the headquarters building is so huge.* He looked at the disc they had given him. *silly to call it a badge... it's more of a fancy kind of tag.* The small round disc had a hole so it could be hung on the Buddy Board. They pulled one from a big tray of blank ones and wrote his name in the center. That's the way they kept track of whether you had checked in or not. *nobody's allowed to sneak in or out, either... there's only one gate.*

Julian looked at his name. *printing is sort of goofy looking... too bad I couldn't letter it myself... oh well.* With a shrug, his attention returned to what was up ahead; there were five lines on the long boardwalk—you could pick any one you wanted. Each line had a staff member or Senior Counselor who told you when to jump in and swim. Waiting in line with Norman was okay—Norman, the Wolf's Assistant Patrol Leader, was assigned to be his Swimming Certification Buddy. Julian liked him pretty well, but he didn't really know him... *he's kind of tall... maybe he's a basketball player.* Norman had done all this before, so he helped Julian along. They found a cubbyhole easy enough, but Julian's boots were too big; he had to put them on top. He figured they'd be safe.

Once the line was clear of the cubbyholes, he could see what was coming and why it took so long: they wrote down your name and watched you swim. If you were a beginner, you had to swim twenty-five feet out and back and float for a full minute; your badge got colored red on the top. If you could swim out fifty yards to the platform, dive off into the deep water and swim back, they colored the bottom half blue. That meant you were an Intermediate. That was almost the same as First Class, so almost everyone got their badges colored in. If you could swim out to the platform two times, and backstroke back, they colored the first space on the outside edge of the badge green, which meant you were a distance swimmer. That was part of the merit badge requirement. Then there were notches for longer distances, up to a mile, even. There were a couple of lifeguards out on the platform keeping watch, as well as along the dock and out in rowboats. You were allowed to rest for a minute on the platform, then you had to dive in and swim back. If you had to rest too long, they made you leave the water. They let you try again on a later day.

About one of the worst things that could happen would be to have an all white badge. Nobody wanted to be one of the "wading pool scouts" who had to take swim lessons. So far, two scouts from Troop Nine had flunked. Julian sure didn't want to be the third. But he had made First Class a month ago, so he wasn't too worried.

While they waited, Norman had him stand under the pull chain shower. That was sort of like the pool back home, only here it was strictly cold water. No soap or shampoo, just cold water. *brrr!* It was supposed to make sure that diving into the cold lake wouldn't cause a sudden shock and give you trouble. It wasn't hot today, but Norman had him go under it anyway. *giant goose bumps!*

One thing that Julian did like about this place was no bathing suits. He didn't know why all swimming was in the nude. Evidently it had always been like this. *it's really interesting to see what different guys look like down there...* he didn't want to get caught staring, but some of those **guys**! *especially Tom! he and about three others ought to have a contest or something.* Julian figured he himself was about average, except for the fact that he didn't have much hair down there yet. He had a lot of company in that; probably a fourth or fifth of the scouts were just as hairless as he was. He was self-conscious at first, but after a while it was no big deal.

Sid's line moved forward, allowing him to give Julian a friendly prod in the ribs. "So, you think you can make it all the way out there and back without a nose full of chlorine?" Julian always had trouble with that at the swimming pool.

Julian was startled out of his preoccupation. He could never match Sid's wit, but sometimes he tried. "I've been sleepless for a week, worrying." Sid put a strap on his glasses. "What's that, anyway?"

"This is supposed to stop me from losing my glasses to the fishies… without these, I need a guide dog. You're too busy to fill in there, so I made sure to have this along." He put his glasses back on and blinked his eyes happily. "See? I **knew** you were still here!"

Sid's swim buddy was Gary West from the Lynx patrol. Julian didn't know him at all. Sometimes these assignments were a mystery. He planned to ask Sid about it later.

"I wonder if we'll get to do this any time today?" Sid smeared some more sun cream on his face. Standing here was a real drag.

Julian wasn't concerned. The line behind them was still growing. It looked like Troop 9 was about in the middle, actually. Now he understood why Tom was in a hurry to get here. He stood on tiptoe to see up ahead… maybe Mark would be coming to the lake too; the guys in the water— were all older, swimming teachers or maybe scoutmasters. *boy! I just realized—when Mark goes swimming, I'll get to see all of him. now **that** I would like.* He pondered about that… *oop. bad idea…* he started to get that tingle. *I have to think of something else quick… there's no way to hide a stiffy out here! come to think about it, I don't see anyone who has one, either… that would be awful.* The thought scared him back limp.

hmm… how can I draw this up for the scrapbook? it's hard to see everything from here. I have to get it all into my memory… my tablet is over in that cubbyhole with my clothes and towel. what's that over there? looks like a couple of branch docks or something.

"Julian Forrest," the Counselor at the table called out.

that's me! Julian stepped forward. He looked over the edge of the boardwalk. The water was about two feet below. A pipe ran along the edge just above the water.

"First time qualifier?" He reached out his hand for Julian's badge.

Julian noticed the coloring pens and his name on the long list; he nodded.

"What's your level?"

level? Julian drew a blank.

The counselor looked at Julian impatiently. "Non-swimmer, Beginning, Intermediate, or Advanced?" He'd only had to explain that a thousand times today.

"Oh. I can do the Intermediate. I passed First Class a couple of months back." Julian was pleased with his water ability—except for diving.

The counselor nodded and pointed toward the open water. "You swim freestyle to that platform; then you dive and swim back, also freestyle. We're not doing any special strokes today—just do a regular crawl. A lifeguard is there if you need him—all the guards have on a blue t-shirt so that you know who to signal if you need help. You may rest for a minute before swimming back. There's no time limit, but if it looks like you can't make it, a lifeguard will come to help. If you know you can't make it, just stop and tread water. Okay?"

Julian nodded. *am I supposed to go under the shower again? I'm all dried off...*

"Mr. Brady will give you your start signal and be observing your performance." He gestured toward the edge where Sam Brady was waiting.

Julian stepped to the edge. The staff man in the water raised his hand. *gosh... I'm not so sure now... it does look like a long way... this is a lot different than the pool... the platform is probably three pool lengths away, maybe four...*

> > ***tweee-eet!*** < <

The whistle chirped faster than he expected; he dove in, clumsily. *I have got to work on my dives.* It had been a while since he had gone swimming, probably three or four weeks. *doing okay... water is warmer than I expected... that shower was a lot colder.*

His arms began to complain. *better slow up a little... breath is holding up okay.* He looked up to see how far. *darn... I thought I was closer—looks like I'm about half way there... stick with it... keep your mind on the motion of your arms, Julian...* That's what his swimming teacher said... 'keep your knees stiff...' It worked; he forgot about his tired arms.

The water got a lot colder all of a sudden... *must be deep out here.* His hand struck the platform. *wow... I'm here already.* That surprised him; he looked up at the lifeguard.

"Doin' fine, kid. The ladder is over to the right. Take a two minute break; I'll give you a ten second warning before you have to dive."

"Thanks." Julian was a little short of breath, but he was pleased with himself. He climbed up onto the platform. For a while he'd been worried he might not make it. Now he knew he was okay. 'All in your head,' he remembered some long ago advice vaguely. He looked back at the boardwalk. *it **is** far out here! man, I did great!*

"Ten seconds; you ready?"

Julian nodded, and stepped to the edge. He pointed his hands and held out his arms. He wanted this takeoff to be better than the last one. He dove in.

> > glurb! < < well, maybe next time. one day I'll learn to do that without getting water up my nose. boy, do I hate that.

arms are okay right now… they must keep going better if they get a little rest. He did the concentration thing again… that really worked.

Julian was focused and his confidence took over—he put his head down and gave it his all. He was pleased at how well this was going—*this isn't hard at all!*

*> > **tweee-eet! tweee-eet! tweee-eet!** < <*

a whistle!! … he looked forward. They were waving at him— oh-oh… he had started to go at an angle, and was about to bump into another swimmer. He corrected and got back where he belonged... *pay better attention, dum-dum.* He made it back to the boardwalk fine, energy to spare.

"Sorry about that." Julian figured the man in the water by the boardwalk must be a scoutmaster, somewhere. He's older than the Counselors. "I got a little off course."

Brady laughed. "You want to watch that if there are any boats around, son." He gave a signal to the Counselor. "Congratulations. You have a good stroke style. Practice, and you will do well in the water." He smiled at the eager face. "The Counselor will give you your badge." He patted Julian on the back and gestured for him to get out of the water.

yay! I passed my swimming test! Julian pushed himself out of the water and stepped up to the table. *sure enough! the badge is all colored in!* He looked around... still no sign of Mark.

"Hey, good work!" Norman had just qualified in the next line over. "Let's talk about our swim schedules at breakfast, okay?"

Julian nodded. He wasn't clear about this Buddy thing. *do I always have to go swimming with Norman? hmm.* He got dressed and went out of the swim gate. He hung his badge up on the board, just like Norman had; he made a mental note of its location. *I'm supposed to remember where it is when I come to swim again.* He stepped up the slope and sat next to Jeremy. The grass made a fairly good cushion—it was still green and springy.

"How come they don't time you when you do this test?" Jeremy felt cheated; he had worked real hard to show how fast he could swim. His super fast time went unrecognized.

"Dunno… I thought it would be harder." Julian glanced over at the guys that had flunked. *whoa!* Cory had just sat next to them. *that's really surprising… he's is a year older and a lot stronger than me. he's gonna be my partner in Archery. oh! that's why he's still a Second Class! kind of embarrassing…* Julian looked around for Sid… *ohboy… still waiting in line. this is going to take a while.* "Norman was my Buddy. Who was yours?"

"Brad Fisher. He's a Tiger." Jeremy pointed to the group over at the right. "The one with the extra short haircut." He was a little scared of him, to tell the truth. Brad wasn't especially friendly; he seemed annoyed to have been assigned to Jeremy, who wasn't in his patrol. He only did it to get some points. Jeremy overheard him say that's why he volunteered.

Julian looked at Brad… he seemed okay… the guys around him were tuned in to whatever he was talking about. Guys like that didn't always appreciate the new kids—especially if they're smaller, like he and Jeremy were.

Julian shifted his attention to the long body of water. *it's beautiful… this is the biggest lake I've ever seen. maybe there's a poster…* he could see a big picture of this on his bedroom wall. The way the sun reflected on all the teeny waves and ripples was fascinating… *hard on the eyes, though.* He opened his tablet and began a sketch of the waterfront layout. He could see those branch docks clearly from here. *they must be for the swim classes. the canoe racks are interesting. hmm. should I draw this scene with or without all these scouts?* Lack of swimsuits could prove to be a problem. He had never tried to draw any nude stuff before—except for his special sketches of a certain person's backside; he did **not** flip back to those. *I'll leave people out of this sketch for now… this wants to be a* *regular drawing, not a cartoon.* About three months ago he had started to do both types. Some topics were simple, and a cartoony style was best for that—like the bus one... no point in spending a lot of effort on one like that.

$$\dagger$$

After almost two hours had passed, Tom stood in front of the loosely scattered troop. Confident that everyone had completed the certification process, he beckoned to the patrol leaders. "Time to count heads." When they had reported back, he convened the group. "Troop 9, gather 'round."

at last... Julian was eager to get back to camp. Besides, he had another case of teebee; it was a relief to stand up. Tom's order meant they could just gather into a bunch. Getting into standard formation on this hillside would be awkward. He slipped the pencil into the spiral and turned toward Tom. *I'm ready to let the drawing rest for a while.* He massaged his backside with his left hand as Tom began his talk.

"We have almost an hour until we have to be back at HQ for supper. Patrol leaders, you need to get there five minutes early to reserve a space for your patrols. Danny will be there to give you directions. We'll sit as a group for this meal. Remember, it's full dress, so look your best. Scouts who are here for the first time will come with me for a quick tour of the grounds. We'll go directly to the mess hall from there. The rest of you can return to camp if you want. Just don't be late. It's a barbecue, so everyone has to go through a line. Questions?"

"Can we take these back first?" Sid held up his towel and sun cream.

"Hmm... give them to your patrol leader to take back for you." Tom looked for any others. Jeremy had raised his hand. "Yes?"

"My hat is back at camp." Full dress meant wearing his scout cap.

Tom was not amused. "Anyone else have that problem?" Eight hands went up. "Okay: Patrol leaders, this is for you to fix. You'll need to get those caps and bring them to the chow line." He paused for a few minutes while the patrol leaders made the needed arrangements. Many, including Julian, dashed over to hand off their towels.

"Okay. First timers, follow me." Tom headed off to the west along the fence.

Julian wondered if he should tell Sid about his hair… it needed to be combed. He smoothed his own down with his hands. He had forgotten his comb too. *aha! I can put on my cap!* He slipped it out from under his belt.

Tom stopped: "Anybody here going to do either Rowing or Canoeing?" Half a dozen hands went up. "You will report through the swimming entrance, but you turn left and hang your badge on the special board on that side. You stay dressed for those activities, including recreational time. A Counselor is there to check you in and out."

Jeremy raised his hand. "Can anybody do that?" He thought you had to have the merit badge to check out a canoe. That's why he had signed up to work on it.

"Only swimmers with their blue half filled are allowed to check out a boat. Otherwise, yeah." He thought about it a minute. "Remember, though: you have to have a Buddy for that too." Tom led the group toward the trail at the edge of the forest. He stopped again. "Anyone working on the Swimming badge?"

Three hands went up.

"Okay. You go through the gate too, and dress down as usual. Your Buddy Badge goes on the swim side, in the area marked in a red box." Tom didn't think this applied, but he liked to be complete: "If you're working on distance ratings, you do that in the period before Swimming Badge class starts, at the same time as the beginning swim class."

Julian found Tom's tour very helpful. There was an ax yard where they taught how to use an ax and hatchet properly. Next to that was a ropeyard. That's where they taught tenderfoot scouts how to tie all the different knots they needed to know, as well as advanced level merit badge work on lashings. Those were on the west side, along with the merit badge class areas. There was a special space for Tenderfoot scouts to work on advancement to Second Class, and a space for Second Class to work on First Class. Those were a cluster of small clearings with tables and benches lined up under open-air pavilion roofs. Skits could be worked on in some too, or whatever was needed. They had to be reserved by a scoutmaster in the HQ building. The spaces were labeled A, B, C, clear through to G. They learned the location of the Archery Range and the Rifle Range—way over on the east side of the camp, against the hillside.

Julian was glad he wasn't working on the Fishing, Hiking, or Climbing badge. They met at HQ—those scouts had to ride in one of the camp crummys to get to their badge areas. Julian wasn't sure what a crummy was, actually.

At the large space set aside to work on handicrafts like Woodcarving, Leatherwork and Basketry, Tom stopped. "Okay. You've seen most of it. On the other side of the HQ building are the Counselor and Staff cabins, strictly off limits to scouts. The assembly area is next to the lake just on the other side of the swimming fence. If you're signed up to work on something we didn't see, ask me, or your patrol leader about it after the barbecue. A word about that: we sit together at this one. The troops get graded on their table manners and cleanup, so tuck your shirts in and look sharp at the meal. Remember: the cap goes to the left of your plate, on signal from me. I'll give that when everyone is seated. No early bites." Tom looked at them closely to make sure they had paid attention. Silent commands always made them look especially sharp.

"There's no program—that's saved for the big campfire tonight. We'll sit together there too, but not by patrol. There are no seats, just a hillside. The Tigers will need us to cheer and holler after their act. It's not a contest, but we might as well show the other troops what they're up against with a good Troop 9 cheer or two. So! Let's get to the chow line!" He gave a shoo gesture, and everyone took off running.

This was the best part of the tour… Tom enjoyed seeing all those cute little butts running down the trail… *very nice… going too fast to pick one out… a couple of fresh ripe pairs are there someplace.* He wanted to be their first. It was something he did very well, breaking those in… *I'll get a chance soon enough.*

8 *formal supper*

Suppertime, finally! Julian was starved… *lucky we're eating in the main dining hall the first night… that means we won't have to spend time getting supper ready. just as well, because the patrol didn't even meet yet to figure out who's going to do the cooking.* Up ahead, two lines led up the main trail to an open area adjacent to the HQ building. At first Julian was afraid that he was in for a long wait, like the one at the swimming test. But the line moved along nicely. He soon saw why: up ahead the two lines split into four lanes with identical serving tables. After dishing up outdoors, they were to take their trays inside.

The Troop 9 first timers weren't the last in line for chow, thank goodness, but close enough, as far as Julian was concerned… he wanted some food to be left when he got there. Dozens of scouts were coming down the trail to get into line… *guess we're okay, at that.* The aroma made his stomach seem emptier.

this is fun! the scoutmasters are the cooks today… They had tall cook's hats with a big number tacked on the front. Julian felt a sudden thrill: *there's Mark!* Julian was so **glad** to see him. A big 9 was on his hat; it tilted to the left a bit. *he is so cool…* Julian bounced on his toes unconsciously. *ooo! what a luck out! I can pick the right line.* In a minute he would be in front of Mark. *wow… how many guys… one… two… three… four… only seven in front of me.* Julian hurriedly did his usual look-my-best-for-Mark prep routine. He smoothed his hair, checked to make sure his shirt was tucked in, his kerchief all straight and smooth. He grabbed a tray and plate.

Troop 17's scoutmaster was the first server, spooning out mashed potatoes; Troop 29's was next, ladling the gravy. Then came Mark, serving barbecued spareribs—a pair of big tongs in his right hand. *he looks so cool with that apron—* Sauce drip marks and smudges testified that Mark had been at the task for a while.

"Hey, Wolf Number Six!" Delighted to see Julian at last, he grinned wide. *look at that big smile, that downy face...* "So, will it be two, or three of these? Did you work up a big appetite today?" It had been a long day.

"Yeah, I'm hungry. Did you guys cook all this yourself?"

"Sure did! Well, we had a little help from the kitchen staff, but we did most of it. The kitchen has the right equipment, so it's not hard to do." He looked left and right, feigning innocence, and forked over a small third piece. He gave Julian a wink—he loved the effect that had.

Julian blushed, sort of embarrassed. Every time Mark winked like that he got goose-bumpy all down the back Camp had been interesting today—but everywhere, except here, there had been no Mark around. He just had a scary thought: *what if it's like that all camp long?*

"Beep-beep!" Sid nudged Julian to keep moving.

Reluctantly, Julian moved on to the veggies.

Mark smiled at Sid gratefully. He came in handy at times, keeping Julian on track.

Julian waited for Sid, and they went into the mess hall together. They followed behind a couple of guys from the Badgers. They went in a side door that led right to the tables.

> > *squip-p-p-p... squip-p-p-p squeep-p—* < <

Julian looked down at his feet, embarrassed. He'd forgotten about his new boots—he didn't expect to make such a racket. A clear impression of the tread appeared on the freshly waxed asphalt tiles.

Sid looked down. "Nice... you got the no-skid tread. Good idea."

Julian spotted the Wolf patrol pennant—Stu had clipped it onto the front edge of the third table. *at least it isn't that far away.* Regular cafeteria tables filled the room, just like at school—only here they had folding chairs instead of benches. Each patrol was assigned one side of a table. He took his seat next to Jeremy. The rest of the patrol was seated already, waiting for Tom to give the order to start eating. Julian looked around... *weird. everyone else is gobbling away. we must look funny, just sitting here. ooo. here comes Tom.* On his silent command, Troop 9 began to eat with enthusiasm—that was free-style.

After supper they did organized K.P. duty at their troop's section. Tom took charge. *this is so neat!* Just like at the awards banquet last month—in a couple of minutes the plates, glasses and silverware were rounded up and taken to the collection table.

Julian's patrol was assigned the used napkin pick up. As each patrol finished their assignment, they returned to their place at the table and stood at ease. Several troops were still eating. Julian could tell they were watching what Troop 9 was doing. That made him feel good... he paid attention to his task and worked with care—walking as lightly as possible... the boots didn't squeal as much that way.

Since Mark had to remain seated with the other scoutmasters, Tom was in charge. He did a quick inspection tour, then with silent signals, he called them to attention. He saluted and dismissed them to return to the Meadow. They needed to freshen up and get their camps all squared away while there was still some daylight. They didn't go in formation, but left the dining area in an orderly, evenly spaced single file. As each scout came within six feet of the exit, he put his scout cap back on.

—m—

"Schaefer, you are something else!" Ted Soames, scoutmaster of Troop 6, shook his head in frustration. They had all been checking off the points earned during the meal on their clipboards. Mark's group was so much better it wasn't even close. Their outstanding performance brought in twenty-five points. Several at the table shook their heads. Troop 9 was ahead already!

Mark blushed slightly; he was enormously pleased with the boys, naturally—and of Tom. He sensed a degree of resentment in the compliment and wanted to smooth things out a little. "Don't blame me completely. Things are looking up for you guys next year. My JA will likely be replaced; he's off to the real world next June. I won't have another one like him for a while."

"Baloney. You must have given him all that Marine Corps snap-to." Harold Carter from Troop Two had observed all the commands carefully... they had been silent, and executed perfectly. The boys had even waited for a signal of some kind before starting to eat—he'd missed that one. Every move was **well** rehearsed.

"No, really. I've never been in the service. The boy is a born leader, that's all. I'm going to miss him a lot. I get to work at this full time again, starting next June." Mark had been smart enough to keep the tradition he had inherited when he became scoutmaster; his predecessor and mentor **was** ex-military. But next year would be a challenge—he had no one in the pipeline that could match Tom's leadership skill. He'd been trained by his older brothers—Tom came from a long line of Eagle scouts. Mark did have half a dozen who were on the verge of earning their Eagle, though… picking the best one was going to be his biggest problem. He did have a legit brag if he wanted one: for over a year now, all the boys in the troop had joined under his leadership.

From previous years the other scoutmasters knew that Mark was the true leader of the outfit, and they had to respect him. The trouble was, he was such a good guy. Often the Top Dog was someone they could enjoy trying to sabotage. Not one of them was inclined to do anything like that to Mark. All the same, they would not mind one bit if they could whip his butt somehow, fair and square. His three year winning streak had gone on long enough. Not one thought they could compete with him, though.

Director Jorgensen smiled to himself. He had expected this. He'd watched Troop 9 form and head out this afternoon. That had more than compensated for the late arrival. If that had been in the troop point tally, these men would really be bellyaching. He saw no reason to doubt that Mark's boys would stay on top.

Julian and his Wolf pals walked leisurely up the trail to Barr's Meadow. It felt good to be free and loose for a while. *come to think of it, it's the first time we've been on our own since we got here.* Over an hour remained before the campfire. *it's only six thirty… the skits are supposed to start at eight o'clock sharp—half an hour before sunset.*

Julian paid close attention to the trees along the trail this time. *they're different up here at four thousand feet.* He stopped in place and watched the treetops for a minute—they looked happy up there in the breeze. He turned slowly to the right; he did this sometimes, turn in a complete circle, just to see a complete picture of a place. The air was cooler, fresher than in town… this place was very different from home. It didn't scare him any—it added to the excitement. *this trail is nicer than the one coming in from the road... not so dusty... grade isn't very steep at all... extra wide. they must use a Jeep or something...* Tread marks showed in a few places. He looked back down the trail to see if Mark was coming. *nope... probly still sitting at that long table with all the other scoutmasters. oh well... oop*—Sid and Jeremy had gone ahead, as usual. He ran to catch up. They were close to camp already.

"Gotta go." Jeremy cut left to the latrine.

Julian decided to go too, as long as he was here; he nodded to Sid, inviting him to tag along. *so... six stalls.* He chose the third unit; he could tell it was free because no feet were visible underneath the door.

> > **praanng...** < < *umf! wow...* The long spring at the top of the door was stiff—required a real tug.

> > **whap!** < < *oh... it keeps the door closed. has to, the hook is missing. hinges are sure rusty... they need to repaint this place... it's pretty old.* Exposure to the weather year around had taken its toll. Julian focused on his task. It didn't stink as bad as he expected, but he didn't like this place. *well, it's better than having to find a spot in the woods behind some bush. at least it's far enough from the patrol camps. the Panthers are closest if the wind comes in wrong.*

After finishing, he was curious... he peered down to see what made it sound like that. A white powder covered everything... *huh... that must be why it doesn't smell much.*

> > **praanng... whap!** < < *man! why do they need such a powerful door spring?* He was glad to get out of there.

"Everything come out all right?" Sid was examining a strangely shaped acorn.

Julian didn't reply—it was a tired old joke. Jeremy was still in the end stall; they waited as a courtesy. It didn't take long.

"Thanks..." Jeremy was expecting a jibe from Sid. He was mildly surprised when it didn't materialize.

They ambled up the meadow to their camp. Sid did an impromptu wolf call as they crossed the small footbridge.

Stu poked his head out to see who it was. He waved back instead of giving a call.

"I thought all good Wolves were supposed to bark when they came back home." Sid poked Jeremy.

Jeremy gave a wolf cub yip and nudged Julian.

Julian gave an extended moon howl. That broke Sid up.

Stu gave them a mini-salute as they came by his tent. He was generally happy with his pups—that's what he called his youngest patrol members.

In the tent Julian moved his towel onto his backpack. *nice… Stu plonked it where I'd find it easy. Stu's a good patrol leader. so: how do I do this?* He unfolded the cot. *boy, it's a handful once it's opened up. why are these things all folded up, anyway? must be the first camp of the summer or something.* He admired how it was designed; all folded it was very compact. *it's easy to figure out, once you look at it.* He straightened it out along the back wall and pulled it open. He sat on it good and hard and bounced up and down a couple of times so that it would unfold completely and snap into place. *must be fairly new… still tight and stiff.* He rolled out his bag and fluffed up his pillow; it was all scrunched up from being wrapped up tight in the bag. *ug…* His fingers felt a little sticky from supper. He needed to wash them off before unpacking the duffel bag.

"Hey, Sid—do we wash our hands in the creek, or what?"

"Nah, don't get caught doin' that. You're s'posed to use the washbasin over by the Lynx tent. It's their duty to fetch the water. You gotta take your own soap and towel, though." Sid unraveled his new air mattress with a flourish—he wasn't bragging, **exactly**. He shook it a few times to unfold it completely. *color is kind of cool—sky blue. must have been Mom that actually bought it.* His father would have snagged an army colored one. They had both kinds.

"Thanks." *Lynx tent… how'd I miss that? 'Prob'ly because you were looking at Mark again,'* his conscience scolded. Sometimes he didn't pay very good attention when Mark was standing close by. He opened his duffel and fished out his new toiletry kit. *You gotta pay better attention, dum-dum.* He wrapped his towel around his neck and slipped past Sid— he was unscrewing the cap on his air mattress valve. Jeremy's side was blocked off; he was sorting out all his stuff.

this place is really something; lots fancier than the places where we go for campouts. we even have a stove instead of a campfire! Julian paused to examine the two burner propane camp stove stationed in the stone fire ring. *so this is how we'll be cooking... cool.* He crossed back over the footbridge... the washing area was to the right, near one of the Lynx tents.

A folding table made of wood slats stood on a flexible steel mat platform. A stand for hanging towels and shirts stood at the left, next to a small table. One guy was washing his hands and face. Julian didn't know him at all; he was older, had muscular legs... a Panther, maybe? He couldn't see the arm patch. *this is lucky... I can see how he does things. like everything around here, this place is different—a washroom without any walls.*

Alex was in a great mood this afternoon—Gary, his patrol leader, had just paid him a terrific complement about his performance at the dinner cleanup... *if only I could get that kind of recognition from the Major.* Somehow the Major was never pleased. He always found a small error—or if not, he just nodded and never said a word. Alex had hoped that his father would be pleased that he was in scouts; the troop he had joined was well known for its marching and military polish. But no— when he met Mark, all he did was size him up and shake his hand. The Major kept his opinion to himself, as usual. Alex tried once to talk with Mark about it, but they got interrupted. *maybe I can find a way this week. Mark seems interested in everyone personally. oop...* he glanced at the mirror—*someone is waiting to wash up.*

"Hey, don't be bashful, come on over... plenty of room." He shifted to the right. Alex made it a point to be very friendly—the Scout Law was something he took very seriously. He could recite it from memory. "Hey, you're the kid that does the scrapbook, aren't you?" He rubbed his face dry and dumped out his dirty water. It slipped right through the slats and disappeared into the mesh. His father had told him about the efficient way to use this area—always tip the basin to the side. It was similar to the facilities the Marines used in their field training. "Good work, kid. Somebody shoulda thought of that a long time ago."

"Yeah, thanks a lot." *this guy knows who I am! whoa... look at that! the entire table is a drain... so is the floor. better stand back when you empty the wash pan though—huh... nothing splashed on this guy...*

"So you just take water from that can over there?" He pointed to a rectangular five-gallon can with a spigot in the bottom.

"Yah, that's it. First time here!" He stuck out his hand for a shake. "Alex is the name, Alex Trent. I'm from here at the Lynx patrol." He shook Julian's hand firmly.

"I'm Julian. Julian Forrest." He smiled. "Wolf."

"Great. Glad to meet you, Wolf. You're in the right outfit. This troop's gonna win again this year… we got started at lunch today!" Alex noticed the First Class patch. *all right! that scrapbook is pretty impressive, him only being a First Class.* He grabbed his shirt off the rack. *I need to get with it…* He put on the shirt and buttoned it carefully, leaving the neck open, the collar turned under. He stood back. *I don't need the mirror; the kid can go ahead.*

Julian took the basin over to the water can. Elevated so that the basin could be filled without being held, the small spigot was simple and easy to operate, but slow—the output was les than a quarter inch. While the basin filled, he watched Alex put on his shirt and kerchief. *he's so… what's the right word? organized, or something. putting on his shirt looks like a performance… the Star patch looks new. he's younger than I thought— super muscular legs. probly an athlete… broad shoulders… football player I bet.*

"Later, 'gator." Alex turned to leave. *maybe I can wangle a spot next to Max at the assembly… or Gary. too bad we're not in the same tent this year… I was put in with Paul and Sandy for some reason… maybe it will work out. too early to tell… Sandy's the new one—that must be why. maybe Gary is wise to Paul, then.*

Julian returned Alex's wave and watched him disappear into the tent next to the wash station. *strange I never noticed that guy before.* He took the basin over to the table and put it in front of the mirror. The steel mat felt odd to walk on; he bent over to look at it closely. Small serrations were cut or punched out along the top of opposite sides of the individual metal segments. *be nasty if you were barefoot.* The table was wide enough for two, but there was only one washbasin. *was I supposed to bring one over from the Wolf camp?* He examined the table… *looks like it folds up. it's sturdy enough. these slats are ingenious… I can see straight down to the ground… who invented all this stuff, anyway?*

He pulled his brand new bar of Lifebuoy soap out of his toiletry kit. *hmm… no place to toss the wrapper—wait. I need it—I'll keep the soap in it when I'm done.* He tucked it back into the kit. As he soaped up his hands and rinsed his face in the cold water, he speculated about the opening night campfire. *it has to be great, because every troop is going to be showing off its best. what will Mark be doing? prob'ly has to help run it, or something. what about tomorrow? maybe Mark will be helping with merit badges or something. when will I get to see him? I didn't think there'd be so many scouts around. he'll prob'ly be busy all the time.*

Julian wasn't discouraged, but he was a little worried. He figured there would be lots of times at camp when he could find a chance to be alone with Mark. He'd been counting on that. *man alive… all these hundreds of scouts! it's hard to figure when that might be… wait—the scrapbook! he's always interested in that… and in the chow line he gave me that special wink… hmm. this is one of those times, Julian when you have to be patient and pay attention. something will come along…*

"So, you gonna scrub your skin all off, or what?" came the question from behind.

Julian snapped out of it and rinsed his face real quick. "Sorry, Sid. I kinda let my mind wander off, I guess." He tucked the soap into the wrapper and was about to toss his water out—*wait…* He tipped it to the side the way Alex did. *amazing.* Not a drop went astray. He handed the basin to Sid. "Did you blow that thing up already?"

"I decided to go halfsies; I'll do the other half later." Sid was kicking himself for not bringing along his tire pump. He wasn't about to ask for help—that would mean having to share the air mattress. *no sir-ee.*

Julian noticed the comb tucked into Sid's back pocket. *good idea—I better do that.* He returned to the tent and finished unpacking. He arranged everything in the footlocker so he would know exactly where things were. He tested his flashlight, just to make sure it worked. He stood back and looked his area over: *ready for inspection, just in case.* They weren't supposed to inspect until tomorrow after breakfast, but there might just be a surprise one; he didn't want to be the dummy that lost points for the patrol.

He sat on the cot and reviewed the sketches he had made during the day. He'd been able to do a lot after Certification; *there's always something to add or improve.* He flipped back to the first page. *maybe the bus tires could use some rounding. hmm... not enough light in here.* He stepped out of the tent and sat at the table. *hey—I'll start one of the Wolf camp... Stu's tent. the patrol pennant waving at the corner is cool...*

Barr's Meadow   Eldot

the bus tires could use some rounding. hmm... not enough light in here. He stepped out of the tent and sat at the table. *hey—I'll start one of the Wolf camp... Stu's tent. the patrol pennant waving at the corner is cool...*

9 *opening night Campfire*

"Wolf patrol! Front and Center!" Stu called urgently. "Time to hit the trail." He looked across the creek. The Lynx were well down the slope. The Tigers were long gone. *maybe we're later than I thought.*

Julian closed his tablet at once; it was getting hard to see well enough to draw anyway—the sky was turning orange. He poked the pencil into the spiral and dashed into the tent; he slipped the tablet into his footlocker and re-joined the group.

"'Kay, guys… I'm gonna show you a shortcut…" Stu held his hands in a shush position. "We're not supposed to go this way… something about not wanting us to start a trail or wreck the natural setting. Anyway, fan out so you don't mess up the slope—and step careful, step light. And don't **tell** anyone." He waited for a nod of understanding from everyone.

He led them to the shortcut route that went down the hill behind the Tigers' camp. It cut the distance to the amphitheater almost in half. There wasn't a trail—the ground was open like the meadow with random clumps of bear grass. It was much steeper than the legal trail. Between the setting sun and the moon, it was easy to see where to step. The ground dropped nearly fifty feet, enough to keep the Barr's Meadow camps out of sight from below. The lake latrine was to the right, near the small pine trees at the bottom of the slope—twice as many booths as in the meadow.

The campfire event was held in a large natural amphitheater located uphill east of the swim area. Scouts sat all across the slope; the arc was about a third of a circle. Space was ample—it would take twice the number attending this camp to fill the expanse. An open area at the bottom served as the stage… it was backed by tall yellow poplar trees a few feet from the ledge above the lake. No platform, no side entrances—only a large level area in front of the fire pit.

A sunken circle five feet across was lined with large stones. Fires were reduced to three feet because of the dry conditions. Technically, this part of the state had been in a drought since last fall. On windy nights, camps were required to substitute white gas lanterns for open flame.

Seating was random; the uneven grade was interrupted by patches of grass and small irregular rocks; no chairs or benches. Moderately steep, the slope was sufficient to provide good acoustics and visibility, but gentle enough to resist erosion. Small white pines bordered the rear and east sides. A good view was available from any vantage point, making it a logical assembly location.

Troop 9 sat on the northeast side, behind another troop. When Sid and Jeremy decided to move closer to the performers, Julian hung back. He felt like having some space around him—but he had another reason. *it's hard to keep a lookout for Mark if I'm all huddled up in a bunch with the other guys.* He found a soft grassy spot up toward the top… nice and roomy. *I can stretch out up here—lay down, even.* A few scouts over toward the center were doing just that. Unconsciously, his artistic eye took over: the view was outstanding. He shifted into his pre-composition mode.

For some time now, whenever he saw something new and interesting he automatically began to frame it as a drawing. It helped him remember what he had seen, and it usually added to his enjoyment of the moment. Sunset always enhanced things, and the orange glow in the western sky was reflected on the lake—the cottonwoods on the far side of the fire pit were black silhouettes in front of a magical sea of glistening patches of orange and deep blue. The setting was as perfect as it could be. *Mom would like this a lot if she was here.*

The evening began with the pledge of allegiance, followed by the Scout Oath. John Jorgensen, the Camp Director, was master of ceremonies. He had been doing this for many years.

Julian paid attention at first. The opening commentary was a little boring, and his attention faded. He looked around at the audience. *where's Mark sitting? he's tall… should be easy to spot… it's hard to make out faces in the twilight.* He surveyed the crowd carefully… seeing an individual was nearly impossible—all the shirts and kerchiefs were so alike… the moon wasn't much help; it was near the western horizon, chasing after the sun. Soon the fire would be the only light—barely enough to see some kerchiefs and faces. *man alive, this is a big camp! hundreds and hundreds of scouts! way too many to count. at last!* Off to the right of the fire: Mark was in a huddle with the Tiger patrol. *our skit must be about to come up or something...* Julian felt better now... he returned his attention to the program.

The acts were good, so far. The first one was about Indian creation myths; that really grabbed Julian's fancy—*maybe that's a good merit badge to work on* Next was a solo act, a mime. It was fantastic: how did that scout make everyone believe he was climbing an invisible ladder? *and the way he opens the door! you can almost see the knob turning. are those sound effects? this guy will be on TV someday.* The gospel quartet was boring. Half the time they were off key. *barbershoppy stuff always sounds sour or something.*

The Tiger skit went off well—Tony was a riot, as usual. It didn't get as big a cheer as the mime, but almost as good. Tom stood below and prompted them in the Troop 9 cheer. That almost made up for it.

Julian looked around, but couldn't see Mark anywhere. *too dark now to see any distance at all... getting cool, too.* He drew his legs up and held his arms around his knees. The short sleeved shirt and short pants weren't going to be enough to keep him warm much longer... the long socks helped some. *hmm... they're only four acts into this. how cold does it get here at night, anyway? when the sun goes down, so does the warm air.*

A duo stepped into the performance area below. They were from Troop 76. The guy who announced the acts didn't talk loud enough. Julian couldn't make out the name of the song. The tall one had a guitar. *he's really good—*

!!!

Someone had sat down on the grass behind him; he felt a hand on his shoulder. His face flushed—he recognized the exciting odor at once. He started to turn his head—

"Eyes front." Mark spoke softly, just above a whisper.

A rush of sensations, impossible to sort out: Julian was suddenly warm, tingly, his heart was going a mile a minute, he was holding his breath, his eyes were about to pop out, he was growing rock hard down below, and he couldn't think. He could feel his face flush red... his legs had turned into a mass of goose bumps. What could this mean? He wasn't sure about much, but he always knew that odor—unlike anything else… electrifying. It made him tingle. He inhaled as deep as he could, through his nose… so musky, so sweet.

Mark's voice caused a trace of that exotic tickle—*just like when he pinches my shoulder.* It ran up the right side of his neck to the back of his head. His forehead and temples were burning. If Mark weren't holding on to him, he'd probably tip over.

"Can I talk with you for just a minute?"

Julian nodded eagerly.

"How is your camp set up?" First off, Mark had to know if his idea was feasible.

Julian didn't understand the question. "I'm in a tent with Sid and Jeremy…"

"How would you like to be assigned to the Flaming Arrow patrol?"

Julian was at a loss… this had come out of the blue. *I don't know anyone in that patrol, but if Mark wants it, there's only one answer.* "Sure."

"It would mean leaving the Wolf patrol. I wouldn't want you to be unhappy about that."

I don't want to leave the Wolf patrol… but there's still only one answer. He remembered his own sage advice to himself a little while ago: 'something will come along.' *sure enough: here it is!*

"I think they can get along all right without me." He shrugged. His mind was buzzing, searching for some reason for this incredible development.

Mark took a deep breath. This was the tough one. "I want you to understand that there is a small problem. The Flaming Arrow crew tent is full. That means you to will have to stay in the cabin." Mark was confident this was no problem for Julian at all—yet it was essential to be a known pre-condition.

Julian couldn't believe his ears! *stay in Mark's cabin?!* Suddenly the one problem he had been wrestling with had been solved. *don't mess up now, Julian!* "Uhh… that's okay. I don't mind." His mind raced… *who else is going to be in there?* He wasn't sure who all was in the Flaming Arrow Patrol.

Mark spoke softly, slowly. "There is a second problem. It would be best if you could move into the cabin tonight rather than tomorrow. Do you think you can do that?"

move tonight? what does that mean... Julian's heart sank. *by the time this assembly is over, it might be too late... it's almost dark already.* He didn't know what to do. "How can I do that?"

Mark hated to be conducting this conversation in whispers and from behind—but he didn't have much choice, now that he had begun. "Unfortunately, it means doing it now; you'll have to miss most of the assembly."

Julian was elated. *I don't mind that, one bit! most the acts are kind of boring, anyway.* "That's okay... I can always find out about them later."

"Good." Mark was pleased at how this was going. "Go and get all your gear, and the folding cot from your tent and put everything in the cabin. Be sure to move your footlocker too. Leave nothing behind. I'll help you set everything up when we get there later. Leave now—as if you're going to the latrine. Come back as soon as you've moved it all. I'll be sitting right here until then. Do this as fast as you can." Mark released his hand so Julian could stand up.

Julian couldn't believe it! His head was swimming—his wildest dream was coming true. He did exactly as Mark instructed. The hardest part was not breaking into a run and shouting for joy.

Mark watched Julian hasten across the top of the amphitheater. His heart rate was up a little... he was pleased with how easily that had gone. He scanned the area cautiously... *is anyone paying attention to me instead of the program? looks okay...* he glanced behind... no one was seated there. *excellent.* The nearest was a group from the Panther patrol, about fifteen feet down to the left. Julian couldn't have picked a better spot to sit. When Mark saw him all alone up at the top, he made a snap decision then and there to go with this tonight—it was too ideal to pass up. The uncertainty was Julian's ability to get the move accomplished in time— *he's new to the camp. there's still some moonlight left. the trails are wide and clear... he should be okay.*

—⟋⟍—

it's too dark... Julian stumbled a couple of times—he didn't know this way very well—he'd only come this way once, just a few minutes ago. His eyes were still adjusting to the low light... it got easier to see as he moved farther from the glare of the campfire. *let's see... you go down toward the lake, then... ah... latrine booths are ahead on the left. this is where to scoot up the hill.* The Meadow was a good ten minutes away. *what if Stuart hadn't shown us this shortcut?* The regular trail would take half an hour in the dark, at least.

He hurried up the hill as fast as he could. *it'll be easier to see once I get to the top. boy, this is steep when you have to go up.* He stopped suddenly. *is this the right way?! nothing looks right... I don't recognize anything.* He turned around and looked back. *huh. the latrine booths look the same as before... this has to be right.* He started to climb again. *it's just farther up than I thought. hurry up, dum-dum.* He could see a little better now—the starlight was getting stronger. *too bad the moon isn't higher...* It was about a third full, but about to disappear behind the trees.

ah... the crest at last: I can see better up here—the light reflects off the grass in the meadow. the paths are easy to see... the Tiger camp was just ahead. "Thank you, Stu!" *I can do this!*

He was short of breath, but didn't stop—he turned left onto the trail and ran right over to the Wolf camp. *the flag's waving at me!* "Hee-hee!" He waved back. His tent was the first one.

"Ow!" He banged his shin on Sid's footlocker. *man, it's dark in here!* He felt his way to his own footlocker... thanks to his careful preparation, he was able to locate his flashlight in an instant. He rested it on the end of Jeremy's cot and aimed it so that he could see what he was doing. *there. eee, that bump hurts.* He sat on his cot and pulled down his sock carefully... *amazing! there isn't a cut. good thing I have on long socks!* He rubbed it gently. *maybe it won't hurt too long.* "Slow down, dum-dum," he scolded. "You don't want to mess **this** up!" *okay*—he rolled up his sleeping bag, blanket and pillow, and put them in a wad over on Sid's cot. He flipped the cot on its side and folded it up. *this is a lot easier than unfolding it was...* He made the cot his first load. It wasn't too heavy, but it was an armful. He was careful to avoid Sid's footlocker on the way out.

lucky the little footbridge is easy to see—otherwise I might step into the creek. After the cot he toted over the footlocker and pack. *ugg: they're heavy... shoulda made two trips...* He put them down on the landing and opened the door. He set them inside just past the threshold and shoved hard—he did not turn on the light.

> > **crash!** < <

yikes! it tipped over! everything spilled out! He froze in place—lucky no one is around. *how could it make so much noise? must be a slick floor in there. should I turn on the light and fix everything? geez... I have to hurry. I still have to fetch my bedding and flashlight. Mark will understand... he said he would help set things up.* Julian returned to the Wolf camp running full out.

He stopped for a second and held his pillow. He addressed it somberly. "This is a miracle, y'know. We have dreamed about this." He buried his face in it and yelled as loud as he could. "**Miracle!**" That felt better. He took a deep breath. *oo... maybe I shouldn't have shouted so hard.* His throat hurt a little.

—⁓—

Mark's attention to the pageant below faded gradually. Reenactments of famous moments in history were awkward at the best of times. In front of this small campfire, they had little chance; if the characters hadn't been identified by name, it would have been a total disaster. He took advantage of the opportunity to think through what he had done more carefully—Julian would be gone for half an hour, at least. *missing the assembly is unfortunate, but I doubt if he'll be bothered by that. time for some careful thinking... no surprises are allowed tonight.* Julian being gone for a few minutes was a big help. He checked his watch again: *he's been gone over fifteen minutes now. hopefully, he'll be back in another fifteen or twenty.* Mark took a deep breath and exhaled. *with any luck, the program will still be going when he returns.*

During the barbecue he had watched the boys eat together and socialize—it came to him suddenly that important relationships at camp were set on the first day—they were foundational. Whatever he came up with, it would be wise to have the camp start with it in place... making a change midway would be disruptive. It might even invite speculation.

That's why tonight was so much better than tomorrow, as he had originally planned. Better that Julian not have to make a visible move after spending a night in the tent with his buddies. *there won't be a lot of time tonight to talk, unfortunately. but the essentials can be handled—they're all that's needed tonight anyway. we'll have lots of opportunity to confer; we'll find a solution to Julian's obsession, eventually.*

The entertainment program was well past the halfway point. *all right: I need to run over my instructions to Danny again, just to be certain. the announcement I make tonight will deflect speculation.* Mark was aware that once it was known Julian was staying in the cabin, questions could arise. *best to avoid those from the start.*

—⁂—

Under normal circumstances, Julian would probably stop to think about what was happening and work out what he should be doing to make it easier. But his instinct had taken over the second that Mark told him what to do. There was no time for questions or considerations... the fact that Mark had told him to do exactly what he'd been dreaming about for **years** served to remove any hesitation he might have had. *besides, the clock is ticking. I have to get back before the assembly is over!* He buried the flashlight in the middle of the pillow and ran to the cabin for the last time.

if only I had a watch—how long have I been gone? It seemed like he'd been taking way too long—**three** trips from his Wolf tent. He placed the sleeping bag just inside to the right and closed the door. *done!* He took off at a trot... the starlight helped make it bright enough to see. *in no time I'll be taking Stu's shortcut south of the Tiger camp.*

Julian ran as fast as he dared... he didn't want to trip. *how is this going to be allowed? well, Mark's the boss, so it must be okay!* He started down the drop off carefully... the growing darkness made it seem steeper. He slowed down suddenly: he just had an inspirational thought. *what if I'm the only other person in there? darn! I should have turned on the light and looked around at least. I have no idea how I'm going to...* he shook his head, disgusted with himself. *you don't want to be kicked out before the night is over. just behave and take your time. something will come along. that must be a new motto or something. yeah... goes perfectly with Be Prepared.* Julian smiled at his cleverness.

He glanced toward the opposite slope. Part of the amphitheater was visible. *lucky it's this dark—otherwise I might be spotted.* He could barely make out the sea of faces watching the assembly... he could hear their laughter clearly enough. *what luck! the assembly is still going.* He moved forward again, slowly. "Careful... you don't need a twisted ankle, dum-dum."

Julian's eyes had adjusted to the dark... he could see Mark up at the top of the slope. He circled around from behind; that way he wouldn't cross in front of anyone. *sure glad I sat way back here. 'something will come along...'* he giggled softly. Julian's imagination had begun to work on some possibilities.

Silently he approached from behind. *where should I sit? in front where I was before, or beside?* He looked around... nobody's paying any attention. He inhaled deeply... there's that smell. It gave him a tingle below. I better sit down quick or I'll get a stiffy. He inhaled as deep a breath as he could and sat down on Mark's right side. He wished at once that he had sat a little closer.

Mark was impressed by how soon Julian had returned... *this bodes well.* He patted him on the thigh and whispered, "Everything taken care of?"

Julian nodded yes eagerly. *mmm...* Mark's voice tickled.

Mark was reassured at once. "You did very well, Julian." *I doubt that I could have done that any faster.* He returned his gaze to the performance below. It was a very shopworn skit... *someone does that one every summer about. their scoutmaster needs to get a new catalogue.*

Julian wasn't at all interested in what was going on down in front of the fire pit. He wondered if Mark was going to say anything more about the move—maybe why. But he didn't want to be a pest... Mark is watching. *oh... he probably needs to see these things.* He shrugged and put his arms around his legs again. It was growing a little chilly.

Mark noticed Julian's discomfort. *that's one of the realities at this altitude. it cools off at night.* He glanced at his watch. *we won't be here much longer.* "We'll be leaving soon. If you get cold, give your legs a good rubbing to increase the circulation."

Julian followed the advice. It helped at once. "Thanks." *hmm. I guess he isn't going to say anything. I have to wait until we get there. hang on Julian, be patient.*

"Sit tight… I'll be right back."

Mark stood up carefully… he walked down and over to Danny Laskey, the Senior Patrol Leader. Fortunately, he wasn't in the middle of a group. Mark was very grateful it was this dark… without attracting any attention, he had to ask Danny to make some additions to the announcements he would be making after the campfire. The vast numbers here tonight were a terrific asset—almost a shield. Occasional movement was not apt to attract any notice. The olive green uniforms were almost black in this light. He got down on one knee and tapped Danny's shoulder.

Danny wrote down Mark's whispered instructions carefully. He had to tilt his tablet to get enough light to see the page. It was tricky… the moon was disappearing already. He couldn't stop to think about what he was writing down. It didn't make sense to him exactly.

Mark had Danny read it back—he had to be certain it was exactly right. He had already spoken to Jorgensen about holding the troop for a brief meeting after the assembly. He planned to do the announcements here so they wouldn't have to assemble back in the meadow. So far, everything was going perfectly. His mind was more settled about what he had put into play… *I don't have a tiger by the tail as I had feared.* He was relieved by Julian's cool and collected behavior. *maybe this will be easier than I expected.*

Julian watched Mark with confused anticipation… he wanted Mark back, right now! He had forgotten completely where he was or what was going on around the fire—that was static in his ears that he was ignoring. *why is he talking to Danny, of all people?*

Danny lived right behind Julian's house, across the tall fence. Julian used to think about him a lot. *he's really hot, actually.* But he was over a year older, so they never had much direct contact. After he fell so madly in love with Mark he had stopped thinking about Danny completely. *wow! that's why I don't think about Danny any more… all I think about is Mark.* He just had a realization about himself.

Mark returned uphill; he glanced around—no one was paying attention; he settled down beside Julian once again.

Julian expected Mark to say something... but he wasn't in a hurry to talk for some reason; he had leaned back a little and rested on his hands. Julian was confused... he looked over. Mark just smiled and nodded his head. *everything is okay, I guess.*

Mark moved into a cross-legged position. Sitting in one place for long was uncomfortable on the irregular slope. The grass was dry and a little slippery.

Julian was disappointed... he'd been hoping Mark would sit a little closer, actually. *other than talking about the scrapbook, I never get to sit by him...* Julian had no idea what was going on down by the fire; his mind was swimming with chaotic ideas about what might be going to happen in the cabin. He couldn't focus on any particular scenario... he had never imagined anything like this. A sudden burst of applause snapped him back to the here and now. He heard the old scoutmaster bring things to a close. He had completely missed what was going on down there.

Director Jorgensen finished his complimentary remarks and closing announcements. "Last of all, Scoutmaster Mark has asked that Troop 9 stay for a short meeting down here by the fire. Everyone else is dismissed to his troop's camp. The fire crew will stay and completely extinguish this blaze. Good night, everyone."

After a good stretch, the Troop 9 scouts shuffled down the slope and clustered at the bottom as the other troops moved out. The four man suppression crew began their attack on the fire. They worked as quietly as they could so the Troop 9 meeting could go ahead. They were efficient and finished before the meeting was over; the breeze was from the east— the smoke and steam didn't interfere.

One of Danny's regular duties as Senior Patrol Leader was to give announcements and last minute instructions for the morning activities. Someone held a flashlight so he could read from his notebook.

Julian missed some of what Danny was saying—it sounded like instructions about getting water from the creek or something. He felt so strange... even though Mark was right behind him, he was glad it was dark. Suddenly, what Mark had been talking to Danny about became clear.

"Effective tonight," Danny read, "we have a new Assistant Scribe." He held the tablet close up so he could read it exactly; his handwriting was uneven because it was so dark up there. "It will be his job to work with Mark and Nick to write up and print the **Troop 9 Notes** newsletter. He is a member of the Flaming Arrow patrol, starting tonight. The new Assistant Scribe is Julian Forrest."

Mark nudged. "Wave your arm and smile."

Julian was startled… he held his hand up about halfway—*oop*. He just remembered to smile. He was kind of scared… so many faces were turned to look at him… some were smiling. A small token applause made him blush. He didn't entirely understand what Danny had said… it was all so unexpected. It was too dark now to see anything very well… he didn't see Sid or Jeremy anywhere. *what are they going to think?*

"Now, here's Mark to finish things up."

Mark stepped forward and took Danny's place. "I need to remind the patrol leaders about reveille. Since Frank isn't here this year, we have no bugler to sound it in the morning. You will each have to be responsible for that in your patrol. It's still a seven o'clock wakeup. If any of you are up earlier, please be respectful of those who are still sleeping. By the way, you did an excellent job cleaning up after the barbecue. You picked up twenty-five points!"

The troop did a cheer.

"Now, about the new appointment… Julian will be a good Assistant Scribe. Most of you have seen the scrapbook he has been making this year. The next issue of the newsletter will be mostly about this camp, so I encourage you all to get to know him and tell him your stories." Mark stepped forward one step and came to attention. "Troop, Attention!"

The Troop stood up snappily. They knew the end ritual well.

Mark held up his right hand and gave the cue to begin the Vespers Song. The Troop sang from memory:

Softly falls the light of day as our campfire fades away.
Silently each scout should ask, 'Have I done my daily task?'
'Have I kept my honor bright and may I guiltless sleep tonight?'
'Have I done and have I dared everything to Be Prepared!'

"You have started off well. Remember, lights out is ten o'clock. Dismissed!"

The troop hurried off to the Meadow. Many had brought along a flashlight; the string of lights moving up the trail had a mysterious exotic quality. Everyone used the established trail—the few who knew about the shortcut also knew that major demerits would be awarded if Mark saw them take it. The moon was past the tree line of the forest on the ridge to the west; it's light would be gone completely in a few minutes. They had twenty minutes before the ten o'clock lights out. The trail was wide and gentle, so many ran ahead.

Mark and Julian fell in behind the rest… they did not talk.

Julian wished it was darker… he was afraid to look at Mark. He was anxious to not do or say anything wrong; he just froze his mouth. The wide trail meant that they could walk side by side… *wow*.

Mark was glad it was this dark; he preferred that their action tonight remain unnoticed. He knew these paths well… *we'll be at the cabin after the lanterns start up, but the boys will be busy.*

10   *first night*

"We've got the light for about five minutes." Mark opened the door and flipped the switch. "So let's get you set up." The overturned footlocker caused a chuckle. "You must have been in a hurry!" He watched closely as Julian jumped to it... *what's going through his head? as far as I can tell, everything is okay.*

Julian squinted; the sudden light from the bare overhead bulb was brighter than he expected. His overturned footlocker and its contents had spilled across the center of the room. *why didn't I straighten that up? I had the time after all. oh well...* he stepped in and headed for the cot. *where am I supposed to set it up?* He looked around the room. *boy: a big double bed... a table and chair to the right, next to an open door—must be the bathroom.* He hesitated momentarily as it registered in his head: *no one else... just Mark and me!*

He got down on one knee and unfolded the cot. Before he could open it up, Mark took it from him, snapped it open effortlessly and put it in place against the wall. Julian watched in awe—in the Wolf camp that had taken him several minutes and all his strength. For Mark it might as well have been a folding chair. Julian didn't have time to think—Mark seemed to be in a hurry, so he fetched the sleeping bag and unrolled it, zipper side out; he fluffed up the pillow and put it in place. *shucks...* being close to the big double bed was out, for now at least. *best to be quiet for now...* He spread his extra blanket over the bag and pillow, and made the regulation corners at the foot. He was still afraid to look Mark in the face for some reason. The overturned footlocker was next. *stupid klutz...* All his stuff had spilled out when it tipped over in the dark. He slid the footlocker over to the head of the cot. Mark handed things to him, and he put them in place. He tucked his empty pack and tennies under the cot.

Mark glanced at the clock... *three minutes... I may have to fudge a little...* He needed to go over the ground rules before he could turn off the light. "Are you ready for the guided tour?" His instinct was in charge more than anything, but he was keenly aware that starting off on the right foot was essential.

Julian turned around and smiled. "Sure!" *just what I wanted, actually.*

"Right. Your cot is on the northwest wall. The entire wall is now your responsibility. There is one window," he gestured.

Julian turned to look. The curtains were pushed to the side and the window was wide open. It faced the forest, so nothing could be seen but darkness.

Scoutmaster's Cabin

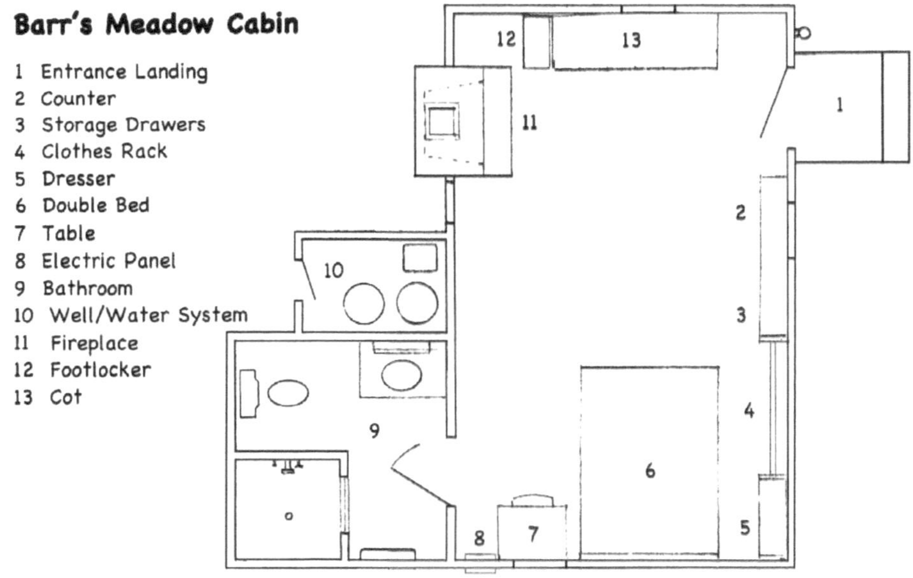

"We will have to work together on its use. I learned last year that it has to be open if air circulation is needed—and it is, most of the time. If it's too cold at night, it's best to close it tight. I usually did that after campfire last year. It's wise to close it at night—otherwise a raccoon or packrat might get a little too curious. The cabin holds the day's heat for about two hours. I don't think this place is insulated." Mark stepped over to the fireplace. "This is never used in the summer. The camp is open year round; this is here for fall and winter activities. I've never started a fire in it." Mark gave it a second glance... *it must draw well; I don't see any soot streaks... the andiron has seen a lot of use.*

Julian formed an image in his mind... a winter night, a foot of snow on the ground outside... huddled in front of the crackling fire were two people wrapped in a heavy quilt, keeping warm and cozy. The one on the left was taller... probably around six foot if he were standing. The one on the right was shorter; he had wavy blond hair...

Mark stepped back toward the door and pointed to the right. "This widow faces northeast." He gestured above the counter. "As you can see, it's just like yours... each wall has one; they're all the same."

Julian checked the other walls. *sure enough.*

Mark shut the window and closed the curtain. "I always close the curtains at night. That way the sun doesn't wake me up early." He gestured to Julian to do the same to his window.

Julian turned to the window. He leaned over the cot and poked his head out. *can't see much...* he looked each way... *the forest and the trail...* he looked up. *wow... the Milky Way is so **clear**.* He pulled back in and closed the window part way—*the slide is **stiff**.* He tightened the knob, but left it open an inch. That way a little cool air could get in—his sleeping bag got kind of hot. *curtains are sure heavy... real thick.*

Mark continued the tour; it was a useful way to get past the awkward stage. He wanted Julian to feel safe and at home. The serious subjects would have to wait... *just as well.* He pointed to the counter and storage cupboard and drawers under the window. "These are full of supplies and miscellaneous items. We won't be using any of this." He moved on. "The clothes rack is for you too. Which end would you like?" Mark reached up and grasped the pipe. The hangers he had appropriated from the staff lounge swung back and forth, as if eager to serve.

Julian had no idea about using such a thing. He looked back at Mark blankly. He never hung up his clothes on campouts. At home either, actually. *Mom does that, mostly.*

Mark was amused. "You've never had a roommate, have you?

Julian shook his head.

"Well, roommates have to get things settled first thing, or they could have problems later on. The same thing was true in your tent. Everyone has their own space, and it's important to know where things belong or don't belong. Here you get to hang up your shirt—that's a bonus; keeping your shirt looking fresh and neat is easy when you can hang it up." Mark pointed to his extra shirt and long pants, hanging in the center.

Julian was still processing all this in his head, and trying his best to keep up—the concept of roommate was beyond his understanding. Besides, what he wanted to know most of all was how he was going to find his way into that **huge** bed. He forced himself to think about Mark's question. "Oh… left end?" *that's closest to my cot.*

"Sounds good to me." Mark slid a couple of hangers to the very end of the pipe. "Those are yours to use." He knew Julian wouldn't need more. He moved his clothes toward the right.

The sound of hangers sliding on the pipe sounded so strange… everything about this was strange. Wonderful, but strange. Julian's eyes glanced up. *Mark's Sergeant Preston hat!* It was on the shelf above the clothes pipe. *I want to try that on…*

Mark backed up a few steps and put his hand on the chest of drawers. "This is mine. I have this instead of a footlocker. Sorry about that." He gave a mischievous grin. Mark realized that he could have made a drawer available, but thought it unwise.

Julian's eyes wowed. What an idea! Sharing a dresser with Mark?! He stifled an urge to giggle out loud. He smiled with a shrug instead. "That's okay." *what does he keep in there? underwear! ooo-ee.* Julian wondered what brand it was.

Mark didn't think to mention the bed. He walked around the end and gestured to Julian to follow along. He stopped behind the table. "This is where you'll be working. The lamp is very good—better than the overhead."

Julian looked at the table. A large wood chair was pulled up in front. A single shallow drawer extended the full width of the table. Big… solid and heavy, the chair looked like the ones at school the teachers use, except for the color. This one was army color—almost like the olive green of the scout uniform. The paint was worn in places... *must be pretty old. that table is excellent. I can use that when I draw stuff. it's like the one at home, only smaller... mine has two drawers.*

"In here is the bathroom." Mark stepped inside and beckoned. "This is one place that has special rules." He opened the medicine cabinet. "First aid supplies are on this shelf. Ignore the top two—that's stuff that has been left behind. Probably not much good anyway. I have my shaving gear on the bottom shelf." Mark glanced at Julian. *he **is** a lot shorter.* "I'll move it up one. You can have the bottom shelf. Okay?"

"Whoa..." Julian exclaimed in a whisper. ***shaving** stuff!* He was captivated by the sight. Shaving was something he had wanted to see, to know about, for a long time—ever since Mark first visited, it had been something he wondered about. Instantly he set himself a goal: *I will see Mark shave at least once before camp is over.*

"Do you have a toiletry kit?"

Julian nodded.

"You can use this instead, if you want. It's up to you." Mark pointed to the now empty bottom shelf.

Julian had a toothbrush, toothpaste, sun cream and a bar of soap. Plenty of room for those. *kind of like home, actually. am I supposed to move that stuff now?*

Mark had closed the cabinet and was pointing to the toilet. "This is the special secret: you don't have to run down to the latrine all the time."

"Wow!" Julian liked that. He liked that a lot.

"There are two rules: first off, you need to flush every time you use it. There is no window or fan in here, so it's important to keep this fresh."

Julian was annoyed by that rule. It implied that he wasn't careful about that. *I always flush at home.* One time he forgot, and his mom raised the dickens. He never forgot again. He didn't say anything, though. *Mark didn't mean anything personal by that...*

"The second rule is that you are not to invite any of your friends to use it. They still have to use the latrine." Mark paused. "I recommend you keep this privilege a secret." Mark looked Julian in the eye and raised his eyebrows, expecting agreement.

Julian felt a thrill suddenly... he wasn't expecting Mark to look at him directly in the eye. It had the usual effect. He blushed and found it hard to say anything for a second. He could feel his erection beginning. *not now, not now, please, not now...* he didn't want Mark to see anything.

Mark noticed the blush. *I should have expected that.* He moved on without waiting for an answer... *it won't be a problem.* He turned around and pushed the shower curtain open. *get a move on, Mark: we're past lights out.*

"I usually take a shower before going to bed. I sleep better when I can do that. You are welcome to use the shower too. We just need to schedule it. It's a little too cozy for two, as you can see," Mark laughed. *hmm... I don't know how big the water tank is... two showers close together may be a problem. I must remember to check that.*

Sirens, whistles, noisemakers of all sorts went off in Julian's imaginary world: taking a shower with Mark! He nearly swooned at the idea. He noticed the shampoo bottle and soap dish hanging from the showerhead. He realized suddenly that Mark was talking again.

"You can have one of these to use." He pointed to the wall rack.

Two large towels and a floor mat hung there neatly; they looked pressed and clean, just as if his mom had been here.

"You want the top one or the bottom?" Mark was pleased, generally at how this was going. *Julian seems to be in control of himself.*

Julian shrugged... he couldn't see a difference.

"I'll use the top one, then. Just be sure to hang yours back up when you're through—same goes for the floor mat."

Julian nodded.

"Oh—always leave the door open when you're not in here. Remember there's no window or fan. I usually leave it open all the time, actually." Mark hesitated. "I leave it open when the shower is running too. The mirror steams up fast if you don't."

That information sent Julian's imagination into high gear. When Mark took a shower, the door would be open. *this keeps getting better, Julian!*

"Let's go back into the main room." Mark gestured to Julian to lead the way. He stopped at the table and picked up the clock. "I always set this to go off a little early. I like to be wide awake and ready for breakfast." He checked the setting. "This will go off at 6:45 a.m." He pulled out the alarm release. "I warn you, this is **very** loud. You can hear a click about thirty seconds before it goes off. I always grab it and shut it off before it has a chance to sound, if I can." Mark wound the clock until the spring was good and tight. He glanced at the face: *five after... not bad. I doubt if the camps notice the light is on—they're all supposed to be tucked in now, anyway.*

Julian just noticed the ticking sound. He grimaced. *that thing might keep me awake.*

"Okay. Time for a short meeting." Mark gestured toward the cot, indicating that Julian was to go there. He grabbed the chair and dragged it over.

Julian felt a sense of relief, now that he had an idea about things. *this is going to be great!* He sat on the cot and watched Mark pull the chair over. *ooo. Julian: do not look there. not now.* He was usually able to behave when he knew he was being watched. Only... *what if I look into his eyes? try not to do that either.*

"We're past lights out, but I won't tell if you don't," Mark joked. *this is going smoothly enough... I don't know why I was worried, actually.* He cleared his throat. "I need to set out the rules of the road, so to speak. I don't want you to have any misunderstandings or confusions about staying here. Do you understand?"

Julian nodded.

"Good." He paused a second. "By the way: if you have any questions, please ask them, okay?" He saw Julian nod again. "That includes now. Any questions?"

Julian shook his head.

Mark looked at him narrowly. Julian had been mostly non-verbal the entire time. "Julian, you have hardly said a word. You have to have a question of some kind."

Julian flushed. The trouble was, he had dozens—but he couldn't put anything into words. "Umm... well..."

"Okay, when one comes to mind, interrupt, okay?"

"Yeah. Thanks, Mark." Julian felt better… off the hook for now. *get it together, Julian. you look like an idiot. you don't want Mark to be sorry he brought you here.*

"Tonight is special because we're just getting started. After tonight, that light switch gets thrown to off at ten p.m. sharp." He watched Julian's face closely… *I'll stop if he looks confused.* "That means that everything needs to be ready. Any paper work, any getting ready for the next day, any bathroom visits, showers, the works. We have to follow the same rules here as the rest of the troop."

Julian nodded. "That's only fair." *should be easier, actually. there's seven in the Wolf patrol. that's lots harder than two. oh, that's right:* "What am I supposed to do in the patrol?" *probably KP, being the new kid.*

"You will be Danny's Kitchen Buddy in the mornings. You'll help him prepare breakfast and be on clean up detail. That means you'll also help inspect the patrol campsites. It's his job to grade them on how well they cleaned up. You can keep track of all that for your newsletter story. Then you and Danny will join the rest of the troop at the morning free swim. I get to go to a meeting with the other troop leaders." He grimaced; that was business as usual… it would take most of the morning after the waterfront briefing and swimming qualification.

this is gonna be cool! Julian felt a sense of relief. *so far everything is easy as pie.* His eye landed on the table—the drawer stood out since the chair wasn't there. "I don't understand about the assistant scribe job."

"Good for you. That's the main reason you're here." That wasn't true, entirely, but it would do for now. "Nick is the Scribe and you will meet with him to plan and put out the newsletter. He knows all about this; we talked about it last week. He will fill you in. I don't know when he plans to do that. Be sure to ask him at breakfast."

"Oh; I don't know him, but I know who he is." Julian pictured Nick reading out the minutes. *seems like a good guy.*

"Anything else before the light gets turned off?" Mark was pleased with how this had gone. But something nagged. *what have I forgotten?*

Julian thought for a minute. He wasn't sleepy at all, but he didn't have a question ready. "Guess not." *I bet I'll think of one after the lights are off.*

"Okay, then. First, let's get settled about the shower. Do you need to take one tonight?"

Julian shook his head without thinking. "I took care of that during Qualifications at the lake." It seemed silly to take a shower now, actually. He hadn't done anything to get dirty, all day. He never took a shower at home unless he needed one; he always took one after PE class.

"I'm glad, because I need one in a big way. So after you're through in there, I'll take my shower." Mark stood and grabbed the chair; on the way back to the table he restated the sequence more precisely. "When you're all tucked in, I'll turn out the light in here. You can start catching winks while I take a shower." He slid the chair tight against the table. He looked at Julian, expecting a comment or question.

Julian was kicking himself for not thinking… *I could have taken a shower!* For some time now he had been of the opinion that if Mark had a chance to see a little more of him, a little more than his head poking out of his silly scout clothes, he might… *well, he might start to think of me as a person, not just a scout.*

"Hello?" Mark snapped his fingers. Julian's startled look was comical. He pointed at the bathroom. "Do you need to do anything? Brush your teeth, say? Now is your last chance."

"Oh! Sorry." Julian hopped up and went to his footlocker for his toiletry kit.

Mark stepped around to the other side of the bed and watched Julian hustle. He bounced on his toes unconsciously. He had faced the unknown here and it had gone very well. *I was right about this.* He felt sure that if he faced Julian with a real task, being close up would actually help. Julian did blush once, but the hungry stare never took hold. *maybe there won't be a need to talk about his crush at all. I'm betting he can manage it and learn control by himself.* He inhaled deep. *I hope so.* He reviewed what he had gone over… *did I skip anything?* He heard the medicine cabinet door open.

"'Erv o gaav!" Julian exclaimed. He needed to rinse his mouth.

Mark hastened over to the bathroom and looked in. Julian faced him with his toothbrush in hand, a look of frustration on his face. Mark laughed. He looked comical with a ring of toothpaste foam around his mouth. "Sorry about that… you have to use the faucet like a drinking fountain."

Julian was embarrassed. *next time, dummy, put a small glass in your toiletry kit.* He bent over and rinsed as well as he could. "Yechy-yech!"

Mark closed the remaining windows and curtains while Julian finished up. He went to the dresser for a fresh pair of briefs. He had just realized that he couldn't sleep in nature's own as usual. *I can put up with that for a couple of weeks.*

> > **scree-eeep!** < < *blast this drawer.*

"All done!" Julian announced happily on his way out of the bathroom. He just noticed that his boots were very loud in here. They didn't squeal though, like before.

Mark stepped over to the light switch. "Tell me when you're ready."

Julian put his empty toiletry kit into his footlocker. He stood for a minute and looked at the cot. It didn't look inviting at all. *oh well…* He took off his kerchief and sat down on the cot. *time to take these things off!*

Mark watched Julian unlace his hiking boots. "Those are very good boots. Maybe you'll be able to go on one of the long hikes. Those would be perfect. Some sections of the trail are rocky and uneven."

Julian nodded. "That's one reason Mom bought me these." The registration packet had a picture of guys crossing over a creek under a big waterfall. "I like hiking. There's always neat things to see." He tucked the boots under the cot alongside his tennies. *boy does it feel good to have those off!* He stood and unbuttoned his shirt. Midway he paused… his eyes widened. *I'm supposed to hang this up! wow.* He turned and finished unbuttoning on the way over to the clothes rack. He hung it up and straightened it carefully… *this rail is higher up than the one in my closet at home. oh, wait.* He ran over to the cot to get his kerchief. *I'll hang that up around the shirt!* He giggled happily as he straightened it up. *Mom always does that.*

Mark was charmed by this activity. It was an unexpected glimpse at his own past. He recalled his first night at scout camp. *two of us in that tent. we had to odd man for everything… clothes were plopped in a heap on the footlockers. Wally Butts was my buddy that summer. what a slob… but a great pal.*

Julian glanced at Mark. *looks like his mind is somewhere else. hmm. am I supposed to hang up my scout shorts too? how do you hang those up, anyway?* He shook his head. That's a silly idea. He went back to the cot and took off his shorts. He folded them neatly and placed them on top of the footlocker. *there.* He looked at the cot. *here goes…* he flipped back the cover and unzipped the sleeping bag. *just in time…* the overhead light went off suddenly.

Mark had pushed down the light switch. The room was dark except for the bathroom light. He didn't need to supervise Julian taking off his socks.

Julian removed his long scout socks. *say, it's starting to get cold in here. I couldn't tell that before. sometimes these longies are a good idea.* He climbed into the sleeping bag. The cot was very firm… *it isn't exactly hard… maybe it won't be that bad… feels kind of cozy, actually. huh.* He scootched around a little. The bag was beginning to feel warm already. It usually did. He fluffed the pillow and settled on his right side as usual.

*ohmygosh! the shower is running! what did I miss?! you are an **idiot**, Julian!* He frowned. His first failed opportunity. *well, I'll make sure to pay attention from now on. did Mark undress out here, or in the bathroom? cripes. okay… get ready. maybe I'll get to see something.* He gazed over to the bathroom doorway. *this is a good angle, actually.*

Mark worked up a good lather and shampooed his hair. *what a good idea, this.* "Mmm…" he hummed contentedly. *hot water is nearly instant here. I wish I had a showerhead like this at home.* He turned his back and indulged himself briefly, letting the water pound away… *this is almost like a massage.* This was the incredible bonus of being assigned to steward Barr's Meadow. Aside from the staff quarters, this was the only facility at Camp Walker with electricity and hot water.

He would have enjoyed a good long shower, but he needed to be considerate of his new roommate. *what could be going through his head right about now? maybe he's asleep… well. nothing to worry about, and a giant load off my mind.* The next thing he had to face was that mattress out there. Lumpy and uneven, the rope web underneath was a poor substitute for a set of springs. *Julian might have the best bed in the place. amazing they haven't brought a decent bed up here.* Mark had hoped, but not expected to be assigned here; he didn't even think of bringing his air mattress.

He turned the water off and stepped out onto the floor mat. Being rid of the trail dust and dried sweat was **so** nice. He felt fresh again.

Julian enjoyed the shadows projecting from the bathroom. The husky muscular action of Mark drying himself was fascinating. Julian's tingle had begun again. *I love the way that feels.*

Mark stepped over to the sink. *hmm. I'll shave in the morning.* He brushed his teeth rapidly. *Julian's right: we need a pair of small juice glasses up here. I'll see if Pierre has something in the kitchen. sucking up to this faucet isn't much fun.*

The door swung closed a few inches. *Mark must be hanging up the towel and the floor mat. get ready Julian... what's that sound? an elastic slap! he's putting on his undies!*

Mark picked his clothes up from the toilet seat. *silly man, you could have undressed out there. now you get to hang things up in the dark. well, I'm new at this. I just didn't want to feed Julian's fantasy any more than I could help. looks like that isn't as big a problem as I expected.* He carried his clothes out of the bathroom and headed for the clothes rack and dresser.

Julian was in heaven: Mark had just left the bathroom carrying his clothes—and he left the light on! Julian watched every movement like a hawk. *wow.* What he was seeing wasn't the vague bulge he'd studied on the bus. *no sir, this is outstanding. even though it's undies, you can tell a lot. boy, is it ever big...* He watched the backside as it crossed over into the dark part of the room. *wow... that's not flat, either.* He was getting a good idea of just how effective a pair of pants could be at hiding things.

Mark opened the third drawer down—that was his hamper. In went the socks and briefs. He hung up his shirt—he followed Julian's example and draped his kerchief over a shoulder. *never thought of doing that... good idea.* He folded his short pants flat and placed them on the counter. *these things don't hang worth a darn.* He had to get his boots and turn off the light. *Julian is silent—maybe he's asleep. I'll walk quietly.*

Julian was ready for this: *he's heading **into** the light this time... wow.* The contents of Mark's briefs shifted from side to side as he walked. Julian studied that carefully. Of special interest was the slit in front: a small gap opened every few steps. *well, now: Mark's skivvies are a lot better than mine—they don't keep everything hidden so tight. if only he was walking in slow motion...* Julian watched Mark return to the bathroom. The loose cotton accented what they were covering very nicely. Julian approved highly. *my old ones were like that. I liked them a lot better—more freedom, easy access when I'm in a hurry.*

Mark retrieved his hiking boots from the floor in the bathroom. He paused by the door and double checked the room—everything is in place and ready for the morning. He snapped the light off and walked over to the bed slowly... *no need to bark my shin over here.* He put his boots at the head, pulled back the covers and crawled in. *let's see where those lumps are.*

Julian was thrilled. Mark had paused by the door when he checked the room. For a minute he had a very clear view of Mark's mid section. A fresh bank of images for his fantasy file, the best ones ever, were ready and waiting. He closed his eyes and got right to work.

Part 3: Monday

It is the first full day of regular camp activity. **Julian's** new routine as a member of The Flaming Arrow is established. **Tom** Dawson, the Junior Assistant Scoutmaster, is accustomed to being the kingpin. His friend **Nick** Harrison has been assigned to mentor Julian as a troop journalist. **Danny** Laskey, the boy that lives behind Julian, was promoted to Senior Patrol Leader recently. Also new to the Flaming Arrow, he is assigned to team with Julian in camp operations. Each of them has a private, personal agenda that hinges, one way or another, on Julian.

Each camp is furnished with a cooler chest and a sideboard cabinet with utensils and basic condiments. The unusually dry climate condition has forced the camp to replace all outdoor cooking fires with propane stoves.

Introducing **Leonard**, the staff member in charge at the lake. The lake is a major center of what happens at the camp—much of that is because of Leonard's benign rule.

Merit badge study is a primary part of the scout camp, and Julian attends his first class meetings. Introducing **Justin** Blake, a younger scout that Julian has been mentoring, and **Cory** Summers, his Archery partner.

The first troop campfire showcases creative talent, and sets the stage for the after hours entertainment as well.

The second night in camp is special for two members of Troop 9 in particular. Unexpectedly and unplanned, both **Julian** and **Nick** achieve success in a longstanding personal goal.

11 *waking up*

so warm... cozy... Julian became aware of unusual sensations... unfamiliar sounds... his dream about Sid huffing and puffing into his new air mattress morphed into a soft irregular sound... *it's the curtains.* The friendly nudges of the morning breeze caused them to wave gently... the transition to consciousness was seamless. He opened his eyes... daylight streamed through the slit in the curtains; the gently moving panels admitted irregular surges of brightness. ...*this isn't my bed—where... ?? it's so **dark**... **the cabin!*** He turned over and faced the room. *wow.* He could see the outline of Mark's form in the big bed.

It wasn't easy to sort out what he was seeing... too dark. Once in a while the curtain over the table waved slightly, opening a bright shaft of light. That allowed a glimpse... *Mark is still asleep.* Julian inhaled deep, in hope that maybe he could smell something... *poo. too far away. ooo! I'm about to pop open!* He wanted to watch Mark for a little, but he had to take a piss real bad.

Reluctantly, he flipped back the sleeping bag and swung himself to a sitting position. *ai! the floor is **cold**!* He hurried across the room on tiptoe. He stopped to look. His heart began to beat faster. *Mark is asleep...* Julian could see his face clearly. He wanted to stand here all day. *why do I have to go **now**?!* He hurried in to the bathroom and closed the door. He thought to do that as quietly as possible... *don't want to disturb Mark.*

>> ***klack!*** << the light switch was uncommonly loud.

yow! blinding! The overhead light was unshielded, just like the one in the main room.

He squinted and stepped over to the toilet. *boy! that's a **little** better... the light is behind me.* He pulled down his waistband. *man oh man, does it ever want to go! you hafta **wait** a minute!* He lifted the seat and bent slightly so he could aim just right. His stiffy had saved him from wetting the bed. That happened a lot at home too. He watched it soften as he began to urinate… what a relief. He finished, finally.

>> *sssp… ssp… p-plp.* <<

He shook himself good and pulled his waistband back out and up. Using the built in opening in front never made much sense… *especially these new ones. too hard to get my willy out in time.* He liked his old saggies best—all he had to do with those was pull one side or the other open. *somebody's going to invent a good front opening some day and get rich. all you need is a flap.*

"Be sure to flush, dum-dum," he whispered. The warning about that still rankled. He closed the seat and pushed down the handle. *it's not too noisy, at least. maybe it won't wake Mark up. what time is it? I forgot to look.* He leaned against the wall while the tank refilled. The shut off valve had a high pitched whine. *good thing to know…* Julian planned his exit carefully while the water came up to the shut off line.

at last… all filled up. He stepped to the door and carefully turned off the light—he tried his best to keep the switch silent. That helped quite a bit. It had made a loud sound when he turned it on. He waited for a minute for his eyes to adjust to the dark. He knew where to look and what to look for, but he didn't know if his noise had awakened Mark. *with any luck, I'll be able to get a good look before I go back to bed.* He turned the knob slowly… he pulled the door open slowly too… *careful, Julian, it might squeak…* Luck was with him: the door was silent.

It was still very dim out there; the curtains were closed, and the knotty pine walls and ceiling helped keep it dark. *it's so quiet… birds chirping… different from the ones at home…* An occasional waft of air let more light in. With care, Julian peeked around the doorway. *yay!! Mark is still asleep! he's lying on his back now… ooo.* Julian's gaze ran to the left and focused on a pronounced midship bulge. *is that just a fold in the covers, or… hum.* Julian wanted it to be an accurate profile of what he knew was underneath. *no way to tell for sure.* He returned his gaze to Mark's face. That profile caused a wonderful buzz too. *how could I be this lucky? just look where I am and who is right there!* Julian glowed with love. *someday, Julian, someday.*

A wave of goose bumps ran up his right arm—it was the cool breeze, not the view. He tiptoed back across the room. He crawled back into the sleeping bag. *dumdum! you forgot to look at the clock! nevermind...* he turned on his right side and renewed his study of the mini mountain in the center of the big bed.

"Mmmm…" Mark hummed sleepily. A distant creaking sound had entered his awareness… *army cot...* He wasn't fully awake yet. He'd awoken a short while ago when a noise in the bathroom broke into his dream… *what was that about? they vanish so fast, dreams.* He figured that Julian was relieving himself. He'd need to do that himself before long. He wanted to wait for as long as possible. It had taken a long time to get to sleep last night, and he didn't rest very well. *good old Lumpy Louise.* That was his nickname for the mattress. He dozed briefly, wiggling to maintain the patch of comfort he had discovered.

Julian was rapt. *look at that...* the blanket stretched tight as Mark moved under it. *boy. that's the best yet. what would that look like from the side?* His stiffy was getting started again. *a great way to start the day, wagging a good one.* He reached down with his left hand and freed things up a little.

Mark drifted back into consciousness… he didn't want to wake up. Thankfully, the curtains were trying to help out there. The birds, on the other hand… *I slept so soundly!* He glanced over at the clock. A few minutes before the alarm. No point in fighting it. He flung back the covers and stretched his arms wide. He yawned and rubbed his eyes. *my turn to visit the room.* He swung around and sat on the edge of the bed. *one good thing about this place is the cold floor: forces you to wake up all the way.* He stood and glanced over at the cot. *too dark... can't tell if he's awake... no matter.* He stepped over to the bathroom. He headed straight for the toilet, then stopped. He just remembered that he wasn't alone here now. He turned back to close the door and flipped on the light. "Ouch!" *the light in here is cruel... must be 150 watts. I wonder if I can get a smaller bulb in the warehouse. add that to the list, Mark.* Some overachiever had installed a sunlamp bulb.

Julian had stuffed the pillow into his mouth to smother the exclamation that was desperate to burst out. He had just seen the most **fantastic** profile. *even bigger than I thought. how am I going to keep my eyes off it? whoo!* He turned onto his tummy and pressed tightly against the cot. He gripped his pillow and stared blindly at the dull brown fabric that lined his sleeping bag. His mental catalogue of Mark views was busily reshuffling itself.

Mark stepped over to the toilet and lifted the seat. It's going to take a while to urinate—his erection did not want to recede. That's one thing he had never learned to fix. Roger always had a mind of his own.

think about the day ahead; that will help. how long before the alarm... what did the clock say? I need to let Julian sleep as long as possible. I hope his night went better than mine. He chuckled... *maybe I can talk him into swapping places some nights.* He yawned one last time. *I wonder if I have time for a run? I didn't think to set out my togs...*

Julian was almost back in control. A good thing, because Mark was about to reappear, and he didn't have a plan. *should I pretend to be asleep?* That didn't feel right, somehow. *maybe I should be getting up? that's dumb... should I be staring at the door? that's what I want to do, but... you have to learn to be cool, Julian. if you don't, Mark will toss you back to the Wolf patrol. you sure don't want that.*

He frowned. *so, I have to pretend. I always do that... about the only thing I'm any good at.* He scratched his head unconsciously, trying to settle on what exactly to do, what to say. *ooo!* The toilet flushed!

Mark opened the door and stepped into the room. Still dark. *these curtains are terrific..* He picked up the clock and looked close: a minute to go. He held it still and waited... > > click. < < He smiled victoriously and pushed in the button. That was like winning a footrace. It always meant the day would go well. He put it on the table and headed for the dresser. *cold feet are no fun at all. I need to put on some socks.* As he rounded the foot of the bed he glanced at the cot. "How are you this morning?" He could see that Julian was awake.

"Umm... fine." He was doing better at containing himself, too. This most recent exhibition was just as glorious—maybe more. The whole time Mark stood looking at the clock, his protruding not yet limp massive glorious wonderfully large one pushed outward, making the profile a wonder to behold. The flashes of light from the slit in the curtains were like a spotlight. Julian was, naturally, in full attendance.

> > **scree-eeep!** < < *put that sandpaper on your list, Mark!*

He pulled out a pair of socks and a T-shirt. He sat on the edge of the bed and put on the socks. "Time to rise and shine," he announced. "I already turned off the alarm." He slipped the T-shirt on and bent forward to open the bottom drawer. He pulled out his notepad and travel case. He always used this time to get the day organized before the breakfast leadership meeting.

Julian threw back the sleeping bag and crawled out. *lucky Mark isn't looking... hard to hide this stiffy.* Giggling, he stepped over to the footlocker. He put his scout shorts to the side and pulled out a Troop 9 T-shirt. *mmm. smells so fresh and clean—I just love that.*

Mark walked around the bed again—he doubled back and opened the curtain. He was pleased to hear that giggle. *all is well.* He pushed the window open... *might as well get the place as cool as possible. it will warm up in no time.* On his way to the table, a novel sight: Julian's wavy blond hair poking up out of a Troop Nine T-shirt as it was being pulled on. It drew his eye to the poster behind. "I forgot to mention the chart next to your window last night. If you ever need to check out what's going on at camp, it's all there, the whole two week schedule."

The T-shirt Julian had pulled over his head was an Oglivy's excusive. *I got a super deal on those.... the boys get them at a very good price, too. too bad I can't get the distribution rights for all their official clothes.* He put his case and tablet on the table. Usually he shaved at this point... *I'll wait. Julian might need to use the bathroom.*

Julian's gaze followed Mark... he'd missed the front this time, but seeing Mark's behind in those skivvies was a special treat. *man, he is so hot! the way he stands there... so cool.*

"You all squared away for the day?" *maybe Julian could use an encouraging sendoff.*

"Um... I think so. 'Cept I don't know where to go, exactly." *where is the Flaming Arrow camp, anyway?*

"Oh, I'm sorry. I forgot that you're new around here," he laughed. "It's right up the trail a few yards. When you leave, turn left on the path, and you'll see the flag. Danny is supposed to meet you at seven o'clock. You have about ten minutes or so." Mark pulled out the chair and sat at the table.

ten minutes: that's plenty. all I have to do is finish dressing and comb my hair. Julian reached over for his short pants. He pulled them on and made all the usual adjustments... he turned to see if Mark was watching. *nope. I can see why. when I go limp, there's nothing to see.* He pointed it down, since it was fading fast anyway. He zipped up and finished tucking in his shirt.

He spotted his comb poking out of the travel kit. *ooo, that's right...* He ran it through his hair quickly. That's all he had to do when it was dry. His floppies peeked out from under the orange towel. *perfect! lots better than those big boots. I can use those at the lake, too.* He grabbed them in one hand and stepped around the cot to slip them on.

Mark started his daily work list. *let's see... the meeting after breakfast. we need to juggle Danny's assignment a little so he can take Julian in hand... oh: tonight.* "Julian?"

Julian looked up. "What?" He hurried over to see what Mark wanted. He had been trying to figure a way to go over there and look down over Mark's shoulder; his new motto was right again: *something will come along if you're patient.* His gaze aimed downward... he controlled his eyes. They wanted to open wide and assess the potential for that slit to open... the other side would be a better vantage. *next time I'll be sure to remember that.*

"Let's have a little conference tonight after the campfire. I think it would be smart to go over things regularly. Save up any questions that come up during the day, you know," he turned to look at Julian with a smile. The interested eager face was reassuring.

Julian had indulged himself; his nostrils needed to take in as much as possible. *Mark in the morning!* No words to describe it; his tingle was returning. "Yeah... I'll start a page in the back of my tablet. When I think of something, I'll write it down... that's a good idea. I'll start a page in my tablet just for that!"

Mark was delighted. Julian had just made one of the rules, all by himself. *I'll make a list too.*

Julian avoided looking Mark in the eye. This close, that would be way too risky. Instead, he took notice of Mark's face: *he has whiskers now!* His eyes focused closely... *I've always wondered about those. they look different than I expected...really rough.* He wanted to stroke Mark's cheek gently with his left hand.

"Nothing formal, you know, just a friendly open chat about any and all. There are lots of things at camp that will be new and strange. No need to let anything bother or confuse you." Julian's confidence level looked in good shape... *remarkable.* Julian's self assurance was one factor that made this arrangement possible. *Julian is more mature than his peers... self directed in so many ways.*

Julian felt great. *Mark isn't sorry about letting me say in the cabin.* He nodded. "Anything else?" He just looked at the clock. *two minutes! time goes fast here.*

"Nope. Oh, wait. As soon as the coffee is perked, run a cup back here, okay?" *that's what I need right now: a full cup of black coffee. I'll drink a toast to Louise.*

Julian gave the okay signal and headed toward the door.

"Oop! Forgot my tablet!" He raced back to the footlocker, floppies slapping the floor. He lifted the locker lid and grabbed the tablet. He checked to make sure the pencil was already inserted into the spiral. He paused and tilted his head. *forget anything else? nope. scoot!* He stopped at the knob and turned. He looked at Mark a last time. He waited to see if... *yes: Mark turned to look back!* Julian flashed his Cheshire grin. He giggled as he went out the door. Mark had smiled back. *this morning went great!* With a skip he headed up the path.

Mark chuckled. Julian always gave that toothy grin. *okay: to business.* He turned to the notepad. *mm... still dark in here.* He stood and opened the curtain above the table. He swung the window open as well... a habit developed last summer. He went to the window by the fireplace and opened it up next. Julian was skipping happily up the trail. He watched briefly. *what was I so worried about? Julian did fine, both last night and this morning.* He went to the other wall and opened the window above Julian's cot. Julian's blanket wasn't pulled tight. Mark fussed for a minute, making Julian's cot look perfect.

12   *first breakfast*

Danny awoke with a start. *did I sleep in? it's sunup already! I'm supposed to get breakfast this morning with Julian! I don't want to mess that up!* He jumped out of his sleeping bag and got dressed fast. Tom and Nick were sound asleep... *must be okay for time. where's my wristwatch, anyway?*

last night Mark told me that Julian was being promoted to the Flaming Arrow! not only that: I'll be teamed up with him to do breakfast and inspection duty for the whole camp! what could be better than that?

What Mark didn't know was that Danny had developed this huge crush on Julian. He lived right across the fence. Danny had watched him building his little clubhouse. *the kid is so darn cute! he's a couple of years younger, true—but that means less all the time. I always thought Julian was cute, but lately "hot" is a better word. now we'll be working together in the same patrol! it will be so easy to become friends—really close friends. Mark is brilliant!*

Everything was going so **great**. He was now in the Flaming Arrow Patrol: he was the new Senior Patrol Leader of the best troop in the Council. Scoutmaster Mark was the best of the best, and if he promoted someone, they must deserve it. That's why the news last night was a double bonus. *boy... am I ever glad we had that training campout last month. otherwise, I'd be just as green as Julian this morning.*

—⁓—

Julian left the cabin with a skip and headed up the path to the Flaming Arrow cooking area. He could see the Troop 9 flag flying by one of the tents, just like Mark said. *that has to be it.* A light dew coated everything, but it wasn't cold. He looked up into the sky: no clouds in sight. *it's going to be a clear day.* A hawk was cruising gracefully off to the right. "Looking for breakfast, I s'pose." He waved at it and picked up his pace. His floppies made a silly noise when he hurried. *gosh... still quiet—nobody seems to be up yet. only two tents.*

Julian wasn't sure what to do; he went over to the open sided hutch that housed the stove. *wow! a regular stove! that's right... the Wolves have a camp stove. guess nobody's using campfires... huh. I've never seen one of these before... Mom's stove is way different. it's electric.* He pulled out the drawer under the oven. A square pancake griddle, a very used frying pan, and a set of kettles with lids. *what would...*

?!? Suddenly someone came up from behind and gave him a hug.

"Good morning!" Danny held Julian briefly, then jumped back, pleased with himself. Hiding in the supply tent had been exactly the right thing to do. The second he heard that drawer pull out, he knew it was okay to peek out.

Julian turned around. "Hi, Danny." He hadn't expected a hug, but it was nice. He had always looked up to Danny, and it meant a lot to be accepted. Even though Danny lived just behind, he didn't know him very well. Not that he didn't want to: for a long time he was sort of fascinated by him; it wasn't a crush, exactly. *when I saw Mark, I sort of forgot about Danny.* Besides, he had lots of friends in his own grade, and they pretty much hung out together. *I used to think he was very cute. he's still good to look at.*

"Hi, Julian. Pull out the griddle and fry pan." *man, he is **hot**! just smell him!* Danny wanted to hug him again and maybe hold on a little longer—but he didn't dare. "We're supposed to cook pancakes and sausage this morning." *glad it's a simple one the first day.* "Have you done that before?" He grabbed the aged skillet from Julian and slid it onto the right rear burner. He pointed to the left burner for the griddle. He took a wooden match from the box on the shelf.

"Sure, lotsa times," Julian fibbed. A couple of times on campouts would be more accurate. He watched Danny light the stove... *huh. look at all those little teeny flames.* He took the pancake mix off the shelf above the stove and read the instructions. He **had** done this before, but he wanted to be sure he was doing it right. He didn't want to foul up on his first morning. "Where do you get the water?"

"There's those big gallon canteens over there." He pointed to the portable sideboard cabinet in front of the supply tent. *good thing Tom and Nick showed me the ropes yesterday.* This was his first morning in this campsite. Last year he was a Badger, and all they had was a stone fire circle with a thirty inch wide steel grate. *here they have classy equipment—the stove even has four burners and an oven.*

Julian crossed over to the sideboard cupboard and pulled out a large stainless steel bowl. The drawer had all the tools and measuring cups. He assembled everything on the table and started mixing the batter.

Danny took the roll of sausage from the cooler chest. *when did they stock this up? feels cold enough...* He snagged a knife and took the small chopping board to the front of the stove. *let's see... two patties apiece... that means divide the roll into ten slices.* "Julian, we'll make six pancakes apiece."

"Okay." Julian calculated this... *there are five, counting Mark. that means thirty! wow.* He double-checked to see if the recipe was for that many. *at home Mom only makes three each... oop. I better add, lessee... half a cup of flour, a little water...* he stirred it some more. *what's so hard about this? all you do is add water and a teaspoon full of oil.* He made sure most all the flour had dissolved. *Mom said smallish lumps are okay.* He added a **tablespoon** of Wesson Oil, just to be safe. It made a funny amber pool that went deep into the middle of the batter. He stirred it outward in a spiral... *that looks so neat.* He mixed it all in and carried the bowl over to the stove. He passed his hand over the square griddle, carefully. *ooo... plenty warm already...* he spooned out enough to make four cakes at a time. *cool how they spread out just far enough to avoid touching... oop!* "Darn it!"

"What's the matter?" Danny looked over. "Ya burn yourself?"

"Nah. I forgot to make a test cake. You're always supposed to make a test one first. I hope they'll be okay." He felt like slugging himself. *if these are a flop, I don't know what I'll do.* He watched them very closely.

"Hmm." Danny looked over Julian's shoulder; he got close enough to get another whiff. *yum! why does he smell so good? so sexy?* "Watch for the bubbles; wait 'til they're half covered with bubbles, then flip 'em. They look okay to me." He got busy sprinkling salt and pepper on the sausage patties. *mmm...* He felt himself start to swell down below; *Julian is turning me on!* He wagged his butt unconsciously.

"Have you made coffee before, Danny? Mark wants me to bring him a cup as soon as it's made." Julian had never paid any attention to making coffee. He didn't much like it, himself. He grabbed the spatula from the table and went back to watch for bubbles… nothing seemed to be happening.

"Oh, it's real simple. I'll show you. First, you take that small pot over there…" Danny pointed to a ten cup aluminum percolator.

Julian handed the spatula to Danny; he fetched the pot quickly.

"Now, take off the lid and remove all the insides."

"What do I do with these?" Julian held up the basket and post.

"Just put them on the table while you fill the pot with water." Danny came close and pointed to the lines stamped into the pot. "Fill it up to that line there, and put the pot on a burner and turn it up high. Then you take that basket and fill it half way up with coffee from that can over there by the boxes and cans." He pointed to the food stores where the coffee was on the second shelf. "Then you put the lid on the basket, and put the whole thing into the pot. When you see the bubbles start up into that glass thing on top, you turn it down real quick so it doesn't boil over. Six or seven minutes, and it's done. Easy as pie, really." Danny had been making coffee in the morning for his dad a couple of years now. *nothing to it— 'cept it takes longer up in the mountains.* He turned on the right front burner and moved his pan onto it. He pointed to the rear. "Put it there. It will heat up and brew while you make those pancakes."

Julian looked at his pancakes; only a few little teeny bubbles so far, so he stepped over to the table and set about making the coffee. *phew!* He wrinkled up his nose at the pungent air that escaped from the can… *this stuff sure smells strong!* A small yellow plastic stem poked up out of the dark brown granules… a little scoop. He dipped in and filled the basket halfway, like Danny said… *I can hardly wait to take Mark his cup of coffee!*

Danny watched Julian fill the basket—he didn't want to get caught staring. He wanted to make sure Julian did everything correctly… but even more, he just wanted to **look** at him. *he gets hotter by the minute!* When Julian looked up to see if he was doing it right, Danny smiled and nodded, and gave him the okay sign. He turned and checked the patties— *not quite ready to flip. goody. I can watch Julian some more.* He was seriously risking getting a boner, but he couldn't help it.

Julian finished assembling the coffee and got back to his pancakes just in the nick of time: huge bubbles covered the cakes. "Oo! I need the flipper, quick!" He grabbed the spatula from Danny and started flipping. This was something he knew how to do, because his mom always had him do it at home—they often had hotcakes on Sundays. *yes!* He smiled with pride: a nice medium brown. He loved the way they always plumped up after he turned them over. *wowee, these are super puffy*...the cakes pulsed up and down—

> > *pfff... pff... ff... pfff...* < <

An occasional little jet of steam tooted a soft, happy song. *they puff more than usual... is the stove getting too hot?* He peeked underneath... *looks okay...* Julian continued to monitor their progress. *this square pan is cool. can I actually eat six of these? four, maybe... they're smaller than ours...*

Danny patted him on the back. He let his hand rest there a minute. "Those look great! I bet they taste as good as they look, too!" And he was impressed. He looked at Julian's eyes. Those dark lashes were incredible—*his eyebrows are dark too, but his hair is a wavy golden blond. sexy, that's what.* All the other blonds he knew had blond eyelashes. He opened the oven door and pointed. "We'll keep everything warm in there on those platters." He took the spatula back and flipped the patties.

Julian studied the pancakes... he didn't want them to burn. The morning sun had a fascinating effect. It made the detail in the brown rings on the cooked side of the pancake so clear. They were much more intricate than he remembered. He looked into one of the bubble holes that had popped open... little spokes were holding up the surface of the pancake. Watching these cook was a good assignment... it helped free him to reflect a little about last night.

The magical feeling of Mark's hand on his shoulder at the campfire... *that was so special, so mysterious. I didn't know what was going on. it turned out I was mostly wrong. still, it was hot to think about anyway. someday, Julian, someday.*

Danny indulged himself by watching Julian concentrate on his pancakes. *what a beauty.* His dick was starting to wake up again. Standing close at the stove like this was so wonderful... sometimes he got a whiff that went straight down to his crotch. *if only I could hug him again.* He turned to the side and made an adjustment… he didn't want Julian to notice his growing problem.

At last the sausage patties and pancakes were ready and waiting in the oven. Julian helped Danny put out the OJ and milk. *oh! a bubbling sound—the coffee!* He rushed over to the stove to watch. *I should have done this first of all. it's way too late to take Mark a cup—breakfast is ready to eat.* He could see the other patrol members moving around in their tent. He turned the heat down a little, as Danny had instructed. *how long is it supposed to do this?* The bubbling slowed gradually. *is it done, or not? how do I tell?*

"Smelling good, men, smelling good!" Tom Dawson strode into the mess area, his arms in a grand, wide morning stretch. Tom was the Junior Assistant Scoutmaster, and the oldest member of the troop… only one badge to go for his Gold Palm. He marched up and grabbed an empty mug from above the stove and poured himself a cup of coffee. He looked over at Julian and raised his eyebrows. *who's this?* He did a double take. *hmm. oh yeah! the announcement last night… wasn't paying that much attention. too busy fooling around with Nick… so… it seems I have a new challenge. this is going to be interesting.* He looked closer… *very interesting. where has this one been hiding? last time I looked, this kid was just a little cub not worth noticing. hmm…* His game plan for today just might have taken shape.

Tom was seventeen; his senior year was coming up in a couple of months. His big brothers had moved on at last, and it was now his turn. He wasn't the little brother any more. Randy joined the Explorers and was gone. Wilson and Charlie were in college. Charlie was his oldest brother; he had been the JA of Troop Nine six years ago, and his reputation and honors were a part of the Troop's history. Now Tom was the Junior Assistant. The responsibility was invigorating, and he welcomed the challenge. He also relished the privileges. He liked being top Eagle on the totem pole. He figured it was part of his job to keep the young ones in line—his line, mostly. He earned his Silver Palm last December, and as Mark's JA, he was set. He was a football player, bigger than anyone else in the troop. He was first string wide receiver on the squad at school, but being top dog around here was more fun. He hadn't planned out exactly what he was going to do after high school... probably the Navy, but he wasn't too sure he wanted that. His brothers were against it, too. There was plenty of time to think about it, anyway. He had a whole year.

Nick Harrison came to the table whistling a tune. Nick was fifteen going on sixteen. One more badge, and he'd make Eagle. Mark had talked to him last week about Julian. Nick was the Troop Scribe; he looked forward to having Julian's help with the newsletter. He stepped up and gave a friendly punch to the right shoulder. "Hey, welcome aboard, new assistant! Can you type?"

Julian blushed; he did **not** know how to type, in fact. "Er... well, I haven't taken a class in it yet." This hadn't come up before. *what if I have to know how to type?* He brightened, "But I can draw pretty good cartoons!"

"Boy, I'm glad to hear that! Okay, you can take notes and draw things. I can type real fast, so we'll be set!" He took Julian by the hand and they did the Troop handshake. *Mark was brilliant to think of this.*

close call... for a minute Julian was afraid he'd be bumped back down before he even got started. Mark said he had to get that **Troop 9 Notes** newsletter ready to mail out every month. *wow: this month is a third gone already. I better talk to Mark about it tonight.* Julian watched Nick go over to the table and sit next to Tom. This was the first time either one of those guys had ever talked to him... the Big Cheeses of the troop! *Tom's sort of quiet... Nick's super friendly though... he didn't take along a mug of coffee.*

"Coffee... coffeeee!" Mark did a staggering in the desert act as he came in. He lurched to the table dramatically. "Where's my coffee! Quick, before I..." he feigned a collapse on the bench.

The patrol laughed; it was a familiar act. But Julian jumped. He felt awful. *how could I be so...* he stepped back to the stove and grabbed the coffee pot. He took it straight to Mark with a big grin.

Mark looked at the pot, then at the big grin on Julian's face. It was hard to keep a straight face. "Why, that's more like it... but... do I have to drink it straight from that?"

The group was delighted. New kid moments were fun, as long as they were someone else's.

Julian was embarrassed; he could tell Mark wasn't mad. He was red faced, but bounced back as well as he could. He stood at attention. "Why, Sir, no Sir—not unless you insist, Sir!" He gave the scout salute with his left hand and raised the coffee pot in his right. His wide Cheshire Cat grin was automatic.

Applause and cheers.

Mark was impressed… such a delightful, nimble move. *Julian will fit in here just fine.* He looked at Danny, tilted his head and raised an eyebrow.

Danny slowly nodded his head three times.

Mark took his seat at the far end of the table—his folding canvas stool was ready and waiting. Danny brought the food from the oven. Julian filled a coffee mug for Mark. Danny had gone to the cooler for the butter and jam, so Julian sat down on the end, next to Mark. Why not? He could tell that Mark wasn't mad about the coffee. *tomorrow, Julian, you do the coffee first.* He did a double take: *Mark shaved! he did that while Danny and I made breakfast. huh… how am I going to see him do that?*

Tom kept his eye on Julian—he'd seen those cute little buns scurry after the coffee mug. *a truly nice pair…* a discovery that had made his day already. He looked at him across the table. *yeah… after the meeting this morning? I'll be ready to move if things look right.* He sniffed at the hotcakes. *these look terrific—need some butter and jam.* "Pass the blackberry jam, Danny…" It came to him at once: *I'll do the old Panther initiation routine. that will simplify everything.* "Hey, since Julian is a new member, he should be our **go-for** and get things we want if they aren't on the table."

There was a momentary pause. That was a lead balloon.

Julian blushed; he'd never heard of this custom. It didn't seem right.

Danny was pissed. Tom could really be a pain. What was Julian's reaction? He glanced over—*he looks okay. maybe Mark will stop this.*

"No… Everyone in this patrol is an equal. Julian will take his turn at whatever has to be done just like everyone; no more, no less." Mark had always been opposed to any form of hazing or initiation nonsense anyway, and he wasn't about to let Julian be bullied or taken advantage of. This was probably meant well, but it was off target. "In fact, I think we owe

Danny and Julian a big hand for such a great first breakfast." He applauded briefly.

Nick nodded his head and mumbled in agreement; his mouth was full.

Tom shrugged... *the day is still young.*

Danny was glad Mark had stepped in. "It was Julian who did the pancakes. I just cooked the sausage."

Julian looked at Danny; *why did he say that?*

Danny smiled, a little sheepishly. Everyone continued eating without another word about it. Danny watched Julian closely. *sitting right next to him is terrific...* he watched his lips as he ate... watched him smile at Mark. *the kid has no idea what a favor Mark just did him; Tom would have tried the slave master routine, and then it would only be a matter of time. the Panther patrol was famous for doing that go-fer thing, and Tom used to be a Panther.*

Soon breakfast was finished. Mark ordered the patrol to fall in formation so he could tell them about their daily activities, officially. Even in a small group, Mark set things off in an orderly way on the first day—it caused them to focus and remember who and where they were: the top.

"At Ease. Nick, you take over for Danny as acting Senior Patrol Leader this morning. You will help Tom and the patrol leaders get the younger ones squared away while Danny and Julian are on cleanup and inspection detail. All the scouts know what they have to work on for advancement. I'd like to see all the Tenderfoot boys make Second Class rank by the end of camp—I want to know if any of them have trouble with compass reading. This is the best place to pass that. Many of the Second Class will able to move up to First. First Class and above will be working for at least two merit badges, as always."

"We have six that have to take swimming."

"Six?" Mark was surprised it was that many. "I hope they get that done. I want it to be zero by the second week." *maybe Tom could use some of his freedom this year to take them under his wing...* Mark didn't make it an assignment. "I have a leader's meeting and workshop down at camp headquarters. I should be through in time for lunch. I'll be in the upstairs conference room if you need to find me. Lunches are down there, as usual... you'll need to remind the patrol leaders to brief the Tenderfoots on how that works. Also, the next troop meeting will be tonight at our own campfire. Tom, you need to get a couple of volunteers to gather the wood and get it up here. You are to get it from the new central supply over by the main equipment shed. They don't want us picking through the woods any more. Any questions or comments?"

"Did they find more lifeguards yet?" Tom hoped he didn't have to get stuck with that so often this year.

"Good question; I don't know. But I'll find out at HQ. Be ready to keep an eye out, just in case. We may have to put up with that some. I'll see how many others have qualified. I don't want to see you trapped there either. Thanks, Tom. Okay, then. Let's have a super first day! Dismissed."

Mark checked Julian out of the corner of his eye... *looks like all is going well so far.* Danny was a good choice for Julian's supervisor. *he's honest, reliable, and doesn't have a mean bone in his body. one day he'll be an excellent Junior Assistant. lining up leadership talent is more than half the job done.* Danny had made Star rank in record time. "Meet me at the cabin, Tom..." he headed down the trail. He had to get his case.

It just dawned on Tom: *not only is it the first full day of camp, I have a new job this summer—I'm a free agent who helps with the merit badge classes instead of taking them.* He didn't know how many classes he'd help with yet. It was supposed to be better than being one of the counselors... more like being an assistant teacher. *no sweat there—I already have all the badges being taught.* He didn't know if anyone else would be doing this... *maybe there'll be one or two others.* He was about to ask, but Mark was halfway to the cabin already. ***cri-miny, Tom! get a move on!***

He hustled over to the crew tent. *I need my sunglasses*—he felt vulnerable somehow, without those. He rummaged in his footlocker for the glasses case. *where **is** it? **crimanentlies**! I don't want to keep Mark waiting. why do I have this many socks? mother. I let her pack the clothes.* He shook his head. His Mom had a thing about smelly socks. He had to admit that she had a point. Left on his own, he'd probably stink up the whole tent by the end of the week. *did Charlie ever have to put up with Mom's fussing like that... aha!* He felt the hard shell and pulled the glasses case free. They were at the very bottom. He opened the case and put them on. He was transformed. He looked out to see if Nick was paying attention. *Nick likes these shiny goggles... nope. well, time to jet.* He slammed down the lid on the footlocker and emerged from the tent.

Nick was uncertain about this new assignment. *what is the Acting Senior Patrol Leader supposed to do? it means tagging along with Tom, evidently, so I won't complain.* He scratched his head unconsciously... *what will I need? take along the notebook, as always... whoa! Tom is heading out!* Nick scurried to catch up.

The hike down to HQ took less than fifteen minutes. Mark was in a fabulous mood. He hadn't felt this happy in a very long time. *I'm even going to enjoy the staff meeting. why not? Tom and Nick seem fine this morning... evidently the problem on the bus ride has been solved, whatever it was. the leadership assignments will keep them busy.* His mind replayed Julian holding the coffee pot up... *wonderful. Julian was fine in the patrol this morning... the boys accepted him without any questions. this is working out perfectly. Julian didn't have any time to oogle and stare. he's going to be kept good and busy.*

"See that fence?" Mark pointed. "That's the new wood supply. Be sure to get a good, big pile early. There'll be a lot of competition."

"Yeah, I see it. Do they have any carts, or is it the old fashioned way?

Mark hiked his shoulders in a "search me," and headed for the lake. His first task today was to re-certify. *a good swim this morning will be perfect—makes up for not doing a morning run... I had one pancake too many, too.*

Tom had no reason to believe they'd have a bunch of carts. "Go back to camp and tell each patrol leader to send one scout with a packboard and rope to meet me over there." He pointed to the fenced wood supply.

"Now?" *that's pretty annoying; we just came from there.*

"Yeah... sorry about that. Tell them now. But they should meet me there right at the beginning of the free swim period. I'm going to try to make this a one time thing. Each pack board will carry fuel for two campfires." *that ought to do it... we don't need any wheels.*

"What am I supposed to do after that?"

"Help get the Tenderfoots squared away. Assemble them into a single group first. Some will need to be taken to Ropes, others to the Second Class area, and some to swim lessons. The distance swimmers should know what to do—they have to be on the boardwalk in half an hour." Tom had no idea where they were going to assign him this morning. *First Aid would be nice.* "I have to go over to the amphitheater to find out what they want me to do." He looked to see if anyone was watching. He gave Nick a quick goose. "Jump on ya later," he whispered.

Nick loved it when Tom did that. He watched him jog toward the amphitheater... *he looks so sexy with those Marlon Brando sunglasses.* He turned around and headed back to the Meadow. *being the Assistant to the Assistant is going to be fun.*

13 *Danny in charge*

Danny set about directing the cooking area cleanup. *I'm in charge of Julian for almost an hour and a half!* He rubbed his hands together. "So, you have any place you want to start? We've got dirty dishes and we've got the stove, and we've got the table and the leftover jams and stuff to put away."

"I can wash up all the dishes and fry pans, if you'll clean up the stove and table." Julian thought it was right to do the hardest part, since he was new. He wanted to prove himself, and he looked forward to working with Danny.

"Great… the big wash pan is behind the stove." Danny could hug Mark for setting this up. *The cute kid he had oogled at across the fence is a big boy now.* He watched Julian get the big basin and load it with the dirty dishes. *man! check that out!* He admired Julian's backside. "I'll go over to the creek with you and fetch some water to heat up for rinsing."

"Thanks!" *yep… Danny will be fun to work with. better than Tom, probably… Danny isn't as strict or as big. he's very handsome now…* When he was a Cub he used to peek through a secret spy hole once in a while and watch him mow the lawn or do other stuff in his back yard. *his super curly hair is kinda special. a lot taller now, too—two or three inches probly. I always was sort of a secret Danny admirer.*

Danny grabbed the big six-gallon aluminum pot from its place under the stove apron and they set off for the creek. It wasn't far, maybe forty or fifty feet across the gentle slope behind the three-man tent. Danny balanced the empty pot on his head as if he were on a safari. He bounced up ahead… he felt playful this morning.

Julian laughed at Danny's unexpected gamboling… he would have joined in the fun. but the pan full of dishes was too awkward. *at least everything is either plastic or metal—so it isn't that heavy. Danny's cool!*

Julian loved the way he held his arms out level and kept the pot balanced as he walked—and the way Danny sort of wagged his butt as he walked ahead.

Danny's hair made a good cushion; it was fun, doing this. *the spring isn't far... oh no! it's slipping—* **"whoops!"** He overreached and lost his balance. He rolled head over heels after the pot.

> > ***boorng-ng!*** < <

The pot banged on the turf with a dull metallic sound.

Danny sat up happily and laughed at himself. He and the pot were unhurt.

"It's a good thing you weren't close to the water!" Julian laughed.

In fact, the creek was only a few feet ahead. Danny stepped to the edge and dipped the big pot into the nice pool—the current was very gentle. "Hupf!" he couldn't lift it out. "Man, this is heavy; can you grab one side?"

"Sure." Julian put his load down between a couple of large swamp grass tufts. He stepped around and grasped the other handle; the pot was well over half full. "Ooo! This **is** heavy! I better take this side all the way to camp with you. Then I can run back."

"Yeah! Thanks a lot. Besides, you forgot to bring the soap."

"Oh, yeah..." *second foul up today! well, it's the first day on the job. I'll be perfect tomorrow.* "ugggh!" *maybe we could put in less water after this.*

Danny loved the way Julian looked when he concentrated... his tongue poked out of one corner of his mouth. He didn't mind the fact that it took a little while to tote the pot back to camp. "Help me put it up on the stove... thanks. The dish soap is on the shelf by the big tent."

The bottle of detergent was near the coffee can. Julian grabbed it and a washcloth from the drawer. "See ya later."

Danny waved back. "Rinse water will be ready..." he watched Julian's cute little butt exit. *yum. maybe I should have figured a way to work with him by the spring.*

—※—

Julian ran back to the creek. His floppies slapped noisily… running was awkward. He slid the pan near the bank and kneeled down. *ooo. the moss on the rocks is super thick! soft when you push on it; tender, too. like a wet sponge.*

A brown salamander with orange spots peeked around a rock on the other bank; it stopped to look at the intruder. It blinked its eyes and froze in place.

"Good morning!" Julian was delighted. He hadn't seen this variety before. He watched it briefly. *maybe I can pet it…* he reached over slowly.

> > sploopsh! < <

It dove into the creek and zipped out of sight.

oh well… "Sorry." *didn't mean to scare it.* He looked at the pan. "How am I gonna do this?" *I need a dipper. aha!* He took an empty aluminum tumbler in each hand and used them to dip. *that works.* He squirted in some detergent and got started. Plates first; he was used to using cold water for this… *that's what we always do on campouts.* This creek was a little bigger than some he'd had to wash up in. He'd never had a big pan full before; usually on campouts he washed up right in the stream like Stuart had taught him. The sand and fine gravel always worked perfectly to scour away the crud. *that's a no-no here. this is a fairly easy batch of dishes. enameled plates are a cinch.* The only thing that argued about getting clean was the frying pan that Danny used to cook the sausage. That one had to soak.

—⚊—

Danny's mind was busy while he cleaned the stove. *we have more time than we need to do both cleaning and inspecting. what are the chances that Julian might like to "mess around?"*

"He's **almost** the same age I was…" he spoke to himself softly. A year ago Tom pulled him into that empty tent. *it was a shock, but I liked it, after a while. it did hurt at first. but I really liked it, the more I thought about it; I have to admit that…* He hadn't done anything with Tom since; *Tom moves around—he doesn't want a regular boyfriend.* Danny decided over a year ago that he did, but none of the guys he knew attracted him that way. It would never be Tom, and that was okay. *anyway, a lot of guys* *play around*—Danny chuckled: *I came across Andy and Doug once... it looked a little suspicious; I pretended to be dumb and not notice. Frankie and I goof around some, but... I don't see Frankie as an actual boyfriend, not as a steady. anyway, he isn't at camp this year.*

He had fantasized about Julian when he first joined the troop. But Julian had so much fun with the other kids in his patrol; they seemed a little silly. Typical Tenderfoot scouts, fresh out of Cubs... he sort of stopped thinking about it. *but now, he's a real grown up First Class scout! and here he is: the prime candidate, in my own patrol, after all!* "Thank you, Mark!"

The sound of his voice startled him. He looked around—*whew!* Nobody was there... *could be somebody over at Zebra... better not lose my cool.* He continued to think about this challenge. He swabbed the table, lovingly... *maybe I'm falling in love at last. what to do, what to do?*

—⚅—

It didn't take long for Julian's hands to get used to the cold water. His mind wandered to last night. He shook his head in disbelief. For a moment he thought maybe Mark wanted to... Julian blushed. "Sometimes you let your imagination go wild, Julian!" He didn't usually mix up his fantasies with real life though. That usually wrecked things. Every time he got into a hurry, he fouled up. *this time, Julian you are going to think first. that's an order.*

His train of thought shifted to the frying pan. *yucko, this one will be work.* He scrubbed hard. *gotta let this one soak... do the easy ones first.*

"No, Julian, you have to prove yourself first." *Mark didn't invite you to the cabin because you are special. sure, you can draw stuff and all that. he even said so—that's what the table is for. you have to figure out what will make you special as a **person**. you have to pay attention better.*

Julian devised a KP scheme as he went along—*put the finished ones on one side... no sense washing things twice.*

He blushed and shook his head in disgust. "Dum-dum!" *forgetting to take Mark a cup with the coffee pot! you have to prove yourself, not look stupid all the time. you have to show him you are worth paying attention to. yeah...* he paused and looked up. *what does Mark like? what turns him off?* He nodded... *keep track of that too. that only makes sense when you look at it: take advantage of staying in the cabin.   I bet there's lots to learn if I keep my eyes open.*

right now I'm just a silly scout... there are lots of guys like me. you don't see Mark messing around with any of them, do you? no. just as well, actually. at least I don't have any competition. or do I? hmm. come to think about it, I never thought about that before. maybe I better keep an eye out.

The sudsy water made him think about the shower… *boy did I want to watch that! fat chance of **that** ever happening.*   Julian burst out laughing. *just imagine two of us in that teeny shower! we'd be bumping into each other all the time. no way could you bend over and wash your feet.*   Julian's imagination got to work on that idea. *what an idea!* He laughed hard. *we'd probly end up washing each other, half the time! hoo!*

He enjoyed playing with this idea as he swabbed out the tumblers. *what an idea... there are some parts I'd like to wash.*   He attacked the frying pan again. *I need one of those scrubber thingys like Mom has... I'll have to scrape it with a fork.*

I could tell this morning that he had taken a shower... he smelled nice and fresh on top of how he always smells. what's the word for how Mark smells? I always want to park my nose close by... I'd like to park it there forever.

there!   Everything was washed, even the sausage pan and the chopping board. He splash rinsed them, making sure not to dump any suds into the creek. *on the grass only, dum-dum. the moss wouldn't appreciate any soapsuds—the salamanders either.*   Carefully, he tipped the pan upward so that the dishes couldn't spill out.

"Catnip!" Julian sat up suddenly. "Catnip! I'm just like Lucy's cat." One of the fun things he got to do was tease that cat with the little catnip cushion Lucy had. Julian laughed merrily. He could see himself swooning and rolling around on his back after smelling Mark. *oo: what if somebody noticed me looking weird when I sniff the air like I always do whenever I'm close to him.* "That's a warning, Julian!" *besides... I'm not a cat. I'm more of a puppy. that's what Stu says... I agree.*

Julian didn't look around when he talked and laughed out loud—he figured he was well away from everybody.

Technically that was true; no one could hear Julian—the Badger and Wolf camps on the other side of the spring were far enough away. But Tom was getting an eyeful through his binoculars. He stood by a large red oak just beyond the meadow clearing. He'd watched Julian for a few minutes, hoping for another glimpse of the view he'd gotten at breakfast. No luck there… *but the day has barely started. it's a sure bet that this kid will tag along with Danny to the lake in an hour or so…* "Yeah!" he spoke softly. "I'll see this one at free swimming!" He lowered his sunglasses and hurried back to his duty assignment. He was supposed to help the Counselors set up the First Aid merit badge area for its first meeting. It was only a few hundred yards from the Meadow as the crow flies, so he ducked out for a minute on the off chance. It almost paid off. Tom knew a lot of shortcuts at Camp Walker—as well as where to snag a set of binoculars.

14 *playtime*

Julian lifted the tub of soapy dishes onto the stove next to the big pot—there was just enough room for both. The water was steaming already. Carefully, he dipped a plate in. "Ooo-oo eee-ee, this is **hot!**" He turned the burner off. *that was close! almost dropped the plate into the pot.* He pulled the small saucepan from the drawer to use as a dipper. He rinsed the dishes in the large pan then spread them out on the table to dry in the air. Danny had done a good job of wiping it clean.

"Should we save this water for later, or dump it out?" Danny was just emerging from the center split in the supply tent's flaps.

"Dump what you used." Danny had decided to try a move like Tom, only not so pushy. He was a little scared, but Julian was driving him **nuts**. "There's a place over here beside the supply tent." He had just come out of there, in fact, after making his "arrangements." Nervously, he watched Julian rinse the last item. He went over to help lift the pot off the stove. "Tom can use what's left of this tonight after supper." He fished for the big pot's lid in the drawer—"that will keep out the crud." He stood in front of the stove, rocking on his heels, watching Julian finish up. He had just created a playpen and didn't know for sure how to lure Julian into it. He tried not to show how nervous he was… he clasped his hands behind his back and watched Julian carefully carry the sloshing dishpan of water across the camp.

The spot near the southwest corner of the supply tent had been used for this for a long time. *this is easy enough.* After dumping the pan, he carried it back to the stove and put it away behind. He stepped over beside Danny and looked around for something else to do. Everything was shipshape; he looked at Danny for instructions.

"It's all done, except for letting the dishes dry." Danny exhaled loudly. "So now we deserve a break." He put his hands on his hips, still mustering his courage. He held up a finger. "I just had an idea. Wait right here." He went over to his tent... he couldn't tell if he was more scared or more horny. *I've never tried anything like this.*

Julian watched... *Danny seems to like me. it was stupid to be scared to talk to him. I was afraid I'd look silly, and he wouldn't want me around.*

Danny came back in a second with his sleeping bag draped over his shoulder. "Let's go in there." He led Julian into the storage and supply tent where all the winter camping gear and supplies were kept. He had cleared an aisle in the center of a collection of large storage crates, and shifted them to the front of the tent. At the back he'd spread out the campsite's canvas tarps. Danny unzipped his sleeping bag and laid it out flat. "Come on, let's sit down and take a break." He slipped off his shoes, got down on his knees and sat on his heels.

Julian stepped out of his flip-flop sandals and sat down Indian style. He didn't feel tired, at all. *this is a little strange; why didn't we just sit down on the grass out in the sun?* The plaid flannel lining of the bag was very soft; he smoothed it with his hand. *oh... maybe it's still damp out there.*

"This is really nice; it's all puffy and soft. It's a lot nicer than mine," Julian nodded. "Christmas colors, almost." Julian's bag was a muddy brown color inside.

"Thanks. Yeah, my dad just got it for me. My old one was starting to fall apart... it's a little too warm, maybe." Danny directed his left forefinger along one of the narrow white lines in the pattern. He couldn't figure out just how to get this started.

Julian noticed that Danny seemed a bit nervous. *maybe he had trouble going to sleep last night. tents are kinda strange to sleep in, actually.*

Sensing that sitting upright might not be a good way to get things going, Danny reclined on his left side and gave the flannel an invitational pat.

Julian's eyes widened; did Danny have a secret or something to share? How intriguing. He lay down on his right side.

"You know... Tommy and I used to see you and the Cubs once in a while, playing in the back when you were just little twerps..." Danny stopped at once and blushed. "Sorry, that was dumb… I mean, when you were a lot younger, you know…" *damn! I can be so stupid sometimes! is Julian pissed?*

"That's okay," Julian laughed. "I thought I was a twerp too." *twerp! that's funny.* He was delighted that Danny had even seen him… he was happy to be a twerp. *hmm… what is a twerp, anyway?*

Danny was afraid he'd blown it already. He glanced back and forth between Julian's face and his forefinger as he moved it in small squares following along another narrow line in the soft flannel; this one was orange. "But… even back then, I thought that you were a… well, a good looking boy."

Wow. Julian was surprised to hear such a thing—from Danny, of all people. He was a little embarrassed. He didn't know what to say.

"When you got old enough to be a member of our Troop, I told Mark he should recruit you. Ever since you joined, I've thought you were the most handsome boy in our Troop." Danny was amazed at himself for saying this… maybe it was too bold.

Julian was speechless. He was shocked and enormously pleased. "Thanks, Danny." He looked down—the intense look on Danny's face was too much to understand, really. Julian felt his face blush. "I didn't think you even knew who I was." *this is strange; I thought I was the one doing the looking, at Danny.* He felt a little guilty… *I stopped doing that a long while ago.* He looked up into Danny's face again.

"You told Mark to recruit me?" Julian was amazed. "Wow! I sure owe you one. Joining this troop is the best thing that I have done ever!" He meant that with all his heart. *I never knew Danny had anything to do with it.*

Danny was so relieved! He hadn't scared or offended Julian. An unexpected emotional surge made him want to cry all of a sudden. He sat up sharply. "Roll over… and I'll massage your shoulders." Looking at Julian's face was something he dared not do right now.

Julian rolled onto his stomach. *I've never had a massage. I saw it in a movie once on TV…* it had never occurred to him that he could have one. *it's probably a good thing, though… now I'll find out. might as well. but why is he suddenly saying such crazy things? I'm not handsome. Danny saying so sure makes me feel good… that's a nice surprise.*

Danny kneeled on the left side and started giving a massage. He breathed deep, trying to calm himself... *I almost lost it.* He didn't know how to do this like an expert, but he'd been studying about it a little. It was supposed to be a good way to start out what he wanted to do. *now I'll be able to see if it works... it's a better way to start than trying to talk.* He was never too good at figuring out what to say. He started at the neck and then worked his hands down to the back. *oh... this isn't any good.* "Umm—you need to take off your shirt." Pushing a shirt around wasn't going to help anything. "You lose all the benefit if your skin is covered up."

"Okay," Julian pushed himself up and sat on his heels. He glanced at Danny and slipped off his Troop 9 T-shirt. It was getting warm in the tent anyway. He lay back down on his stomach. "What should I do with my arms?"

"You can stretch them out wide or leave them along your side— whatever feels comfortable." *that's probably the right answer.* He rubbed Julian's back gently, methodically. He made big circles, then small circles; he kneaded the sides. "You're supposed to relax. Take big long deep breaths." He worked his way down toward the belt of the scout shorts. *it's hard to believe I'm actually doing this.* He had fantasized about it, so he pretty much knew what to do. *I haven't studied very many backs close up like this... any, actually. this one has to be about perfect. his skin is so soft and smooth!* He inhaled through his nostrils: *mmm... the smell!* He wanted to sniff up close, but didn't dare. *it's mild, but still so very sexy. I've never known anybody who smells like this.*

Julian wanted to giggle... it tickled a little. It did feel pretty good, but Danny was off center; *kneeling on his left side must make it hard to do an even job.* He didn't want to say anything. *maybe it's supposed to be this way.* He took those deep breaths. His elbows were bent slightly, and the left side of his head rested comfortably on the soft flannel. He closed his eyes. He felt a little drowsy—*the big breakfast, probably.* He relaxed and didn't think about anything. When Danny reached over to take his right arm he opened his eyes. He kept them looking straight ahead, so they ran along a straight arc and followed a seam in the canvas as Danny turned him ... an old stain in the roof... *looks like a giant doughnut. a small patch is peeling loose near the pipe ridge at the top.* Gently moving shadows... the birch tree branches... receding. That meant the sun was well up already. *oh... must be about to do the front side.* He glanced at Danny; a few beads of sweat had appeared on his forehead.

"Maybe you should take off your shirt too. It's getting plenty warm in here."

Danny grinned wide. "Yeah; thanks." *perfect!* His heart leapt... *this is going better than I thought it would.* He took off his T-shirt and moved in between Julian's legs. He doubted if Julian could see his raging boner—*as long as I don't have to stand up, I'll be okay.* His voice quavered a little. "How's it feel, so far?"

"Good... Real good. It's relaxing; I might go to sleep." Julian wanted Danny to know that he was pleased. It amazed him that Danny would go to all this effort. A nap wouldn't be a good idea, though.

Danny worked on the front side as he had on the back. Neck first, then the chest. He moved the heels of his hands over to rub the nipples gently... they started to firm up. *mmm...* He looked at Julian's face. His eyes were closed... *he's so beautiful!* Julian's chest muscles were just beginning to take shape. The pectoral form was shallow still, but clear. *his skin is flawless.* He worked on down to the abdomen—the top of the olive green scout shorts was at hand. *look at that belly button!* Gently, he stroked on both sides with his thumbs, inscribing an invisible parenthesis... he did it again, above and below. He was just above the belt now... *here goes...*

He sat back on his heels and unclipped the buckle on Julian's scout belt; he folded the belt back and unfastened the top button. He glanced at Julian's face again briefly... his eyes were still closed. Danny pulled down the zipper... A brand new elastic band appeared with the bold red letters running across. It was a brand he didn't know. He wore Jockeys, himself.

Julian had become so relaxed he was in a twilight. He wouldn't go to sleep, but he was half way there. When the zipper went down, he didn't think anything about it. He opened his eyes and looked at Danny. He saw a reassuring smile. He closed his eyes again for a second then looked Danny in the face again. Seeing his whole face, surrounded by those beautiful black curls in this soft warm light hit him suddenly. Danny's naked chest, shoulders... Danny looked sexy all of a sudden. Julian could feel his willy coming to life... a blush developing... He closed his eyes again, quick. He didn't understand what was going on. *maybe the best thing is to let Danny go ahead; he seems to know what he's doing. maybe if I get a stiffy, it won't bother him; maybe it will go back down.* He thought about Mark's coffee—the first thing that popped into his head.

Danny's heart raced. *Julian looks so ready. he seems to be willing, at least.* Danny decided to keep going according to his plan. He sat back on his heels and on both sides tucked his fingertips under the waistband. Julian's eyes were still closed... *don't stop now...* he tugged at the underwear and started to pull, along with the scout shorts. *I don't believe this—he's lifting his butt to help... he's cooperating!* Danny's heart beat faster. He pulled the shorts down to the knees, then the rest of the way off. He placed the clothes to the right and paused to catch his breath. *man alive! looks like... is Julian getting a boner too?*

Lifting up was automatic. Julian did it without thinking; he was just being helpful. He had figured out that Danny planned to do the massage all the way down to his feet, and the shorts were in the way. There was no way to hide a stiffy now, anyway, if it happened. *it'll go down eventually... probably when he works on my knees.*

Danny massaged around Julian's midsection briefly, stealing glances at what was growing below. Julian's eyes were closed, luckily... but Danny had to pretend for a while longer that he was only giving a massage. He started to work on the thighs. *oboy: he's almost completely hard now.* Danny's pulse raced. He didn't know what to do next. He had to stop himself from making a sudden move to suck on Julian; that sure was what he wanted to do... he wanted to stroke the contours of the lower abdomen as it swept gracefully over to the ridge of his hipbones... He swallowed suddenly, automatically—*don't drool all over him, idiot!* Salivating like that was completely unexpected. It served as a reminder that he didn't really know what he was doing, and he could ruin everything in an instant. But he had always been more courageous than careful, so he pressed on.

Julian wondered if he should apologize for getting a stiffy... *I couldn't help it. it wasn't on purpose. why did I get one now, anyway? I don't know what to do. Danny's massage isn't helping any, either.*

Danny sat up and started to massage the chest again, slowly. He looked at Julian's beautiful face. *how can he have eyelashes like that!* He could wait no longer: he leaned down and kissed Julian right on the lips.

Julian didn't expect Danny's kiss at all. He did not know why, but it was wonderful. He returned it... then thought to open his eyes. Danny's were closed. *this isn't part of the massage... hmm. Danny sort of tastes good!* He couldn't believe *how* good! *my willy sure likes this; he's standing tall and proud—and hitting Danny right in the butt.* Julian blushed suddenly: Danny had opened his eyes.

"Was it okay, really, for me to do that?" Danny sat back and breathed deeply. He was worried suddenly—*what if Julian is mad at me?*

Julian couldn't believe the question. "Well, yes. I guess so. Yes." *is he going to do it again?*

Danny couldn't stop his blush...this is one of those awkward moments. "I... I've wanted to do that for a long time." There. He had confessed it at last.

Julian's eyes widened. *did he really say that?* He didn't know what to say back. This was all very unexpected. The only person he had ever kissed was his mother. This was **very** different.

Danny looked down at Julian's pulsing cock. He reached forward and touched it lightly. "Lookie here!" He looked at Julian with a grin. "Okay if I touch?"

Julian was surprised. It had never occurred to him that anyone would want to—Danny, of all people. He nodded yes. He watched Danny gently stroke him... Danny pulled the skin up and down, and started to hold it more tightly. *oohm... it feels good. does a massage always have this?*

Danny had wanted to do this for so long—he looked closely at the skin as it slid up and down. *Julian is beautiful down here too!* He looked up. "You jack off sometimes, don't you?"

Julian nodded yes. 'A lot,' he said to himself. He didn't want Danny to know that, especially.

"Can I jack you off?" Danny asked, almost pleading.

Julian was astounded. *what a question.* "If you want to... sure. Yeah, I'd really like that." He'd never thought about anyone doing that to him. *whoa!* It came to him suddenly! He watched Danny lovingly pull and stroke: *Danny's just like me! Danny likes boys too!* Julian had not thought such a thing possible. *handsome guys like Danny always got taken away by the girls, never to be seen again! oooh, this is wonderful!* He watched a little longer. *strange, someone else doing that.*

"Can I…" Julian interrupted. He looked into Danny's startled face. "I want to do it to you, too." He saw Danny's eyes go wide. "Can I?"

"For sure!" Danny stood and took off his scout shorts and underwear.

Julian propped up on his left elbow and watched. He looked in wonder at Danny's hard, dark cock. It bent to the right a little. *it's bigger than mine by at least an inch! what an amazing thing to see. ohmygosh! look at all the hair. now **that's** what I want.*

Danny knelt down beside Julian, his heart racing. He was amazed at the expression and interest he saw in Julian's face.

Julian touched the tip and it bounced up out of his reach. He grinned at Danny and took a more secure grip and moved the skin up and down slowly. *gosh this feels… good. it's uncircumcised!* He squeezed a little harder and stroked it a few times. *very different from mine. so warm! I want to see it shoot!*

"You have a nice one, Danny… I wish mine was this big."

Danny was so relieved! He giggled, happy and nervous. "Thanks, Julian." *I hope you get to know it a lot better.* "I call him Little D." He reached over and stroked Julian again. "Does yours have a name?" *this is a perfect cock… just like the face above it. in a year or two it will be a masterpiece.*

"Little D! I just got it!" Julian laughed. *that's **perfect**.* "I never thought about having a name for it." He thought for a second. *Little J… makes sense. yeah…I like that.* "From now on, he's Little J." *cool. why didn't I think of that?* "Can I sit up all the way? I want to use both hands."

Danny shifted his weight and settled opposite Julian, with his legs stretched out. He was unsure suddenly. He had not thought it through this far. He watched in amazement as Julian moved in front of him, sat on his heels and reclaimed his hold. Julian cupped his balls in one hand and was stroking with the other! He had not known his balls could feel good like that.

"What's it like, Danny, to have all this hair? I only have a little." *boy… feeling Danny's cock… wow. foreskin is **interesting**. there's so much of it…*

"It's okay, I guess. I never thought about it much. There just gets to be more of it gradually. It gets itchy when you sweat, though." Julian's fascinated study of his cock was so unexpected! Feeling him caress it, pull up and down, squeeze… *mmm this feels so good. this is the best day of my life!*

Julian memorized the rich dark treasure in his hands. He went slowly, then faster, then softly, then tightly. He stopped stroking and tested to see what happened when he twisted the loose skin to the left and right. *look how far around it can go!* He stroked it up and down again briefly, then held it still in a firm grip. He looked up at Danny's face, delighted. "Danny?"

"Hm?" Danny had to swallow suddenly—he was salivating again.

"Can I jack you off and watch you shoot?"

Danny was surprised. He grinned wide, "Yeah! Yeah, and then you'll let me, right?" *what a hot thing! Frankie and I never did this!*

Julian nodded his head eagerly. "Wow, Danny, this is going to be so…. I've always wanted to see one up close!" Julian was fascinated. *Danny's cock is wonderful!*

Julian scooted closer on his knees so that he was directly in front; he stretched Danny's legs farther out on either side. He took Danny's cock into his hands and began a loving stroke. *ooo…* A whiff of something… sort of pungent… *that's a new smell—Danny's foreskin sliding up and down seems to produce it…* He wanted to see what it looked like when was about to shoot.

Julian pulled the skin with his right hand for a while and cradled the balls in his left. Then he massaged the balls gently as he stroked. He used both hands to stroke for a while. *that feels really neat!* He looked up Danny's eyes were closed tight and his lips were working. *whoo! he really likes this…* seeing that made his own cock pulse instantly.

He held the base tight with his right hand, and with his left twisted the skin as far to the left as it would go, then to the right. *amazing! how thin the skin is, and how flexible.* He did a few short pulls down at the base, only an inch or so… he moved up halfway and did that again. Then he went just under the head and did it, gently bumping the ridge. *yow! it pulsed back!*

He took both hands and wrapped the cock tightly. He did a slow up and down from the base to as far over the head as the skin would stretch.

He did this seven, eight times… he could feel Danny pulsing his shaft in response to his rhythm. Obviously this felt good.

He held it tight at the base with his left hand and softly feather stroked with his right hand, ever so lightly. He looked at it closely… it throbbed, the head swelled slightly… a bead of clear fluid appeared in the widening hole at the tip.

"Uhhmm!" Danny moaned.

Julian's eyes went wide. He grinned, and looked up. "Danny… are you going to come already?"

"Man, I will if you keep that up! Mmm. Julian, that is fantastic!" He looked at Julian in wonderment. "Should I hold it and do you for a while?"

"I don't know; I guess so, as long as you can hold it, I guess." Julian wanted Danny to work on him again, for sure. But he didn't want to miss seeing the great jet. "No fair going by yourself, okay?" He let Danny loose.

"Ohh-hh! Man! Julian. I am really on the edge. Let me wait a sec."

They both watched with interest; Danny's cock went through a half dozen involuntary spasms. Pre-cum had started to spill over onto the shaft.

Julian bent down to look close. He had never seen anything like this… *look at it throb… boy, that smell is stronger now. is it that shiny stuff? what would it taste like?* He resisted the temptation to lick it; that would send Danny off in an instant. It settled down at last. He sat up. "Wow! You were really close, weren't you?"

"You know it! I've never been that close without going. I sort of want to, now."

"Oh! Okay," Julian reached out. "Let me…"

"No." Danny put his hand on Julian's shoulder. "I want to get you up to the same place first. Let's just wait a sec, though. Now that I've stopped, let it back down a little more. Right now the slightest touch might set me off."

Julian was ready to continue, certainly. He looked at Danny's face; his cheeks were flushed, but his breathing had calmed down. *Danny's chest is really beautiful… muscle lines are fine and delicate, small dark nipples.* He saw Danny a whole new way from before. *I really like him now, as a person; a real person.* He was no longer the big kid from across the fence.

"Okay, your turn!" Danny got onto his knees and addressed Julian's cock. He would follow Julian's excellent program, too. "Sit back, like I was... thanks."

Danny had never thought about doing this sort of thing before. Maybe it was first grade stuff, and maybe he was in the third grade already, or maybe even more—but this was going to be an absolute treat. *who would have thought this jewel would invite me to perform this close examination? this **road test**? zowie!*

Danny took Julian's balls into his left hand. *pretty good sized... just as big as mine. I forgot what it was like to have only a layer of fuzz down here... balls are a lot tighter than mine.* He bent close to look at it the way Julian had. *it **is** interesting... look at the blood vessels throb! man, that's hot.* Julian responded to a slide up to the head; *it's really hot to see the head swell... how can it get this hard? skin's a lot tighter than mine.* Danny tried the twist back and forth... *won't go very far. I don't want it to hurt. he sniffed silently... ooo... **ooo**! this is what I've been smelling all morning!*

"Is that okay, Julian?" Danny looked up.

"Mmm, yeah." Julian smiled back. "I like the way your fingers feel... so nice and smooth."

Danny renewed his tour enthusiastically. *the things that felt so good to me must feel good to Julian—his cock is too small to use two hands, though.* He put his thumbs and forefingers together and pressed on each side of the shaft instead. He worked it up and down... he looked at Julian to see what he was feeling. His head was back with his eyes shut, so it must be good. He stroked up and down slowly, then gradually picked up the pace. When he hit the head on the way up, Julian quivered—his thighs began to jiggle. *that is so hot!*

"Mmm! That is so good. I never tried that! Mmm."

Danny felt his own cock begin to pulse again. *doing Julian is such a turn on!* He spread his knees apart so that he could hang loose... he had a lot more to do before he wanted to shoot. He examined the perfectly shaped instrument in his fingers up close. *it's so smooth and fine... and* *red on top... really **red**.* It was very tight anyway, but he did Julian's hold the base with one hand while stroking with the other move.

"Ooo—oo!" Julian flinched. "Maybe a little softer." He looked down to watch. The top of Danny's head was interesting. *I always liked those dark curls. his nose from above is... wow, this feels so wonderful... except if he holds it too tight. did I squeeze Danny too hard? I'll be super careful when my turn comes back. man, this feels so intense.*

Danny lessened the pressure... he felt Julian approve of the change. *how close is he? there isn't a drip yet... does Julian have pre-cum too? I didn't used to... well, he'll say when he's getting close.* He massaged the balls ... *it's fun to roll them back and forth.* He tickled right under the head. Julian sure liked that! He held the balls and ran his fingertip in a trail around the rim and down the shaft to its base. Julian's moans were wonderful.

He did the two sides stroke again. The thighs started a small quiver. He used one hand... he fully wrapped the cock into his cupped fingers, and slowly went up and down as far as the skin allowed. He saw the head pulse; he felt it too... Julian's scrotum began to contract. *this has to be it.* He looked up—Julian was squinting real hard. "Now?"

"Yesss! Oh. Please don't stop—I can't hold it!"

Danny bent close to see. Julian grabbed his shoulders. *wow...* the rhythm was driven; Julian's thighs were clenched—he started to thrust his hips forward and back involuntarily. Suddenly he froze in place and a jet burst out... it splashed onto Danny's shoulder.

"Nnnm!" Julian grunted as he thrust each shot. *boy, is this intense.* On the last one he seemed to be stuck in a forward thrust. He took a deep breath and sat back. After a moment he opened his eyes wide. "Wow, Danny. That's probably the best shoot I've ever had!" He grinned. He took several deep breaths. He blinked his eyes, and laughed. "Okay! Now I get to do it."

Danny was overjoyed to see Julian this happy. He sat back. *it won't take long to get off.*

Julian was back where he wanted to spend the rest of the day... *it'll only take a couple of minutes, but maybe I can talk Danny into doing this again sometime—he is sure good at it.* He took the cock into both hands and did the slow up and down as far as it would go—*Danny liked that.* He went up and down several times, wondering if his hold was too tight. He bent closer... *it's dripping again.* He watched for it to pulse; *it's slick and shiny in places... it isn't very thick.*

"Tighter, Julian. That's perfect, only tighter. Mmm, yeah!"

Julian gripped harder; he could feel the underside hardening, he could see the head flare. He bent close and focused on the hole. Danny began to thrust along with the strokes; a natural, almost automatic rhythm took over, assisted by the slippery patch of pre-cum spreading down and around the head... it made his fingers slide smoothly. He saw it happen! The thick white stream erupted with force and hit him on the chin.

"Waah!" Danny's hands clenched the sleeping bag and twisted tight. He pressed his eyes closed and threw his head back as he shot.

Julian stared... it continued to splash on his face. He didn't count, but there must have been five or six enormous shots. *wow, is this ever wonderful!* Danny's cock continued to constrict and dribble.

He sat up and looked at Danny's face with complete admiration. He had just seen something truly miraculous; it's an image he would never forget. He still held Danny's beautiful tool in his hands. A little cum ran over the back of his right hand. He wanted to lick it off... *do I dare do that?*

"Julian, Julian! That was incredible. How did you think of doing that?" He looked at him fondly. *yes, I've found who I want.* He laughed. "I shot all over your chin!" He reached over and grabbed his underpants. He swabbed his cum from Julian's face. "Sorry about that," he chuckled. He swiped across his own shoulder.

"'Sokay, I don't mind. That was cool to see, Danny." He wanted to ask when they could do this again; *I better see what Danny wants to do...*

"Uh, Julian?"

"Hm?"

"Did you know you're still holding me?" He was amused, but this was going to keep him hard... *we don't have time for a second round.*

"Oh..." He looked at his hand. "I like to hold this, Danny." He tilted his head. Reluctantly, he released it. His mind raced... *how can I lick my hand without Danny seeing?* "Maybe you could let me hold it again sometime."

"Julian, **that** is a promise!" Danny was unable to describe how he felt at this moment. He had to talk a few things over. "You've never done anything before, you know, with another boy, have you?"

Julian looked a little sad. He bowed his head, but looked up at Danny. "I know I don't know what to do, Danny. I'm sorry if I did anything wrong. I've thought about it so much. I never knew what it would be like. All I could do was pretend." He looked at Danny's cock; it was still swollen, but going soft. It had a drip hanging off the tip. He pointed: "Lookit," he giggled. "You're still coming!"

"Oh!" Danny cupped his palm around his cock; *I don't want to get any on the new sleeping bag. I just now thought of that.* He grabbed his undies and carefully wiped the tip; he looked around for any other splashes. *stupid idiot... didn't think to bring a towel along.*

Julian took the opportunity to lick off the back of his hand. Most of it had run off onto Danny's leg, but a little taste was there. *maybe I'll get a chance to get a bigger sample. maybe it has to be tasted right away, before the air has a chance to wreck it.*

"Listen, Julian, I have to tell you some things." Danny tilted his head... *I'd better be careful about how I say some of this.*

Julian sensed something was wrong. Danny had gone all serious.

"First off, there are some other boys here that..." Danny paused, looking for the right way to phrase it. "well, that like to have sex with other boys. In fact, they do it a lot." *I just wish I was as busy as some of them are.*

Julian was stunned at this news. His eyes went wide... *there isn't anything wrong, after all!* He was happy again. "Really?" he grinned eagerly.

"Yeah, **really!** They're pretty cool about it, mostly, but you need to know a few things. Am I ever glad I'm the one who gets to fill you in— and you'll be glad you found all this stuff out, too!" Danny wanted to shield him from Tom, more than anything. He also wanted, if at all possible, to gain an edge with Julian's affections.

Julian figured Danny was right. He sat upright, crossed his legs Indian style, and paid full attention. *boy, am I lucky. Danny's even more handsome, the longer I look at him.* Julian felt a little different now... he couldn't quite identify what was going on in his head… *but it's good, I know that; I feel it.*

"Tom and Nick are also into boys." He grinned… *I'm the first to know that the entire leadership patrol, except Mark of course, is into this, including Julian, the newest member.*

Julian had a little trouble understanding the significance of this. It must be good, though, because Danny seemed to think so. His eyes darted back and forth as he tried to sort this news out.

Danny paused to look at Julian's face. *he's so beautiful…* "Julian," Danny spoke softly. "I just think you are the best looking boy in the world; and I think I …" He was afraid to say it yet. *what if Julian freaked and ran out? what if he told Mark?* He looked into Julian's beautiful eyes. *I could do that all day, too…*

Julian figured he had to say something, but he didn't know what or how. This was all so new and sudden. "But I'm not, really. I think you are. You don't know this, but…" he paused; *should I tell this? okay, I will.* "You know that little clubhouse hut I built? In my back yard?"

Danny nodded; he had indeed watched that being built—*from my upstairs window vantage point.*

"One reason I did that back then was so I could watch into your yard. When you were outside, like when you mowed the lawn? Or played with your dog. Some days I would sit out there just waiting for you to come outside." He felt silly about that, now. *it was over two years ago, but it's true! I did think Danny was handsome.* He shrugged. *maybe Danny won't laugh.* He looked up shyly.

Danny was at a loss for words, now. He looked at the puppy sweet eyes across from him. They embraced—it was a little awkward. They lay back down in each other's arms. They were getting hard again.

"What if somebody comes in? We're still naked."

Danny flinched. "Oh, yeah! That's right!" He laughed hard. He had a sudden picture of Tom barging in and finding them. *oh… we need to rejoin the scout camp.* "I wonder what time it is!" His watch was still in his footlocker. How long have we been here? He didn't know—they had inspections to do. "We better get up." He looked at Julian. "Is it okay with you if we come in here again tomorrow?"

"I was hoping you'd say that. What about…you know," he pointed down to the two stiffies.

"Hmm…" Danny looked down at the problem. Now that he seemed to have Julian's affection, he didn't know what to do about it. Julian had swept away all the barriers he'd expected to be there… *I have to think some about this now.* "You trying to tempt me into something?" He giggled.

Julian thought about that. He didn't know if he had anything left, but he wouldn't mind finding out. He opened his eyes wide and grinned.

"I have to admit I'd like to. But we better get dressed and go do the inspections. And remember, after that we have free swimming!"

They sat up. Danny thought about getting some clean skivvies… *nah. these will dry pretty quick when I move around… my right bun will get a special "lotion" today.*

Julian pulled on his t-shirt. His stiffy was going down. Just as well. He pulled on his skivvies and pants.

As he folded up his sleeping bag, Danny thought of something: *I need to instill some caution, especially about Tom.* He just remembered the go-for trick Tom tried during breakfast. Tom was famous for another thing: initiating unsuspecting new scouts. Julian wouldn't stand a chance if Tom got hold of him. "Listen, Julian—let's play it cool, especially in front of Tom, okay?" He looked at Julian… he didn't want to go into detail. That would take too long. *It has to be done very carefully—Julian is way too green to even hear about Tom.*

Julian froze—he thought of Mark. *what if Mark found out? I don't want Mark to be mad at me. I'll have to be super careful.* He looked at Danny and smiled. He made the zipper sign across his lips.

15   *first inspection*

Julian followed behind Danny; he had been given the job of keeping score on the form as they inspected each patrol's camp. Danny explained how everything was supposed to look as they went along. Stuart had told the Wolves about this, so he already had a good idea about it. He used the chart on Danny's clipboard. There was a list of patrols across the page, and down the side was a list of what they were being inspected for—like, "things all put away," "bed neat and straight," and individual stuff like that. Patrol things like clean stove, emergency kits handy, and water channels in case it rains. It wasn't a hard thing to do. All of the scouts below First Class were off at their morning classes, and others were off to the special long distance swimming... so the camps were half empty or more. That made inspecting real easy... but this was a new thing for Julian. They didn't have these inspections on campouts.

In all the patrols there was only three things to mark down; Julian thought they were kind of picky. They couldn't select a winner—all the camps were in great shape. So Danny told him to take off a half point each for the Badgers, Tigers, and Zebras.

One place was not inspected yet, of course.

"Hey, what about my camp?" *I'm going to enjoy this.* He had figured out that Danny did not know where he was bunked.

"Yours? Didn't we..." He swiveled around. "That's right! You aren't a Wolf any more—where **are** you?"

"Where's one place we didn't inspect?" Julian smiled, sweet and innocent.

Danny frowned; he took the clipboard. Glancing across the meadow, he tallied off each patrol's site, including the Flaming Arrow... then he noticed the Scoutmaster's Cabin. His eyes went wide. "You mean..." He looked at Julian. *!!!* He didn't believe it. "Really?" *how could this be?*

"Yeah. Isn't it lucky? I'm supposed to use the table to draw and to work on the newsletter. Mark will check my work and make suggestions."

"Wow... What's it like?" Danny's mind was going a mile a minute about this.

"It's really super. There's just one big room and a small bathroom. That's what's best—I don't have to run to the latrine! And it has a shower, too." *ohmygosh! I forgot! I hope I didn't foul up by telling that*—he just remembered what Mark said about not inviting other scouts to use it.

"But..." he did not dare to ask, but he had to know. "Is there a bunk in there for you?" He looked at Julian very closely.

"Nah. I just have my cot. There's plenty of room on the west wall for that and my footlocker."

Danny was still a little amazed.

Danny's reaction worried him. *maybe telling that I'm staying in the cabin wasn't a good idea.* "There's a big wind up clock on the table. It ticks real loud at night. I finally got to sleep though."

Danny looked at Julian again... *he's **so** clueless. no way could anything be going on...* Staying with Mark was one thing he had never imagined. He didn't know if it would be bad or not. *maybe Mark snores... hmm. is it a Big Ben wind up clock? those are real loud... sleeping in Mark's cabin might not be so great, at that.*

"So, do I get inspected, or what?"

Danny laughed. "Why not? We'll just see if Mark follows the rules like everybody else!" *what a nifty surprise! I always wanted to see what it's like inside that cabin. think of it! a bathroom!*

Julian's cot and locker were in perfect shape. He figured a plus mark in his column would be a good thing. They sauntered down to the cabin.

Danny entered close behind. He paused and took everything in. Sure enough, Julian's cot was all set up with his footlocker at one end. It was immaculate. It made sense suddenly—*maybe Mark is smarter than I thought. maybe he put Julian in here to keep him safe! does he know about Tom? hmm... probably has suspicions, anyway.* He glanced across the room. The table had a small lamp and... *yep! a Big Ben alarm clock.* He went over to it... *Julian's scrapbook is sitting right there.* He looked back and smiled conspiratorially as he went into the bathroom. Two king sized bath towels hanging on the wall rack! "Man! You have your own towel, too?"

Julian nodded with a grin. He noticed the razor and shaving cream on the back of the washbasin. *darn! I didn't get to see Mark use that this morning. I'll have to do that tomorrow, for sure.*

Danny went to the center of the room. "All in order here. Top marks." He glanced at Julian's cot. *not for me... Mark would catch me beating off the first thing.* The cot was only twelve feet from where Mark slept.

"Hey, man!" Danny pointed to the clock. "Let's go swimming! You can go in as my Buddy." He punched Julian in the arm and broke into a run for the door. "I'm going for my towel. I'll catch up with you on the trail." Danny had a big plan, and getting to the lake early was crucial.

what a relief! Julian stood for a second, watching Danny's hasty exit. Passing the inspection was not a surprise—but seeing Danny's reaction to his being in the cabin was what counted—that was really what mattered, and until this minute he didn't understand that—he didn't even know that. *wow.* He went back to the bathroom to get his towel. He'd used the big one Mark had assigned him last night after washing his face. *it's almost as big as a beach towel.* He draped it around his neck and headed for the door. He double-checked to make sure his pencil was still inserted in the spiral—he planned on adding to the sketch he started yesterday.

He headed for the lake—right away he had trouble running. *this is no good at all... it's a long way to the lake: too far for floppies. it will take an hour to get there in these things! tennies would be a lot smarter. won't take long to swap these out.*

He hurried back to the cabin; he opened the footlocker and took out a pair of crew sox. The long scout socks were reserved for full dress events. *besides, it's plenty warm out.* He returned to his cot and reached for his tennies. *these are the way to go—plus, they'll fit into the cubbyholes.* He sat down and kicked off the floppies. "I'm going to give you a long vacation: two weeks, at least." He put on the socks and slipped on the tennies—*much better. no wonder I haven't seen anyone else in the patrol using those. they make my feet feel all dusty too.*

He returned to his footlocker and tucked the floppies at the back behind the flashlight. *hey—there's my towel, the salmon orange one I brought from home... it's a lot smaller than Mark's. that would be better at the lake—those cubbyholes aren't very big.*

He paused for moment. Danny's reaction about the cabin before the inspection just filled his mind like a flashing yellow light. *what was Danny thinking?* Frowning, he returned to the bathroom to hang up the towel.

whoa. He understood something, suddenly: *without thinking, I put Mark in danger—if Danny figures out what I feel toward Mark, it would be Mark who got into trouble. it worked out okay, but... I better be more careful.* "You need to think about things first before opening your big mouth." *I couldn't stand it if I got Mark in trouble.*

Out of habit, he stopped to look at himself in the mirror. Hair's all messed up. He ran his pocket comb through it, then looked at himself in the eyes briefly. "We haven't talked about moving in here yet, you know."

He smiled... talking to himself was sort of a habit at home; *maybe at camp it isn't too smart. but it's true: I need to figure things out.* A lot had happened in the last few hours, and he hadn't had time to think about it at all yet. Up to now, he'd been kept busy all the time. *and now, there's this thing with Danny.* What a surprise that was!

"You don't want that to get in the way," Julian told the mirror image. *still, it was fun... and interesting. besides, I could learn stuff that will help me know what to do with Mark someday.* He never did have a clear picture of that anyway. All he knew was that he loved Mark and wanted to be with him forever. He had never spent much time on he details of what they would actually do; he figured that when the time came that would take care of itself. He always figured that Mark would know what to do anyway, so why worry about it?

"It can't be that big a deal to learn." Playing with Danny wasn't hard to figure out at all... *I never thought about that beforehand.* The face in the mirror nodded agreement.

A light came on inside his head: *that's it! I can learn lots of stuff from Danny.* It had always bothered him, not knowing anything. When the big kids talked about stuff like this all he could do was pretend he knew what they were talking about. *I haven't heard all that much, actually. a few words here and there is all... they always clam up when they see me around.*

He looked at himself again. "Here's the deal: whenever we get the chance, we'll compare notes about stuff." *Mark wants to have a talk every night about things—we can do the same thing. that way I can be ready.*

He smiled at himself sagely. His confidence had returned to its former level. It always felt good to have a plan. He always had a conference with himself when he was confused or uncertain—silly, maybe—*but it helps, that's all.*

"Are you ready yet?!" he scolded. "Maybe you'll be organized by tomorrow!" He grabbed his tablet and towel and started for the lake at a run.

16 *free swimming*

Danny arrived at the lake running full out. He expected to catch up with Julian, but didn't even see him. He looked back to see if he was coming. *huh. nowhere in sight. we have to go in together. Leonard is at the gate today... he's strict about things like that.* He retraced his steps until he saw Julian coming down the trail. He reached high and waved back and forth. He was eager to get a start on his suntan. The lake was crowded already. *should I wait here, or... how come he took so long, anyway?*

Julian spotted Danny waving. *man. I hope he isn't mad or anything. I didn't think he'd be there already... he must have run all the way. I better hurry up.* In the distance he could see that dozens and dozens of scouts were already splashing and having a great time in the water. *that's good... a crowd made him less self-conscious. I won't be the only hairless kid. wow... a lot more guys today. at least there isn't a line like yesterday.*

"What took you so long?"

"I had to put on shoes." Julian felt a little silly.

"I wondered why you had those things on."

Julian was embarrassed. He didn't especially want to admit that he was a stupid new kid. He always wore his floppies to the pool, that's why. His mom always dropped him off in front, that's why. He hated to wear sox, that's why. Nobody told him not to, that's why. He hurried over to the board to get his badge.

Leonard was less interested in the badges than he was in the boys who had just put them down on his table. *what a remarkable pair! so different, yet nearly equal in beauty.* He was partial to the curly haired brunette—a familiar one from last year... but the blond: a new treasure, just now coming of age. *in a year or two... well. when the body grows into that face, watch out, world!* He smiled, affecting an official air. These two would add to the quality of his day.

After they checked in, they hung their badges next to each other on the swimming Buddy Board.

"I'm gonna swim out to the platform and lay in the sun for a while," Danny announced as he looked for an empty cubbyhole. "What are you gonna do?"

"I need to work on my dives." Julian checked out the long dock. "If I can find a place to do it, that is." *so many scouts here today...more than I thought!*

"Here's some open ones." Danny had stooped down at the end of the second cubbyhole unit.

Julian found one nearby and undressed. *boy—we got here just in time; only a few of these are left.*

"When they blow the Buddy Whistle, look for me out on the platform." Danny looked down along the F dock. "How deep do you want to dive? You want to go out the platform too? You can dive real deep out there. I just might do a few dives myself, if the sun gets too warm." Diving was one skill that Danny had made a specialty.

Julian wasn't sure. "I think I'd like to be closer in. I'd just as soon be able to stand up once in a while. Probably 4 to 5 feet or so at first would be best. I'll work my way out. About all I can dive now is a cannonball."

"Start out about the middle of the F. You'll probably have to wait some between dives—it's real crowded today. At the whistle, make sure to point at me when you raise your arm. That way they can tell we're Buddies." He glanced out to the platform... *boyoboy! I have to get out there quick while there's still room.*

"Okay. That's what I'll do then." *this Buddy thing is a bother, to tell the truth.* He just remembered Norman, his Buddy yesterday. *Norman must have found someone else to be his buddy today, or something. there's no way to tell if he's even here, it's so crowded.* "I might do a sketch or two first, come to think about it, for the scrapbook. This place is a lot more complicated than I remember."

"See ya later." Danny gave Julian a small pat on the left bun as he headed over to the F dock. He planned to swim right out to the platform.

Julian looked after him, surprised. *how come he didn't get under the cold shower rinse? hmm... that means I can wait to do that too. I'll walk around the place first... I didn't see half this stuff during Certification. nobody's giving tours... I'll just explore on my own.* He returned to his cubbyhole to get the tablet... *gotta make sure it doesn't get wet. finding a safe spot where I can draw is gonna be tricky.* He walked over to the edge of the boardwalk first. *about twelve feet wide. the cubbyholes and Buddy Board are on the west side of the gate.* He calculated that the whole boardwalk must be about sixty or seventy feet long. Mark would know about that. *a lot bigger than the pool; probably four or five times bigger.*

The lake was shallow at the boardwalk edge—three feet deep. Depth marks painted along the edge of the dock showed where it dropped another foot. *good idea... so the lake bottom slopes down gradually to the deep water... to twenty feet at the end of the dock. wow... the pool is only twelve feet. what is it out by the platform?*

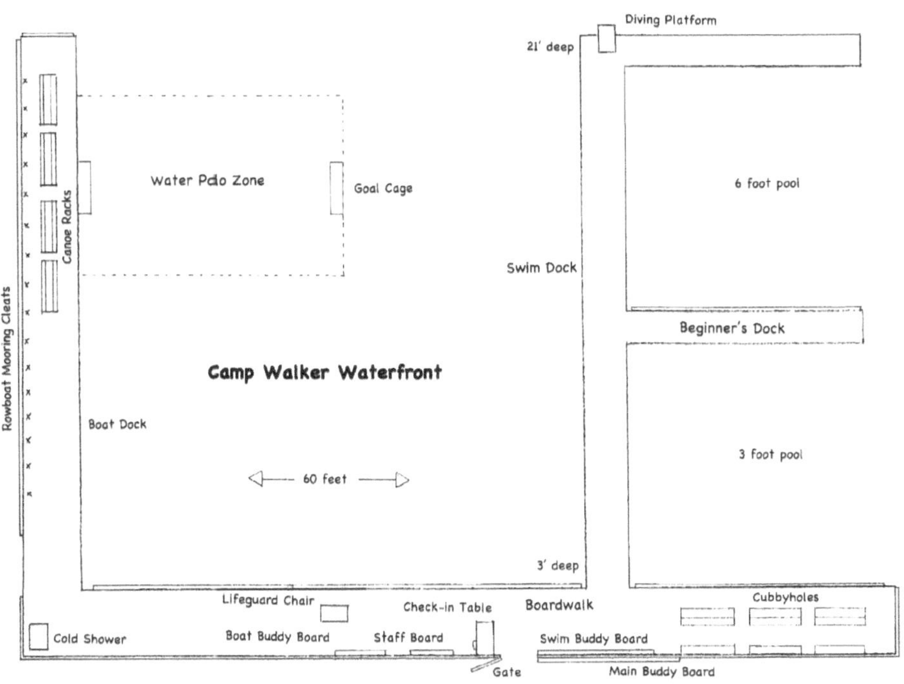

He stepped toward the dock on the west side. It was six feet wide and extended out into a big F. Crowded all along the way, some guys were diving, others were sitting on the edge. He stayed on the right side—safer from all the splashes. At the center he stopped to reconnoiter. Beginning swimmers were practicing laps on both sides of the F dock. The area to the right was marked three feet deep... the left six feet. Both were almost as wide as the pool back home—twenty-five feet or so... *boy, those kids have to work.* Counselors were helping them... in the shallow half, scouts were working in pairs practicing how to float. He walked out to the end; a raised diving platform poked out a couple of feet. Only a foot high, a dozen or so scouts were in line to dive; Julian moved farther out... he needed to stay clear of the splashes.

From this vantage point the central swim area was a blurry swarm of splashing scouts. *not very interesting...* The dock on the far side was different. Four long racks housed the canoes and paddles. *Mark told Jeremy about those on the bus.*

Julian counted five lifeguards... *must be Senior Counselors.* One occupied a high tower chair on the boardwalk, the others walked back and forth, two on each dock. They wore visors and sunglasses; large whistles hung around their necks. *hmm... blue Speedos... makes sense I s'pose. sort of makes them look sexy, actually.* Fifty yards out in the lake a floating platform, twelve by eighteen feet, was anchored in a fixed position. *looks different... no one on duty out there today... no boats, either. looks like four or five guys are out there. Danny is stretched out on his back, getting a tan for some reason. huh... I didn't notice the diving platform yesterday. like the one at the end of the F dock... it hangs over the east edge. no diving boards... that's okay by me. I have a way to go before I'm ready to use a board.*

A view that made sense for a drawing wasn't likely from here... *too big... so many scouts! hmm... maybe... yes!* He walked back to the boardwalk, and headed for the other dock.

nice...not nearly as crowded over here... He walked to the end and looked back. Large lifesaver rings hung on the ends of the A frame canoe racks—Camp Walker was painted in large red letters around the bottom. The end ring had a large number eight on the top. *not a bad location for a sketch. angle isn't that great for showing the F part, though.* He sat cross-legged close to the outer edge and began a sketch. The lifeguard tower made a good focus point. Miss Connor taught him about that long ago: always identify a focus point first. It made perfect sense when you thought about it. *everything fits in easy once you do that, even the horde of swimmers.* He could fill in the center later—plugging in a few kids splashing around would be easy. The canoe racks helped the composition... *that's why this dock is wider*—three canoes hung on each side. Paddles hung vertically like a row of baseball bats, wide end down. *say, that's clever: rowboats are tied up along the lakeside edge... all those boats in a line look interesting... that's a drawing all by itself...*

About ten minutes passed—Julian had roughed in compositions for both views. *there—enough for now. time to join in the fun out there.* He looked back across the swim area... still very crowded. *oh well... hafta put up with it.* He slid the pencil back into the spiral and headed back to his cubbyhole. *obviously it will take two or three sketches of this place... there's just too much stuff to pack in... the lifeguard tower would be nifty...*

> > ***bleet! bleet!*** < <

The shrill sound of a whistle sliced through the merry waterfront ruckus like a sabre—the splashing and laughter went quiet suddenly.

Julian stopped in mid step: he looked over to the tower. The lifeguard had blown the Buddy Whistle. All activity had stopped and swarms of arms stretched up out of the water. *yow!* He looked out to the platform for Danny—there he was, waving his arm just like he said he would. Julian raised his arm and pointed back happily; he happened to be between the two Boat Dock Lifeguards. The one closest to the boardwalk gave him a strange look.

"My Buddy is working on a suntan out there." Julian assumed that information would help the guy. He looked kind of frowny, but with those sunglasses on, it was hard to tell. He seemed to look out at Danny, then returned his focus to the swimmers.

This took a while. *a **lot** of scouts out there...* Julian wasn't in a particular hurry; he watched the process. Many of the kids in the water were actually holding their hands together. *that must help speed things up.* When the lifeguards finished scanning the lake, the one in the tower blew a three tweet signal, and everyone went back to swimming. *how could they possibly tell everybody is okay? I get it: each lifeguard is assigned a section, the one closest to me only looked from here to the boardwalk.*

that must be how they do it. even so, there must be hundreds of scouts out there… that's why it took so long. He decided not to apply for the job.

He stopped by the shower. *dry underneath…* Nobody was using it. He went over to the sign-in table. "Excuse me, but am I supposed to use that before going in, or not?"

Leonard glanced over his shoulder. "You can use it whenever you like…" he took the opportunity to look at Julian's incredible eyelashes more closely. "Usually when it gets into the 90s, or if the humidity is over 85 is when it's strongly recommended." Leonard glanced quickly at Julian's midsection. *nope. not ripe enough, quite.*

"Oh." Julian saw the point of it now. "Thanks…"

"Leonard. You may call me by my name, if you like." Leonard smiled. *this is one I would like to know.*

"Leonard! That's a new name. I'm Julian." He smiled brightly. *Leonard is nice… his name is sewn onto his shirt.* The spelling was interesting too.

"Good to know you, Julian." *my, yes.*

Julian gave a small wave and hurried over to tuck the tablet into the cubbyhole. He made sure the towel covered it completely. Then he stepped over to the waterside edge of the boardwalk and took advantage of an opening: his cannonball splashed a bunch from another troop close by. They responded instantly with a water fight. They splashed back energetically; he cupped his hands and pushed several big splashes. Lots of scouts were having fun doing this. After a while the fun was over and he swam toward the center of the F dock where it was a little less crowded. He swam back and forth along the dock a few times; when there was room on the dock, he pulled himself up and waited for another space to open.

He was able to make a few practice dives at the four foot mark. Sometimes he had to wait for an opening, either on the dock or in the water. It was crowded—as bad as the pool during the no reserve hours. He experimented opening his eyes under water. The muted sounds were strange; *so that's what fish hear—I don't see any. prob'ly isn't room for them around here; too many scout legs. this is a lot better than the indoor pool: no chlorine. that stuff always makes my eyes sting. this is great: I can keep my eyes open all the time here—there's a lot to see! trouble is, it's hard to see any detail without goggles. nobody seems to have those—or fins. come to think about it, there aren't any 'tubes or water toys either. just as well, with all these scouts.*

Whenever Julian couldn't find a space to dive, he spent time swimming under water. It was fun to look around. Looking at the other swimmers' equipment wasn't as good as he expected; they had to be real close up or they blurred out. *still, that's something I can't do at the pool... 'course, the water shrinks everybody up mostly, so it's no big deal.* Once in a while a longish one waved as he paddled by; he waved back at one just for fun. *mine is so shrunk up it's almost disappeared.* He just remembered about the name. *I wonder if any of these other guys have names? I'm glad Danny gave me that Little J idea, actually... I mean, he is my closest friend.* Julian giggled at that and gulped some water by mistake.

He surfaced, choking and laughing. A lifeguard looked at him closely. Tensed, he was ready to jump in.

"I'm okay," Julian waved happily. "I just swallowed some water by mistake." He got himself under control quickly. "No problem, really." The lifeguard waved his okay and moved on.

Julian bounced up and down briefly. The water was only four feet or so here. *closest friend.* He chuckled. *trouble with jokes like that is you can't tell them to anyone.*

so... what's next? He looked at the jam-packed swim area. *it's just too crowded to do much diving... maybe I should work on underwater skills. I can learn to hold my breath longer, at least. yeah. good idea.* He took a deep breath and submerged. He counted to himself: *one thousand one, one thousand two...*

—w—

Nick watched the scouts splashing in the lake. His perch at the top of the grassy slope was as good for visibility as any—the downside being no shade trees anywhere close by. *Tom has to run by here on his way to the gate. we'll go in as Buddies, as usual. incredible, how many are packed in there this morning—it's always a mob at the first free swim. last night the Camp Director said it was a record attendance this year.*

His morning had gone very well, considering. All the Tenderfoot scouts made it to their destinations on time. Cory helped out by taking all the beginning swimmers in tow; it was a small group—*Cory still has his trouble with swimming. why does he have such an aversion to water? maybe this year he can conquer it. must be awkward, still being a Second Class.* Mark had made it clear that he couldn't advance any farther in rank without that swim rating.

Nick wiggled in place briefly—something embedded in the ground had begun to assert itself... he scooted up the slope slightly... *there... grass is a little softer here.* He checked his watch again... *a lot of extra time this morning. that will probably change.* No one had told him yet what all he'd be doing as Tom's assistant. *maybe it's a one-day thing.* Today he spent some time in the rope area with the Tenderfoots Scouts. *sort of surprised myself, I was so good at it. some things just stick with you. maybe tomorrow I'll go along to the compass and map reading class. wouldn't hurt to brush up a little there.*

how long will I have to wait? Tom was leading the firewood detail. *he said it might take half an hour. maybe I should have gone along. no matter, except that sitting in the sun is getting old. sort of annoying, not having any shade.* He glanced down to the lake. It was so crowded today there wasn't much point in hurrying—*it doesn't look too bad out past the docks. we might have fun finding a cubbyhole, though. boy, the sun really glares on the water—hard to look down there without dark glasses.* He moved his eyes down toward his feet to relieve the discomfort. *too bad I don't have a pair of those Brando sunglasses.*

Nick was a little concerned about Tom lately—*sometimes he's hard to figure. he can be moody, like he was on the bus.* Nick had a pretty good idea about what was behind that, though... probably something to do with his sex life. It often was. In fact, he was a little horny at the campfire last night. *I half expected him to figure a way to sneak off into the brush after hours.* Once they were in camp Tom's attention had shifted again. Nick knew better than to ask any direct questions. He had learned over the years that, as long as he was cheerful, handy, and made no demands, Tom was happy to have him around. He had done whatever he could to make Tom depend on him without realizing what was going on. Now that he was actually Tom's official morning assistant for this year's camp, he couldn't be more encouraged. *it won't be necessary to do so much managing, and arranging excuses to be around, things like that. be smart to have a few suggestions ready for my new job, just in case.*

17   *Tom's first move*

Tom ran down the trail at full speed... the others weren't far behind. The firewood loading detail had gone very nicely, but it had taken a little longer than he wanted. He was all set to move on his game plan, but Mark threw a curve with that firewood assignment. *no problem... he was fairly sure Julian would be there for the first free swim period. that's one choice set of buns I saw this morning. they need to be broken in properly. that means by me! good! Nick's right where he's supposed to be. excellent. he always comes through.*

"Sorry to keep you waiting." Tom came to a distance runner's stop. He had to catch his breath. He bent over, hands on knees and looked back—his crew of firewood packers was just coming around the junction. *hmm... they should have done better than that.*

"No problem." Nick stood and massaged his backside back to life. He watched Tom panting heavily. "Did you run all the way from camp?"

"Yeah..." Tom stood, hands on hips. "Nathan did a brag, so I had to show him." He checked again—they were just now passing the amphitheatre. Tom still reigned supreme. *I'd feel better if it was a contest. I expected one of those guys to make me work.* "Let's go swimming."

They stepped down to the Buddy Board and snagged their badges on the way to the gate. This was a familiar routine.

"Hey hey! It's Big Tom!" Leonard quipped. He didn't enter Tom and Nick's names; they were faces he knew well. He returned their badges. "I thought last summer would be it for you." He eyed Tom with appreciation. *it was nice to see him again—Tom always enriched his fantasy life.* It was good to know he had another lifeguard handy if needed, too. This afternoon, in fact: the lifesaving qualifications needed a tower guard. He looked forward to springing this.

Tom removed his sunglasses and winked. He knew what was happening in Leonard's lap. *too bad he's sitting at this table where he's all hidden from view.* Tom had seen him in previous camps, and he was pretty good stuff, probably. Tom had never played with any of the Counselors. He preferred the smaller buns, the new ones.

"My fee for lifesaving duty has gone up, you know." Tom tried to be off-handed.

"I'll pass that on." Leonard kept his response even. "Meanwhile, plan on a short one this afternoon."

"Huh?!" Tom was stunned. He did not expect to be hit this soon. He had no escape plan in place.

Leonard pulled the other clipboard over, found Nick's name, and put his fingertip on it. "While Nick here is qualifying." Leonard relished this. "Everyone is on duty, and we need you in the chair." He was pleased to see that Nick was still in favor… Tom didn't seem to stick with anyone else for very long.

blast! Lifesaving again. I should have known. He looked at Nick.

"Yep… One last hoop to swim through." Nick expected to get his Lifesaving merit badge this very afternoon. He had done everything except the mock rescues in the water. That would make him eligible for Eagle in the fall.

"Oh." Tom was mollified, somewhat. *I don't mind helping Nick out.* "Okay. I'll do this one free. For old times sake." He tried to imitate Leonard's smile.

"Thanks. Briefing at 3:15." He returned a "ta-ta" wave and watched Tom and Nick try to find an open cubbyhole. Leonard was **very** pleased with himself. One of his secret pleasures was corralling Tom. His attempts to get him on staff had all failed. This was his consolation. He adjusted himself as he watched Tom and Nick undress. *lordy! I had forgotten just how big Tom is. this table is a blessing. sweet dreams in the night, what a tool!*

Tom was mildly annoyed… he had thought arriving late would shield him from getting stuck with lifeguard duty. *I lucked out this session, anyway. at least it won't be a full shift this afternoon.* It made sense to have an experienced crew today… it was the first free swim. *I'm lucky they didn't put me on as an extra this morning: the place is really packed. last year they drafted me on the first day to man a special rowboat—ruined the whole session.* The Counselors on duty today were familiar faces, as far as he could tell. *they can handle it.* He folded his sunglasses and tucked them carefully under the towel. He wasn't worried about them being lifted, but he didn't want them to get broken. He had that happen once down here because he'd been careless. *the Trading Post stocks them now, but man do they cost a bundle.*

He stepped out of the cubbyhole aisle and moved to the edge of the boardwalk. How to locate Julian? *look at that sea of splashing arms and bobbing heads! it's going to take forever to do the Buddy checks. so...* He began a systematic search, starting from where he stood at the boardwalk. *if I don't spot him in the shallows, I'll go along the F dock.*

"So, what are you planning?" Nick needed to know where to find Tom when the Buddy Whistle blew.

"I'm going to find our new patrol member. I want to know more about him."

oh-oh. Nick had forgotten about the slipup Tom made at breakfast. *I should have expected this. Julian's little butt is just what Tom likes best. that's a very bad thing nowadays. Tom has outgrown this hobby and doesn't realize it... he's almost nine inches now. even big butts have trouble handling that. well, then... I'd better keep an eye out... might have to do some blocking moves. Mark is counting on me to work with Julian on the newsletter.*

The Buddy whistle blew. Tom and Nick raised their arms, hands clasped. After three years at camp it was a reflex action, on dock or off. Tom used the opportunity to scan the area. He was in his element: stalking the game was a major part of the fun.

Julian tried doing some underwater breaststrokes, but he kept hitting legs all the time; he resorted to a modified underwater dog paddle, scooting along close to the bottom. He couldn't stay down for very long; having to come up for air all the time was a bother. He did this for quite a while, trying to improve. He scooted along, dodging legs... *it's kind of a dirty sand down here. out of breath again...* he surfaced near the boat dock. *yow!* Everyone had his arms raised.

I don't hear the whistle when I'm down there! He looked over at the platform. He waved at Danny—he was standing up looking around. Danny saw him at last and waved back and pointed. Julian pointed too and looked over to the lifeguard he'd talked to before. He got his attention, finally. *boy, it sure takes a long time.* Seeing all these guys with their arms up in the air was odd; but it made sense now... especially with so many swimmers. *I'm sort of glad now, actually; a real lifeguard knows I'm okay. yeah.*

Tom spotted Julian at last. *terrific. over near the first bank of canoes. I'll watch what he's doing, then make my move. where's Danny? must be a ways off, with Julian waving like that.* Tom looked around for a matching waving arm... *ha! on the platform. ideal. Danny won't get in the way, then.*

Nick had seen Julian as well. This told him how to shape the rest of the hour. *I'll keep watch from a distance. Tom has to go back to the tent before lunch, so Julian is relatively safe for the time being. there isn't much Tom can do in this crowd.* It wasn't likely that he'd take Julian up the trail this morning.

"I'll work on my speed some today. I'll do laps out to the platform and back."

"Got it. Thanks." Tom squatted down on his haunches to watch. *Julian is practicing something... at the whistle he ducked back under the water; what's he doing?*

Nick watched Tom's focus, briefly. *I should have expected something like this. if he's true to form, I should be able to delay him, at least.* Nick went to the end of the dock to dive. *no way to make a running jump today... too many bodies in the way. I'll work on my speed anyway. I need to be in good form for the test this afternoon.*

Tom did a quiet entry off the boat dock near the shower. He moved along the edge like an alligator. His prey was in sight. He'd been watching for a while, planning his approach. After Julian surfaced from a shallow dive, he came up alongside. "So, how far can you swim under water?"

"Oh, hi!" *wow.* Julian was flattered that Tom would pay him any attention. *maybe he can give me some good tips.* "I've never actually measured it. I can only stay under for about 30 seconds, I think."

"Not bad, not bad. Keep practicing and you can get it a lot better; I got up to a minute and a half a couple of years back."

"Wow! What's the record?"

"I don't know; some of those pearl divers can stay down for three minutes or so, I've heard."

"Do they have gills, or what?" Julian was amazed to hear that. He couldn't imagine being under water that long—*I can't do a minute even.*

"No, really. They do it in their families for generations. They learn to swim before they can walk. They even live on the boats." Tom was somewhat proud of his knowledge of matters aquatic.

"Wow. I bet you're a good swimmer. Can you swim across the lake?" Julian studied Tom's face. He hadn't done that yet. The beginnings of a mustache... *nifty*—half a dozen small fine black hairs ventured out just above the outer edge of his upper lips. *almost as tall as Mark... shoulders are just as broad. is he heavier? he's more muscular.* Julian fell into his pre portrait mode automatically when he studied a face closely—came in handy at times. *nose... sort of looks like the Indian on the nickel. straight black hair—not too short.*

"Yeah, I can do pretty well, I guess. I've never tried to swim all the way over there." Tom pointed to the dock on the opposite shore. "I think I could—I know I could. But getting back—that might be a problem." He laughed... he had swum almost halfway once to avoid being drafted as a lifeguard. He hated to be stuck in that chair, so he made them search for him when he could.

Julian bobbed up and down... he kind of wanted to swim some more. *it's important to be on Tom's good side... sometimes he's a little rough on young kids like me... a lot stricter than Mark is about things.* He didn't know what to say, exactly, so he just looked at Tom and smiled.

"I have an idea. How about I help you learn some things, like how to hold your breath, and dive. Do you like to dive?"

"I don't know any dives. Except the cannonball." Julian was impressed... *getting personal help from the troop star? yes! another benefit of being in the Flaming Arrow patrol.* "I could sure use help. The trouble is, all the diving spots are filled up." He pointed at the dock and boardwalk. They were jammed full of scouts. There was space out on the platform, but he didn't want to go out there.

"No problem. We can practice a few right here!"

Julian frowned. That didn't make any sense. *we're standing in three and a half feet of water.* "I don't get it… where would I jump from?"

"That's easy. I just make a stirrup, like this…" Tom held his hands up, locked together. "You raise your feet and I slip my hands under; I lift you real fast out of the water." He demonstrated, miming a lift. He squatted down so only his head showed above the water, then stood up fast. A rush of water flowed through Tom's hands.

Julian saw instantly that it would work. The water would make him light, and Tom was so strong he would zoom up. "Wow, that looks great. You wouldn't mind?"

"Naw, I've done this lots of times. We do this at the pool a lot to break in the little kids when they're learning to swim." He looked at Julian and raised his eyebrows. "You want to give it a try?"

"Sure!" *sounds like fun.* "So what do I do?"

"Just bend your knees and kick off the bottom with both feet as hard as you can. I come up from underneath with this stirrup hold and lift you up real fast. When I do that, you hold your arms into a point, so that when you enter the water again it will be smooth. Be sure to lower your head. You zoom under water as long as you can hold your breath, then you come up." Tom looked at Julian as if this was the easiest thing in the world to do.

"Yeah, I get it! Cool! Tell me when to start."

Tom moved around behind Julian. "Okay: when I say go, you count to three and then jump. That gives me time to get my hands in position. Ready?"

"Yeah!" *this is great! Tom is super!*

"Go!" Tom ducked down behind Julian in the water. *oh! look at those **cheeks**! as nice a pair as I've ever seen!*

'One. Two. Three.' Julian put his feet together and jumped. He felt Tom's hands slip under his feet and lift him fast. He forgot to keep his hands together and nearly lost his balance by wobbling to the left. His point was really bad—his elbows were bent. He came all the way out of the water, but only just. He got a mouthful of water before coming back up. He laughed and shook his head. "I really messed that up. Sorry. Can I do it again?" He felt silly, but maybe Tom didn't mind. *it felt so different from what I expected.*

"You bet; nobody does it right the first time." He got behind Julian again. "Be sure to kick off as hard as you can—go!" Tom submerged— *how long can I tempt myself like this?* Julian's crouch before kicking off brought that cute butt tantalizingly close to his face.

This time Julian did it much better. His arms were pointed, he kept a good balance, and he remembered to keep his head down. He zoomed out of the water completely, then came back down in a smooth arc into the water... *I forgot to start counting!* When he felt short of air, he surfaced. "Wow!" He was delighted. *what a sensation!* "I want to do that again!" He swam back over to Tom eagerly. "That's fantastic, Tom!" He was a little short of breath. "How many seconds do you think that was?"

Tom grinned ... *this is going well.* "I didn't count. Probably a good fifteen or twenty." *six more times should do it... I never used this ploy before. makes for a longer preliminary, but spending some time with this view is worth doing in its own right.* Julian was a little heavier than he liked, but he could handle it.

"Isn't that hard to do?" Julian didn't want to impose, but he wanted more of this—the catapult sensation was fabulous. *Tom is so strong!*

"Nah, piece of cake! We can do this all day. You ready?" He was perilously close to putting his nose too far forward... well within an inch when Julian bent his knees under water. *if this was Nick, I'd do a rude tongue jab.*

Julian nodded his head eagerly and turned around. He heard the 'Go!' and he was ready.

>> ***whoosh!*** <<

Wow... he could tell that he had reentered in a perfect arc. He looked ahead at his pointed hands... *that's the secret! I didn't get water up my nose!* He counted the seconds; at 25 his lungs were bursting and he came up for air. He breathed deeply and grinned back at Tom. He looked for Tom's reaction.

"That was a lot better! You learn fast. I'm really impressed."

Julian paddled back again, happy with his progress.

The Buddy whistle went off again.

"Who are you Buddy with?" Tom looked for Nick… *there he is, just pushing up onto the end of the F dock.* He raised his arm and pointed. He was glad to get a break; Julian was a little heavy for this.

"Danny," Julian waved his arm. "He's getting a suntan out on the platform." He saw Danny wave back. The lifeguard nodded at him. *boy, those guys are smart. how can they tell who is who out here? especially when they move around? the sudden quiet helps, probably. even so, there are a lot of arms stretched up.*

After the whistle they did a couple of lift-ups. Julian continued to improve. He could almost predict how he would do.

Tom had a revision to make in the process. "Okay—I have an idea. Instead of grabbing your feet from behind on the bottom, I'm going to come down over your head this time with my hands already clasped. When you feel my hands touch your toes, then jump. Okay?" *phase two.*

Julian nodded his head eagerly. They did this a couple of times. It did seem to go smoother; the leverage was improved, and he sailed out farther.

Tom had to turn his head when he did it this way… he had to avoid brushing his nose in just the right place. He wanted to save that surprise for later. *I have to concentrate on making the contact around in front just right. I can't see… it would be easy to bump Julian too hard.* His palm needed to make contact at just the right angle.

Julian noticed that Tom's hands brushed his cock on the way down. It didn't hurt… it was just an accident.

oop… that contact was a little too sharp. Tom adjusted it outward slightly on the next lift. *this is tricky.*

The hand brushed by again, not as strong. *hmm… Tom's trying to miss, at least. but the dives are going great!* "Wow!" Julian needed to catch his breath a second. He looked at Tom to see if he still wanted to do this.

"I think you're up by ten seconds from when you started," Tom was enthusiastic. "Do you want to go for a couple more?" He was ready to go to the next level. His arms were tired.

"Sure, if you want to." *it's fantastic that Tom would do this... he is sure strong. I'll try to last another two or three seconds on the next one.*

Tom slowed the speed that his hands dropped. This time he almost stroked that little cock on the way down.

Julian noticed that Tom's hand brushing him had sort of become regular. He wondered if Tom could be doing it on purpose. *problem is, I might get hard... I like getting hard—but I don't want to get a stiffy out here!*

Tom could feel that his "accidental" brushes were having the desired effect. *he's ready for the next step: phase three. it's time, too; my arms are about done for.* On the next one, he did not go to Julian's feet. He stopped halfway down and took the semi hard cock into his right hand and squeezed; he massaged the balls with his left hand.

Julian took a surprised breath.

"Don't sweat it." Tom spoke softly behind Julian's left ear. "Later on I can show you how to do other things." He let go.

Julian turned around and looked at Tom in surprise. He didn't know what to say. Suddenly things had changed. He tried to smile anyway… "Umm… okay…"

Tom reached out and squeezed again, briefly. "Count on it, you'll really like it."

Julian did not want to look ungrateful, but he was a little turned off. This was very different from Danny. He **didn't** like it. But he figured he'd better play along, for now. He sort of smiled… and gave a small nod. He tried to show that it was no big deal. He didn't know what to say.

Just then, the whistle blew. The lifeguard signaled that the free swim period was over. Julian was glad about that: he didn't want Tom to squeeze him again.

Tom gave the okay sign. "I gotta go back to camp." He looked at Julian for some kind of reaction… he'd gotten the message. Tom wasn't that impressed by the size of what he had felt. But he was interested in the other side, anyway. His plan to add Julian to his list of conquests was on schedule. He turned and swam to the boardwalk.

—⁓⁓—

Nick had paid attention to what was going on as well as he could, but he was a long way off. At least Tom had stayed in one area. He lifted himself onto the end of the F dock and walked rapidly back to the cubbyholes. He looked at Julian out of the corner of his eye, and saw a confused look on his face. *so Tom did something after all...* his brain got to work at once.

Tom was waiting for him at the Buddy Board. They'd checked out; Tom lowered his sunglasses onto his nose and tapped him on the shoulder.

"Beat ya by ten yards!" Tom took off running for the Meadow. He was in a great mood now. *this is how it's supposed to be.* The fresh image of those incredible cheeks in his mind had transformed the day! *I'll figure out the next step this afternoon—yeah! that will make duty in the guard chair go fast.* He pressed his mental speed button; he could hear Nick catching up.

Letting Tom win the usual footrace was one of Nick's routine gestures. It kept him connected, if nothing else. He pushed himself anyway—he had to look like he was trying. Tom was clearly satisfied with himself. *good. that will keep him off guard when the time comes.* Nick's experience was that when Tom was happy, he could be maneuvered and outsmarted without much difficulty. *I'll be able to keep a step ahead most likely; I need to keep Julian out of Tom's reach—for a while, at least.*

—⁂—

Julian was troubled. He didn't know whether or not to talk to Danny about this—*I just remembered! Danny told me this morning that Tom and Nick liked to goof around with boys. I thought he meant with each other! gosh, gossh! is everybody in the patrol going to play around with me or something? this is getting complicated.* Julian walked back through the shallow water to the boardwalk. He lifted himself up and sat on the edge for a minute. *hmm... what did Tom mean by "other things?"* He kicked his feet in the water briefly, puzzling about the unexpected event. He swung around and stood up; the boardwalk was swarming with scouts. He couldn't even see the cubbyholes... the crowd was too thick.

I have to wait; he leaned against the lifeguard tower. *hmm... things* were starting to click. *maybe he meant sucking! ooo! maybe Danny wants to suck me too. hmmm! now* **that** *I would like to do. but Tom? I'm not so hot for that idea. 'course, I haven't had a chance to see Tom's* *equipment, other than at Certification yesterday... kinda big.* Besides, that unexpected underwater grab was unwelcome.

Danny pulled up out of the water and walked up the dock to the cubbyholes. He could see Julian leaning against the tower chair. "Hey, Julian," he waved happily. *I'm glad the swim is over; my back feels a little warm.*

"Hi," Julian waved back at Danny... *hmm. maybe I won't mention what happened yet.* The crowd had begun to thin out; he went over to the Buddy Board and got the badges off their hooks. He made his way to the cubbyhole. *now there's room to get dressed.* He handed Danny his badge.

"Hey, thanks. We're supposed to be in uniform at lunch, you know." That meant they had to go to the Flaming Arrow camp and get dressed all over again. He snuck glances as they dressed... *Julian is still as pretty as he was this morning.* Remembering things when he was out on the platform had caused him some trouble. He had to spend most of his time on his stomach. Too many guys kept coming and going, and he didn't want them to see his persistent boner problem. He walked over to the check out line with Julian. He held his towel in front just to be safe.

Leonard noticed Danny's interest in Julian as they approached. He also noticed that his bulge was in transition—going down or up; he hadn't seen him dressing. He's probably receding now. *delicious.* He winked at Julian. It was just a friendly gesture, not a tease... *oh...* his gesture went unnoticed. *he's preoccupied. problems?* "Have a good swim?"

Julian's eyes focused. He saw Leonard's friendly face. He smiled automatically. "Oh—hi. I practiced my dives some... yeah." He was glad to have his attention shifted.

"Well, that's something, with this crowd today! How did you do?"

"I got up to 35 seconds at holding my breath!"

Leonard was delighted by Julian's tone. *he's okay.* "Good for you! Well, the lake isn't always this busy... next time you'll have more room to practice." His wink was seen this time... Julian's smile charmed.

Danny nudged Julian as they went out of the gate. "You want to race?"

"Nah. You go on ahead. I don't feel like running right now." *I'd just as soon be by myself for a little, actually.* He waved a last Buddy wave and sent Danny on his way. He turned and waved at Leonard too. Leonard made him feel good, for some reason. *he doesn't have on those sunglasses like the lifeguards, for one thing. he has interesting eyes. you can tell he's a good guy from his eyes.*

He started back to camp, thinking as he went. *does Mark know about these guys? probably not. should I tell him about Tom? maybe I should... I don't want to be a fink though. I'd better just think about this for a while. the afternoon is going to be a lot of fun... I don't want to get distracted.* Julian looked forward to the merit badges. He picked up his pace back to camp. *I don't need to be late for lunch. I've screwed up enough for one day already.*

18   *lunch with Sid*

Back at the cabin, Julian took off his tennies and crew sox. He didn't like to wear his long scout socks, especially when it was this warm. *oh well; dress is dress.* He put on his long socks. *oh*—he just realized: *I didn't bring my brown scout dress shoes.* His mom wanted him to take real good care of those, so he left them at home. She said he wouldn't get another pair until his feet grew too big. *I'm sorry my scout stuff costs so much... I'll outgrow everything again before another year goes by.* He pulled his boots out from under the cot—*hum...* he didn't want to put them on, especially. *they aren't any more dress than tennies, are they? these things are so heavy and clunky... and they squeal when I wear them indoors.* The solution was obvious: "Tennies it is!"

He tucked the boots away again and stood. "Get a move on, Julian!" He took off his Troop Nine T-shirt, folded it neatly, and with a grin, put it in the footlocker—he had reserved a space for used clothing. Normally, he wasn't this organized. But his mom had gone on and on about keeping his dirty clothes and his clean clothes separate, so he promised—anything to get her off the subject. Mothers had funny ideas about some things, that's all—especially dirty clothes. *too bad I don't have a camera so I could show her this.* He went to the rack to get his scout shirt and kerchief. *amazing that Mark lets me hang these here.*

ooo! He leaned over and sniffed Mark's shirt—it was a few inches to the right. *oh: smells fresh. he hasn't worn this one yet... that's nice, but I wanted to smell Mark. shucks. maybe I'll get to do that tonight!* He shrugged; it made sense for Mark to have a duplicate shirt. He reached for his scout dress shirt—his eye caught the hat, sitting on the shelf above. *wow...* gently, he took it down and held it carefully in front of his face. The rim... *so firm.* He felt the contours on the crown. It was strange and wonderful. He couldn't resist: he put it on. *oop... a little big.* He giggled: *I gotta look...* He held it on with his right hand and went to the bathroom.

huh. He was surprised, actually. He wasn't at all sure about how he felt. It looked so impressive on Mark. *doesn't make me look impressive at all...* he let his right hand fall to the side, and the hat settled an inch down his forehead. He burst out laughing at the sight. He took it off and went back to the rack, feeling very silly. Carefully, as if it was fragile, he returned the hat to its shelf. He grabbed the kerchief off his shirt and flopped it over his shoulder. He took his scout shirt off the hanger and slipped his right arm into the sleeve. "Maybe if I'd had this and the kerchief on..." he chuckled again. *at least no one was here to see that.*

As he buttoned up, he stepped over to check the schedule Mark had posted. Lunch at the main hall today, then merit badges. Those all had the dress uniform star next to them. He looked down the list... *Forestry is in space F. after that I go to Archery at the range.* "It's sorta like school only a whole bunch better!" *one of the benefits of staying in the cabin: I can always see what's up.* He hadn't seen his badge partners yet today, but he was sure they'd be there. Dress uniform meant he was supposed to wear his kerchief. He pulled it off his shoulder, spread it out on the cot and rolled it to the six-inch point. He turned up his shirt collar and took the kerchief and slide into the bathroom. He enjoyed the ritual of donning his uniform.

As always, he looked in the mirror while he put the kerchief around his neck. The red and yellow colors made the official patches on his shirt look so cool. Dark olive was an ideal background color. The logo on his slide was centered just right... he winked at himself. "You look just fine without that hat." His hair was still damp and messed up. He dried it with his huge bath towel; he smiled at the towel, then re-folded it reverently. *I haven't figured out yet how to use this. all that swimming makes taking a shower stupid. hmm.* "Maybe one of these days I won't swim so I can give you a job." He hung it on the rack; whether he used it or not, it was a special towel.

He pulled out his pocket comb. *oh!* the safety razor caught his eye. He picked it up and looked at it closely. *huh. such a thin blade... you twist the knob on the end to open and close it...* he felt the edge... *whoa... sharp!* He ran it across his cheek gently... *wow, this **is** sharp.* "Don't cut yourself dum-dum... mmm..." He grinned and did a pretend shave stroke. He laughed and put the razor down; it looked funny to do that. *I can hardly wait to watch Mark do it.* He finished his hair, and returned the comb to the back of the washbasin. *wait...* he slipped it into his back pocket—he planned to swim after merit badge classes were over. *I'll need it at the lake.* He hightailed it to the door—no need to straighten up the discarded sox. *won't be another inspection until tomorrow. time to scoot! maybe I'll see Mark at lunch!* He grabbed his tablet and the orange towel *oo! has Danny gone already?*

The line going into the HQ wasn't very long—twenty guys or so. That was good, because his appetite had kicked in. *hmm... I don't see Danny... must be inside already. nobody else I know, either. oh well.* He was curious about this big building. *didn't have much of a chance to look at it yesterday at the barbecue. style is clever—they use wood and logs outside to make it look like it's in the frontier wilderness; inside it's pretty much a modern building—tile floors just like at school, lots of big windows, rows of fluorescent lights overhead. doesn't look new, just well kept. walls are knotty pine, just like the cabin. good style for a camp in the forest.*

The guy in front of Julian was kind of big, hard to see around. When the line turned the corner he couldn't see ahead. The kitchen aromas weren't very strong... hard to tell what was coming up, actually. *I'll know pretty soon... the line is almost to the pass through window.* He took a tray off the stack and inched forward.

Lunch was pretty basic... choice of tuna or bologna sandwiches; Julian decided on tuna—lots of guys took both kinds; carrot and celery sticks, milk or lemonade... *ooo! chocolate chip cookies! one of my favorites. especially the ones Hazel makes.* He looked close: *fresh baked! mmm.* No utensils needed... this is like the cafeteria at school. The crew was friendly. Their shirts were bright yellow... *cool: you can tell what a person does by the color of his shirt.* The camp symbol was printed on the back. *I wonder if they sell those in the Trading Post—I might be tempted to get one for a souvenir. look...* A man in a big chef's hat was in there working away. *must be getting things ready for supper. what a funny mustache! wow... that's about the fastest lunch line I've ever been in. better grab a napkin.*

Danny was nowhere in sight... *maybe I can spot somebody from Wolf patrol... aha!* **perfect!** *Sid's over there, close to the trash bin. odd to see him all alone... where's Jeremy? oh, there he is, talking to Kurt.*

that's right—on the bus he told Mark he was doing the Canoe badge with Kurt. Julian trotted over and put his tray on the table next to Sid.

"Hey, Wolf!" He gave a friendly elbow to Sid's side as he pulled up a chair. He was tempted to give the Wolf call, but thought that might be silly in here.

"Julian!" Sid was surprised. "So what's up? You never came back to the tent after campfire. This morning I saw your stuff was gone."

"Mark moved me over to the Flaming Arrow last night." He looked at Sid and did an eyebrow raise. He grinned wide and munched on his carrot stick.

"Oh yeah, that's right! Danny told us at the end, that's right. Wow! What's it like, being with all the big shots? Do you have to stand on a bench to be seen, or what?"

Camp Walker Headquarters

1	Main Entrance	15	Pillows, Blankets, Tarps
2	First Aid	16	Moveable Worktable
2b	Recovery	17	Sink
3	Trading Post	18	Delivery Entrance
3b	Supply Room	19	Dishwashing
3c	Office/Security	20	Kitchen
4	Rest Room	21	Dry good Stores
5	Stairway up	22	Walk-in Cooler/Freezer
6	Laundry	23	Prep Tables
7	Instructor's Office	24	Grills
8	Camp Director Office	25	Ovens
9	Foods Office	26	Food Assembly
10	Camp Ranger's Office	27	Pass Through
11	Workbench	28	Assembly/Dining Hall
12	Supplies and Equipment Warehouse	29	Safety Exit
12b	Hand Carts	30	Table Storage
13	Tool Cage	31	Waterfront Director
14	Featherbed Storage	32	Activity Director

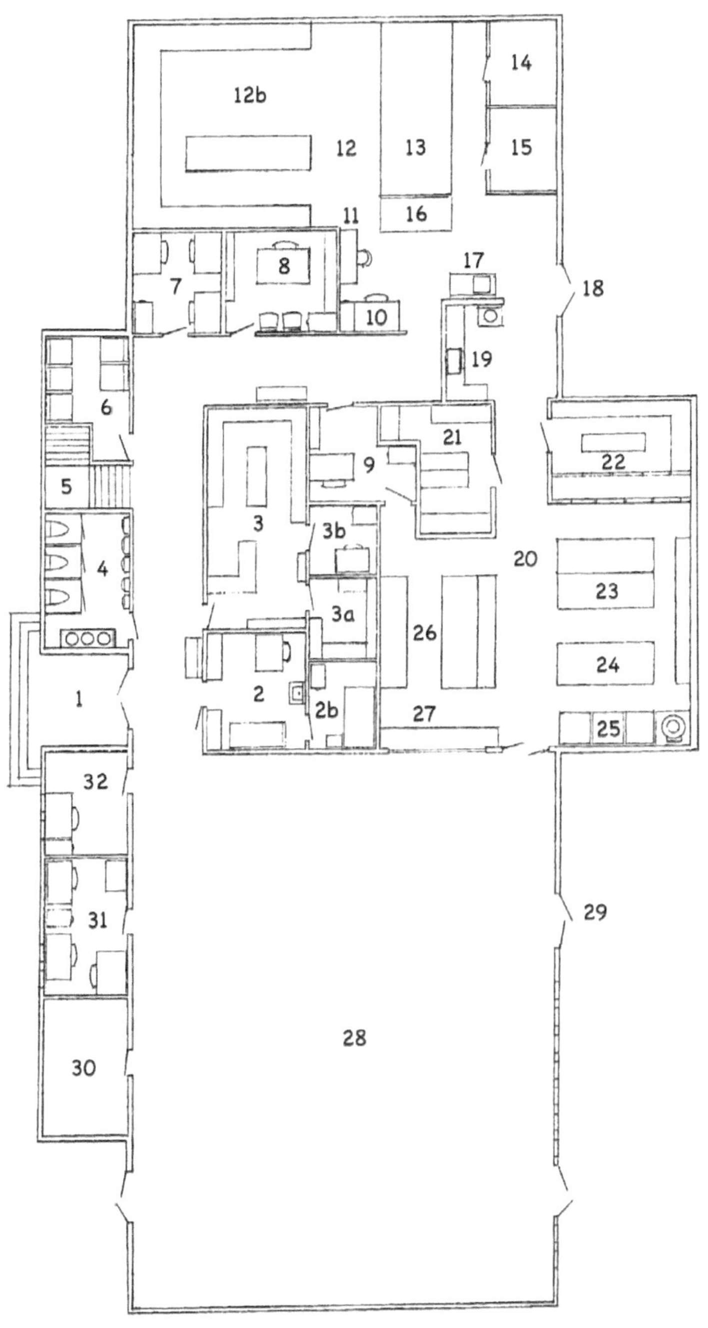

Julian laughed. *I love Sid's jokes. it's true: I am the shortest in the Flaming Arrow, as well as the youngest.* "It's really cool. I got to make Mark's coffee this morning." No brag, just fact. He looked at Sid smugly.

"Well, I'm glad you got there in time!" Sid scarfed down a big bite of his bologna sandwich. He grinned back, a little envious. "Really, though. What's it like? What do you have to do?"

"This morning I helped Danny cook breakfast. I guess I get to do that all week, maybe all camp, I don't remember exactly. I'll tell you this: they have the fanciest stove of all. It's propane and has four burners and an **oven**. We could cook for the whole troop on it, I think."

"Hmm. Ours is on loan from a playschool… so what did you fix?"

"I did pancakes, and Danny fried sausage patties. We had OJ and milk. No big deal." Julian examined the cross section of his sandwich: *different from Mom's… the sweet pickle bits are interesting… no hard boiled egg chunks. tastes different, but it's okay… more fishy maybe.*

"Mmm, sounds just like ours. Casey is the Wolf patrol's breakfast cook. Maybe everybody has the same menu around here."

"Prob'ly. Makes it easier to shop for a bunch this big. They prob'ly get it wholesale," Julian opined.

"Makes sense," Sid nodded. He glanced across the room full of scouts feeding their face. *there must be over five hundred in here… how many quarts of milk and OJ would that take every morning? the camp must get a pretty good discount, at that.* He looked over at Julian. *Julian's pretty smart to think of that.*

They chewed some. Julian regarded his tuna sandwich again. *not that great.* "What's your favorite food?"

"I got a lot of those… I got so many it's a miracle I'm not a major chub, like Bruce." *I could use a few of Bruce's extra pounds.*

Julian had to laugh. Bruce was very round. Joining scouts was supposed to help fix that. He had a ways to go.

"Lasagna. Whenever my mom makes that I want to really stuff myself. That's a likely number one. Why?"

"I dunno. No special reason. I was just thinking about how many different things different people like. I think we've had lasagna a couple of times in those frozen dinners. I like it."

"So what's yours?" Sid polished off the last bite of his bologna sandwich. *needs more mayo.* He started on his first cookie.

Julian pondered… *either fried chicken or baked ham.* "Tie prob'ly between chicken or ham 'n peas." *there's meatloaf too…* "How about dessert?"

"Gotta go with lemon meringue pie on that one…" That made his eyes close for a second. He really did like that. "I get it! You're gonna be the magic chef over at Flaming Arrow. Dream on. Maybe if you could secretly order out…"

"Say, that's an idea! Do they have a cooking merit badge?"

"Are you kidding? They got a merit badge for everything. No way could you ever get 'em all. Cooking's gotta be on the list. If they have beekeeping, they gotta have cooking! Sid consumed his first cookie in two bites. *mmm: fresh baked!*

"Beekeeping? Seriously? Who'd ever do that?"

"I saw it on the list. I guess it's big down in the orchards." Sid searched for another wisecrack, but none was handy. "You still gonna do the Forestry?"

"Sure," Julian was enthusiastic. "Right after lunch. All that other stuff is the same. The only real big deal is I have to work with Nick and Mark to get out the newsletter." He nibbled at the chocolate chip cookie… *mm. as good as I thought. nice…* he dunked it into his milk. "Gaah!" The cookie broke apart!

"Way to go, Joe!" Sid laughed. "I hate it when that happens."

"S-D-H." Julian muttered, tipping his glass to look at the chunks. *dissolving already. I need a spoon.*

"What's **that** mean?"

Julian looked around to see if anyone was paying attention. "It's a demerit-free cussword I invented."

Sid thought about it. 'S.' *that's obvious;* 'D' … *well, duh!* 'H.' *the simplicity is very nice.* "That's cute. That I will steal. Shakes!"

They faced each other and did the Troop Handshake.

The cleanup crew came through collecting debris and dirty glasses. *huh… we don't have to take our trays to the cleanup table? that's pretty deluxe.* Julian said a silent goodbye to his drowned cookie. *at least I have one left;* he tucked it into his shirt pocket for later. He and Sid got up and set out for the merit badge workshops.

19   *merit badges*

"See ya later, alligator." Sid turned off at the A sign.

so, that's the entrance to the First Aid space.   Julian was sorry he hadn't signed up for that, but he'd already agreed to be Justin's partner in Forestry. He continued up the trail to the space F path. Justin was a year younger; Mark asked Julian to be Justin's guide and helper when he first joined. *he's a Zebra... very shy.* He finished his Tenderfoot and Second Class early. Mark said how pleased he was with Justin's progress; *gave me a big chunk of the credit.* Julian knew it wasn't earned—Justin was a hard worker and serious about scouts. *I didn't have to do a thing, really. I have to actually do something to show Mark I deserve the compliment. working on this badge will help a lot.*

The trail into space F was farther than he expected; the pavilion and worktables were not visible outside the clearing. The scoutmaster of Troop Seven handed Julian a fact sheet as he entered. He was the fifth to arrive... three picnic style tables were arranged in a U. *looks like there'll be around eighteen in the group...* different plant samples, pinecones, leaves, and some flowers were placed on the tables.

there he is... Justin was studying the handout sheet at the left table— in front of him a small vase held a white flower. Julian walked up behind quietly... he felt mischievous all of a sudden. Crouching, he reached slowly toward Justin's neck... just above the kerchief, he tickled very lightly with his fingertip.

Justin felt a fly trying to land on his neck. He brushed it away automatically and returned his attention to the plant list handout. A second later that pesky fly was back. He shook his head sharply. A second later it was there again! *okay then...* Slowly, he moved his right hand across his chest. *I'll slap it quick before it sees my hand coming.* Came the tickle, and **whap!** he struck.

!! that isn't a fly! He turned around.

"Good shot, Ace!" Julian laughed, and patted Justin on the shoulder as he sat down. "How's it going?"

"Hi, Julian. You fooled me at first! I thought it was a fly, or something." He was happy to see Julian. He pushed his glasses up on his nose. "It's really different from what I thought! I like it, but there are so many scouts here! At swimming it's solid bodies almost."

"I know! But it's run really well. You don't have to wait very long in the chow line, at least." *Justin is still shy in large groups.* "You'll get used to it pretty soon. I was a little worried at first, but everybody's so friendly! What about the Campfire last night? Was that cool, or what?"

"Yeah! That guy going up the stairs! How does he do that?"

"Yeah! If I see him around I'm going to ask. Wouldn't it be great to pick that up while we're here? Wouldn't you just love to do that at school next fall?"

That is something Justin would **never** want to do. He was much better suited to being in the audience, thank you. "I wouldn't mind if I could do it at home." Justin was thought of as rather talent-less at home. He could use something to raise his rating there a little. Even his little sister didn't take him seriously.

Julian looked at the handout. "Man, do we have to learn all these words by heart?" There were three columns. The left was real technical terms, the second was sort of understandable, and the third was labeled "slang name." He skimmed down that one; he recognized lots of things… a bunch were new.

"My name is Henderson," said the tall man in front of them.

Everyone was present and ready to start. Julian looked up at Scoutmaster Henderson; he hadn't looked at him closely on the way in. *half bald… pretty old, maybe in his forties. looks like he knows what he's doing… look at that sash—covered with merit badges!* He'd never seen that many.

"Thank you for signing up for this badge. I know you'll be glad you did. First, I want each of you to think of how many different plants you saw as you came into this area. I'll give you two minutes to think about it, then I'll ask you to tell the group how many. You may look around from where you are, but you have to stay seated. Ready?" He looked at his wristwatch. As the second hand reached the top he said, "your two minutes begin now!"

Julian sat up... he looked straight ahead and counted three kinds of tree. *one is a pine. not sure about the other two—oak? I've heard of oak.* He turned his head and began to note grass, then a small flower. *we did some of this when I was a Bear, but I mostly forgot it... this is interesting.* He folded down a finger every time he spotted a different one. *do the ones on the table count?* The label by the vase read "Trillium." *that's a silly name—there are only three petals. oh, wait: I was thinking of trillion. never mind.*

All the boys were on task. Scott Henderson was pleased with what he saw. A good looking bunch out of the gate; no reason to think any wouldn't get it done. He watched the second hand.

After the Forestry session, Julian had to hurry down the trail. The short forest tour that Mr. Henderson had taken them on went a little overtime, because they had stopped to watch a wild turkey poking through the woods. It was a lot smaller than Julian expected—more like a big chicken, actually. *didn't have that big fan around the back. Mr. Henderson said that was because it was a young hen... kind of a boring bird, really. didn't even go gobble-gobble.* He started to run... it didn't help that the Archery Range was all the way past the HQ building, about as far away as it could be.

When he got there, Cory was waiting, his arms crossed, "Thanks-a-lot!" written all over his face.

"Sorry, man, I couldn't help it." Julian caught his breath. "The last guy let us go late! What's going on?"

"Not too much, but you got to check in. Hurry back, 'cause I'm not supposed to use this until there are two of us here." He held up the bow in his right hand. "You better..." *too late.* Cory was about to tell him about the bow sizes. Julian had missed the opening instructions about that.

Julian hustled over to the equipment shelter, where the Junior Counselor assistant, clad in a green staff T-shirt, was slouching in a folding chair with his arms folded across his chest. There was a clipboard on the table; Julian saw his name on the list. "That's me... I'm kind of late." The counselor looked sort of grouchy. "Sorry."

"What weight?"

"109..." Julian tilted his head. *what an odd question.*

Junior Counselor Mason gave him a dark look.

Julian had done something wrong. He didn't know what... he waited to be told.

"The **bow**, not you," Mason smiled, condescendingly. He looked at Julian. *probably needs the smallest one, but I'm under orders to not make recommendations.* "You can have a ten pound, fifteen pound, or twenty pound."

Julian was still in the dark. He looked at the rack; three sizes were mounted on the display, along with several styles of arrow. He pointed to the middle one. It seemed as good a guess as any. *how could it weigh that much?*

"Fifteen it is. Sign your name on the center clipboard." Mason reached back and pulled a fifteen out of the bin. "You'll start with a single end. Wait for the signal before retrieving any loosed arrows." He handed Julian three arrows and smiled thinly. "Don't forget to take a rule sheet." *hard to believe this one made First Class.*

that's it? I can go back to Cory now? I feel like a complete dunce around here. He smiled at the counselor, but it didn't do any good.

"Time's a-wasting." Mason made a slight shooing motion. He had his doubts about this kid's prospects... *a little slow, to say the least.* He glanced at the clipboard. *at least they're all here now. I can sit back for an hour. this is one of the most boring duties they could have laid on me. at least I didn't have to do the first period class session.*

Julian's arm was so **sore**... massaging it didn't help. *Archery is supposed to be fun. not today.* The bow was incredibly hard to pull. Plus, the string sometimes hit his left forearm behind his wrist. *that doesn't feel good at all, either. I need one of those sleeve things some of the guys had on. will my arm get better by tomorrow? I had to let Cory have some of my shots. I'll probably get the ten pound bow tomorrow. Cory had a*

fifteen pound too; he said it didn't matter which one you used. He rubbed his right arm again. *I bet Mark could use the big twenty pound one.* Missing the opening instructions hadn't helped any, either. *the counselor thought I was a real dodo... I can't figure out why they call them by pounds. they don't weigh anywhere near that much. sure are a lot of odd words to learn.*

Julian's fantasy about becoming one of the merry men in the forest seemed pretty far-fetched, now. He used to watch Robin Hood every week when he was a Cub... *it looked so easy when they climbed up the trees and ambushed the Sheriff's posse. they could go through a whole quiver full of arrows without batting an eye. how could they do that? I could hardly pull the string back.* He walked slowly toward the lake, massaging his arm. Cory had run on ahead; he had to go to the Trading Post.

another thing: how come the arrows here don't make that cool whooshing zip sound? you could always tell when an arrow was Robin Hood's—it made that twangy sound when it hit, too.

After Archery the afternoon free period started. He knew from looking at Mark's chart that today was a little special. He had a choice between doing some more archery in the free shoot or volunteering to be a rescue victim at the lifesaving session at the lake. *that would be best... I can rest my arm, at least. besides, the archery isn't free at all: you have to buy your own target sheet.* That meant running up to the Trading Post and back. *I don't have any money with me, anyway.*

20   *Lifesaving test*

When Julian reached the lake they were busy doing something over on the boat dock side of the boardwalk. Others were being directed to the cubbyhole area. *they're just getting organized. since Archery is so close by, I got here in plenty of time.* He grabbed his Buddy Badge and went through the gate. He smiled wide—*Leonard is there telling people what to do. I like Leonard.*

"Hello, there!" Leonard was delighted to see this one again. "Are you going to join in?"

"I thought it would be fun. Besides, I'm trying to improve my swimming all I can. This might help." He handed over his badge. It was a relief to see Leonard after being with that sourpuss guy at the Archery Range.

"You won't need to put that on the Board unless you plan to stay for Free Swimming. Do you have a Buddy?" It looked unlikely, unless someone else was coming along later…

Julian shook his head.

"I'll keep it safe here. After the Lifesaving tests, you can put it back—or on the swimming side, if you hook up with someone." *my word, this boy's eyelashes are…* he caught himself. *behave, Leonard.* He watched Julian head over to the volunteer group. Troop 9 on the arm patch; *one of Tom's flock. interesting.*

Julian grinned happily and headed for the cubbyholes with a skip. *I didn't even think about getting a Buddy; lucky I don't need one to be a rescue victim. I can work on my sketch if they don't need me. so few scouts are here… opposite of this morning. no problem finding a cubbyhole…* he chose one near the top and tucked in his tablet and towel. *they ought to find a better way to deal with towels around here. carrying it around all afternoon is a nuisance. why couldn't they build more cubbyholes? if they had more, you could just reserve one and leave your towel here… maybe I'll ask Leonard about that. he's so nice about things.*

After Julian and the others undressed, a man named Matt Smith assembled all the "victims" at the boardwalk end of the F dock. *a swim instructor—very muscular—name embroidered his blue T-shirt pocket, just like Leonard's.* He gave a general set of instructions. They were supposed to swim out past the dock ends into deep water and pretend to be in trouble. An advanced swimmer would swim out from the boardwalk and rescue them. The victims were supposed to perform different scenarios. In some they would be limp and out of it with faces down. In others, they were supposed to pretend to be panicked and to struggle and have to be calmed down. The rescuers would be graded on everything they did. When the judge thought they had shown proficiency, they would be awarded the rating and get the Lifesaving merit badge. It was one of the hardest to get—required if you want to be an Eagle.

Julian bounced up and down on his toes—*this is going to be fun!* He looked around briefly: *whoa! Tom's sitting up in the lifeguard chair… why is that?* He hadn't had time to think about Tom yet. *is he going to be up there the whole time? maybe keeping clear of him would be a good idea—especially since I don't have a Buddy this afternoon. I don't need any more under water squeezes. hmm… maybe I won't look for a Swim Buddy—*

"Ow!" Someone punched Julian right on his tender arm.

"Sorry…" Nick hadn't hit hard at all. "I get to rescue you!"

"Cool…" Julian rubbed his arm. "But go easy on the right arm." He was surprised to see Nick here—*he has on some old school clothes. they're all wet.*

"What's the matter?"

"I just spent over an hour trying to shoot arrows, and my arm really aches. I never thought it would be so hard."

"Oh yeah… I know what you mean. You picked too big a bow." Nick rubbed Julian's arm gently. "I'm sorry… pick the next size down tomorrow. After the third or fourth day, maybe you can try the bigger size again. he bigger ones have more power and range, but the small ones work fine."

"Oh. I used the middle one."

"Ah, the fifteen… use a ten. It's a matter of basic muscle strength. You might want to get some weights and work on the biceps in your spare time." He pinched Julian's bicep gently. *yep… spaghetti arm.* "You could spend some free time at the range with the ten pound and build up that way."

"Oh." Julian didn't like that idea. He didn't want to buy a target, especially. He said a mental S-D-H. He looked at Nick's wet shirt and jeans. "What's up?"

"We've been doing the emergency floatation tests and undressing in the water. We're done with that part now. The last thing we have to demonstrate is our ability in a distance rescue. We have to shuck our clothes to improve our mobility and swim at least twenty yards to the victim. I brought this outfit along so I wouldn't have to do all that in my uniform."

Julian was taken aback. "Do I have to put mine back on?" He looked around—all the other volunteers were undressed too.

"No, you're fine. You know what to do, don't you?"

"I think so… where do you want me to drown first?"

Nick laughed. "Pretend drown, please. We have to go to my slot at the end of the boardwalk. Mr. Franklin will give us the signal to go." He led Julian toward the boat dock. "Officially, I'm number eight today." He looked out toward the lake. "You'll swim out there, as soon as we get the signal." He pointed to the line of rowboats stationed about thirty yards away.

"Are you doing the face down kind or the wild and crazy one?"

"Let's start with a passive. I'm supposed to do two of those. That means you pretend to be unconscious and face down in the water. I'm supposed to turn you over and bring you to shore." Nick looked at Julian to see if he understood. *he seems bright enough.*

"Okay. Face down. I swim out there, take a deep breath and go under. Then I hope that you get there in time for me to take another breath. Right?"

"Right."

Julian looked out to the lake... *the end of the dock is a long way from here. good thing I practiced holding my breath this morning. I got up to thirty seconds with Tom's help. can Nick get there in thirty seconds?*

Nick watched for the signal... Mr. Franklin gave a nod for him to go. "Now is the time. I'll be keeping track of you, so don't worry. You are guaranteed to be rescued because I'm gonna need your notes." Nick slapped Julian on the left bun lightly. "Take off!"

ooo... that little pat surprised. *odd... felt kind of good.* He hopped into the water and started swimming. *hey... in the water my arm isn't that bad.* Out about two yards beyond the end of the boat dock he tried to stand.

blurp! Over the head deep... *that was pretty stupid! I know it's deep out here...* he bobbed back up. About fifteen feet away a rowboat caught his attention. *the lifeguard is looking at me... I hope I'm doing this right.* Julian turned around and looked back to shore. Nick was poised, and watching. Julian waved his hand—he saw Nick start to undress. *man, he's moving fast. he must have been practicing. gosh!* Danny had just taken a big step off the boardwalk into the water. *huh... how come he didn't dive?*

Julian took a deep breath and let himself slip downward. He pretended he was moving in slow motion, like in a dream. He rolled onto his stomach and looked down... *too deep to see the bottom. maybe I went out too far... I don't want to run out of breath completely before Nick shows up.*

strange, sort of fun, letting my arms float out... relaxing... The motion of the water lifted one arm, then the other. *I must look odd from shore*—Julian had a sudden urge to laugh: he pictured his butt poking out of the water like an iceberg. *showing my butt to all these lifeguards would be fun. trouble is, my buns won't float up to the top. poo. only my head and arms poke out of the water... next time I'll take a deeper breath.* He felt the water lapping against his ears. *I'll pay attention to that... hurry up Nick! my 30 seconds are about gone...*

Just in time he felt Nick take his arm. He pulled it around in front and twisted just right—Julian was forced to turn on his back. "Blub-blub..." he said happily. He took a quick breath just as Nick put a hand under his chin.

Nick chuckled. "You okay?"

"Yeah," Julian took another deep breath. "Your timing is perfect. I was just about to change to the panic lesson." Nick's swimming was smooth and powerful; impressive, considering he could only use one arm. He had a good rhythm. About every third stroke, they bumped... *that part's nice. I'm as limp as Lucy's stupid rag doll—feels weird, being pulled through the water on my back.* It was enjoyable, actually—except *for having my chin forced back like this.* "Am I still supposed to be unconscious? Can I open my eyes, at least?"

"Leave 'em closed. We're almost there." Nick was doing okay, but talking took too much breath. *this is tougher than I expected...* ten more feet to shore.

"Nice turnover, Harrison." Franklin made a note on the clipboard as they approached the boardwalk. He stepped to the right and addressed the next candidate. "Next we have... ah, it's Mr. Jenkins. Ready, CJ?"

Nick released Julian and they paused briefly at the bar pipe that ran along the boardwalk. He shook his head and breathed heavily. *I did not expect to be this short of breath. man, am I glad I was required to shuck those clothes.*

"Was that good, then?" Julian expected the coach to say more.

"Yeah, I guess so! That's one down and two to go. The passive one, like we just did, is harder to do, that's why I'm doing them first."

Julian was fascinated. This badge might not be too hard after all. *except for my puny arms. maybe I couldn't pull someone else along very far.* He watched the next guy being rescued. "Is that what we just did?"

Nick frowned. He hiked himself out of the water and sat on the edge of the boardwalk. "Not exactly. He's bringing in the same way, but the turnover was across the chest." *I'll do that one next.*

Julian joined him on the boardwalk. They watched a few others finish their first rescue. He chuckled to himself.

"What's so funny?" Nick toweled himself dry. *time to get dressed again.*

Julian looked at him with a sheepish grin. "I was just looking out there—I wondered what I might look like from shore," he pointed, "if my rear poked out of the water as well as my head. I couldn't get it to float up, though."

Nick chuckled. "I never thought about that! That's funny!" *that would make other turnover techniques possible—the bun grab from the side maneuver. Tom would like that one.* He stood and dried off his legs.

They heard Mr. Franklin call out: "Six! You're up!"

Nick dressed again... *these wet clothes are so hard to put on.* He sat back on his heels to wait. "How's the arm?"

Julian rubbed it. "Better. Yeah, better!" He looked at Nick. He'd never paid much attention to him before. *seems to be a really nice guy. I'll be working with him on the newsletter.* He studied Nick's profile. *not handsome like Danny... but he isn't bad looking, either... he's average... yeah, a truly average looking person. huh. I've never thought about that before. they're okay, average people... yeah, really okay. I'll give them more credit in the future. huh. average is a stupid idea, anyway, if you think about it. everybody is different in some way.*

"So we do another like the last one, right?" He stood; he could see that his turn was coming up again. He was ready...

Nick nodded yes.

"Say, why didn't you dive before? Wouldn't that be faster?" Julian had seen him step off the edge of the boardwalk just as he went down.

"I'd flunk the test instantly if I did that. You're supposed to keep your eyes on the victim at all times. That way you know exactly where they are, especially if they go back under, like you did."

"Wow." *this isn't as simple as it looks.* Julian watched another rescuer bring in his victim. His head is pulled back so hard... *kind of rough... Nick is better at this.*

The call for eight came, and Julian dove in. As he swam he noticed that his arm was even better. *surprising... water must help.* Soon he was close to the rowboat again—there was a whole string of them. He turned around. *if you didn't go so far out dum-dum, Nick could get here quicker... oh well.* He looked at the shore, and Mr. Franklin signaled okay. This time he practiced taking a deep breath twice before going under. Nick just walked into the water—*that looks very odd, actually.* He waved his arm and sank out of sight.

Julian opened his eyes... he let his body relax completely. He floated to the surface. *my butt still won't go up out of the water. that was as deep a breath as I could take, too.* He looked below. *any fish out here? must be, because there's a Fishing merit badge group. they probably stay clear of the swimmers... it's roomy enough for them out here this afternoon, though.* He felt his arms float up... his hands broke the surface. This time he spread his legs slightly as they floated up. *I can't tell how much is visible above the water. I bet my balls have shrunk completely out of sight—the water is cold, must be a cold stream out here.* The water lapped at his ears. *must be waves from the next rescue over or something...* the slapping sound was annoying. He felt his hair floating. *I can almost picture it, waving back and forth in the water. I'm starting to enjoy this— ooop! Nick's here already!*

Nick ran his arm under Julian's chest and turned him over in the water. He started to swim, keeping one arm over the chest this time, his hand high up against Julian's chin—it forced his mouth to stay closed.

Julian could tell Nick was trying a lot harder. *must be tougher to do this one.* He didn't want to distract, so he closed his eyes again and pretended to be asleep. *I just realized something! I wasn't out of breath. how can that be? two bumps, now three. I didn't count last time.* He focused on being relaxed and limp... *it's interesting to let my arms flop in the water; they only move because of Nick's back and forth movement. huh... Nick is breathing kind of hard... he's lost his rhythm all of a sudden. something isn't going right. he's working harder than last time. maybe...* they stopped abruptly—he felt the top of his head touch the bar.

He was pulled out of the water suddenly—they stretched him out on the boardwalk, face down. His arms were pulled out... he felt someone sit astride him and push down on his back. His eyes opened: *do they think I drowned?* He flinched and giggled: whatever he was doing, whoever it was, it tickled. They turned him over onto his back at once.

Julian looked around—half a dozen people were standing around staring at him. Mr. Franklin had been the one kneeling over his back. "What's the matter?"

"You're okay?" Nick was on his knees, staring.

"Yeah, sure. Did I do it wrong?" He sat up and leaned on one elbow. A few hands went onto hips. *have I screwed up again?* He saw Tom stand up and look from the Lifeguard's chair.

"Well, son—" Roy Franklin regained his balance. "You had us believing you were in real trouble."

Whoa… Julian paused at this. He looked at Nick, then at Mr. Franklin. He sat up all the way. "But they said we were supposed to pretend we were unconscious and really make the swimmer work hard to get back fast." He frowned, still not believing this. He paused, looking for something else to say. Nothing came to him. He looked at Mr. Franklin and shrugged. "So I that's what I did."

Everyone laughed. "Well you did that better than anybody ever has. Maybe you should consider becoming an actor." Franklin was genuinely impressed. He reached down and took Julian's hand to pull him up. "I may have a problem, though." He planned to pass Nick anyway, but was slightly concerned. "You did everything correctly, but you seemed to be uncertain at the very end. Can you explain that?"

"Well, yeah. We were getting close to the dock, but Julian hadn't made a peep or anything, and he was as limp as a wet blanket, and getting heavy. Then I realized he hadn't gulped for air like he did before. I was afraid he could be drowned." Nick blushed. He glanced at Julian, then looked at the instructor and shrugged, holding his hands out. "So I really put on the steam. I didn't panic, really, but I was for sure sweating it."

The other Lifesaving candidates put themselves in Nick's place… he had done the right thing.

Franklin put his left hand on Julian's shoulder. "Thanks for the great act, Julian. You got everyone to pay better attention." He nodded to Nick that the rescue had passed.

There was a cheer and a small applause.

"Okay, then: number nine! You're up." Franklin and the others moved on.

"I guess I owe you one." Nick led Julian to the edge of the boardwalk. They sat again and let their feet dangle in the water. They watched number nine. Nick shook his head and laughed.

"Did you **really** think I had drowned?"

"Well, yeah, in a way. You were so **limp**. A lot more than you were before. Then, when I realized you didn't say "blub-blub," I tried to tell if you were breathing, and I couldn't." He looked at Julian. "I gotta tell you Julian, I was worried."

"Wow." He pondered this. It was a little scary. "Okay. We have the wild panic one next. I don't want to foul that one up. What should I do?"

Nick paused. *boy am I lucky to have Julian here for this.* "Good question. This one is very different, because you are conscious but out of control."

"Okay…" Julian imagined a sequence. "When I go out there, I'll sink, like before, but then I'll come up for air. I'll wave my arms a couple of times. Then I'll take a breath secretly, and sink again. I'll count to ten before coming up again. Okay so far?"

"Yeah…"

"I'll keep an eye out, and I won't sink again until I see you move; I'll just wave and start hollering 'til then."

"That's good, yeah." Nick pictured how this would appear. "What are you gonna yell?" *does it matter? they didn't say…*

"Hmm… I know! If you hear anything besides the word 'help,' you'll know I'm in trouble. If I'm okay, that's all I'll yell."

"Good. Good. I think that will work… keep thrashing around as hard as you can, and ignore me as much as you can. It's supposed to look real. I'll probably take a lot longer than you want, okay?"

Julian had it pictured in his head. "I'll swing wide on purpose, so I don't accidentally whap you one." *boy is this fun!* "Oh—is there a time limit?"

"No time limit. They grade on the other stuff." *Julian will probably wish there was before this one is over.* Nick was confident that this would be a one shot deal. *oop!* He stood up and put on his clothes—no time to spare. My turn is coming.

"Number eight!"

Julian had stopped attending what was happening; he wasn't expecting to be called up this soon. He sat up quick and looked at Mr. Franklin.

"Well, are you going to go, or what?"

Julian slipped off the edge and swam out. He hurried this time. His arm was about the same. When he thought he was out far enough, he turned around for the go ahead. Mr. Franklin was shaking his head no. He made a "go out farther" motion with his arm. He cupped one hand and shouted, but Julian couldn't hear; too much hollering and splashing from another rescue close to the F dock. He swam out farther, almost to where the nearest lifeguard rowboat was parked—*that's right! the lifeguards are probably helping judge all this—that's why they're out here.* He turned around again—the instructor gave the okay sign.

Julian took a deep breath and raised one arm. He let himself sink down a few feet. He came up after three seconds and waved both arms briefly. He took another breath and sank again, because he had seen Nick move off to the right. He followed his plan exactly. Since he couldn't hear the instructor, it figured that he could be shouting anything at all and the shore wouldn't know what he was saying either—unless he screamed super loud. So on the third time out of the water he yelled as loud as he could. "Help!" *not very original... I can hear another guy hollering the same thing... looks like two rescues are going on at the same time.* He thrashed some and hollered again.

Nick had come up with a unique plan. He waited for Mr. Franklin's signal to go. When the whistle blew, he surprised everyone who was watching: he moved to the left and ran full speed out to the end of the boat dock. He grabbed the life ring off the end canoe rack and tossed it out as far as he could toward Julian. Then he undressed quickly, keeping his eye on Julian. He grabbed a canoe paddle off the rack and did a stride entry rescue jump at the corner of the dock in a straight line toward Julian. Doing a crawl stroke with the paddle was awkward, but he didn't have too far to go. Running out on the dock had eliminated well over half the distance.

Julian was having a ball. He hollered away merrily. *better sink again to keep things believable..* He had lost track of Nick's whereabouts. *oho! I can see him approaching... he's almost here!*

He flailed his arms wide as he surfaced. Nick looked at him, concerned.

"Helpety-help," Julian said cheerfully. He pounded the water erratically.

Nick tried not to laugh, but it was hard. "Okay, keep pretending. You have to get all tired out. Pretty soon I'm going to push a life ring at you. Ignore it for a little, then pound on it a few times. When you figure out what it is, you can stop swinging and look like you're getting under control."

"Helpety help, sure thing, helpety." Julian swung his arms randomly.

"Calm down… No, don't yet, for real. I'm supposed to talk and get you calmed down so I can get you relaxed. So I'm gonna say calm down a whole bunch." Nick was aware of the rowboat nearby—he assumed the lifeguard was paying close attention.

Nick caught the rope on the life ring with the paddle and pulled it over between himself and Julian. Gradually he nudged the ring with the paddle and pushed it toward Julian's splashing hand.

Julian nodded his head. "Help, help," he continued flopping his right arm. It hit the ring at last. "Ow. That's hard!" He lightened up his swing.

Nick kept pushing the ring with the paddle and reached for the rope with his other hand. The ring was pressed to Julian's chest now, forcing him backward—he had to grab hold of the ring to stop from being pushed under the water backwards.

Julian laughed. *this is fun.* "Do I just hold on now?"

"Exactly. Okay, now slowly stop and look like you're calming down. Yes… that's perfect. Now, take a couple of real deep breaths… yeah; now, nod your head yes."

Julian followed the script perfectly. "So do you take me back the same way?"

"No, that way is for unconscious victims. You're conscious, but weak. So you have to hang onto the ring while I pull it to the shore. I'll look back at you once in a while to make sure your head is still out of the water. Let me do all the work except keeping your arms around the ring."

"Ooo, I see… so I just cling on for the ride?"

"Yep. Are you ready to go?"

"Yeah! Mush—or what do you say in the water?" Julian giggled. He looked at the ring. *perfect! the number eight is between my hands! Nick is number eight too.* He glanced to the left. *looks like Nick will be the first one back in this group. not only that, I'm the only one who got to ride in on a lifesaver! it's like riding a water sled, sort of, only a little jerky.* He was about to kick his feet—but remembered what Nick said. *s'posed to pretend I'm all pooped out—more rag doll stuff. this is great! what a fun ride. watching the dock get closer is interesting. when I don't do the swimming, the dock almost does the moving... weird. oh... we're at the boardwalk already... it went too fast!*

"Now, you need to stay calm, stay in the water, and hold on to the edge." Nick gave his instructions for the benefit of Mr. Franklin, who was standing over them with his clipboard. "You need to stay here until you feel strong enough to lift out of the water under your own power. Okay?"

Julian nodded, grateful. His arms were pretty tired after all that flailing.

Nick smiled back... Julian had done that perfectly.

"Good work, Harrison. You did a very clever throw and reach there. You've just passed the last Lifesaving tests. Congratulations. Your name will be posted in the morning." Franklin held his hand down and shook Nick's firmly. "And you, mister actor, did another excellent performance. Thanks for helping out." He shook Julian's hand too, and flipped to the next page on his clipboard. "Okay, on we go! Ready Jenkins?"

They leaned against the rail pipe and rested, savoring the achievement.

Nick laughed. "Helpety help?"

"I don't know why I said that," he chuckled. "It just came out. Maybe I was thinking about a cartoon character." Julian replayed the rescue in his mind. "But I'm glad I did this. I'm better prepared now, if I do get in trouble. I have a way to go to be a really **good** swimmer, like you are."

"Yeah... The old Scout Motto makes sense, even if they sort of overdo it sometimes." Nick plopped the paddle onto the boardwalk and pulled himself up. "Hand me the ring, will you?"

Julian handed up the lifesaver and pulled up onto the boardwalk. He walked back to the boat rack with Nick. "Say, I just thought of something. How come you don't have to practice the respiration stuff? I was the only one that even got pulled out of the water."

"We've already done that part; they make us practice that on each other in class, the pushing and pumping. They have dummies there for us to do the mouth-to-mouth part, too. We do that after we empty all the water out by pushing on the back." *I was sure glad they had that dummy. I could think of only one guy in the class who I wouldn't mind kissing. I could hold off kissing him without any argument, actually.*

Julian had not thought about the mouth-to-mouth thing. *wow. what if I hadn't opened my eyes when I did?* He looked over at the instructor.

He did not particularly fancy the idea of Mr. Franklin blowing air into him through a long kiss on the boardwalk in front of the whole camp. *I can just hear Sid now. that's one I would never live down.*

They watched number ten do his rescue. It was pretty good.

"Ohmygosh!" Nick pointed. "Look—Bruce is the next victim! We **gotta** watch this one!" *so that's who Jay paired up with.*

"Bruce?!" Julian remembered Sid's wisecrack about the troop's roundest scout. "I didn't know he was doing this, too."

Bruce stood on the edge and paused briefly before diving in. His attempt to be graceful was compromised rather badly by his profile. The attempt was valiant enough. They watched him swim out. Bruce raised an arm dramatically and sank. He went down like a boulder.

"Oh-oh. I hope he took a nice deep breath!" Nick chuckled.

Bruce was out of sight for a long time. Julian and Nick looked at each other.

"What if he's not faking it?" Nick wasn't worried.

They watched with interest. Bruce surfaced at last.

"Hmm. He sure splashes good."

"That he does." Nick sat down on the edge of the dock to watch. *how will Jay handle this? he doesn't have a dock close by.*

Julian sat down next to Nick. He chuckled, thinking back to the picture in his mind of Bruce standing on the dock before jumping in. Being mostly submerged was somewhat better for his image, but he was still a pretty good size.

Nick looked over at Julian.

"I was just wondering if the life saver ring would be enough to keep him afloat."

"To be honest, I don't know what they'll hold. I should know that, too."

"I wanted to sit in the hole while you towed me in, sort of like riding an inner tube." *they don't have any 'tubes here, do they?*

"Wow, that would have done me in. I'm sure glad you didn't. You did great, by the way. It looked real. Maybe you **should** be an actor."

Julian giggled again.

"What?"

"I was just thinking of Bruce's buns riding back in the lifesaver ring."

"Yeah!" Nick laughed. "He'd get stuck."

"You could tell if it was big enough to keep him afloat!"

They both laughed. Then they felt bad because they had been making fun of Bruce. His flopping arms had calmed down. It looked like Jay would bring him in on his back.

"Your buns, by the way, are about a **fourth** his size. You'd probably fall right through the hole."

Julian blushed. "Come on. I've got buns." He was suddenly self-conscious. "Don't I?" He looked at Nick for an explanation.

Not thinking, Nick laughed. "Listen: you don't have buns. You have Choice Buns." That was an understatement, in fact.

Julian could tell he was being complimented, but he was a little confused. This was a term he had not heard before. "What does that mean, Nick?"

uh-oh—better stop right there. I don't want to pull a Tom. for all I know, Julian is still as pure as the driven snow; I'm not about to be the one to spoil anything. besides, Mark's counting on me to train him to be my assistant and make the newsletter something classy. I don't want to foul that up... Nick searched for a safe answer. *hmmm. tricky. buns...* He cleared his throat.

"Well, it means just that. They are choice: well shaped, cute, all that kind of thing. Look at me, for example." Nick poked his right cheek through the wet skivvies. "Plain ol' buns, that's me. They're okay for sitting on, but..." *darn! I'm having trouble here. I was about to say 'not at all sexy.' I don't want Julian to think... well, to be worried or anything. he probably has no idea what being sexy is, to look at him. how can I talk about buns any other way?*

Julian was unsatisfied. *I still don't get it. I won't press, though... he's just being a typical big kid. they always clam up whenever things like this come up. I like Nick anyway. in fact, I'm starting to think that he's the kind of guy I want as a friend. probably already is. yeah...* that made Julian feel good all of a sudden. He turned back to watch the rescue.

whew. Nick was relieved… Julian seems to be satisfied. He took a deep breath. Just then, his eye caught Tom leaning forward in the Lifeguard Chair. *that's right: I need to come up with a plan. Tom will be off duty in about fifteen minutes.*

Julian watched Jay working to bring Bruce in; *he might not like having so much of a load.* "Was I very heavy out there?" *I'd like to try another ride, this time in the ring, if I could figure an angle. I haven't seen any inner tubes here, come to think about it. I noticed that this morning—no water toys. no swim fins, either. I don't remember seeing any rule against them. usually there are all kinds of rules posted up about stuff. ah: Leonard will know. I'll ask Leonard about that.*

"Weight in the water doesn't mean that much. You will need stronger arms, though." He remembered feeling the spaghetti arm. Julian had work to do there, for sure. *I had a bad case of that myself when I was his age.*

They watched Bruce ride in and get dropped off. "You want to watch the rest?" Nick was a little worried. He'd seen Tom checking out Julian's butt earlier; it would be a good idea to find something else for Julian to do. *he'll have half an hour after his lifeguard duty—I know just how he'd like to use it. I have to head that off.*

"I don't care. I thought you had to stay." *maybe this isn't like a class.*

"Nope. I'm all done, thanks to you. Why don't we go and do some planning for the great newsletter?" The perfect reason to leave, he realized suddenly. He glanced over at Tom: *he's behaving himself, watching the rescues. this is one overstaffed activity.* There were fewer scouts in the water during this activity than any other time. *Tom is going to be free real soon.*

"Sure!" *I want to get a better idea about that anyway.*

Nick grabbed his wet clothes and walked with Julian over to the cubbyholes. They dressed quickly and checked out at the table.

"Thanks, Leonard." Julian picked up his Buddy Badge—there were six others.

"Not staying to swim?" Leonard refrained from asking about the incident on the boardwalk… he expected to be told something.

Nick patted Julian on the back. "We're going to have our first editorial meeting. Julian is my new assistant in the troop newsletter."

"Well, congratulations!" Leonard extended his hand for a shake.

Julian felt a slight blush. He smiled quietly and shrugged. *Leonard is so thoughtful. he's at the top of my friendly list when it comes to camp staff.*

Nick tugged at Julian's sleeve… time to leave. He didn't want Tom to notice their exit. *if he follows us, I won't be able to do much to hold him off.*

Julian waved briefly at Leonard and skipped over to hang up his Buddy Badge. *lucky I have my notebook all ready—I don't know anything about newsletters. but Nick's very friendly; it will be easy enough to learn the ropes. yep. hurry up dum-dum*—Nick was headed for the Meadow pretty fast.

Nick glanced over his shoulder as he and Julian left the lake. Tom was still looking the other way. *we have to hurry… get out of his sightline as fast as we can. should we take the long way?* The little "rescue" experience with Julian had reinforced his intention to be as protective as possible. As he watched Julian return his Buddy Badge to the board, it was clear to him that that he'd never known a kid as talented and bright, and so obviously innocent. Tom would be real bad news. *I like Julian; working with him on the newsletter will be fun. we have more than half an hour—it will be time well spent.*

He glanced back to the lifeguard tower—Tom was using his binoculars, checking on something. *think fast, Nick…* He looked up the main trail to the HQ building; if they took that they'd be visible all the way to the Barr's Meadow junction—five minutes at least, maybe more. Knowing Tom, he'll discover we're missing—he's certain to look up the trail. *the shortcut is lots faster… safe enough. Tom might not check there. maybe we'll get lucky, and he'll be stuck in that chair.* Nick looked in every direction… *no one is around the latrine… no one in sight. that's the smart way to go.*

Besides: he was ready for a little action of his own. He planned to keep Tom busy tonight himself; an inactive afternoon would make Tom **real** needy. *it's Code Green tonight.* He stopped to wait for Julian, jogging happily up the slope. Nick was not used to seeing such a genuine, engaging smile. *this kid is not at all what I expected...* he reflected briefly about Mark's choice... *this will be fun.* "Is that your newsletter tablet?"

"I guess; I use it for the scrapbook sketches, mostly." *the writing tablet is in my footlocker, actually.*

"Let's take the shortcut—" Nick was about to steer them left, toward the latrine, but Julian turned first. "You know about this?"

"Yeah. Stu showed us last night... we were a little late leaving for the campfire." *ooo... I hope Stu won't get in trouble.*

"Well, don't let Mark catch you... twenty five point demerit."

whoa... Stu didn't tell us that.

"We should have plenty of time before supper to plan out how we're gonna do this. It's great Mark picked you to help out—I have to do all the minutes of all the meetings, and man, sometimes I don't have time for much else."

"Wow! I didn't know you did all that; I thought you just had to read them."

"No such luck!" Nick glanced back—*the chair is out of sight; we must have made it.* He crossed his fingers... *I don't know what I'll do if Tom shows up in camp too soon.*

Julian smiled a secret smile. This patch of ground is where he had adopted his new motto last night. *ooo. that's right! supper isn't that far off; I get to see Mark at last. I haven't seen him all day! huh!* He just realized something: *I didn't even worry about Mark; all day, not even* **once**. *now that's a first!* Julian watched Nick step carefully to avoid leaving footprints in the thin ground cover... *kind of tricky where it's this steep... we're near the top already! this shortcut is amazing.*

Tom watched the last rescue. The best part of this duty was seeing first hand that there were seventeen newly qualified lifeguards. *I get to climb down from here at last! next time Leonard tries to spring his trap, I'll hand him the list. my butt's tired; this seat cushion has seen better days.* He could hardly wait: he'd been stuck there for way over an hour. His patience was about to be rewarded—*I'm going to get that bubble butt*

off by himself before supper. I have to find a way to lose Nick, but that's doable. Tom played back his memory of Coach Franklin pushing down on Julian's back. *woof. that whole thing was odd, actually. I'll get the details from Nick later.*

He sat up as the last "victim" was brought to the edge. All the docks were clear now; Leonard was about to reassign the guards for the afternoon Free Swim. Tom looked over to the check-in table where everyone was clustered. A pretty good sized crowd was waiting to get in. *where's Joey, anyway?* He was on the platform duty station. *he's supposed to take over the chair for the free swim.* Tom stood up to look— *can't see him anywhere. now he's gone off somewhere... maybe he's at the latrine. well, five minutes, then.* Tom sat back down. *he'd better show in five minutes. blast.*

looks like I have to give the open swim signal. yep... Leonard just waved the go ahead. The guards were on their way down to their dock stations. Tom blew the whistle and glanced over to check on Julian and Nick. *what! where did they go? they were on the edge of the boat dock!* He swung his head right, then left. *gone?* He looked back to the cubbyholes. *I don't **believe** this. I've been watching carefully. not a trace!* The scouts were jumping into the lake already; he leaned down to look under the tower. *nope.*

Tom took a minute to think. He looked back at Leonard... busy talking with the instructors, Franklin and Smith. *double blast! I'm **stuck**... I have to keep my eyes on the swimmers. maybe it won't be for long; Joey will show eventually. but where did Nick go? maybe they're swimming.* He flipped up his sunglasses and scanned the water... *I can spot them easy from up here. hmm. these binoculars aren't that hot...* he looked at the power stamp on the back plate: only 7 x 35. *they should have an 8 x 50 up here.* Where would they be swimming? Tom scanned the swim area rapidly—there weren't too many in the water yet.

okay... Plan B then... even if Joey shows, I'm out of luck. Nick and Julian were gone, who knew where. *only half an hour left. it'll be time to fix supper by the time I find them—and **I'm** the cook. rats. hmm. plan B. oop...* Tom checked his watch. Five minutes to the buddy whistle. *don't want to be late on that.*

well. the day isn't over yet. there'll be a good two hours after supper... yeah... there's plenty of daylight; sunset isn't until nine thirty or so.   I can figure something out. meantime, I can keep my eye peeled for another prospect... I noticed a few this morning... if Joey ever gets here. hmm... can't tell that much when they're in the water. when they lift up onto the dock for a dive, that's when they show it off...

❧❀☙

21 *afternoon wrapup*

Mark found it difficult to keep his attention on the assigned duty—it was a bore: time keeping for the first free-time afternoon at the Archery Range—very busy today because Free Swimming wasn't open until the Lifesaving tests were completed. All the equipment was checked out. The scouts were limited to ten ends per pair, which took roughly fifteen minutes—two arrows per minute, give or take. So he had to pay attention, and give them time to swap out their target sheets. He glanced at his watch: *a minute to go on this round.* He raised his arm to signal that the whistle was about to blow. *there.* He gave the signal. *if I were doing some instructing, it would be worth my time. maybe I can pick up a few tips just watching—too far away from the action to see much, though.*

A few minutes ago Cory had given him a brief report on Julian's first archery lesson. Mark shook his head again; it must have been tough for him… *I'm sorry he didn't stick with Cory this afternoon... maybe I could have helped out.*

Uncertainty about moving Julian last night had begun to nag. He hadn't had an opportunity to think about it, which made him somewhat uneasy—it began to compete for his attention more and more as the day went on. Between signals he was able to give the matter a little thought, but Cory had to nudge a couple of times—saving him from the embarrassment of missing his cue.

we had so little time to talk last night and this morning... so much had to be taken for granted. I have to make up for that tonight. Even so, there was one welcome aspect: *Julian's crush seemed to disappear when I was really close. I'm not sure what to do if that changes. I hope I pre-empted that with this move. that's what I had in mind.*

This was a new kind of challenge. No other scout of his had ever had Julian's problem. Lots of them got involved with one another, of course.

That was only natural. For some, it was fairly serious. *for most, it's simply a stage in growing up—playing around a little… or a lot.* Mark smiled. *I certainly did my share when I was a scout.*

The dark cloud reappeared in his mind—events intruded from the past that did not bring a smile… not every kid is ready to play at the same level, and some of them get an unpleasant surprise. Let's face it: that was the other major reason for the move. Julian had to be protected, pure and simple. *Julian is so **absolutely** attractive that he'll draw attention at some point. may well have already. over six hundred boys are here… it stands to reason that several will look closely… some would make a move if they got the chance.*

Mark was certain that Julian had no experience in these things. *Francine has done an excellent job of keeping him safe. maybe too good. he's been completely sheltered. I doubt that he's had any education or guidance in the basics. he won't take a health class at school until next year.*

Last night's toothpaste moment came to mind… comical and special. *he's kind of like a little brother, I suppose. I never had one.*

Mark saw movement out of the corner of his eye—he glanced at his watch. *how could the time move that fast?* He raised his arm again, poised to blow his whistle. *two more of these.* After this duty, a short break at the HQ staff lounge was in order.

I need to pay some attention to some of the other boys. Tom needs some advising. and there's Alex… Justin… Sean. each had a different problem that needed some kind of helping hand. *most of them have buddies in their patrol, but they need an adult's attention as well… I have to be on my toes. Alex in particular: his hardline Prussian father is something else.* Mark shook his head. *that one is a real tough nut.*

Mark slouched in his chair and exhaled. *what would Erik do?* He shook his head. *what made me ask that? I haven't thought of him for nearly a year. I don't know if he was ever a scout, come to think about it.* He sat up straight. *shape up, Mark. don't dig in the past for answers. all you get is bad memories and no help. you are on your own.*

what about tonight? I have no plan ready. maybe that's why I have this unsettled feeling. He shrugged. *on the other hand, maybe I don't need one.* He glanced at his watch. Ten minutes to the next set. *sure be glad when this is done. I'm getting hungry.*

—∿—

In what seemed no time, Julian and Nick were seated at the west end of the Flaming Arrow table. The dishes were still where Julian had put them to dry. "Am I supposed to put those away?" Danny had set them out for breakfast; Julian wasn't sure where they went.

"Heck no, this saves me some work! I have to set them out again for supper, anyway. Did you wash 'em?"

Julian grinned and nodded yes.

"Then they're ready to use." He gave a double ok sign. "So, what have you got so far?" He pointed at the tablet. Nick just realized that he was extremely uncomfortable… the clothes were still very damp. He stood and took off his shirt. "I'm gonna get out of these wet clothes… go ahead." He took off his pants. He laid out the clothes along the bench. *the sun might dry them out before supper.*

Julian skipped through to page five; that's where he had his notes from today. "Today's inspection results." He flipped the page. "I wrote some notes in the Forestry merit badge… flora, fauna, stuff like that… that's it so far." He didn't mention the scrapbook sketches he had started. He was planning the archery one in his head.

Nick pondered about this while he went over to his footlocker to get some dry clothes. He spoke on the way. "What about the opening campfire?"

"Oh, wow, can't forget that! That's the best thing so far!" He flipped to a new page and wrote that down. *I have to remember to ask Mark about what I missed.*

Nick stopped to think: *Julian has no idea what to do. well, why would he?* Nick put on his scout shirt and gathered up his shorts, dry socks, undies, and his kerchief. *this meeting is a better idea than I thought.* He returned to the table so that he didn't have to yell. "Okay. Here's what we'll do. Let's make a list of everything we've done, from the time we left home, and decide which of those we should write about."

Julian nodded his head and began the list:

1 Bus ride

2—

"I doubt if camp inspections are going to be super interesting to read about." Nick shed his damp underwear... *too bad we don't have a clothesline around here.*

Julian had to laugh. "Yeah. We had one crooked footlocker, a wrinkled top blanket, and half a Kleenex hiding under a cot this morning."

"See what I mean? Next, we make a list of contacts in each patrol. We have them tell us if anything is going on that ought to be in the newsletter. Since they get points for being written about, they'll bring us stuff automatically. All we have to do is pick the ones we want." He slipped on his undies and short pants and sat down to swap his damp socks for dry ones. Just enough room remained for him to sit.

Julian wrote all this down... *man, this is great stuff. usually all I do is put down ideas for a sketch. now I have to consider other things.* "Wow, Nick, you are really smart! And I can use some of this for the scrapbook, too!" *I had trouble getting information from some of the patrols during the year. Nick just told me how to fix that.* "No wonder you're in Flaming Arrow!" *boy—this changes things; I'll transfer all this to my writing tablet later... I need to keep this one for drawings.*

Nick blushed briefly... *I've just been complimented!* he looked at Julian— *what a surprise.* For the first time in months, he felt very good. He looked at Julian more closely. It took a minute to recover.

mmm... the dry clothes were a very good idea. I'm warm again. the evening breeze would have been super bad. "Say, do you have a camera?"

"Nope. I sure want one, though. That's why I draw most things in the scrapbook. Ben Jasper gave me some extra pictures after last Christmas, but that's all I have." *Mom told me I had to wait; she's saving up to get a good one. she has an old one of grandpa's, but it's hard to get film for it any more. besides, it's too old for scout camping trips.*

"Me neither. I know what! We'll have Mark or Danny announce at campfire that we need some photos. Lots of guys in the troop have a camera. Maybe we can give out points or something." *Andy used to have a Hawkeye Brownie...*

Julian scratched his head. It might be a choice of either photos or drawings; *I hope one of my drawings gets in the newsletter.* "How many pages are there?" *I hate to ask that—I should know. Mom always reads the newsletter...* He hadn't given it more than a glance. *I always figured it was meant for the parents.*

"Either four or eight pages—they print it sideways and fold it in half—so a regular sheet of paper has four pages. Two sheets equals eight pages. Pretty neat, eh?"

Julian began to comprehend the dimension of the project... *this won't be as hard as I thought. I do a lot more than that for the scrapbook every month.* "Tell me about the typing part. How do you do that?"

"Oh, that's easy. My dad has an extra typewriter that he lets me use. He has a new electric one now. It has a magic ball that whirls all over the place. It works a lot better. The keys never get jammed if he goes fast. Of course, I don't type fast enough to have that trouble. Anyway—when I'm done, I turn it in to Mark, and he does the rest."

Julian was baffled; he had no idea what Nick was talking about. *keys? balls?* He'd never paid any attention to typewriters. *they have them in Geraldine's office. the secretary at school has one...* He still didn't quite get what he would be doing.

"So, I make some notes in my notebook..." *maybe Nick will finish the sentence...* He didn't especially want Nick to know how ignorant he was.

"Well," Nick was patient... "like I said, we go over all the stuff you have written down and all that has been handed in, and we pick out what will go in. We write it all up, then I type it, and hand it to Mark—all done!"

It sounded better; Julian was still uneasy, though. He was not prepared for this job. *but I'm not afraid. Nick is nice as well as smart. Mom has a typewriter. I played with it once... I'll talk to Mark about it tonight. he'll help me figure this out. I can do this, eventually.*

—⁂—

Danny's goal of getting a tan was well underway; the lake platform was ideal. Frankie had convinced him that a good tan was the best way to attract the kind of attention that mattered. They had a bet going about who would have a better tan by the Fourth of July Parade. *Frankie has to work in the store all day—he doesn't stand a chance.*

The afternoon sun was a little too warm—*a lot more intense than this morning. this swim period is a lot shorter, so maybe it's okay. with two free swimming periods every day, I can get a super tan by the end of camp.* He had forgotten the lotion bottle again. *I better wrap it in my towel when I get back to camp... then I won't forget. I sure don't want to get a burn; that always makes me peel. I hate that... it's always so itchy.*

His thoughts returned again to that incredible after breakfast session with Julian. It had preoccupied him on and off all day. *wow. oh-oh... I need to quit thinking about it... getting hard again.* He turned onto his stomach; he didn't want his problem noticed. *I don't know any of these guys out here... they're all from other troops.* He turned his head toward the F dock. *yep... Tommy's still there.* Tommy had agreed to be his Buddy after the merit badge quals. *I always get along with Tommy. he was buddy a lot last summer. something is bugging him, though. he didn't say what—probably still annoyed about the Flaming Arrow promotion. well, what could I do about it? besides, Arnie doesn't hold it against me. true, he deserved it more. but Mark had his reasons. he made Arnie patrol leader instead. that's a bigger deal in a lot of ways. it was fun to be a Badger.*

Danny was so relieved—and **happy**.... *Julian likes me... is he the one? am I lucky enough to snag him to be my boyfriend? the possibilities are endless! he lives right there, across the fence. what's that clubhouse like inside? I almost asked about it this morning.*

He wasn't sure, though... he'd hadn't expected such early success. it might a good idea to wait a little. *I want Julian to be my boyfriend, but I still think about some of the others. not as a boyfriend, especially... but I still want to have some fun if the chance comes along. Julian **is** sort of undeveloped.*

A few other guys at the lake were pretty hot, actually... *one out here on the platform this morning was something. but my chances with any of them are slim to none. I'm such a coward. that's where I envy Tom. whenever Tom sees one he wants, he just goes for it.*

But Julian was the best, hands down, in the long run. *the possibilities, the possibilities! uh-oh... lying on my stomach helps make me harder.* Before very long, he'd have to figure out what to do: showing a big stiff one out here would be a very bad idea... *when the whistle blows I have to be super careful.*

Rumination about the days and weeks ahead continued... *we can do something tomorrow morning. Julian even said so, didn't he? should we do the same thing, or something else? he has a lot to learn... to think that I'm the one who gets to show him the ropes! all I have to do is keep him away from Tom. boy, it's sure lucky that he's staying in the cabin. he'd get jumped on tonight for sure, otherwise! if Tom had his way, he'd jump on every little butt in the camp. the Arrow camp only has one tent, and it's full. I'm using Frankie's cot, actually. if he'd come this year, we'd have to put up a second crew tent—Julian would have been in for it for sure.*

He twisted and flexed his back... an annoying burning sensation ran across his shoulders. This was the first time he'd ever set out to get a full body tan; *maybe there are things I should check on, like which way my head should be pointed. right at the sun? or should I be at a ninety-degree angle? maybe I should I rotate every so often... I ought to let my front side get more sun; thanks to Julian, I can't seem to stay limp. maybe I'll be able to get that under control tomorrow.* He swiped the small of his back unconsciously... it burned a little like his shoulders. *I can't cool off by diving in right now—no way to hide my problem.*

Nobody else out there seemed to be working on a tan yet— between dives they all sat for a while, talking. Danny didn't pay attention to their conversations; they ignored him too, which was okay. Once in a while one would shake his head after a dive, causing a few drops of water to land on the back of his legs. *be nice if one of those sprinkles got me between the shoulders... I'm pointed the wrong way... hmm... maybe Leonard can tell me what works best—he always has a nice tan.*

>> bleet! bleet! bleet! <<

oop! whistle already—time to head back to the Meadow; just as well. He looked around: a couple of guys from Troop 7 were still here... *one is **hot**. big, too, like Tom.* Three others he didn't know. *I didn't see the others dive off. I'll wait until they're all gone... a slow crawl through cold water will fix the problem. I need to do that before I go back to the cubbyhole... **especially** since Tommy is waiting.* Always ready with a wisecrack, he didn't want Tommy to see his condition—Tommy never messed around. *just as well... he isn't exactly hot... fun, but not sexy.*

there—the last one jumped off at last. Danny stood briefly, then dove in. *wow!* The cold water was a real shock... his back and buns were glowing hot. *maybe I did get a slight burn. I'll get someone to put some lotion on my back first thing.* He felt himself shrinking up fast. *cold water helps do that.*

22 *supper and campfire*

Tom wasn't in a hurry to get back to camp… he was thoroughly pissed. His plan to get Julian after the second swim period had been foiled, and the yummy that had come up to him at the lifeguard tower ran off before he had a chance to do anything. *boy, does Leonard owe me—Joey never did show. Leonard promised he'd make it right, somehow. just wait until they need me again, that's all. I best cool down before returning to camp; otherwise, Nick and Mark will wonder. don't need that.*

Tom turned left… *might as well make a stop before heading up.* The lake latrine had several open booths. *great! might as well get that out of the way—could save time for later on, after the campfire.* The hinges were quiet, compared to the Meadow's. He lowered the hook into the eye to secure the door. *eew…* he twisted his nose. *maybe stopping here wasn't such a hot idea.* He shrugged. *I'm here, so down with the drawers.*

He sat for a minute… no urge. He twisted his torso back and forth a couple of times… nothing was moving down below.

>> firrp. <<

mmm… baby farts are no help. maybe it isn't ready. He waited a second and pushed again: "**hoi**—" *nope… don't want to force it.* Obviously his inside crew wasn't prepared to deliver at the moment. *have to wait after all.* he pulled his pants up and headed out. *supper will get things moving. I'll do my usual race to the latrine after the campfire.* He rubbed his nose… *how often do they put lime in there, anyway? for only two days into camp it's pretty ripe… that's one reason the Meadow latrine is better, even if it is older: fewer customers.*

Tom went up the regular trail. The shortcut was for emergencies. Besides, taking the regular trail would give him some thinking time—not that it would do much good. *I usually leave the thinking to Nick. it's only the second day... maybe I should just cool it and snag Julian at free swimming in the morning.* That made sense. *in fact, at breakfast I can arrange to be his Swim Buddy! yeah! that way, instead of going through the gate, I can just steer him up the trail past the badge work areas. Marty's hideaway is always there, waiting. how many yums have I taken there, anyway?* He chuckled. That's one thing he never did: keep track. He didn't even have a rough count. He wasn't trying for a record or anything—he just appreciated a good romp in the woods now and again.

He nodded... not that he needed to know, but if he ever wanted to, Nick probably had a good idea how many "romps" he'd enjoyed. Nick was a big help a few times, actually. If one of his "field trips" went wrong, Nick always smoothed things over. He was more than just handy, of course. He could be trusted... relied on. *if I get really horny, Nick's always good about filling in, too. sometimes I don't give him enough credit.* Fact was, Nick never scolded or criticized, even if it was deserved... *he just puts up with me. he's good to have around, that's all. come to think about it, where did he go after Lifesaving? he usually hangs around. hmm.*

Marty's special hideaway—it's practically mine now. perfect for my special "hobby." almost as handy as Hayden Woods back home. When Tom was a Tenderfoot, Marty and Rick took him up there on the second day of camp. Nobody else knew about it. That was the busiest summer of all! *boy oh boy.* Those two were something else—every other day, practically, one of them wanted it.

They taught him well, and he'd been using Marty's hideaway every summer since. *maybe I should check it out just to be sure it's in good shape for Julian's big event.* "Big event!" Tom laughed... *I just made a pun!*

Marty and Rick's frolics always centered around his "big event toy." Remembering that cheered him up. *what ever happened to them, anyway? I never saw them again—they went into the Army at the end of the summer. someone said they went to Germany. why go there, anyway?* He shook his head. If he had to go into the military, being on an aircraft carrier was about the only thing that looked interesting.

As Tom walked into camp Nick was sitting at the table talking to Julian. *so that's what happened: they came up here. I should have thought of that... hey—* Another idea just occurred to him: *that's it! I'll get Nick to swap duties; Julian can help me fix supper... that way I can warm him up some more. okay... how to do this?* First off, he had to clear it with Mark. *just be cool... Mark usually goes along with my suggestions.*

Mark was over by the supply tent wiping sun cream on Danny's back. Tom walked forward casually, as if he had been there a while; he headed toward the cooler. "Mark, could I have Julian help grill the hamburgers for supper?" He asked offhandedly—that usually worked.

Mark looked at Tom; he saw no reason to juggle the assignments. "No, Julian already did breakfast this morning. Keep Nick to help you."

damn! Tom realized at once it was a stupid request. He was disappointed, but he didn't want Mark to wonder about it... *just keep your cool, keep your cool...*

Secretly, Nick was amused. *Mark foiled Tom this time; there's nothing he can do. it's looking good for tonight, at least.* There was no way Tom could lead Julian into the bushes, or anywhere, anyway. The rest of the evening had been scheduled, right up to lights out. He'd had time enough to talk to Mark about the campfire. Once again, anticipating Tom's move had proven wise.

"Hey, Nick!" Tom called out from the cooler. "Burger time! You get to slice the onion and pickles." He grabbed a tomato from the basket on the portable cabinet and tossed it. "Heads up!" He took a large package of hamburger out of the cooler. *I'm hungry. a couple of burgers is the perfect fix.* He squeezed the package... "Everybody want two?"

Everyone nodded yes except Julian. His tummy couldn't handle all the grub these guys ate. At breakfast he'd given half his pancakes away to Tom and Mark. He held up a single finger. *at the Wolf campouts Stu made good hamburgers, but Jeremy and I always got full; Sid could eat two—he always bragged about having a hollow leg.*

Tom glanced over at Julian. Again he recalled the special "diving lessons" he had given this morning. *woof!* His other appetite kicked back in. He grabbed the cutting board and a plate and stepped over to the table to make patties. *last chance will be at the campfire... how can I get Julian to sit in a good place? something will come to me...* He opened the package of ground beef and checked the color… looks good. *what are we doing tonight at the campfire, anyway? I'll be ready…* He wadded up the wrapping paper and made a perfect hook shot into the waste bin next to the stove—bull's eye. *Julian only wants one… so I divide this into nine. no sweat.* He began by forming three big balls.

Nick stepped over to work alongside Tom. Bringing along the cutting board was proof that he wasn't angry… he nudged Tom gratefully. He sliced the tomato, an onion, and a couple of dills. He fetched a platter and assembled the makings neatly while Tom fried away. *interesting how Tom enjoys cooking. he's good at it, too.*

Nick kept his eye on Tom the entire meal; he seemed okay on the surface, but Nick knew him well… Tom was planning something. The burgers were great—everybody thought so. Tom shrugged off the compliments, as usual. *I take more pride in Tom's work than he does himself.*

The entire patrol joined in the cleanup. Julian helped Nick lift the water back onto the stove. Danny and Tom washed the dishes right at the table. Mark pitched in, helping dry and put things away.

"Have a seat, guys." Mark pulled his folding stool up at the end of the table. He needed to conduct a day's end leadership meeting before the campfire.

Nick sat across from Julian where he'd been during supper, expecting Tom to sit next to him. Danny sat there instead—it was the closest spot when Mark called the meeting. It happened so fast there was nothing Nick could do—that meant Tom would have to sit by Julian. *hmm. well, with Mark right there, he won't be able to do anything.*

Julian sat opposite Nick, because that's where they sat while they were planning the newsletter. *what luck! so far, I've always sat in this spot. it's right next to Mark!* He was amazed that he didn't automatically get a stiffy like always… and he hadn't seen Mark all day, either. *oh-oh. I can feel a tingle. don't think about that, Julian.* He opened his tablet to a fresh page. *I'll start the drawing of the Archery Range…* that one had been forming in his head off an on all day… *plenty of daylight left. let's see... there's sixteen of those target stands—or was it eighteen?   this drawing has to be turned sideways.*

Tom saw his chance and took it at once. He sat next to Julian, casually. *perfect. I can lay some groundwork while he's busy watching Mark and making notes. things are going my way at last!*

"Let's go over what went on today. If any changes are needed, or announcements to make at the campfire tonight, I want to get it all planned now." Mark nodded at Danny; his notepad was out, ready to prepare the announcements. "It's going to be a crowded campfire program; after the patrols report, we have to get going on the skit. And I'd like everyone to have some time in camp before lights out. Last night was too short."

Nick had his pad out to record everything for the official minutes. His peripheral vision tuned to Tom... he could read the signals: Tom was getting horny.

Mark asked Tom to report on his activities and the firewood detail. Next, he asked Nick to give a summary report for each patrol's morning start. Nick also gave a report on the planning session he had with Julian on the Newsletter. Danny's inspection report was next; Mark realized that he had not planned for a report from Julian. *I need to find a way for him to take part—put that on the list for tomorrow morning... a leadership assignment with a report component...*

Julian had pretty much tuned out of the meeting... he didn't expect to be called on to say anything. The sketch of the archery range was a challenge. As he formed the first oval in the row of targets, he felt Tom's right thigh press against his left. It was a light touch at first, and he didn't think anything of it. After it had touched him a couple of times, he glanced to his left. Tom was leaning back away from him, his head resting casually on his left arm. It looked like he was thinking about something else. Julian returned to his sketch. *I have to make each target circle a little smaller as I go across the page... that will help show the distance. they can't be round... hmm. maybe I shouldn't try to show all of them... how about just four or five?*

After his report Tom was free to concentrate on Julian. It made him more impatient... *maybe there's a way to diddle just a little before the campfire. I can't do much, but man, I want this one. Julian is a lot cuter than most, but it's that little butt that gets to me. the kid is game... I got him half hard in the lake, no problem. I left the butt alone, though. that's reserved for its own special event tomorrow morning at Marty's. mmm...* the memory of his underwater viewing this morning was vivid... his crotch was sending an early alarm: he was awakening down there. *is there a way to warm Julian up just a little?* One advantage of summer shorts was showing a short stretch of bare leg... he inched his foot closer gradually... his right knee was almost in position.

Julian felt Tom press against his leg again, but this time it was his knee. It stayed in contact. *it's warm... feels nice, actually.* He turned his head to look at Tom, and saw a smile form there. Tom gave his leg a very slight press—Julian felt his dick start to tingle. *wow... what should I do? I don't want a stiffy right now, right here, with Mark sitting next to me and everything. ignore Tom and work on the sketch: maybe if I concentrate on that, I'll be okay.* He just remembered Tom's grab in the lake this morning; *I forgot to think about that today. Tom won't do that here at the table, will he?*

Tom had gotten way too hot. Touching Julian was almost electric. He was three quarters hard already. He adjusted himself with his right hand. Nobody saw. He pressed against Julian just a bit more, and included his thigh. He wanted Julian to look over at him again, but he didn't want Mark to see what was going on. The challenge and danger of the situation turned him on even more.

Julian glanced at Mark; *can he see what Tom is doing? he isn't looking—he's talking with Danny... they're wording the announcements.* Julian took the chance to look. *whoa!* His eyes bulged: *look at that tent. huge!* He glanced at Tom's face: he had a strange smile—*Tom wants me to look at it!* Julian began to get hard. He couldn't help himself—he had to look at it again. He remembered that very special profile this morning in the cabin. *this is bigger!* He looked back at his sketch quickly. *stiffy sure feels good. make it go down Julian. you don't want Mark to notice it.* He tried to move his leg away, but couldn't. *can Mark tell I'm blushing?*

"Looks like we're all set, guys." Mark drained his cup... *maybe there's enough for another refill.* "Tom, you go on ahead and get the fire going. Danny, make the rounds... tell the patrol leaders we'll start in ten minutes. I'm going to talk to Nick and Julian for a few minutes, then we'll be right there."

damn! Tom sat up. "Yessir! On the way." He wasn't ready. He swiveled to the left, which hid his bulge from the others; it would shrink on the way down to start the fire. *it's getting dark anyway. now if Julian will just park in the right place, I might get set up for tomorrow morning. that would be smart, actually. I need to find out what his schedule looks like, for openers: timing will be crucial.* Tom adjusted himself as he went down the trail. Julian's wide eyes were a true satisfaction; *just you wait, Julian: the real thing will really impress!*

Julian was so relieved. *what if he does that at the campfire though? I hafta sit close to Nick.*

Nick had kept track of Tom's little moves at the Flaming Arrow table; he was prepared: he sat next to Julian at the campfire, making sure they sat down right in front, notebooks in hand. Even if there had been an open space near, Tom wouldn't have been able to take advantage of it. Mark's briefing session was a terrific help—it gave him the perfect arrangement to keep Julian occupied. He made suggestions to Julian as the patrols reported in. Tom would not find Julian standing idly around, handy for a surprise field trip.

After the program was well along, Tom got up to get some more wood for the fire. He was annoyed; Julian was located all wrong. He and Nick were taking this scribe business seriously. *well, I can't knock that. I'll bide my time. what else can I do? looks like tonight is a total bust.*

"No more fuel, Tom… we're not going to be here much longer." *Tom is restless tonight.* "How did your day go?" Mark was concerned about his number one assistant. Tom was one reason they always did well at camp. While Nick read the minutes, this was a good opportunity to touch base.

Tom shrugged. "Well enough, I guess. Boring, sort of. The knot tying for three hours was the worst. They need to find a way to break that into smaller chunks." After setting up First Aid, they sent him to the ropeyard. Being assigned as if he were on staff had lost its glamour already. *I might as well be a Counselor.*

"I see what you mean. I'll pass that one on. What's doing tomorrow?"

"There's a special meeting of all the Junior Assistants at HQ tomorrow morning. You know what that's all about?"

"Oh, didn't I tell you? Sorry. They want to streamline the closing ceremonies at the end of camp. You remember last year: a little disjointed, and there were a few awkward dead spots. They plan to use you guys to coordinate and make it run smoother. They'd like it to be less than two hours."

"I'm all for that! Maybe I can get them to sort out the lifeguard duty, too. It would be nice to know when it's coming. I'd like to go for a swim without getting drafted all the time."

"I talked to them about that. Part of the problem is increased demand for staff in some of the other areas... there are fifteen troops this year. Hiring more staff would raise the cost of coming to camp. They don't want to do that."

Tom could understand that… camp was plenty expensive already.

"The other scoutmasters want to help, but some of their star swimmers aren't at camp this year. At the next meeting we plan to fill out a grid. I should be able to give you a fixed duty list by tomorrow night. Is there any other swimmer in our troop we could list?" Several had lifesaving out of the way.

Tom thought about it. "Well, Jay Porter is darn good. He just got his Lifesaving merit badge. He and Bruce did the rescue test today, as a matter of fact. Seventeen guys made it today." He didn't mention Nick. He wouldn't wish that duty on a friend.

"That's great! Anyone assigned the chair duty has to have that merit badge as a minimum." Nick signaled from up front—Mark was next on the program. "I'll keep working on it." He skipped to the front of the assembly.

"Thanks, Nick. Guys, I've looked over the ideas turned in for the last night Campfire. Last night you got an idea of the competition we'll face. There are three skits that could win a prize. First, Max from Lynx patrol has a large group one, then Tommy from Badgers has a promising comedy skit, and Charlie Larson from Panthers has a pageant, which also takes a big group. We'll give each one a look-see starting tonight. On Thursday we'll take a vote. Tonight, we'll give Max his turn. When he's done, we'll have announcements and closing. Max? You're up."

Max Webster was a very talented fifteen year old who had his own band. Everyone knew he would make it in the music world if anybody could. They expected his idea to be a good one.

"This is kind of different, but I think you'll like it. First off, I want each patrol to sit as a tight group, and everybody needs to be on the same side of the fire. So please, you guys on the west side, move around over here. How about three patrols in front, and four right behind them."

The Troop reassembled as Max instructed; they looked like a choir, which is what he was after. He gave each patrol its own pair of words or phrases; Wolf had "Be Prepared" and "Run." Badgers had "Brave" and "Walk," and so forth. When each had its assignments, Max rehearsed them, one at a time.

"When I point to you with my right hand it's the first word. My left hand means it's the second word. The signal will always be to a whole patrol; you will chant your word the number of times that I hold fingers up: one, two, three fingers. It's not a song, but everybody says his word in unison, exactly. Sometimes it will be slow, sometimes fast; sometimes loud, sometimes soft. Okay?"

The Troop understood. He began the run through with the Badgers. He pointed to them with his left hand, and held up three fingers.

"Brave. Brave. Brave"

"Okay, now real soft, as if it was a question," he pointed again, his arm making a shushing gesture.

"Brave? Brave? Brave?" They whispered.

"Then loud and strong!" Max reached high, pumping each word.

"Brave! Brave! Brave!"

This was fun. The troop was eager to find out what was in the skit. After each patrol had had it's pilot run, Max pulled out his script.

"You guys are like a chorus. I'll read this short story—it's kind of a poem. Then at places, I'll pause and point to a patrol and it will chant its word. At the very end, I'll raise both arms, and everyone will chant, "Forever and ever!" Max looked across to see if there were any questions. "Okay, here goes." He held the script to the side so that he could get enough light to read.

Once upon a time, there was a boy scout named Johnny. He was small for his age, and nobody seemed to notice if he was even there. One day, he was thinking about this as he walked along the trail.

Max pointed to the Panthers: "Walk. Walk. Walk," they chanted.

Most of the time that was okay, but he was looking for a way to show his troop that he was there.

"Walk, walk," from the Panthers.

Suddenly Johnny said to himself, *I want them to know I can be brave!*

Max pointed to the Badger Patrol: "Brave! Brave! Brave!"

Mark checked his watch. This was running a bit longer than he had expected, but the involvement was excellent. Even the Zebra patrol was into it—so were the Flaming Arrows, even though they were such a small group. *Tom is right in there too.* He was a little concerned about Tom; *he's a year older than the other boys. it would be good for him to mix with the other Eagle scouts; there must be a hundred or so here at camp. I'll bring that up at the staff meeting tomorrow. a function just for Eagles... something simpler than Order of the Arrow... yes... that's a good idea.* He watched Tom as he chanted enthusiastically.

"Help! Help! Help!" the Flaming Arrows raised their arms as they gave their line.

Tom was sitting right behind Julian. Mark assumed they would get along; he saw no reason to worry. *Julian seems to have fit in fine... being younger doesn't seem to be a problem.* That's one thing he liked about scouts: age levels blurred fairly fast... *able kids aren't locked in place like they are in school. Julian is a typical example.*

The Troop burst out laughing. Mark knew where that was in the script.

"Okay, okay, you guys," Max held up his hands. "If we do this, it's good to know that in a couple of places like that we will have to pause so everyone in the audience can laugh." The laughing trailed off at last. "We're coming close to the end; remember to stand and raise your arms all at once when you say the chant."

Mark walked slowly around behind the group as they worked through the little story. He'd read all three... *this one will be picked.*

"Run! Run! Run" the Tigers chanted. **"Run! Run!"**

He didn't see a single dropout. Amazing how such a simple and obvious fable had all these scouts in its grip. *here comes the finish...*

"Forever, and ever!" the Troop shouted, standing and waving. They burst into applause, and Max bowed, graciously.

Mark applauded as he went to the front. "Outstanding. Thanks Max. Okay—tomorrow we'll see the Badger skit. Danny?"

Danny stepped forward to give the announcements. "Remember to have your patrol contact person picked by noon; Nick will get them from the leaders. And for those with cameras, please tell if they need any extra film. Most kinds are available in the Trading Post. Questions?" There were none, and Danny deferred to Mark for the pledge.

"We've only got about twenty minutes until lights out, so you'll have to hurry a little. Since we're so late, we'll skip the pledge and song. Troop, dismissed!"

The Troop cheered. The final activity of the day was at hand: the race to be first at the latrine.

Nick held Julian at the campfire to talk briefly about Max's skit. Most importantly, he didn't want Julian to come to the Flaming Arrow camp: he wanted him tucked away safe in Mark's cabin as soon as possible. There was just enough time left before lights out to make him uneasy. Luckily, Tom led the race to the latrine. *I'll have enough time to square things away.*

"So, if you can come up with a drawing of some kind, I'll write up the article on Max's skit." He punched Julian in the arm. "You can show me in the morning, okay?"

Julian nodded with a slight wince—his arm was still a little tender from archery. He could tell that Nick wanted to wait until tomorrow to work on this. *I'm just as glad, actually... too dark now to draw without the lantern. the cabin is better—besides it's getting cold out here.* He glanced over at Mark. He was carrying a pail of water over to the fire. "Sure. I'll figure out something." He pictured Max in front of the fire, motioning his arms. *hmm. how do you draw flames?*

Nick took off running for the Flaming Arrow camp; Danny was walking up the trail slowly—*good. I have get there first: I have a plan for tonight.. keeping Danny in the dark would be a good idea.* He raced past Danny without saying anything. He went straight to his footlocker and grabbed his flashlight, towel, and a small tube. He tossed everything onto his cover blanket, wrapped it up and headed for the supply tent. He stopped to glance down the trail... *what luck!* Danny was walking in slow motion, practically. He hurried over to the supply tent and turned on the flashlight... *hey! someone moved everything out of the way already! fantastic! is this my lucky day, or what?!*

He wedged the flashlight between a couple of crates. He spread out the blanket, tucked the tube and towel out of sight behind the end crate, and surveyed the area quickly... everything was ready. *much easier than I expected: didn't have to move any crates.* He turned off the flashlight and put it with the towel. He hurried from the supply tent to the cupboard by the stove and pulled out the Coleman lantern. He was busy pumping pressure into the tank when Danny arrived.

"Hey, Nick. Thanks." Danny had been on his way to start the lantern; this helped. He approached slowly; as Nick lit the mantle, he looked at his watch. "Looks like sixteen minutes until lights out." He sat carefully, facing out—climbing over the bench wouldn't be such a hot idea... his back and legs were very tender. *must have gotten more of a burn than I thought.* The lotion Mark applied before supper was absorbed long ago. He flipped back to the menu page in his notebook; tomorrow morning: scrambled eggs, bacon, toast. *no problem. especially since I have Julian to help. oh yeah... that reminds me: what about afterward? will I be able to play with Julian after breakfast? doesn't look too good right now*—he twisted his back to check. *feels warm, all right. Mark said I was more than a little pink. I'll know how bad in the morning...* He afraid he knew already.

It hurt when he turned his head; the shirt collar band under his kerchief rubbed when he moved... *it's so **rough** when it rubs. I'm tempted to take my shirt off right now.* He twisted to the right a little and stopped quick. *yow, don't do that...* he took in a breath—*tender around the belt line too. how can it be this bad? I wasn't in the sun that long... three hours, all told. it's a lot worse than before supper. walking up here from the campfire was not fun at all.* He performed a tentative touch test where he sat... *ooo. even my arms are sore.*

Tom jogged in, panting. "Not bad; I was third!" He had sprinted to the latrine. Knowing the lay of the land and how to hurdle over a clump of grass made a difference. He put his hands on his hips and caught his breath. Straying from the trail was cheating, technically; tonight there was no other way to pass anyone, and he had six ahead of him.

Nick had been waiting; he walked by and spoke just above a whisper: "Code Green." He turned to see if Tom heard.

Tom looked at him. He nodded his head. "You're on." He checked to see if Danny had heard. *looks like his mind is elsewhere.* He grinned at Nick and raised his eyebrows. *perfect. just what I need. Nick is brilliant at times. after today's disappointments, I deserve this.* He gave Nick a thumb up. He went to the table and sat down next to Danny.

"Third one! Who beat you?"

"Two guys from Zebra: Tad, and Clint. I only beat Jim W. by about six inches. They were sitting the closest to the trail at the campfire, so they had a good head start." Tom was the fastest runner in the Troop, mostly because he was the oldest. But there were a couple of contenders that were going to be right on his heels before long. *especially that Tad—he must be in Track and Field at school.* Tom planned to be first for as long as he was Junior Assistant, then retire, undefeated. Racing to the latrine was a tradition in Troop 9. Only three times had Tom been forced to wait in line—zero times, the last two years. Having six booths helped, of course.

"Well, they'll have a good brag for a while anyway… they can use it. They're the weakest in the points department." Danny didn't know anyone over there very well.

"I'll let 'em have fun for a few days. So: which half do you want tonight?"

"Let me take the Zebras, Wolves, and Badgers." *those camps are the closest—less walking* "The Zebras can whoop it up pretty good before I tell them they lost half a point this morning," Danny chuckled. He glanced at his watch. "It's ten 'til… just enough time for me to make it down there and back." The line at the latrine was probably gone by now. He left his tablet on the table and headed downslope. *the back of my legs doesn't feel so good either...* He walked a little slower.

"I'll wait 'til you get back," Tom said loudly. He looked at Nick. "I knew you were good for something."

"Thanks, Boss." Nick was pleased with himself. "Everything is ready. When you think he's asleep, tap me on your way out. It's all set up right behind the crates in the supply tent—oh: take your pillow along, too." It helped that Tom was in the mood and ready to trot. But then, when wasn't he? "Back in a jiffy; I gotta take a whiz too." He jogged off after Danny.

Tom hadn't expected to be alone in the camp—it felt strange with nobody around. *I gotta hand it to Nick for timing. I'm so horny now… it's all I can do to keep my hands on the table. here it is, the second day, and I haven't made* **one** *conquest. well, Nick knows how to satisfy. he'll make up for things. tomorrow I'll have better luck snagging Julian. things are looking up.*

23   *Mark shaves*

Julian was puzzled by Nick's hasty exit—*why was he in such a hurry to leave?* He wasn't headed toward the latrine with everyone, but to the Flaming Arrow camp—*oh... looks like he needs to talk to Danny.* Danny doesn't do the nightly race. Julian nodded with approval—*I wouldn't either.* He smiled gratefully—thanks to Mark, he didn't need to. He closed his notebook and poked the pencil into the spiral. *I have to think about the Max drawing for a while. nothing's coming into my head...* He watched Nick hurry up the trail... *whoa!* It hit him: Nick had just dismissed him for the day! A curtain opened in his mind: *my time with Mark is almost here. gosh...* he hadn't spent any time thinking about it. *boy o boy...* He stood and turned toward the cabin... *I guess it's okay to go on ahead. I can go in without waiting. that's what Mark said... it's my cabin too.* That thought caused a small buzz... one that felt very good.

Julian's thoughts returned to the last time he got to sit next to Mark... during supper. It was wonderful, but now that he thought about it he was surprised... *I didn't go all crazy like I always did before. I didn't even sneak one look! I've been so busy today that I didn't even think about tonight once. ooo... I was supposed to make a list.* He looked back to the assembly area... Mark was pouring water over the embers of the campfire. *wow... Mark always does his share.* Julian watched him stir the steaming ashes... seeing to it that the fire was completely dead.

Suddenly it felt different to look at Mark... he felt a glow—it started as a blush and turned into prickly goose bumps. *I'm about to be with him at last... better get a move on.* He turned and walked on... he took slow, small steps on purpose... *maybe Mark will catch up. plenty of light to see the trail... moon hasn't set yet.* He frowned.... *should I have stayed to help put out the fire?* His mind was oddly blank; he didn't know exactly what he should be doing, other than going to the cabin. Seeing Mark just now was sort of like a new discovery or something. Why would that be?

Mark hurried to kill the embers... there weren't many, thankfully. He wasn't anxious about tonight, but he wasn't completely confident, either. He got down on his knees and felt through the soup. Past experience had taught him to be thorough... a live ember could dry out the mud and come back to life in the middle of the night. He glanced up the trail. *hah! Julian is lagging behind, obviously waiting for me to catch up.* Mark was pleased... he hurried—he didn't want Julian going up to the Flaming Arrow camp. *we need to have that conference, and we don't have a lot of time. that skit took longer than I expected.*

Julian paused to look up at the sky. *amazing how bright and clear the stars are... I saw that last night too. someday I should learn about them. all I know is the Milky Way. why do they call it that, anyway? it's not milky at all. it's like a splash of glitter or something. huh. the Glitter Way. that's just as stupid. some things are just hard to name, I guess.* Off to the east a quick streak of light dashed earthward. *ooo! a shooting star! you don't get to see those very often.* It felt special, seeing that; almost as if it was doing that just for him to see. Sometimes he had that kind of sensation and it made him feel grateful and happy just to be wherever he was at the time. He waited to see if there were others. *nope... didn't think there would be.* He continued walking toward the cabin.

Mark jogged up the trail, wiping his hands on the back of his pants... the cabin was still about ten yards ahead. *I was right about Julian taking his time.* He came up behind silently and patted Julian's right shoulder lightly as he stepped alongside.

Julian felt a rush—he hadn't been worried about anything, but that soft pat was wonderfully reassuring—it told him instantly that everything was still okay. He glanced at Mark. The moon was still up enough to light his face... *wow is he handsome.*

A spur of the moment idea: "You want to race the rest of the way?"

Julian laughed and broke into a run. The door wasn't locked—he barged right in. He tossed his tablet to the side... he was going to close the door and hide behind it, but Mark was right behind him.

Mark was delighted; starting things off with a light merry tone always made things go well. He turned on the light.

Julian looked at Mark happily. He hadn't expected a challenge like that. *I shouldn't have won.*

"You run well. Do you know Tad?" Mark caught his breath.

Julian shook his head.

"He's a Zebra, new this year. He's the one that's going to keep Tom on his toes. He's on the high school track team already, and he's only a freshman." Mark looked to his right. "You dropped your tablet."

"Ooo!" He rushed to pick it up.

Mark checked the clock. *blast! we've only got fifteen minutes before lights out. I don't want to stretch that two nights in a row.* "Okay, time for our first day-end confab." He looked around for a good place. *only one chair…* he glanced at the bed. *that's out. I should have planned this better.* "Why don't we just sit here in the middle for tonight. I'll try to round up another chair tomorrow." He gestured to the center of the room and sat down cross-legged.

Julian giggled happily and sat down facing Mark. *what could be better than this?!*

Mark needed to know what was going on in that happy bubbling head. "Tell me about your day, Julian. What was best and what was worst."

"It was mostly best! I never expected to do so much, all in one day," he enthused. *boy, where should I start?* He gave a detailed account of the morning, except for the bit with Danny in the tent. He'd made the zipped lip pledge. He always kept that. He told about how Tom had helped him practice dive. He didn't tell about the squeeze. He didn't think he should; at least, not yet. *I don't want to get Tom in trouble.* He talked about Leonard, about the badge classes, the chef with the fun moustache, the sash with hundreds of merit badges, the grumpy counselor…

Mark was delighted. Julian was bubbling over with news and information. It was refreshing, invigorating to witness and share his eagerness and enthusiasm. It took him back to his own early days as a scout—how good it felt just to be a part of it all. It was almost like being a first day for him too… he had come to take the thrill of being in camp for granted. Julian's happiness was infectious.

Julian barely stopped to breathe, he was so eager to share his wonderful first day at camp. "And then, Max had his song…." Julian stopped. He looked at Mark's smiling face. "What?!"

"In other words, you had a great day."

Julian frowned, then realized he'd been talking non-stop. He blushed and looked up at Mark sheepishly. "I'm sorry. I must sound a little silly. And you had a boring day? No fun at all?" He did a little pout with his lower lip

Mark laughed. "You're too much! And forget about my boring day; you just fixed that." This talk is just the right thing. "So you got along fine with Nick?"

"Yeah!" Julian remembered the thoughts he had at the waterfront and at the camp. "He's really a **smart** guy, you know?" He frowned: *the newsletter.* "Do I have to type stuff?" That part was scary. "I'm not sure exactly what I'm supposed to do." He looked at Mark hopefully.

Mark shook his head. "Not right now—Nick can do that part—he can type well enough for the both of you. What you should do is learn from him what things to notice and look for, what things to make a note of. Then you and he can sit together and decide what to put in the newsletter." Mark explained briefly what being an apprentice was all about. He knew from the scrapbook that Julian was a natural journalist. A year from now he can take over the newsletter completely. By then he'll have taken a typing class.

Julian watched mark talk as usual, but it was different this time. *he makes me feel… what's the word? important. yeah… like what I do is important. I never felt that before. huh. Julian focused his eyes… whoa… there they are again—whiskers. I wonder if I should ask…*

"You look like you've got another question."

Julian snapped out of his preoccupation. "Oh. Sorry. It's nothing, really." He was embarrassed suddenly. He'd just broken one of his own rules about staring.

"Julian, it is **something**. No questions should go unanswered here. That's one of the ground rules of being a good roommate, okay?" Mark looked him in the eye. "If I don't know what you need, how can I help? I'm not a mind reader." He kept the eye contact. He felt strongly that Julian could get past his inclination to daydream and fantasize if he was confronted like this.

Julian looked down sheepishly. "It's kind of personal, I guess." He was afraid suddenly that he'd really fouled up. He worked his fingers nervously.

Personal? Mark saw that Julian was afraid of something. He inhaled deep… this could be the awkward moment he'd been dreading. *the sooner it's dealt with, the easier it will be.* "Julian, please. It's all right. You don't have to worry. You can trust me, you know. If I can answer your question, I will. If I can't, I'll tell you why.

"I… um…" *this is hard!* He steeled himself and looked up. "Can I watch you shave?"

Mark was stunned. He paused for a second then laughed. "Shave?"

Julian nodded his head, embarrassed. "I've always wanted to see that." He didn't have to tell about how he enjoyed studying Mark's face. In fact, he had been developing the usual problem again. He was unable to block the effect of Mark's incredible aroma, and that blue eyed dazzling stare had taken over the controls down below… he was up full. *luckily it doesn't show, sitting like this.*

Mark just realized—*how basic. he has no father. of course he needs to see that! shame on me.* "I'm sorry, Julian I shouldn't have laughed. Please forgive me. Of course you can see me shave. You're a few years away from needing to do it yourself, but there's no reason not to know all the secrets." He winked as if it were a confidence. Mark felt a new sensation—a pleasant feeling, really. *this is an honest need, honestly asked.* Being able to satisfy that felt wonderful. He looked at the clock. *what an idea: maybe I can do that tonight!*

Julian blushed. *good thing I'm sitting down.* Mark's winks always made his knees cave in.

"I usually shave in the morning. Maybe I can do that tonight instead. That way you can see what it's all about. Would you like that?"

"Wow! Really?" A dream come true! "Yeah! Right now?"

Mark looked at the clock. *this is perfect.* "Tell you what: you get all your stuff ready for lights out. Set straight what you'll need in the morning. Make any notes you need, things like that. Meanwhile, I'll take my shower. Then, when I'm all dried off, you can come in and watch me shave. I'll bet we can do it by exactly ten o'clock."

Julian looked at the clock. *six minutes! wowee.* He looked at Mark, excited but still unsure about what to do next.

Mark stood; his knee joints complained a little. *getting up from a squat is getting harder; more exercise, Mark. I need to get that chair.* He glanced at Julian and smiled, "Good chat, Roomie." He gave a wink, a thumbs up, and went over to the clothes rack to undress.

roomie! Julian flushed, amazed at the title; he watched Mark go to the far side of the bed. It took a second for his brain to catch up. *oh! I can't just sit here!* He stood and scratched his head… *what do I need to get ready for tomorrow? umm...* he opened the tablet to the last page. *make a list. Nick said to always make a list first...* he giggled happily and skipped over to the table and pulled out the chair.

He opened the tablet and leafed through the pages… *wait. I need the other tablet.* He had figured out that this one had to be reserved for drawing. He raced over to the footlocker.

Mark followed his usual ritual. He disrobed down to his shorts and pulled open the top drawer…

> > *scree—eep!* < <

blast it… forgot that sandpaper. He shook his head. As he rounded the end of the bed the sight of Julian hard at task at the table was reassuring—and affirming. He proceeded to the bathroom—his nightly ritual underway. He pulled open the shower curtain and turned on the water; it usually came up to temperature fast. He stepped to the right and put his fresh briefs on the top of the toilet tank—*out of harm's way there.* This was habit, done without paying any particular attention. He stepped back to the shower, pulled the bath mat from the wall rack and placed it in front of the shower. He removed his briefs, flipped them to the side and stepped into the shower. It didn't occur to him to close the door; he never did that, because it steamed up the mirror.

Julian stared opened mouthed at the shower curtain. *what an idiot! I just missed it!* He did get to see the last bit: only a flashing glimpse of the front side, but he got a superb view of Mark's bare backside before the shower curtain was pulled closed. He was mesmerized by the blurred image busily scrubbing itself behind the semi transparent shower curtain.

Some things are so intense that you have to wait a minute for them to sink in a little before you realize what they are, and what to think about them. This was one of those events. Those bare **muscular** buns… that was a contour and shape that had not meant anything until now. Now they were an imprint on his consciousness that would not fade… *what do they look like with water running off them, soap bubbles being rinsed away…* a good idea of that was visible right now through that plastic curtain. *why do they make those out of blurry plastic, anyway? the one at home is just the same.*

He frowned at his screwup. *sitting right here the whole time and you didn't even **notice**?!* Julian took a deep breath. *that will not happen again.*

Mark felt terrific. *this water is fantastic.* He broke into a chorus of **Catch a Falling Star** as he shampooed his hair. He worked up lather with vigor—he needed to make this a quick shower, or he wouldn't have time for the shaving demo. "…put it in your pocket, never let it fade away…"

Julian froze. *that's the song! that's the song on the radio when Mark came to the door that first time.* It had been a sacred song ever since.

"…save it for a rainy day…"

*how could he be singing **that** song?!* Julian had never heard Mark sing, actually. *I didn't know he could do that…* Reluctantly, he turned back to the tablet. He didn't have much written down: breakfast… inspections. He couldn't think what to write next. He wanted to watch the shower some more but didn't dare. He tapped his pencil absentmindedly, unsure what to write next.

no back brush… it didn't occur to me to bring one along The shortcomings of this shower had just been put on Marks' to do list. *too small… I had no idea I would have the cabin again. I expected to be spending two weeks in a crew tent.*

Mark had stopped singing. Julian turned to look... *yow! what if he catches me watching?!* He looked at the clock. *ohmygosh. I'm supposed to be ready for bed! I forgot about that...* he pulled the chair back and ran to the clothes rack to take off his shirt.

Mark shut off the shower and shook his head back and forth to shed the extra water. He pulled the curtain open and reached for the towel. He buried his face in it as always—starting at the top was automatic. *oh... that's right...* He thought to look out—*good.* For a minute he was afraid he'd be facing Julian in nature's own. Normally that wouldn't bother him, but in Julian's case, caution was probably a good idea. Relieved, he toweled himself off completely, pleased that he wasn't putting on a show. He wrapped the towel around his waist and stepped over to the washbasin. He looked in the mirror and frowned at himself. *why do I always suspect the worst? give Julian a break, Mark.*

Julian undressed as fast as he could. He ran to his cot and took off his tennies and socks. Just as he was putting his short pants down on the footlocker lid, a distant voice was heard through the window over the desk:

"Two minutes, you have two minutes." Tom had approached the Lynx camp on his way to alert the Panthers that it was lights out time. On the other side, Danny announced the same warning to the Zebras.

"You ready to see this?" Mark called out as he turned on the hot water tap.

"Here I come," Julian was there in a second.

"You've never seen this before? Really?"

Julian shook his head. "Only on TV. Does it hurt?"

"Not a bit, if the razor is nice and sharp." Mark gestured with his head: "Come around on the other side. More room. You can get a better view."

Julian scooted around behind... he happened to notice the slit in the big bath towel. *oh boy. if Mark bends over...* he forced himself to pay attention to what he was supposed to be watching. Mark was splashing a cheek with water. "Why do you do that?"

"Helps keep them soft and easy to cut. If they're dried out, they won't cut off as clean and they can catch in the blade. The hotter the water the better." He turned his face and lowered it even with Julian. "Feel the wet side, then the dry side."

Julian reached over and felt the wet side of Mark's face. "Whoa…" *whiskers are so mysterious.*

"They dry out super fast. I just washed them a minute ago."

"Huh." Julian raised his left hand and felt the dry side. "You're right. These are really *stiff*." Unconsciously he felt his own cheek… *I'm a long way from having those. I don't even have much hair below the belt yet.*

Mark dampened the other side and his neck. He raised his eyebrows.

Julian grinned wide and nodded his head eagerly. This was a dream come true.

Mark shook the can vigorously and sprayed foam across his face.

"Whoa!" *what a neat sound! I never guessed it would sound like that. amazing! it just foams up like that!* Mark spreading it around evenly with his fingertips was just like that TV commercial he'd seen… *is it cold? or hot?*

Mark followed his usual sequence, starting below his right ear. That side done, he rinsed off the razor and turned his head. Julian's reflection in the mirror—rapt, miming every move— *this is wonderful.*

The swipes of the razor through the white foam were silent.

I thought I'd hear something, like bitty snaps when the teeny hair stubs got cut off. Julian listened carefully: *nope. total quiet.* When Mark shaved under his chin he thought there was a little sound. *huh. the foam must make it go quiet.*

Mark stretched his upper lip and shaved it both up and down and side to side. He liked to get that shaved close. He did a second run under his lower lip—*there's always a spot that gets missed.* He glanced at Julian's reflection again. Watching him unconsciously imitating the facial stretches was priceless. He reached forward to rinse out the razor.

"Wait!" Julian held Mark's forearm. "Let me see." He pulled the razor close and looked at the tiny hair stubs in the foam. "Huh."

Mark flushed the razor thoroughly; he couldn't resist watching Julian's facial expressions in the mirror while he rinsed. *how could something so ordinary and routine be transformed like this?*

Julian processed it into his memory. *I love Mark so much. this helps.*

Mark pulled the corner of the towel up and dried his face. He bent close to the mirror and turned left and right to check for any missed spots. Under the nose was a tricky spot.

Julian had excellent peripheral vision. It was getting a very special treat in the lower right quadrant. He couldn't help but glance there for a millisecond. It wasn't enough time to study it of course—but for his camera-like eye, it was sufficient.

"There we are." He looked at himself. Hair is still damp... *that's life.* He looked at Julian. "Ready for lights out?"

Julian nodded yes. It was an understatement of the first order. He had to get over to that cot without Mark noticing that he had the hardest, the biggest stiffy in his whole life.

"Go and catch the main light on your way. I'll get this one after I hang up my towel." Mark stepped back and let Julian pass in front of him. *that was really a great idea.*

Julian nodded and did a beeline for the door.

Mark took off the towel and did another vigorous fluff-up of his hair. At home he showered an hour or so before going to bed so he didn't have to put up with a damp pillowcase. *life in the wilderness has its inconveniences...* he hummed another chorus of the song. Somehow it popped into his head at odd times. It was a feel good moment when that happened. He hung up the towel and went for his underpants.

He was about to hit the switch, but decided to check the clock. *I didn't set the alarm.* He stepped over to the table and picked up the Big Ben. He wound it tight, then pulled out the button. He placed the clock just right so he could see its face and grab it quick. Inches made a **huge** difference. He reached back with a twist and pushed the light switch down.

Julian watched Mark set the clock and turn off the light. He was in his maximum viewpoint position and got every minute this time. He was getting good at this.

"G'night," Mark said. "Sweet dreams."

"Good night… you too." Julian had a bunch of calming down and pressure relieving to do, actually. He was about to discover how to do that on this cot. He didn't do that last night… *too chicken. what if it creaks?*

Mark relaxed after finding a good spot. It was easier tonight for some reason. A hot shower before bed made all the difference.

"Mark?" Julian just thought of this. This was Important.

"Yes?" Mark was about to scold that lights out meant no talking too, but he waited.

He paused, feeling awkward. "Thank you." He wished he could say that better, but he didn't know how. Everything tonight was so wonderful, especially the shave!

thank you? what for? He puzzled for a minute but decided not to ask. "You are most welcome Julian. Anytime." *oh… must have been the shave.* Mark smiled. *what a treat today has been, all around.*

He forgot about the interminable meetings at HQ and the tedious session at the archery range. He didn't dwell on his concern about Julian's crush… it wasn't the mountainous problem he'd been dreading. It was there no doubt, but it was a molehill; plenty of time to find a fix. *he's a boy, Mark; he has boy questions.* He yawned and fell asleep in seconds.

Julian turned onto his back and scootched until he felt comfortable. He had never had so much to think about at one time. He didn't know where to start, even. How could everything be so **cool?** So wonderful? *if every day is like this, I don't know if I can stand it!* He spent some time just calming down, not exactly thinking about anything. Eventually a natural order asserted itself; his sub conscious mind set about sorting and prioritizing things.

The last image he saw came up first, naturally enough. Mark was stretched wide reaching for the light switch. The light caught every detail perfectly. Just before that, he stood winding the clock. That part was in the shadow, but a very clear profile was visible for several seconds. Combined with the one from last night, a good picture was developing in his mind of the basic overall shape and size—when it was covered up. He took in a deep breath and exhaled. The underwear shot was quickly replaced by the double set that he got in the bathroom—the ones in the gap between the two sides of that towel. A familiar pressure below seemed to insist on reviewing that one especially. It turned out that Mark was uncircumcised, just like Danny. Only Mark was bigger—a **lot** bigger.

sweet dreams is right.

24   *Code Green*

When Tom and Danny returned from the lights out tour, Nick was already in his sleeping bag. He lay on his back with his hands behind his head, thinking about his plan. It was time for Tom to get a little of his own medicine. Nick didn't know if he ever had, come to think about it. Darkness closed in when Tom turned off the Coleman; the moon had set, but there was still enough light for him to see Tom and Danny going to their cots. While he waited for Danny to fall asleep, Nick ran through his scenario again. *if Tom is true to form, I just might pull this off. if he's super horny and wild... it will be tough. I'll know by how he reacts to the first kiss.*

—ɯ—

Danny was tired—and way more tender than he wanted or expected to be. It was all he could do to undress without groaning out loud. He had to take off his underpants—the elastic waistband hurt something awful. *it keeps getting worse. I have to sleep nude tonight, that's all.* He was too embarrassed to ask either of his tent mates to spread some lotion on... *besides, I don't want my new sleeping bag to get all greasy; I was so stupid not to take the bottle to the lake in the first place. maybe I'll luck out and be okay in the morning. one thing for sure: no tanning tomorrow.*

He crawled in slowly... carefully... and turned onto his left side. *I'll leave my back open to the air... cover up only if I get cold. this soft flannel sure helps...* He started to relax, and think about his day. All told, it had been a great start. He did well at the first Canoeing class. *I'll earn the badge by the end of camp, no sweat.* Backpacking was a problem... *I have to drop it for now... takes too much time. can't do my Flaming Arrow duties if I'm gone on long hikes. besides, on most days I'd lose out on the afternoon free swim. I have to find an opening someplace else tomorrow.* A few other guys wanted to drop out… getting a partner might not be too hard. He yawned.

His shoulders felt better now, but he was aware of them. *this flannel bag is better than a scout shirt, for sure.* He yawned again. *boy, am I sleepy.* He replayed the campfire skit in his memory, and chuckled; *Max is sure good; he can play piano and guitar too…* he tucked his feet into the bag. *that's better…*

At last, the day ended for Danny. The sound of his breathing told Nick that the Fun Hour was at hand. Sure enough, Tom tapped him lightly… *he's headed for the supply tent.* Nick grinned… *Tom is hot to trot. I'm ready.*

The moon was long gone, but there was plenty of starlight. Tom grabbed his pillow and made a beeline for the supply tent. Starlight wasn't strong enough to illuminate the tent—the canvas was too heavy. He felt his way along the crates to the center. *dark in here…* he moved carefully, expecting to run into a crate somewhere. He turned around. Nick's silhouette appeared in the passage. "Man, I am so ready for this! You must be reading my mind, or something." His eyes adjusted rapidly. He could see the open space. *I'm standing on a blanket!* "When did you set all this up?" He tossed the pillow to the far end, took off his skivvies and chucked them over to the crates.

"It was already arranged! All I had to do was spread the blanket." *I wondered about that…* He took off his undies, reached behind the box and grabbed the towel and tube of KY. "I brought a new tube, too."

"Hey, you're the man!" He reached out and grabbed Nick. They embraced tightly and kissed. The feel of Nick's lips was one thing that Tom had no defense against. They mellowed him and they made his cock throb. He hated to admit that, too. Mushy stuff was generally a turn off, but Nick's kisses were dangerous. The frustrations of the day started to fade. He lowered Nick onto the blanket, kissing all the way.

Nick lay on his back and caressed Tom's buns as he kissed. *Tom is unusually gentle tonight… very encouraging. better make the move now before he gets too hot.* Deliberately, Nick moved his arms upward around Tom's back; he grasped them together firmly and performed a surprise flip. He had turned them over and become the top. He broke the kiss and spoke conversationally. "Like I was saying…"

Tom laughed. "I'm supposed to remember?" *I swear, Nick's brain is like a huge computer.* The one thing he could count on was that Nick kept track of everything. He knew instantly the conversation Nick was alluding to, and it had to have been three weeks ago, at least.

Nick sat up and massaged Tom's chest. "I want to have my share this time. You always get to go first, and half the time you're so pooped afterward, all I get to do is jack off and wait for my butt to recover." He bent down and kissed Tom's cock head. He peeled back the foreskin and licked under the tip.

Tom writhed and moaned involuntarily. *man that feels good.* He recalled their conversation—it got interrupted suddenly and unexpectedly by an unsuspecting kid poking around in the brush. *we had to get dressed fast, that time.* "Hmm… I have to admit I've thought about it some. The times I tried it, it was pretty much zero fun." His brother Randy tried it once when he was in the fifth grade. And when he was a Tenderfoot, a couple of times… Neither Marty nor Rick knew how to do it right… *it was a long time ago, actually.* "I always hated the idea of it, anyway. I don't know why."

"Well, forget the **idea**. I'm talking about how it **feels**. Tom, when you do it right, there's nothing better!" He massaged Tom's balls gently.

Tom sensed an implied criticism; he did not like that, at all. "What do you mean? Right?" *those moans of delight I heard weren't faked.*

"Tom, you need to understand something: you have become so **huge**, it's hard to take, and it can hurt a lot—especially afterwards."

Tom was not completely surprised to hear this. He was quite pleased with his cock, especially since it had become nine inches… *well, eight and seven eighths.* Good enough to say nine… he knew of only four others larger, in fact. *it's awkward at times, that's true.*

"Man, Nick, sometimes I get so horny I just get carried away. I'm sorry if I hurt you, though. I've wondered sometimes about it." His new conquests: *sometimes it seemed like… well, it's hard to say; maybe Nick can help me figure that out. my little "surprise parties" aren't as welcome as they used to be. that's what bummed me out the last couple of weeks of school. they all weaseled out, all three of them. I couldn't force them to go along, so I was left high and dry. it's hard to get them lined up, too.*

It just registered. "Butt recover? What do you mean?" Tom was puzzled by that comment. *true, I often get it off first... I can't help it that Nick is so good.*

"Well..." Nick tried to be delicate... "it depends. Sometimes it takes a day, but other times it takes two or three. If you go in too soon, or too far in, it really hurts. The pain sort of quits after a while, and the pleasure takes over, especially when you massage the prostate as you go in and out. That is really intense. But afterwards, the hole is sore, **really** sore. Sometimes I've wondered if it was going to shut again or not. Once I had to walk carefully, and sit down sort of on one cheek."

Tom was surprised by this. "How come nobody else ever told me that? Man, I thought everybody loved it." He rarely wondered if they liked it or not, actually. He just assumed they did. They always came, as far as he could remember.

"Think about it, Tom. You always go for the cute little buns. How are they going to complain? You're the big star, the one who knows, the man to please. You could beat them up good if you got mad." Nick massaged Tom's thighs gently, lovingly.

"But I'd never..."

"I know you wouldn't, but they don't know you, do they? You're a lot bigger than they are, not just in the cock department. Your biceps are a wonder, too, you know."

Tom blushed at the flattery. "Yeah, I guess you're right about that." He still thought of himself as the little brother most of the time. *up to a couple of years ago, I was the short one.* He thought about some of the times he'd had over the years. "It didn't used to be that way, though." *I didn't have any muscles until I started playing football.*

"Oh? Didn't you tell me once that you started doing this in the fourth or fifth grade?" Nick gently massaged Tom's abdominal ripples.

"Well, yeah... third, actually. But then it was mostly with bigger kids. Most of my friends didn't like it. They were too dinky, anyway."

"So when did you turn into Mister Humongous?"

Tom laughed, then realized the implication. "Do they call me that?" *I don't want to be thought of as some kind of monster.* **sex driven stud,** *that's okay.*

"No, I guess not. I haven't heard anyone say that. But can't you see it in their eyes when they look at you, especially if you're hard?" Tom loved to flash it at the bubble butts and brag later about their facial expression.

That was true—*Julian was definitely impressed when he saw my hard-on bulging up a tent after supper.* He always assumed it was awe, envy… something they wanted. Maybe it was fear… Nah. *Julian smiled, didn't he? or was that before he saw it… not sure. then there was Judd at the lake today—he stole a lot of looks while I was stuck in the lifeguard chair. he has a butt just like Julian's. I was proud of myself for staying limp. that's one thing I've learned to control, at least.* "Mmmm…" Nick had begun to massage his cock.

"We wouldn't want to go all soft, would we, now?"

"No, no, no, we wouldn't," Tom said agreeably. "Okay, professor, maybe you could tell me what to do about this." *Nick's hands are nice.*

"As a matter of fact…" Nick pushed Tom's foreskin down as far as he could and squeezed the base. "I believe I can. I have done a bit of research on the subject." *well, I read a porno novel, actually.* But Tom didn't need to know that particular detail.

"Hmm… not in the school library, I bet." *I tried looking there myself once; it's useless for that…*

"Never mind where. The point is, now that I have your attention," he squeezed Tom's freshly hardened cock. "Are you **up** for a lesson?" He pulled the foreskin up to punctuate his question. He held the skin up tight and massaged the tip.

Tom hesitated. This is not how he had expected to get his rocks off. He thought for a minute. He wasn't disappointed… that was surprising. Nick had made perfect sense, as usual. Tom had paid attention, which was **not** usual. His hornies were there, but not mindless like they had been earlier. *maybe I'll indulge Nick… I've never done that. maybe I'll have a good time. no, that isn't true… I always have a good time with Nick.*

"Do I have to take notes?"

"Against the rules."

Tom pushed his hips upwards; he was waiting. Nick could do as he wished. *why not? I can always stop and trade places if I want.*

Nick bent down and pulled the foreskin down with his right hand, and took Tom's cock into his mouth. He sucked it up and down a couple of times. Then he sat back and took the cap off the tube of KY. He greased his right forefinger liberally.

Tom moaned, "Don't stop now… "

Nick held Tom's cock with his left hand and gently sucked again. He sat back long enough to lift Tom's knees. As he returned his mouth to the tip of Tom's cock, he slid the lubricated finger down to Tom's anus. He massaged it gently… as it puckered in response to the upward motion of his sucking, he began to insert his finger gently. He worked them together like this, and Tom began to writhe in pleasure.

"Mmmnn…" *I like this so far… glad I'm on my back… more satisfying.*

Nick let up on the sucking. *I need to make this last.* His finger was in fully now, and he touched the prostate. Tom bounced in pleasure.

"Ohmm!"

"Shhh… we don't want to wake Danny up!" Nick sat up and coated the second finger. He sat back on his knees and repeated the process… *that book seems to be right about this.* He was able now to rotate both the fingers… gradually, he pushed them in and out. He coaxed the anus muscle to relax and flex. He sucked again to trigger the muscle reflex. Soon both fingers were in completely; the anus learned to grab as they were pulled outward.

Tom was amazed—*this is superior!* He wanted that fingertip to land on his prostate and stay there! It was hard to keep quiet.

Nick went to step three… lubricated a third finger. It was much easier to work, because the muscle had learned to stretch and to clasp. Tom's writhing indicated that he was ready. Nick greased his cock and put the tip at the door. He held Tom's cock in his left hand and stroked it gently as he inserted himself. There was no resistance. It slid in as if it were returning home. It hit the prostate and Tom jerked wildly.

Tom was barely conscious, he was in such ecstasy. His attention was fully on his pleasure centers. *think about it later… I want this to last all night.*

Nick leaned forward as he fucked, and kissed Tom on the mouth. The working of their lips was complex and intense. Nick could tell that

Tom was far more involved than he had ever been. *slow down a little, Nick or you'll shoot too soon.* He backed out briefly and lifted Tom's right leg onto his shoulder. He re-entered, and began to thrust with slow, full length entries. Tom lifted his left leg up around Nick's back... the rhythm and contact improved.

Nick held his left hand to Tom's face, and reached his right arm under Tom's shoulder. They embraced in a firm kiss. Tom wrapped both arms around Nick. They began to play with their tongues. Nick's thrusts became more rapid and firm. He clenched his buns hard as he thrust into Tom. He connected with the prostate nearly every time he pulled up. His balls banged Tom's back with the harder pushes. Nick was no longer in control—animal requirements had taken over. His cock swelled and pulsed. As Tom's anus grabbed at him, he went over the edge and shot. Their embrace was tight, their movement spasmodic, random, uncontrolled.

Tom felt, actually **felt** Nick's cock get larger. Nick had embraced him tight; his cock rubbed up and down between their chests. His own pre-cum had lubricated him, and his sliding cock felt fantastic. That and the constant prodding of his prostate took him over the edge; he shot—a second after Nick. The feeling of cum jetting into him was amazing. Nick's pressing on him was fabulous! He shot six or seven times. Their embrace became wonderfully slippery—another new sensation.

Nick didn't count how many shots—this was the absolute best sex he had ever had. It was even better than the description in the novel. Feeling Tom's cum jetting up onto his chest was a delight he had not expected.

They rested in place, heads cheek to cheek, breathing hard. Their heartbeats slowed gradually; they caught their breaths.

Nick remained inside Tom for a time. They both seemed to want that. Nick wondered if his hard-on would ever go down; it wanted to pulse once in a while. He pulled out at last and stretched out his legs. He lay on Tom briefly... wrapped in Tom's large muscular arms like a little brother. It felt so right to do that. Their cocks were pressed next to each other... Tom's pulsed briefly. Nick's replied automatically.

Tom let his legs slide flat. The weight of Nick on him was wonderful. That was new, too. He hugged him briefly and pecked him on the forehead. "You get to do that again." *never thought I'd say that...*

Nick rolled to the side and smiled. He did not expect to get that much pleasure. That was a very new thing indeed, and welcome. "Thanks. But only if you do it that way to me first." That was the idea in the first place. He wanted to kiss Tom again. They didn't do that afterwards. *I'd better not push anything.*

"You mean we have to take turns?" He chuckled.

"Nah, not really. But we might as well have a little variety."

Tom nodded. "Umm-hmm."

They rested for a time. Talk didn't seem to fit in right now. It started to feel a little chilly. They returned to the real world.

"I brought a towel. I hope that's enough."

"Has to be, I guess. I wish we could just stay right here." Tom was surprised at himself. He usually wanted to clean up and clear out afterwards.

"Yeah. It might be fun; what would Danny do if he came in and found us in the morning?" Nick chuckled at the image.

"Well, professor... I'll say this for you: when you research something, you don't fuck around."

They both got the pun at the same time and cracked up. It complicated the cleanup. One or the other would start to giggle, and the other couldn't resist. Finally, they put on their briefs.

Tom hesitated. He felt an urge suddenly to break one of his rules. He reached out and held Nick by the shoulders. "I owe you for that one." He leaned forward and kissed Nick briefly. It was a light kiss, not passionate—but it was genuine.

"Any time." Nick was astounded. Tom **never** kissed afterward. He felt a rush and knew he must be turning red. *I'm so lucky it's dark.*

Tom walked slowly out of the supply tent. He felt super mellow right now... tired, but not droopy. This was a new feeling. He moved slowly, as if on autopilot. Eyes unfocused, he crawled into his sleeping bag without paying conscious attention. Fortunately, nothing was out of place, so habit and rote behavior served his requirements perfectly. He felt a glow or something in his head—as if he was slowly awakening from a nice comfy dream or something.

Nick wrapped everything up into his blanket and walked back to the crew tent. He noticed that Danny's back was exposed to the night air. He put down his bundle and stepped over to listen... asleep. He pulled the sleeping bag over him gently. The night had developed a chill... *don't want him to get a summer cold.* He stepped back to his cot and opened his bundle. He returned the flashlight and tube to the footlocker and put his blanket back in place. Before climbing in, he looked over at Tom—too dark to see his face. *too bad...* he was hoping for a last minute eye contact to verify that he was okay. *it was so different tonight, so...* the cool air asserted itself; his train of thought shifted to the here and now. He crawled into his sleeping bag at last.

Nick wasn't drowsy. The session had been a genuine revelation. It was the first time he knew for certain he and Tom had been truly joined when they made love. It was unlike anything he had ever imagined. *I wonder if Tom will ever allow that to happen again. it was... hum... I need a word for this. this is new.* He yawned at last. *I feel so different... I don't remember if the novel said anything about that. I read it a while ago... I have to check... maybe read it again. it's hidden in a safe place. yep. as soon as we're back home, I'll check that out. maybe there's other stuff I need to check too...* His cock was still half hard—he turned on his side to reduce the pressure. *feels good... mmm.* Recalling the kiss Tom had given him afterward—that overshadowed everything.

Tom turned onto his right side. His butt felt strangely good... tender. *Nick said something about that... but it doesn't hurt at all. what a workout.* Tom didn't understand what he felt. *too bad I can't talk to Nick a little... if only Danny's bunk wasn't right between. my butt tickles.* He felt tired, but it was a new kind of tired. His cock pulsed in an odd, irregular way. It seemed to be protesting or something. It didn't like being confined to his briefs. *what's going on? it's doing that on its own...* It didn't want to go to sleep yet.

am I supposed to beat off now? how can that be? I just emptied a huge load over there! well, it has been a couple of... no, it's been three days! He turned onto his back... his right hand moved into place. *yep... I need to do another one all right.* He pulled off his skivvies and tucked them behind... *mmm... be slow about it...* he had a special memory to follow. Nick's technique was so outstanding! Just remembering what he did was a turn on—so different from what they always did. *not even close to what Marty or Rick did…* After a minute Tom tossed back the sleeping bag. He didn't want to make any noise.

Unaware that the other was also wakeful, both Tom and Nick searched for a way to put his mind at rest. They were in a new place… they were unaware of that. But they knew that something was different.

Nick eased into slumber first… deep slumber, at last.

Tom took longer; he had not enjoyed his hand like this for a long time. *not as good as Nick, but… mmm! soon… soon. after this I can get to sleep.*

The god of sleep has taken control of Barr's Meadow for the night—even the moon has gone down. Our subjects are now free to let their subconscious minds process what has happened—a necessary stage to prepare them for what is coming next.

Julian has completed most of his childhood goals now, including watching Mark shave his chin. His experience in the cabin has encouraged him—he is farther along than he expected to be. In the morning he will discover a world that he did not know was there. For a while, he is distracted from his main objective.

Mark has underestimated Julian. His plan has been to shield Julian from danger, not himself. His success and standing with the camp leaders preoccupies him, and he doesn't understand the impact Julian has on his slowly evolving emotional needs. He has much youth remaining—he is ready to return to life, and doesn't know it—nor that Julian plans to be his inspiration.

Nick and Tom do not yet understand their discovery. Their unconscious minds are hard at work sorting things out. They are not troubled by the enormity of what has happened, but it will take some doing to be in control of the forces that have been set free. Their good fortune is to have made this discovery when and where they did.

The "camera" now zooms out so the reader can assimilate, process, and savor the memories they have just shared—the better to prepare for what is coming next:

Preview

The Poker Club: Julian's Private Scrapbook, Book 2

Tuesday, Wednesday and Thursday: days three, four and five at Camp Walker are full of fun and naughtiness. By the end of Tuesday, the daily routine of camp is well established. Water polo becomes Mark's new challenge. Julian still seeks romance with Mark: will he make any progress? The relationship of Tom and Nick becomes a major focus.

We'll get acquainted with some other members of Troop 9, as well as scouts from other troops. Some have interests and talents that fit nicely with those of Troop 9. There are lots of extra-curricular activities, some planned, others spontaneous. Another serious romance emerges; Danny's sunburn is a complication, but he is a determined scout.

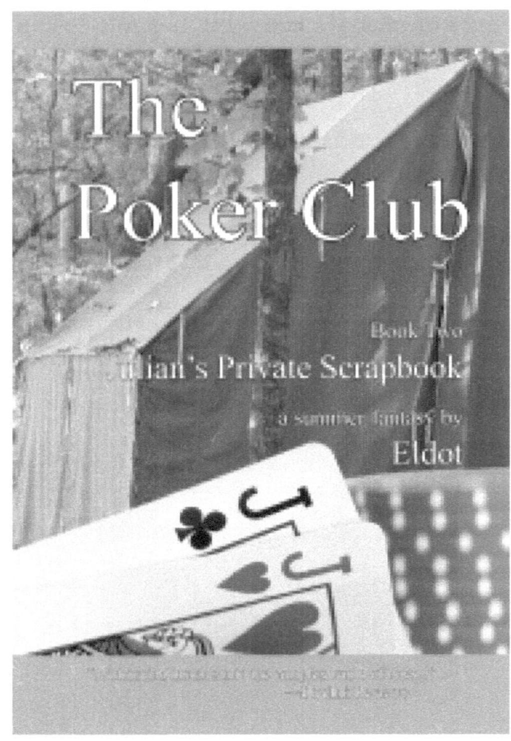

Troop 9   Mark Schaefer, Scoutmaster

1 Panthers

1 Nathan Jensen   [16] L
2 Charlie Larson   [16] L
3 Ryan Kruger   [16] S
4 Calvin Radcliffe   [15] 1st
5 Doug Tucker   [16] 1st
6 Ben Jasper   [14] 2nd
7 Don Bennett   [13] T

2 Tigers

1 Dale Baker   [16] L
2 Jay Porter   [16] L
3 Andy Ashbaugh   [16] L
4 Brad Fisher   [16] S
5 Chris Smith   [14] 2nd
6 Tony Johnson   [15] 1st
7 Shawn McGee   [13] T

3 Lynx

1 Gary West   [16] L
2 Max Webster   [15] L
3 Alex Trent   [15] S
4 Robin Simmons   [16] L
5 Paul Harris   [16] 1st
6 Jason Jones   [14] 2nd
7 Sandy Smith   [13] T

4 Wolves

1 Stuart Walker   [16] L
2 Norman Miller   [15] S
3 Casey Snyder   [15] S
4 Sid Thomas   [14] 1st
5 Jeremy Baker   [14] 1st
6 {Julian Forrest}
7 Billy Bradford   [13] T

5 Badgers

1 Arnie Shaw   [16] L
2 Chuck Nelson   [16] L
3 Tommy Carlysle   [15] S
4 Don Felton   [15] 1st
5 Bruce Ruggles   [14] 2nd
6 Freddy Scott   [13] T
7 Josh Green   [13] T

6 Zebras

1 Jim West   [16] L
2 Kurt Davis   [15] S
3 Cory Summers   [15] 2nd
4 Justin Blake   [13] 1st
5 Tad Benson   [14] 2nd
6 Clint Walker   [14] 2nd
7 open

Flaming Arrow

1 Tom Dawson   [17] E
2 Nick Harrison   [16] L
3 Danny Laskey   [15] S
4 Frank Ferris, bugler   [16] L
5 Julian Forrest   [14] 1st

Ranks

E= Eagle   (1)
L= Life   (14)
S= Star   (8)
1st= First Class   (9)
2nd= Second Class   (7)
T= Tenderfoot   (6)

Position

1-6 Patrol

chronological age in brackets [ ]

Camp Walker Staff [June 1962]

Camp Director: **John Jorgensen**

Camp Ranger/Quartermaster: **"Sarge" Oliver**
    Senior Counselors for camp deliveries and maintenance [3]
    Junior Counselors for camp deliveries and maintenance [3]
Associate Ranger, Purchasing, Trading Post, Laundry: **Gerald Madsen**
    Senior Counselors for Trading Post sales [2]
    Junior Counselors for Camp Laundry [2]
Food Director: **Pierre Arsenault**, Chef
    Senior Counselor assistant [1]
    Junior Counselor assistants [5]
Medical Officer: **Harold Symonds**
    Counselor Assistants assigned when needed

Waterfront Director: **Leonard Stafford**
    Senior Counselor Lifeguards [5] Billy, Joey, Ted, Ken, Lanny
        Adult Staff Instructors:
    Swimming 1: **Roy Franklin**, Advanced and Intermediate
    Swimming 2: **Matt Smith**, Beginning and Intermediate
    Rowing: **Phil Jensen**; *Senior Counselor* Beebe
    Canoeing: **Sam Brady**; *Senior Counselor* Walls

Program Director: **Fred Russell**
    Special Assistant: *Tom Dawson, JA, Troop 9
    Senior Counselor Assistants: [12]
    Junior Counselor Assistants: [18] Mason
        Adult Advancement Instructors [2]*
    Harold Carter, Troop 2 (1st Class),
    Scott Olson, Troop 419 (2nd Class)
    Adult Merit Badge Instructors: [12]*
    Scott Henderson, Troop 7 (Forestry)
    Ed Taylor, Troop 29 (Backpacking/Climbing)
    Mike Fuller, Troop 8 (Basketry/Leatherwork)
    Archie Samuels, Troop 12 (Archery)
    Frank Thompson, Troop 17 (Pioneering)
    Ted Soames, Troop 6 (First Aid)
    Rick Strauss, Troop 13 (Marksmanship)
    Frank Simmons, Troop 152 (Indian Legends)
    Ron Benson, Troop 14 (Reptile Study)

Carl DeBeery, Troop 76 (Fishing)

Sedley Unger, Troop 4 (Wood Carving/Woodworking)
Donald Brimm, Troop 227 (Bird Study)

Recreational Director: **Benjamin Bradley**
    Special Adult Recreational Assistant: * Mark Schaefer, Troop 9
    Senior Counselor Assistants [6]
    Junior Counselor Assistants [6]
    Rope Yard: Adult Supervisor Volunteer*
        (rotating assignment)
    Rifle Range: Adult Supervisor Volunteer*
        (rotating assignment)
    Archery: Adult Supervisor Volunteer*
        (rotating assignment)
    Water Polo: Volunteer Coaches*
        Schaefer, Franklin, Smith, Russell

*   Drawn from Attending Scoutmasters and Scouts

Full Time Camp Employee in boldface
Seasonal employee in italics

Glossary for terms in Julian's Private Scrapbook book 1

Arrow Points: Cub Scout award patches, analogous to merit badges.

Bear: Second year of Cub Scouts. Julian's mother completed that year as a Den Mother; Margery Baker was expecting her second child.

Bobcat: Entry level in Cub Scouts; equivalent of Tenderfoot in Boy Scouts. All cub and scout ranks and levels are awarded after requirements are met. Bobcat is the easiest to meet and held the shortest time.

Big Ben: The Westclox Company made the Big Ben and Little Ben wind up alarm clocks. First sold in 1909, they evolved over the years until 2001. The clocks featured glow in the dark numerals on the face until the late 1960s, when radiumbased paint was discontinued. The clock in Barr's Meadow was a Style 6, manufactured between 1956-1964. 

Blue Ridge Mountains: The eastern portion of the Appalachian Mountain Range that runs from Georgia in the south, and ends in Pennsylvania. The highest point is Mt. Mitchell, North Carolina [6,684 feet].

Brando sunglasses: A poster from Marlon Brando's 1953 movie *The Wild One* was very common. The steel rim aviator mirror style wrap around sunglasses he wore became widely popular. 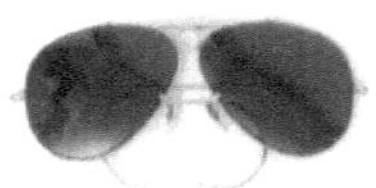

Buddy System: Primarily a safety structure that requires all scouts to remain with another scout at all times when outdoors in the wild. It has broadened to the entire scout program as an expedient in organizing and monitoring progress. At Camp Walker, special Buddy Badges were given to each scout. It showed their swimming proficiency and was required to be presented at the gate prior to lake access.

Cairn: A pile of stones arranged to mark some feature along a trail, such as a junction or a distance.

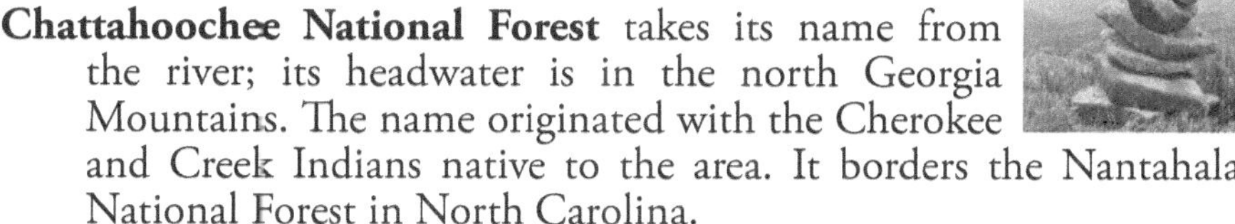

Chattahoochee National Forest takes its name from the river; its headwater is in the north Georgia Mountains. The name originated with the Cherokee and Creek Indians native to the area. It borders the Nantahala National Forest in North Carolina.

Cheshire Cat: A character in *Alice in Wonderland*. The animated film version featured a wide closed tooth open lipped smile.

Crummy: A jargon word that identifies the small hardy off-road bus, van or pickup that transports loggers from the main camp to their work areas. The term is commonly used by Forest Service trail crews and some scout camps.

Den: Small component unit in Cub Scouts, usually numbered, and named after the year/rank of its members (i.e., Wolf Den). All the units combined constitute a Pack.

Den Mother: Adult who supervises and guides each Den.

Explorer: In 1949, the BSA consolidated the senior programs, with the exception of Sea Scouts, into Explorer Scouts. At that time, a boy could be an Explorer in the troop or in a stand-alone unit called the Explorer post. The Explorer advancement program included the Bronze Award, the Gold Award, and the Silver Award. The last Silver Awards were earned in 1966 as Exploring began to turn more toward career emphasis. Venturing was officially created to replace Explorers in 1998.

Gold, Silver, Bronze Palm: Palm branch badges are awarded to Eagle scouts who continue to earn merit badges.

Hawkeye Brownie: Kodak introduced the Brownie Box Camera very early in the history of photography. By the 1950's it had evolved to a Bakelite shell unit that could have a flash attached. The 127 size film was still black and white by and large; the Brownie negative was large, and never had color slide film; later models could take color negative film.

Joliet, Illinois: A community near Chicago. Francine's childhood home. She leaves because she wants to raise her son in a smaller community, well away from urban influences.

Life: The rank between Star and Eagle.

Lion: Third year of Cub Scouts.

Lucy's rag doll: Lucy Graham lived in Julian's neighborhood; she had a floppy Raggedy Ann doll that Julian thought was silly to have around.

Nantahala National Forest: Located in the mountains and valleys of western North Carolina. The terrain varies in elevation from 5,800 feet to 1,200 feet (along the Hiwassee River below the Appalachian Dam). It is the home of many western NC waterfalls. It borders the Chattahoochee Forest in Northern Georgia.

Order of the Arrow: The national honor society of the Boy Scouts of America. Membership is by invitation, and includes individuals from many troops. They are organized into local youth-led lodges that encourage fellowship, promote camping, and render service to Boy Scout councils and their communities. Members wear an identifying insignia on their scout uniforms.

Pack: Large umbrella grouping of Cub Scout Dens.

Perry Como's *Catch a Falling Star* repeats the phrase, "put it in your pocket, never let it fade away." Composed by Lee Pockriss and Paul Vance, and recorded in 1957 by Perry Como it became the first R.I.A.A.-certified "Gold Record" in 1958 and won Perry Como the award for "Best Vocal Performance, Male" at the first annual Grammy Awards in 1959.

Pershing hat: Worn by scoutmasters and scout executives. It is a wide flat disc with four ridges forming a point at the top of the crown. Also called a Campaign hat; made familiar by Army General John Pershing during World War I. Several State Police and the Canadian Mounted Police use the hat. A smaller, modified version was the standard hat for all scouts prior to WW II.

Red Baron: German flying ace in World War I. Julian made a model of his red Fokker Dr.1 triplane.

Secure the Colors: Mark retains some of the military jargon and terminology of his predecessor. This phrase means roll up the flag, separate the pole segments, and put the flag away in the backpack.

Secure your caps: The scout cap was flat when not being worn; it was threaded over the belt, at the ready when needed. The style is similar to the US Army parade cap in use during World War II.

Selectric typewriter: Introduced by IBM in 1961, the innovative machine replaced keys with a whirling ball; the mount made it possible to change balls with different fonts and type sizes.

Sergeant Preston: Radio and Television hero, in the Canadian Mounted Police. The series ended in 1958 but enjoyed years of reruns.

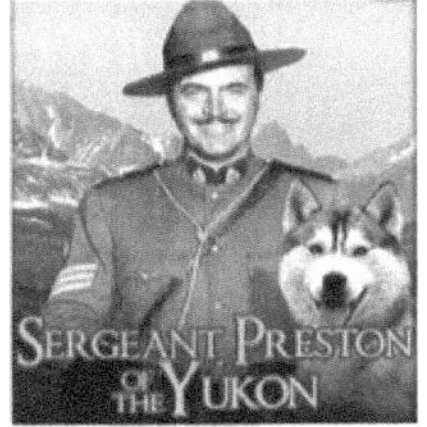

Star: The next advancement in rank after First Class.

T.B.: Slang abbreviation for tired butt, resulting from a long sit on a hard or uncomfortable seat.

Troop Shake: The left-handed scout handshake is made with the hand nearest the heart and is offered as a token of friendship. The handshake is made firmly, without interlocking fingers. Troop Nine used it as an enhanced personal oath, substituting for a salute. The "Solemn Version" in Troop Nine included interlocking fingers and two lateral twists followed by two vertical shakes.

Webelos: Late third or fourth year of Cub Scouts, the highest level.

Song Credits

The songs referenced in Julian's Private Scrapbook were selected because they are representative of the time period and likely would have been on the radio in Francine's kitchen. They are described briefly here, alphabetically.

Catch a Falling Star, written by Paul Vance and Lee Pockriss, is a song made famous by Perry Como's hit version, recorded and released in late 1957. It was Como's last #1 hit, reaching #1 on the Billboard "Most Played by Jockeys" chart but not in the overall top 100, where it reached #2. It was the first single to receive a Recording Industry Association of America gold record certification, on March 14, 1958. The single won Como the 1959 Grammy Award for Best Vocal Performance, Male. Its melody is based on a theme from Brahms' Academic Festival Overture. The Como version features the Ray Charles Singers, who sing the refrain as a repeated round.

Que Sera Sera: (Whatever Will Be, Will Be) first published in 1956, is a popular song written by the Jay Livingston and Ray Evans songwriting team. It was introduced by Doris Day in the Hitchcock film *The Man Who Knew Too Much*, 1956.

Sixteen Tons: a song about the life of a coal miner, first recorded in 1946 by American country singer Merle Travis. A 1955 version sung by Tennessee Ernie Ford in 1955 became a standby on his television program that ended in 1961.

When the Moon hits you eye excerpt from *That's Amore*, a 1952 song by composer Harry Warren and lyricist Jack Brooks. It became a major hit, and a signature song for Dean Martin in 1953. Amore means "love" in Italian, giving a general translation in English "that's love".

Index of Names *in Julian's Private Scrapbook book 1*

Name and Brief description

Adrian Forrest: Julian's father, a sculptor who lives in Greenwich Village, NYC. He was estranged from the family and has remained completely unknown by Julian. He is mentioned only.

Alex Trent: Star scout, member of the Lynx patrol. Son of a Major in the Marine Corps, highly principled and ambitious. Shows Julian how to use the camp wash station.

Arnie Shaw: Patrol Leader of the Badgers, Life Scout.

Ben Bradley: Recreational Director, Camp Walker.

Ben Jasper: Tenderfoot scout in the Panther Patrol.

Billy Bradford: Tenderfoot scout in the Wolf Patrol.

Brad Fisher: Star scout in the Tiger Patrol.

Bruce Ruggles: Second Class scout in the Badger Patrol. Volunteered to help in the Lifesaving final exam.

Casey Snyder: Star scout in the Wolf Patrol. A friend of Robin's; they play blackjack on the trip to camp.

Charlie Dawson: Tom's oldest brother, by nearly six years. He was Tom's hero and role model. He was Troop Nine's Junior Assistant Scoutmaster when Tom was in Cub Scouts. Charlie is gay, an MBA, and lives in Boston with his lover, who Tom met once. That relationship is a major influence on Tom's thinking.

Chef Pierre: Full time chef at Camp Walker.

Chris Smith: Second Class scout in the Tiger Patrol.

Cory Summers: Second Class scout in the Zebra Patrol. Julian's Archery partner. He has been stuck at Second Class because of his inability to master a water phobia.

Counselor Mason: Junior Counselor assigned to assist in the program areas of Sharp Shooting and Archery. His attitude needs improving.

Danny Laskey: Star scout, newly appointed Senior Patrol Leader of Troop Nine, he has passed several able scouts because Scoutmaster Mark sees him as the best leader potential to become Assistant Scoutmaster. He has had a crush on Julian for a little more than a year. Though he lives across the fence, he and Julian have only had a nodding acquaintance prior to this camp. He is assigned to supervise Julian in the daily breakfast and camp inspections, and makes his first attempt to seduce Julian. Afterwards, he gets sunburned at the lake.

Erik: Mark's first love, killed in an airplane crash when Mark was a college Junior. He has been Mark's only romantic partner.

Florence Connor: Fifth Grade teacher. Significant influence in Julian's artistic development.

Francine Forrest: Mother of Julian, daughter of Oscar and Elizabeth Mattson, deceased, of Joliet Illinois. Estranged and divorced from her husband while Julian was an infant, she is making a new life in a new state.

Frank Ferris: (Frankie) Troop Nine Bugler. Not at camp this year; family finances have required him to work full time during the summer. He has been a sexual playmate of Danny's for fun, not romance.

Franklin, Roy: Swimming instructor and water polo coach.

Fred Russell: Camp Walker Program Director.

Gary West: Patrol Leader of the Lynx. Life Scout, twin of Jim.

George: Bus driver.

Geraldine Smathers: Real estate agent, friend and employer of Francine Forrest.

Hazel: Neighborhood friend of Julian's mother. Julian is especially fond of her cookies.

Jason Jones: Second Class scout in the Lynx patrol.

Jay Porter: Life Scout, assistant patrol leader of the Tigers. An excellent swimmer, earned his Lifesaving Merit Badge on the first day of camp.

Jer: Truck driver who transports the scout gear to the camp entrance.

Jeremy Baker: Julian's friend, First Class scout in the Wolf Patrol; was a Cub Scout with Julian.

Jim West: Zebra Patrol leader, Life Scout. Twin of Gary.

Joey: Senior Counselor and Lifeguard.

John Jorgensen: Serving his fifteenth year as Director of Camp Walker.

Johnny: Fictional character in Max Webster's skit.

Joyce Benson: Julian's first Den Mother (his Bobcat/Wolf year).

Julian Forrest: First Class scout, primary protagonist. An only child, unaware that he has inherited an extraordinary artistic talent from his father, a Greenwich Village sculptor whom he has never known. Serious and single minded, determined from an early age to spend his life with Mark, a close neighbor. The first night at Camp, Mark invites him to stay in the cabin. It was not what he had hoped for. His talent for acting comes to the fore the next day when he takes part in the lifesaving class.

Justin Blake: First Class scout in the Zebra Patrol. Julian's protégé and Forestry Buddy.

Larry Smith: Julian's pal who moved out of town.

Leonard Stafford: Waterfront Director at Camp Walker. Has an uncanny ability to remember names and faces.

Louise West: Mother of the West twins, Gary and Jim.

Lucy Graham: Neighborhood acquaintance; Julian likes her cat.

Major, the: Major Phillip Trent, USMC, Alex Trent's father.

Marilyn Carter, Miss: Elderly neighbor of Julian and Mark.

Mark Schaefer: Scoutmaster of Troop Nine, a retail purchasing agent and manager. When he was a senior in college, he was asked to replace his former scoutmaster who died suddenly from a heart attack. His five year marriage is one of convenience; he devotes all his free time to scouting.

Marty Hoffman: Life scout in Troop Nine when Tom was a Tenderfoot. He and his buddy Rick Russell befriended Tom, mostly because of Tom's large penis. Marty had discovered a special hideaway two years earlier, and it became a daily stopping place for the threesome.

Matt Smith: Swimming instructor, Camp Walker.

Max Webster: Life scout, Assistant patrol leader of the Lynx. Talented musician. Author of the *Johnny* fable, proposed as the Troop Nine skit to be performed at the end of camp.

Nathan Jensen: Panther Patrol Leader, Life scout.

Nick Harrison: Secondary protagonist, a Life scout. Troop Scribe, member of the Flaming Arrow Patrol. A talented writer who has had a crush on Tom for three years. Appointed to mentor Julian as a troop journalist. He heads off Tom's plans for Julian and on the second night makes a surprise move of his own for Tom's attention. It is far more successful than he had planned.

Norman Miller: Star scout, assigned to help Julian on the first day at camp. Assistant Patrol Leader of the Wolf Patrol.

Oscar Mattson: Julian's maternal grandfather.

Pat Schaefer: Wife of Mark; a Registered Nurse, studying to become an MD.

Phil Jensen: Camp Walker rowing instructor.

Randy Dawson: Tom's brother, a year and a half older. Randy is Bisexual. He and Tom played sex games frequently. Tom was caught spying on Randy and a pal one day after school. They allowed Tom to join in occasionally.

Rick Russell: Star scout in Troop Nine when Tom was a Tenderfoot. Tom had a brief crush on Rick, but it was not reciprocated. Tom was disillusioned and avoided any further emotional attachments. His relationship with Nick eventually overcomes that problem.

Sam Brady: Waterfront staff; canoe instructor.

Sandy Smith: Tenderfoot, member of the Lynx patrol.

Sarge Oliver: Camp Ranger/Quartermaster.

Scott Henderson: Scoutmaster of Troop 7; teaches Forestry merit badge.

Sherri Harris: Den mother of Julian's Lion/Webelos Den.

Sid Thomas: First Class scout in the Wolf Patrol. Julian's friend from school and Cub Scouts. He is known for his prankster sense of humor and his extremely skinny physique. His mother bought him a new turquoise blue air mattress for camp.

Stuart Walker: Wolf Patrol Leader, Life scout.

Tad Benson: Second Class scout in the Zebra Patrol.

Ted Soames: Scoutmaster of Troop 6. Teaches First Aid merit badge. Annoyed by Mark's continued success.

Tom Dawson: Junior Assistant Scoutmaster of Troop Nine and Eagle Scout. Outstanding leadership ability, but has long had a fetish for fresh adolescent backsides. A secondary protagonist in the series. He relies heavily on the analytic ability of his protégé, Nick Harrison. He helps Julian at the first free swim at the lake as a ploy. But his plan to seduce Julian gets derailed by Nick. His sexual world gets turned upside down when he allows Nick to show him a new way to make love.

Tony Johnson: First Class scout in the Tiger Patrol. He is awarded demerits frequently for a variety of minor infractions. He is the troop's most talented actor and clown.

Wilson Dawson: Tom's other brother, a year younger than Charlie. He is straight and strives to be different from his older brother in every respect. He and Randy shared a bedroom while growing up.

a word about the author

Eldot is a simple cipher: the author's first initial followed by a period,

spelled phonetically [L. = Eldot] Why? When this novel was first published, the subject matter was more sensitive and controversial than it is today. Lest relatives, friends or former colleagues be inconvenienced or victimized, the nom de plume was adopted as a shield. Secondly, the author didn't want media opportunism to distort what the book was seeking to achieve. Media treatment of the subject was the major motivation to write Julian's side of the story in the first place.

All the Julian books received positive critical reviews. The potential for controversy still exists, but the extremist groups have lost their clout—society has evolved rapidly: social media and the cell phone have changed the landscape; the Julian novels are made more topical than ever. In 2018 the subject matter is relevant and openly discussed; a movie on the same theme is a contender for the 2018 Best Picture of the year. For this reason and to satisfy readers' response, the five books have been revised, updated, and re-issued as the five volume *Julian's Private Scrapbook* set.

Thus it's appropriate to let the reader get a peek behind the curtain. Eldot has lived in the Pacific Northwest for most of his life. In order to dodge the draft and avoid the Viet Nam war, he took an occupational deferment to teach high school Drama and English. The interminable nature of the war and the draft lottery kept him in that occupation so long that the refuge morphed into a successful career. Why change a good thing? He became a local and state leader in his profession. After thirty terrific years as an educator, he retired. Now he's taken up writing. The novels are not autobiographical.

Leland Alan Hall

Publications:

1960:   Emperor Commodus Prompt Book: Use of Masks in Drama
[Honors Thesis, a translation from the Greek, housed at University of Oregon Library]
1979-81: Editorials, *Oregon Education*
2011:   *Little J and Roger* [eBook only]
2012:   *Barr's Meadow*
The Poker Club
The Shooting Gallery
Thunder and Lightning
2013:   *The Champions*
Inside Eldot's World: a literary gazetteer [eBook only]
2015:   *You're in High School Now*
2016:   *'56 Scrapbook* [PDF and spiral bound]
2018-19: *Julian's Private Scrapbook, books 1 thru 5*
2020:   *He's kinda tall, Julian's Sophomore Year Part 2*
2022:   *'56 Bookend* [PDF and spiral bound]
2024:   The Julian Novels ATP Special Edition
2025:   *Untitled: Julian's Sophomore Year. Part 3*
2025:   Barr's Meadow–Special Kravitz Edition

Author Website Link: http://www.diphra.com
    ATP website: eldotbooks.com
Facebook: https://www.facebook.com/AuthorEldot/
Twitter: https://twitter.com/AuthorEldot
Tumblr: https://authoreldot.tumblr.com/

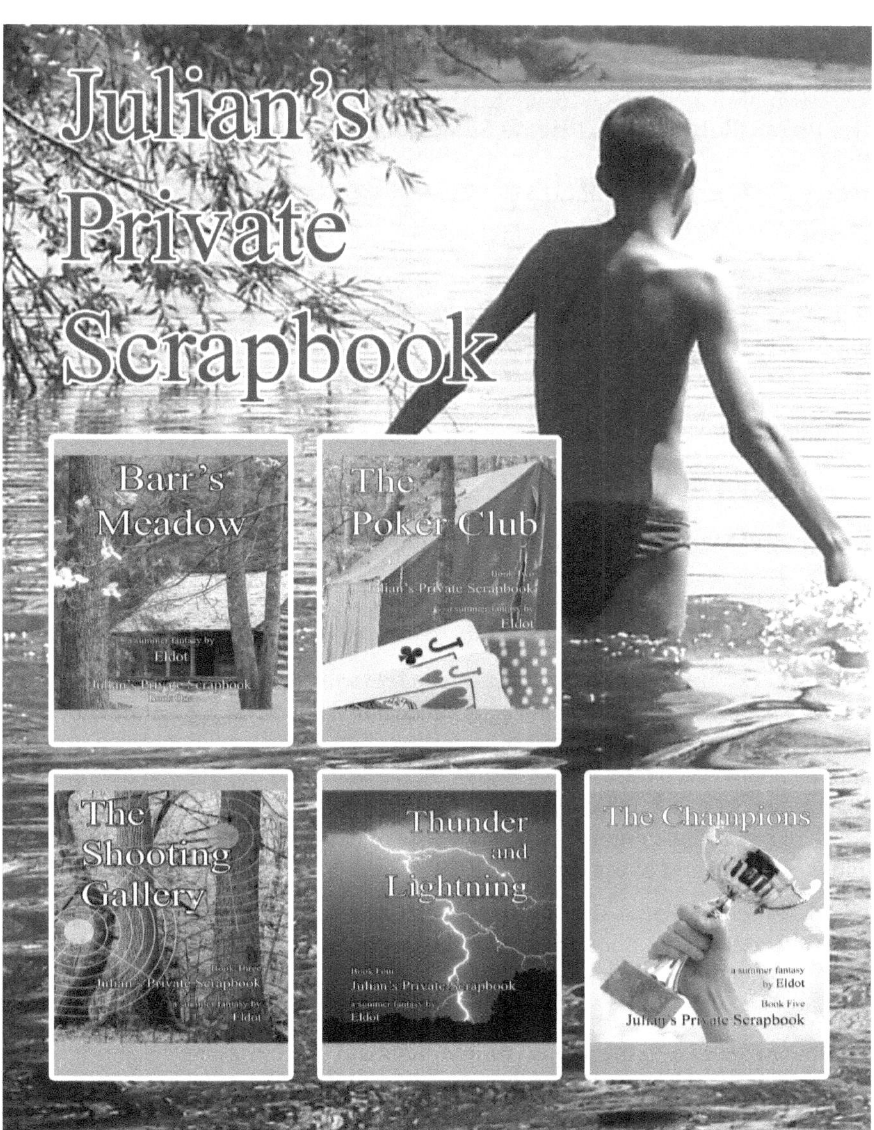
Julian's Private Scrapbook
Barr's Meadow
a summer fantasy by
Eldot
Julian's Private Scrapbook
Book One
The Poker Club
Book Two
Julian's Private Scrapbook
a summer fantasy by
Eldot
The Shooting Gallery
Book Three
Julian's Private Scrapbook
a summer fantasy by
Eldot
Thunder and Lightning
Book Four
Julian's Private Scrapbook
a summer fantasy by
Eldot
The Champions
a summer fantasy by Eldot
Book Five
Julian's Private Scrapbook

The Poker Club: Julian's Private Scrapbook, Part Two

Eldot

Xlibris, 279 pages, (paperback) $15.99, 978-1-4771-1834-4
(Reviewed: March, 2014)

This unusual novel is sure to cause controversy for its subject matter. The second in a projected five-novel series, the book takes place at a scout camp during the summer of 1962, and follows several groups of boys as they form friendships, learn new skills, and fall in love. Much of the book concerns their various sexual explorations; indeed, the "Poker Club" of the title refers to one group's method of beginning such activities – and the author is careful to note on the back cover that the book "is meant for mature readers."

In between the sex, several plotlines start to form. Julian, who has a crush on his scoutmaster Mark, learns more about life matters while interacting with his fellow scouts. Tom, an older boy who has been with many other boys, finds himself falling for Nick, one of his earlier conquests and now a friend. Geoff, a co-founder of the Poker Club, recruits other scouts to join in the fun, including Tom and Nick.

While the extensive explicit sex scenes can feel somewhat exploitative, generally they are handled well, combining experience with innocence in an endearing way. Julian in particular, while certainly experienced in some sexual matters, still has much to learn. His sweet, innocent looks make Mark and the other scouts want to protect him from such things, so that, for instance, while a remark about "choice buns" makes Julian curious about what that means, he doesn't learn the answer until nearly the end of the book.

The developing relationship between Tom and Nick is also fascinating; in the previous book, Tom hoped to seduce Julian but now only wants to be with Nick and feels guilty for his earlier pursuits.

The author includes a summary of the first novel along with maps of all locations. If readers are open to the subject matter, they will find intriguing insights into the complex world of boys in this unique novel.

Also available in hardcover and ebook

The Shooting Gallery: Julian's Private Scrapbook Part Three

Eldot

Xlibris, 287 pages, (paperback) $15.99, 978-1-4771-4986-7
(Reviewed: April 2014)

The Shooting Gallery is the third in Eldot's five-part series: "Julian's Private Scrapbook."We find ourselves in a Boy Scout Camp, where our pubescent hero, Julian Forrest,comes of age in June 1962.

Julian is a prodigy when it comes to drawing, a talent that garners many accolades. As we might expect, there are other skills to be mastered at camp: swimming, canoeing, archery, cooking - and, in this case, sex. In *Barr's Meadow* (Part 1) readers came to appreciate Julian's beauty, exuberance, affability and guilelessness. There, Eldot laid out the rituals and routines of scout camp: inspection and clean-up, naked swimming and campfire sing-alongs. In the midst of this cheery beehive, Julian had his first sexual experience with another scout; another encounter involved two older, more experienced boys.

In *The Shooting Gallery*, the author again presents the everyday activities we might expect, but now, sexual behavior is more frequent. While this kind of intimacy is often explored in fiction, it's much rarer to find it imbued with positive, canny eroticism, as it is here. In *The Shooting Gallery*, the tone is somewhat Utopian; the characters are not influenced by the usual shame or taboos society places on sex between males. Boy Scout Camp becomes a refuge where characters freely (though conscientiously) experiment with same-gender eroticism.

Eldot not only examines male-only sexual episodes, he anchors them in verisimilitude. Unlike more fantasy-driven erotica that sets up outlandish, compulsive scenarios, the sex here arises organically from the plot. The author goes inside the heads of the characters, so that we understand their bashfulness, their longing or curiosity. There is a nonchalant, playful tone that removes the stigma of queer intimacy that easily might have tormented teenaged American men in 1962.

All in all, *The Shooting Gallery* is a satisfying, intelligent story, notable for its warmth and credibility. It's perfect for those who appreciate homoerotic content without the usual overblown raunch so common to the genre.

Also available in hardcover and ebook.

Thunder and Lightning: Julian's Private Scrapbook, Part 4

Eldot

Xlibris, 327 pages, (paperback) $15.99, 978-1-4797-5684-1
(Reviewed: May 2014)

This unusual novel, the fourth in a five-part series, takes place at a scout camp during the summer of 1962 and follows several groups of boys as they form friendships, learn new skills, and fall in love. Much of the novel depicts their various sexual explorations, and the author clearly alerts readers to such content. "This series is meant for mature readers," he writes on the back cover. "...This book should be stored in a place not accessible by persons under 18."

In between the sex, several plotlines progress from the earlier books. Tom, an older boy who had been with many others before committing himself to Nick, makes amends for his past treatment of Kurt, an earlier partner. Nick advises Kurt on how to overcome his fear that his past with Tom will sabotage his relationship with his current partner Sid. Julian continues to improve his artistic skills, drawing beautiful portraits of the lifeguard Leonard and his scoutmaster Mark, while taking on further responsibilities in the campground. In a new development, Geoff, another older boy, becomes attracted to Mark and devises a plan for seducing the unwitting scoutmaster. Meanwhile, Mark begins to confront his past trauma.

While the extensive sex scenes may make some readers uncomfortable, they are handled well, showing the tenderness between the boys. Their relationships are fascinating to watch, as many are now committed couples, yet their emotional bonds are strong enough to allow them to learn new positions and techniques in sessions with more knowledgeable boys. Geoff's pursuit of Mark is handled humorously, leading to a situation where both attempt to conceal their erections. The author helpfully includes summaries of the previous novels, a glossary of terms and characters and more at book's end.

Thunder and Lightning is a charming read in spite of the controversial subject matter. As it shows further growth in the series' characters and their relationships, it sets the stage for the concluding tale.

Also available in hardcover and ebook.

The Champions: Julian's Private Scrapbook, Part Five

Eldot

Xlibris, 375 pages (paperback) $15.99, 978-1-4797-8041-9
(Reviewed: June 2014)

The conclusion to a sexually infused five-novel series, The Champions takes place during the last day of a scout camp during the summer of 1962 and follows several groups of boys as they deepen their relationships, build on new skills, and ponder life after camp. Much of the novel depicts their various intimate explorations, from a final ejaculation contest known as "the Shooting Gallery" to the couples pleasuring each other on the bus ride home. In between, several plots building during the previous books reach their end.

Geoff, one of the oldest scouts, makes his move - even with his injured foot — to seduce the scoutmaster, Mark, in the middle of the night. Julian, while working on his remarkable drawings, befriends Sarge, the camp's quartermaster, and draws out the gruff retired Army man's soft side, even calling him "Uncle Max." Tom, continuing his process of maturing, learns how to get out of uncomfortable situations without the help of his lover Nick, and even becomes a confidante to other scouts worried about their relationships.

Mark comes across as one of the strongest figures in this novel, encouraging all the scouts under his care to become the best that they can be. He makes plans for Julian to receive art lessons after camp, further developing his talent. He shows his tremendous strength, both physical and moral, during his late-night encounter with Geoff. It's no surprise that his troop wins all the prizes at the last day's competitions, or that Julian has a crush on the scoutmaster.

Charming and humorous, with sex scenes that are erotic without being over the top, the novel successfully ends the series, while leaving open the possibility of further adventures. The controversial subject matter may make some readers uncomfortable, but for those interested in a sexual adventure told from a gay perspective, this is a wonderful look at boys transitioning between childhood and adulthood.

Also available in hardcover and ebook.

You're in High School Now: Julian's Sophomore Year, Part 1
Eldot
One Spirit Press, 610 pages, (paperback) $15.99 978-1-893075-77-1
(Reviewed: June 2015)

This charming novel continues the story of Julian, from author Eldot's series Julian's Private Scrapbook. Set in the early 1960s, it follows Julian's coming of age as a gay man through the first half of his first year in high school, as he makes new friends, learns about girls, and navigates this strange but exciting new world.

The title refers to the refrain his mother and her friend continually use when explaining to Julian why he must pay attention to his clothes now and other new "rules." Julian's only real concern is his mother's interest that he take out a girl. Since he is only romantically interested in his scoutmaster Mark, that presents an obstacle. Fortunately, he attracts the attention of Rita, one of the school's prettiest girls, who invites him to the Sadie Hawkins dance. Julian's complete ignorance about Rita's intentions during the dance and the car ride afterwards (as well as his description to his mother later) provides some of the novel's funniest scenes."

Julian is certainly experienced when it comes to sex, however. He continues the explorations he discovered at scout camp the previous summer, both as an initiate in a secret society of like-minded boys, as well as with Randall, recently moved from Washington. Randall, a victim of bullying at his previous school, is instantly drawn to Julian when he sees him, and they form an immediate, deep friendship. Julian introduces Randall to his scouting troop and takes an interest in his photography, and Randall is deeply impressed by Julian's drawing skills. The two bring out the best in each other.

While not every reader will appreciate the sex scenes, they are sensitively drawn and important to the story. The only complaint this reader has is waiting for Part 2, where it seems the situation will become complicated. Well-written, with engaging, likable characters, this book skillfully presents the challenges and pleasures boys who love men face in growing up.

Also available in hardcover and ebook.

You're in *high school* now:

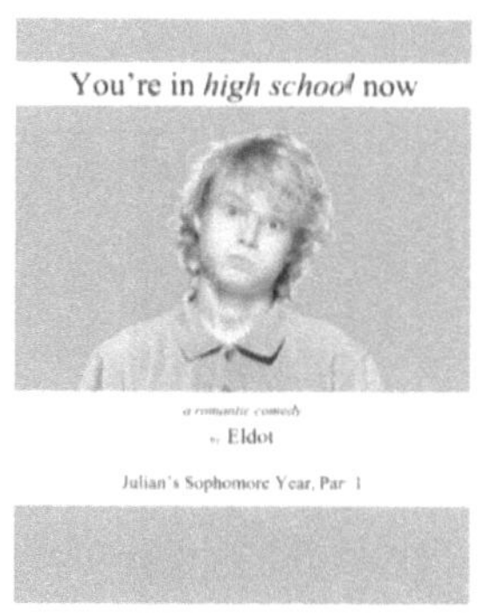

Julian's Sophomore Year: Part 1

Q Press, 626 pages (paperback), 978-1-893075-77-1
Reviewed: October, 2015

KIRKUS REVIEW

The life and times of an adventurous, gay high school sophomore.

In the latest installment featuring Julian, the affable lead in the Julian's Private Scrapbook YA series, author Eldot (The Champions: Julian's Private Scrapbook, 2013, etc.) re-creates the autumn of 1962 as Julian embarks upon another school year full of books and boys at Jackson High School. Amid a backdrop of artistic inclinations and first-day jitters, Julian's romantic feelings for Mark, his Scoutmaster at Camp Walker over the past summer, continue to simmer, with their exploratory fondling lingering in his memory. But his concerned mother, Francine, encourages him to show an interest in girls. When Rita, an attractive, mischievous schoolmate, asks Julian, aka "the blond masterpiece," to the Sadie Hawkins dance, the obvious awkward clashing of orientations ensues.

Humor is one of Eldot's strong suits; he has an impressive capacity for penning farcical, innocently disastrous moments. He also builds a good supporting cast, like Mark, who is in a heterosexual marriage of convenience after his longtime partner died seven years prior; and Randall, a gay virgin and recent arrival to Jackson High. Intimate shenanigans occur at a secret society campout for randy boys, but the author takes care to handle these moments with restraint. Structurally, however, Eldot fumbles a bit. He shifts perspective awkwardly and adds too many disclaimers, style notes, and end matter that are meant to illuminate Julian but result in informational overload. Still, Eldot successfully taps into the experiences of gay youth with a believable blend of engaging characterization, humor, pathos, back story, and teenage angst.

Fun, frolicsome series with good humor and a message of unity and equality; new readers may want to start at the beginning.

You're in *high school* now

Julian's Sophomore Year, Part 1

Reviewed by Amanda Silva, July 23, 2015

This YA romantic comedy reflects traditional coming-of-age themes, further complicated by issues of sexuality and identity.

Eldot's romantic comedy *You're in High School Now* follows Julian, a young gay man in who is getting to know himself while creating his place in the world. This particular world is high school in 1962, a microcosm fraught with prizes and pitfalls, where bullies abound and fitting in is a constant quest. This narrative reflects traditional coming-of-age themes, further complicated by issues of sexuality and identity.

These are sensitive topics for many readers, regardless of age, but Eldot writes with an urgency to connect with those young adult readers for whom these issues might be especially difficult. This story is an extension of Eldot's earlier series, the Julian's Private Scrapbook novels, but can be read in isolation. Readers should be aware it contains sexual content and adult themes layered throughout.

Julian is a sympathetic character, thoughtful and comical in his observations about himself and those around him. His internal struggles and interactions with his peers will likely connect with young readers, regardless of gender or sexual orientation. Selfacceptance rings as a universal desire and pursuit throughout these pages.

Although the writing is clear, the structure is not. While it is admirable for an author to experiment with a new writing style, the clarity of the work can sometimes be compromised. Eldot eventually explains—but not until the end of the book—that the narrative intentionally combines first- and third-person points of view as a means of freeing both writer and reader from "cumbersome conventions" concerning paragraph structure and punctuation. Eldot is a teacher with more than thirty years of experience; his frustration, or perhaps boredom, with convention is understandable. However, the resulting lack of clarity ultimately detracts from his work.

And this is important work. At the very outset, Eldot writes: "The grand social purpose that motivated the *Julian's Private Scrapbook* series lurks in the background, unsolved as always: social change is never as rapid as one would like. There are still bullies … So it's worth the effort to add a positive chapter or two."

Eldot's message is, indeed, as important as ever. When it comes to sharing that message through mainstream media, however, revisions in defense of convention and organization would bring these already bright and positive chapters to greater light.

302

He's kinda tall

a romantic comedy
by Eldot

Julian's Sophomore Year. Part 2

Another memorable snapshot of LGBTQ+ high school life in a bygone era.

HE'S KINDA TALL

BY ELDOT · RELEASE DATE: N/A

The continuing saga of a resilient gay high schooler's adolescent adventures.

Prolific author Eldot picks up where You're in High School Now (2015) left off, with young North Carolina high school sophomore Julian Forrest facing new feelings and challenges in late 1962. The author again succeeds in establishing the era in which his protagonist's youth plays out amid themes of inclusivity, friendship, burgeoning sexuality, and the precarious state of race relations during the school desegregation movement of the mid-20th century. Eldot imparts many life lessons over the course of the narrative; the first is that focused dedication to one's schoolwork will not only garner one good grades, but also beneficial recognition from instructors when one least expects it. Julian's consistently pleasant demeanor, personal flair, and conscientious, hard work make his teachers think of him as a model student. His rare, enviable qualities draw the attention of several teachers who believe he would make an ideal helper for an incoming Black student named Kassa "Kasey" Wood. The son of a prominent Boston scientist, Kasey is a polite, friendly, and impressively talented young pianist who comes to appreciate the time that Julian devotes to helping him adjust to a new town, a new school, and new classmates; in a compelling sequence, Julian even insists on racial equality at a segregated "whites-only" diner. The relationship between these two characters would be sufficient to carry the entire novel, but Eldot has grander visions in mind, carried out by a parade of peripheral teenage characters who take their turns marching through the novel.

Their storylines—some fleeting, some with greater staying power—definitely add some panache to the tale and enliven what becomes a rather overlong tome, as it extends to nearly 600 pages in length. Readers will likely want Julian, a budding artist, and pianist extraordinaire Kasey to remain at center stage, and they often do. However, they're upstaged much too often by other scenes concerned with randy camping adventures, fart jokes, or extended family melodrama. The omniscient third-person narration is often dryly humorous, but the book also explores Julian and Kasey's friendship through the eyes of folks who know very little about them. This narrative twist affords readers a look at what it's like to be observed and blindly judged by casual strangers. As with the other books in this series, the author doesn't ever shy away from the nuances of sexual attraction, which plays a particularly substantial role in Julian's young life. The teens' flirtations and overt physical carnality are portrayed as unashamed and innocently exploratory; they show the characters to be primarily concerned with mutual, guiltless pleasure, but also fully aware of the necessity of social discretion in that time and place. Although the narrative does feel extravagantly expository at times, its overall sense of social consciousness is remarkable. A concluding, expansive glossary, filled with historical references to the 1960s, will be helpful for newcomers to the setting.

Another overly busy but nonetheless memorable snapshot of LGBTQ+ high school life in a bygone era.

professional reviews of independently published books

He's kinda tall:

Julian's Sophomore Year, Part 2

Eldot
Publisher: Diphra Enterprises Pages: 582 Price: (paperback)
$19.95 ISBN 9781732880566
Review: September, 2020

He's Kinda Tall is author Eldot's latest installment of the adventures of Julian, a gay boy growing up in small-town North Carolina during the early 1960's.

Picking up from the last novel, it follows the rest of Julian's first semester in high school, as he's chosen to help Kasey, a Black boy who will be the first to integrate Julian's school next semester. Kasey's family is moving from Boston so that Kasey's scientist father can help develop a cure for a man named Swann's medical condition. As Swann, a millionaire, helps ensure an easy transition for the family and community, he comes to know Julian and his incredible skill at drawing.

Julian immediately befriends Kasey, knowing from his Boy Scout days that "everyone needs a buddy." His friends support him, helping plan the school assembly to introduce Kasey and eating with him at a whites-only restaurant. Julian brings Kasey out of his isolation, joyfully teaching him how to make pancakes at a sleepover.

The sex scenes display a spirit of playfulness and tenderness, employing boyish humor. When some of Julian's friends take a weekend camping trip, they mix sex with tickles and fart jokes. Eldot skillfully combines innocence and experience within the boys, showing both their eagerness for exploration and sensitivity concerning relationships. They have no guilt about sex, just an awareness of the need for discretion.

While all the books in the series can stand alone, several sub-plots here are interesting enough to inspire titles of their own.

The narrative contains one minor distraction: Since Eldot explains in a prefatory note that he tried to "lessen or sidestep the offense inflicted by" 60's racial terms, it's jarring that some characters think of Kasey as "negro," although the word is never spoken aloud or used pejoratively.

Nonetheless, with its well-drawn characters and detailed, nuanced understanding of how boys think, this novel will appeal to readers interested in coming-of-age scenarios told from a gay perspective.